BODY
BREAKER

M.W.
CRAVEN

CONSTABLE

CONSTABLE

First published in Great Britain in 2017 by Caffeine Nights Publishing

This revised and updated edition published in Great Britain in 2020 by Constable

A CIP catalogue record for this book is
available from the British Library.

ISBN: 978-1-47213-266-6

Typeset in Caslon Pro by SX Composing DTP, Rayleigh, Essex
Printed and bound in Great Britain by Clays Ltd, Elcograf S.p.A.

Papers used by Constable are from well-managed forests
and other responsible sources.

MIX
Paper from
responsible sources
FSC® C104740

Constable
An imprint of
Little, Brown Book Group
Carmelite House
50 Victoria Embankment
London EC4Y 0DZ

An Hachette UK Company
www.hachette.co.uk

www.littlebrown.co.uk

*As always, this book is dedicated to my wife,
Joanne, and my late mother, Susan Avison Craven.
Without either, this book wouldn't exist.*

Prologue

Although only one was needed, two men carried the coffin. They walked slowly, concentrating on not getting under each other's feet, tears streaming down their faces. These men were no undertaker's lackeys, paid cash-in-hand as and when required; these men knew the family.

They struggled with their grim task; the smallest coffins really *are* the heaviest.

The funeral cortège silently followed them. There was a pause as the few with foresight put up their umbrellas. It had been overcast, but dry, when they'd entered the church an hour earlier, and the thick walls and high roof had muted the sounds of heavy rain.

The woman was the last to leave the sanctuary.

She had stayed behind to have a quiet word with her God. Despite all that had happened, she remained devout. Her husband was waiting for her. He raised his eyebrows and offered her his umbrella. She stopped him with a small smile and a shake of her head. Together they joined the procession taking their child to his open grave.

The moment she left the shelter of the church she was drenched. Her hair became plastered to her skull, her light makeup ran. The rain bounced off the earthen path and before long her shoes and stockings were spattered with mud.

She didn't notice.

Her husband held her as they crossed the uneven graveyard to the pitifully small, dark slash in the ground.

The priest waited, head bowed.

As soon as they arrived the committal began.

'Fear not; I am the first and the last. I am he that liveth, and was dead; and behold, I am alive for evermore . . .'

She barely heard the familiar words, words that had offered succour in the past but did little to quell the burning rage she felt. A rage that would take her back to places in her past.

Dark places.

She made no attempt to rub away her tears. Her husband reached into his pocket and offered her his handkerchief. She ignored him.

Over one hundred mourners had gathered around the open grave. Standing in solidarity with her. She appreciated the gesture, and would thank them all later, but the intense feeling of isolation was overwhelming.

Her son had died while she'd slept peacefully.

She didn't know if he'd cried out or struggled for breath. She didn't know if he'd been scared, if he'd cried for his mother. That morning she'd woken in a bright and sunny room, far brighter than her bedroom usually was. She'd looked at her bedside clock and been shocked at the time. Nearly eight o'clock. He'd never let her sleep so late before. Instinctively, she'd known something was wrong and ran to his room.

He was already cold.

From the moment she'd touched his cold hands, a piece of her was missing. She was in raw, excruciating pain but felt hollow at the same time. Since his death, her body had been encased in a relentless fatigue, but restorative sleep felt like cheating and she embraced the exhaustion like an old friend. Sitting in his bedroom for hours at a time, she would read from books she'd bought for when he was old enough to have bedtime stories. Other times she would play with his toys. Most of the time, however, she would simply sit and try to remember him. What he smelled like. How soft his skin had been. The sound of his cries and of his giggles.

She embraced the demons that came at night just as she embraced the clumsy friends who came during the day. They arrived with food she didn't eat and cards she didn't open. They left as soon as they could and soon found reasons to stay away, some even crossing the street to avoid her. She neglected her appearance and wore the same clothes for days; the world of vivid colours she'd shared with her son became drab and grey.

When she lost her child she lost her future. She grieved for the lost dreams she'd had for him, for the unfulfilled potential and for the experiences they would never share. The pain she felt was now a part of her. It would define who she was.

It would define who she had to become.

Again.

The coroner had ruled her son had died from natural causes, and although she'd been told that nobody was to blame, she knew otherwise. As she stood on the wet, hallowed earth, she looked to the east.

To where those responsible lived.

As the interment neared its end, the rage she'd felt for days left her, replaced by a cold chill. Some mothers set up foundations in their dead child's name.

This woman had other plans.

One man stood apart from the funeral party. He had never known her son, hadn't seen her for twenty years. But when she called, he came. He hadn't made his presence known yet, but he knew she'd know he was there.

Waiting.

He left her alone with her grief although she never left his sight. He would wait until she was ready. There was no hurry.

The priest said the last words with a grim finality. A few quiet handshakes and the crowd began to disperse, anxious to get out of the rain but not wanting to rush off and leave the woman. She turned to her husband and spoke a few words of comfort to him. She nodded and he joined the group who were now getting into black funeral cars.

As rainwater streamed from her sodden hair, she stared at the handcrafted wooden casket, partially hidden in the shadows of the grave. It was raining and her son was in the ground.

Eventually only she and the man remained in the graveyard.

She turned.

Ready to command him.

4

Chapter 1

Detective Inspector Avison Fluke knelt on the third green of Cockermouth Golf Course and pressed his ear against the closely mown grass. 'Thrombosis Hill' was one of the most difficult holes on the course. It had an uphill approach and a fast, undulating green. From his worm-eye view he could see breaks to the left and to the right. As today was the monthly medal competition, the grain of the grass had been cut back to front, making downhill putts even more treacherous.

The lip of the cup was directly in front of him. There were three markers within two yards of the hole, indicating where balls had been removed to avoid distracting the man putting.

Lying on its side, just off the green, was the flag. The group had removed it as they'd lined up their putts. Hitting the flag when putting meant a two-stroke penalty.

As well as the three markers, there was a ball on the green and it was this that interested Fluke. It was the reason he and the rest of the Force Major Incident Team, FMIT, were there.

The golfer taking the shot had faced three challenges. First was the downhill putt on a green that had been cut closer than marble. The type of putt even pros dreaded. Second, he was on the biggest break on the green. He would have needed to aim at least a yard to the left of the hole to compensate for the slope and, on this green in particular, anything more than a cup to the left or right was guesswork.

However, it was the third challenge that had caused the day's problem, and the reason Fluke was now getting grass stains all over his suit.

Because lying on the green, directly in between ball and hole, was a severed human hand.

Fluke stood and brushed grass clippings from his knees. A green stain remained.

He looked down the hill to where DS Matt Towler was speaking to the golfers who had discovered the hand. If they weren't involved, and if it hadn't been left behind by the group playing ahead of them, then it had been placed there by someone else and, on monthly medal day, the time window between one group leaving the green and the next approaching was narrow. No more than two minutes. Probably less.

Fluke looked at the back of the green. There was a path and a dry stone wall. Was it possible someone had hidden behind it, and nipped onto the green? He walked up to the wall and peered into a farmer's field. A Herdwick sheep stared back.

Someone *could* have hidden behind the wall, waited for one group to leave the green, then nipped out before the next group arrived. He looked beyond the third and fourth holes, however, and saw a problem. The farmer's field was in the centre of a U-shaped part of the course. The golfers on the third and fourth holes might not have been able to see behind the wall but, due to the course's natural elevation, Fluke could see at least four holes on the back nine that had a clear view of the field and anyone in it.

A noise from behind made him turn. Towler had finished with the group playing the green and had joined him.

'You thinking it was thrown from behind there, boss?'

'Too exposed,' he said. He pointed at the group Towler had just finished with. 'What's the consensus? Still saying it came from above?' He frowned as he said it; body parts didn't just fall from the sky.

'Yep. They all swear it wasn't there when they arrived. Geoff Yates,' – Towler pointed towards a middle-aged man sitting on a golf bag – 'says he was lining up his putt when it just landed in front of him. Said he almost shat himself.'

Cockermouth was an affluent market town so the golf club wouldn't be short of professional, middle-class members. He'd be prepared to bet, on a Saturday, in this weather, at least five doctors would be out on the course at any one time. A prank, that was a possible explanation. Someone who had access to medical waste who thought it might be a bit of a laugh. Probably hadn't expected a team of detectives to take it so seriously. It was a flawed theory; it didn't explain why, after the joke was over, they hadn't picked it back up and got on with their round. No one would have been any the wiser.

'You think he's telling the truth?'

Towler looked back down the hill and shrugged. 'He seems a decent enough bloke. Semi-retired. Been a member here for years and plays at least three times a week.'

'But we have no one who can verify he didn't take it from his pocket and put it there?'

'You want me to bring him in?'

'We'll have to. Don't arrest him though. Take him to Workington nick and make sure we get his clothes and his golf bag. If he brought the hand with him, that's where he'd have kept it. Get statements off the others then let them go.'

Fluke watched Towler walk back down the hill. Two uniformed officers had turned up to help although, in truth, the course was emptying. Those behind the group playing the third had either gone home or were back in the clubhouse, and those playing ahead of them were on the back nine by now.

He wasn't sure the green was a crime scene yet. If it were a practical joke then he'd pass it on to local CID. He wanted to be sure though; someone was very definitely missing a hand.

He bent down for a closer look. Like a child demonstrating what a dead spider looked like, it was lying palm up. The index finger was raised slightly higher than the rest as if the hand was flipping him the bird. One final, desperate act of defiance.

The hand wasn't in good shape. There were bloodless puncture wounds on the palm. Possibly defensive wounds? Too small for a knife. Maybe a screwdriver? It had been removed from the arm at the wrist. Not hacked off; the cut was clean but not so clean it looked surgical. More of a butcher's cut than a surgeon's. Fluke bent down and sniffed. He couldn't smell chemicals. If anything, he smelled putrefaction. The hand was rotten, like bad meat.

He was interrupted by the sound of an engine and he got to his feet. A blue tractor was making its way up the hill. It was dragging a complex-looking mower. A greenkeeper.

Fluke watched him approach; surprised none of his team or any of the uniformed officers had stopped him. Fluke walked out to meet him; he didn't want the green disturbed. He held his hand out in front of him. The universal sign for stop.

A spry old man climbed off the tractor.

'How do, lad,' he said, holding out his hand.

He was ancient and gnarled and, despite the sweltering heat, was dressed in several layers of green.

Fluke shook his hand and introduced himself.

'Sam Wilson. Head greenkeeper,' the old man said. 'Gather you've got a hand there.'

Fluke said nothing.

'Fellas down at the clubhouse are saying it fell from the sky.'

'That right?' Fluke said.

Wilson continued. 'Bet it's got you city boys stumped, eh?'

Fluke lived in a log cabin in the middle of a wood. It was hardly Manchester.

Wilson continued. 'They're saying you'll be taking Mr Yates

8

in for questioning soon. Thinking he put the hand there or knows something about it.'

'Seem to know a lot, these "fellas" of yours.'

Wilson smiled. 'Reckon they do. There's nowt worse than golfers for gossip, and this has got them fair excited.'

Fluke was pressed for time. He needed to recover the hand before the sun cooked it.

'I'm sorry, Mr Wilson, but I need to get on. If there's something you'd like to let us know, you should speak to one of the officers in a suit. They'll take a statement from you.'

Wilson didn't move. 'You in charge?'

He nodded.

'Can I look at the hand?'

'Why?'

'I'll be able to tell you if you need to lock up Mr Yates or not, that's why.'

'How?' Fluke asked. Wilson undoubtedly knew things the 'city boys' didn't, and he never ignored local knowledge.

Wilson didn't answer. He simply stared at Fluke, waiting for permission.

'Fine,' Fluke said, 'but you follow me and you don't touch anything. And if you're wasting my time I'm taking the handbrake off that tractor. You can walk back to the clubhouse.'

Wilson grinned. 'Fair enough. It won't take long.'

Wilson bent down and stared at the hand. Fluke was expecting him to get down on his knees and look at it from different angles. As it happened, he didn't look at it for long. He stood up and wiped his hands on his thick coat.

'You can let Mr Yates go,' he said.

Fluke didn't know what to expect but a two-second examination followed by an acquittal didn't come close. 'I'm going to need slightly more than that if you don't mind.'

9

He nodded. 'The hand wasn't placed there. Nor was it chucked from that wall ova' yonder,' he said, pointing at the dry stone wall Fluke had only just dismissed as a hiding place. 'This came from the air, just as Mr Yates said it did.'

'And you know this how?' Fluke wasn't being sarcastic.

'You see those marks on the hand?'

Fluke nodded.

'Those are the marks that mean it was dropped from the air.'

Fluke bent down and looked closely. 'What are you seeing that I'm not?'

Wilson scanned the sky. Eventually he saw something and pointed towards it.

Fluke looked but couldn't see anything. There was a white line in the sky. An aeroplane had passed recently. Was that what he meant?

Did he think it had been thrown from an aeroplane?

It wasn't impossible, but he failed to see how Wilson could know after such a short examination.

But Wilson didn't think the hand had been thrown from a plane. Far from it.

'Those marks are from talons. A buzzard dropped that hand, Mr Fluke.'

Chapter 2

Fluke arrived at the bottom of the hill and walked straight into an argument. Towler had been telling everyone he'd invented the saying, 'Golf is a good walk spoiled.' Alan Vaughn, FMIT's senior DC, was telling him to piss off, Jo Skelton was telling him it was Winston Churchill, and Jiao-long Zhang, their Chinese officer on secondment, was shouting and laughing that they were all wrong, and that it was a Mark Twain quote.

Fluke smiled. Some things never changed. He knew Towler was simply causing an argument because he liked having them. The team gathered round.

'The head greenkeeper tells me the hand was almost certainly dropped by a buzzard,' he told them. 'They get dead rabbits dropped on the course from time to time.'

'Too heavy for them?' Vaughn asked.

'No. That's what I thought. Apparently it's because they're lazy and steal each other's food. He says it'll have picked it up from somewhere and dropped it when another buzzard tried to snatch it. And as they eat carrion, they have relatively small ranges for birds of prey, so we're not looking too far, he reckons.'

'What we looking for though?' Towler said.

'Don't know,' Fluke admitted. He didn't know anywhere near enough. Time to cast a few nets. 'Matt, I want you to go and see Mr Wilson and coordinate searches of likely areas with him. He has the local knowledge and seems to be a bit of an expert. Get uniform to help.'

Fluke turned to Skelton. 'Jo, I need you to go to the local hospitals and find out what happens to medical waste. I don't think that's what it is, but we need to box it off anyway. And while you're there, see if there's any way of finding out if they've amputated any hands recently. But first, get a portable fingerprint scanner up here. See if the hand belongs to anyone we know.'

'Will do.'

He turned to Jiao-long. 'Longy, I want you to . . .' Fluke stopped mid-sentence. 'What the hell?'

Four men were running towards them, waving golf clubs in the air. They were at least half a mile away but he could hear them shouting.

'Matt, get up there and meet them,' Fluke said. 'I think we can maybe cancel that search.'

Towler sprinted off. The remaining members of FMIT watched his long strides eat up the ground. Even when faced with the sharp incline of the hill his pace didn't falter. The man was a machine. He reached them and Fluke could see gesticulating. They were clearly excited about something. At one point both Towler and the group turned to look at something unseen. Towler reached into his pocket and retrieved something. Two seconds later Fluke's mobile rang.

'What is it?' he said.

'They reckon the rest of the body's up there, boss. I'll go and have a look. Give me a minute.'

Fluke waited impatiently.

Thirty seconds later he was back on.

'Found the victim, boss. And we're not going to need the FME to confirm death.'

Fluke said nothing.

Towler continued. 'How are we supposed to phrase it? "Injuries sustained are extensive and incompatible with life."'

Chapter 3

Cockermouth Golf Course's signature hole is the tenth. There are two ways to play it. You can play safe and aim for the fairway marker. A decent drive will put you on the highest point on the course, leaving a short approach shot to the green. Or you can try to cut out the dogleg and go straight for the hole and the chance of an eagle. The danger of that shot being that a slight hook will see your ball drop into the valley below.

With few exceptions, it was everyone's favourite hole, and not just because it was the only real 'stick or twist' decision you had to make on the whole course.

It was because the men's toilets were behind the green.

'Toilet' was a bit generous. It was really just two fence panels set at right angles to each other. There was no plumbing, just a pile of small rocks to piss on. In winter it was treacherous and in summer it stank.

The four men playing had partaken in cups of tea and bacon sandwiches before leaving the clubhouse and had all needed a comfort break when they'd finished putting. The actual toilet area wasn't big enough for all of them so the fourth had wandered off to a convenient bush.

He'd undone his flies and was about to relieve the pressure on his bladder when he looked down.

And saw an eyeless skull.

*

13

Left unattended it is surprising how quickly a dead body becomes part of the food chain. Flies and beetles, rats and foxes, crows and buzzards; they all rush in when death's dinner bell sounds. The bigger animals tear chunks off the corpse, allowing smaller ones to get in and feed as well.

That is what usually happens.

Here, the murderer had given Cumbria's carnivores a helping hand.

The body had been dismembered. There was really no other way to describe it. Someone had taken their time and made sure each part was small enough to be dragged away or eaten in situ.

Unsurprisingly, the skull was the largest piece left and the animals had ravaged it. The eyes had been pecked out, probably by carrion crows. A fox, or something similar, had been feeding on the softer parts. The nose and ears had gone; chunks of flesh had been torn from the cheeks and chin. The tongue had been eaten.

The skull's long hair was the only feature the animals hadn't been interested in. It remained untouched. Blond dreadlocks, covered in dirt and blood.

Fluke saw the other hand – the little finger had been chewed off – but other than the feet and a couple of other recognisable parts, he was struggling to tell what the rest of the bits were. Gristle, bone, offal and flesh were scattered over an area the size of a tennis court. Some pieces were in small pools of blood; they'd either been thrown there by whoever had hacked up the corpse or animals had moved them before the blood had clotted.

Great swarms of flies feasted on the smorgasbord of organic matter on the ground. Fluke knew he'd never forget the sound of their buzzing. It just sounded . . . wrong.

The smell was dense, vile and strangely sweet, and, like the vomit of a drunk, it was overwhelming. Fluke felt saliva fill his mouth and knew he was close to gagging. He swallowed hard and it passed.

14

He thought he was looking at just the one body – there was certainly only one skull – but it would take an expert in human anatomy to confirm it. There wasn't enough left to even guess at what the cause of death had been. Judging by the skull shape, Fluke guessed they were looking at the corpse of a man. Other than that and the dreadlocks there was nothing obvious to help in identifying the victim. There were no signs of clothing among the human debris. He wondered if the victim had been naked when he was killed, or whether his clothes had been removed afterwards.

Large pools of blood stained the grass. Fluke knew he was looking at the murder scene and not a deposition site. He was grateful it hadn't rained recently. It would help with determining a time of death.

The sun had been relentless that summer. Cowpats were bleached white and curled at the edges. Sheep droppings were as dry as dust and moved with the wind.

He heard someone sniff, and turned. It was Alan Vaughn. Even with the summer they were having he was bone white. The man never went outside unless he had to. Fluke was pleased to see him though. Ordinarily he treated criminal profilers with the same disdain as he did consultants – they were people who borrowed your watch to tell you the time – but Vaughn offered perspectives no one else could. He had the unnerving ability to see into the minds of the depraved. Far beyond what was healthy.

Although it was useful, it was also why he'd been voted 'member of the team most likely to turn into a serial killer' at the last four FMIT Christmas parties . . .

'What do you see, Alan?'

Vaughn stared. 'Anger,' he said simply.

A man had been hacked to pieces. Fluke guessed anger was too small a word to describe the rage the killer had been feeling.

'And despite the pieces being small enough to eat, we were

15

meant to find this, boss,' he continued. 'Someone either wants us involved or is sending a message to someone.'

Fluke said nothing. He'd been thinking exactly the same thing.

Fluke sat down on a round stone thirty yards away from the scene. It was rare for plain-clothed cops to be first at a murder scene and there were some tasks he needed to do – tasks usually done long before FMIT arrived.

He phoned HQ to arrange for the coroner to be informed and to request a Home Office pathologist – here he got lucky; his friend Henry Sowerby was free. He then made sure SOCO were on their way.

Finally he called Detective Superintendent Cameron Chambers and told him that the hand on the golf course had escalated into a murder inquiry.

Within half an hour, Sean Rogers, the crime scene manager, had arrived. They shook hands. Fluke hadn't seen Rogers since the Dalton Cross case.

'Makes a change from burglaries,' Rogers said.

Fluke grunted. 'See if you still think that after you've seen it.'

Rogers was travelling with a small SOCO team. They immediately got to work putting down footboards and erecting forensic tents. It didn't look as though it was going to rain anytime soon but there was no point taking risks. Although the media didn't know about the crime scene yet, the tents would also help restrict visual access to their long-range lenses. They also issued forensic suits to everyone who needed them. Rogers had thoughtfully grabbed an extra-large one for Towler.

Rogers and Fluke walked through the crime scene and agreed what needed to be done. The only thing possible for the moment was a video walkthrough and a comprehensive photographic record of the scene. Everything else would have to wait until the pathologist arrived.

While FMIT busied themselves for yet another murder investigation, Fluke found somewhere quiet to sit. A feeling of unease he couldn't put his finger on was crawling up his spine. He'd seen men blown up in Belfast – men who'd had to be swept up with a broom – so the nature of the crime scene wasn't what was bothering him. He just had one of those feelings. He felt on edge, as if he was being watched.

He'd never had a premonition before and didn't believe he was having one now.

Perhaps it was the relentless, beating heat.

It was enough to drive anyone crazy.

Chapter 4

Henry Sowerby was a walking cliché. Tall and thin, it looked like the dome of his head had forced its way through the shock of his white hair. He was wearing his trademark three-piece tweed suit and carrying his brown leather case.

Fluke wasn't fooled by the kindly professor act; Sowerby had the sharpest forensic mind of any pathologist he'd met. The old-fashioned suit was also misleading; he was up to date with every new technique there was, and although the leather case was old and battered, Fluke knew it would be filled with state-of-the-art equipment.

'Got something a bit different, Henry,' Fluke said, after they'd shaken hands. Sowerby worked the north-west of England, which included Liverpool and Manchester; he was no stranger to extreme acts of violence. Fluke doubted he'd have come across this before, though.

They signed in to the inner cordon and stepped into the crime scene.

Sowerby stared for a full five minutes.

'OK, you've got me,' he said. 'This is new.'

Sowerby got to work. He stopped at various pieces of the corpse, occasionally muttering in Latin. Some parts he lingered over, some he ignored completely.

'Where to start?' he said. 'Where to start?'

'We have a hand in a bag in the van at the bottom, Henry.' Fluke explained the morning's events. 'I'm assuming, but you'll have to confirm, that it's from this scene.'

'Is it the right?'

'Yep,' Fluke said. 'What's left of the left is still there. We think it's the body of a man.'

Sowerby grunted noncommittally. Fluke knew he wouldn't offer any opinion until he had something to base it on. It was one of his strong points. Weaker pathologists would cave and start guessing if an SIO pressed for early information. Not Sowerby. You got information when *he* was ready, but what you got was solid.

'The scene is videoed, I take it?'

'And photographed,' Fluke confirmed. 'I really only called to get some advice on how to recover it. This is the first time I've worked a dismemberment.'

'Me too, dear boy. Me too.'

He joined Fluke at the entrance to the inner cordon. A uniformed officer held up the tape for him. In his spare time, Sowerby was a cold-weather mountaineer. He looked uncomfortable in the baking sun. He took a handkerchief from his inside pocket and mopped his face.

'I suppose the only thing we can do is to treat each piece as a separate crime scene. Process them individually. I've counted over thirty different bits so we're going to be here a while. Can you send someone down the hill to my car? I've spare boxes and bags in the boot. We're going to need them.'

They made small talk while they waited for his equipment to be brought up. The slight breeze that had made the heat tolerable and the smell bearable blew itself out, and the suffocating temperature and stench quickly enveloped them. They moved away from the scene and took off their suits. Even ten minutes out of them was a blessing.

A movement below caught their eyes and they watched in bemused silence as Towler jogged up the fairway and met them. He'd come from the clubhouse, so had just run the full length of the course.

In his suit.

Carrying boxes.

On a day when everyone else was drenched, he was barely sweating.

'Henry,' he said, dropping the boxes on the ground beside him. He reached for, and shook, Sowerby's hand.

'You should have got uniform to bring them up, Matt.'

He shrugged.

'We got anything yet, Henry? TOD?'

'Nothing yet, Sergeant Towler. And I'm going to struggle with a time of death, I'm afraid, what with the heat and the nature of the scene.'

Fluke nodded. He'd feared as much.

'I would normally use liver temperature to give a rough TOD, but there are three reasons I can't here,' he said. 'One; the strength of the sun would give a false reading. Two; the liver's supposed to be *inside* the body when I take a reading. And three, and this is the main one, I suppose – something's bloody eaten it!'

It was five hours later and the body parts still hadn't been recovered. Five hours in forensic suits with the sun beating them into submission. Fluke had insisted everyone stop for five minutes every thirty. The last thing he wanted was someone going down with heatstroke. In weather like this, in stifling forensic suits, it was a real possibility.

Sean Rogers, who had to oversee every part of the recovery operation, ignored the catcalls and jeering and stripped down to his boxers just to keep going. Even then he had to change his forensic suit every hour as his sweat was making them sodden.

Sowerby was struggling.

He'd been working flat out and Fluke was worried. Usually Sowerby would express his findings out loud but after an hour he went silent. Just stayed on his hands and knees among the human carnage.

Fluke carried over a bottle of lukewarm water, and tapped him on the shoulder.

'Henry, you need to take a break,' he said. 'And I need you to drink this.'

Sowerby drained it in one go. He handed back the empty bottle and started to put his facemask back on.

'It's not a request, Henry. You're having a rest for thirty minutes minimum. My scene, my rules.'

For a moment he thought Sowerby was going to argue. Fluke didn't want to forcibly remove him, but he would. Instead, Sowerby stomped off without saying anything. Fluke stood at the top of the hill and watched him walk down to the clubhouse car park, which was now full of police vehicles. The air was so still he could hear Sowerby's Jaguar's engine start. The car didn't move. He'd obviously switched on the air conditioning.

No one was working the scene until Sowerby returned and Fluke took advantage of the relative peace. He found somewhere where the air was a bit sweeter and sat down. Except for the incessant flies, the crime scene was still. There were six body parts to recover. With their food source diminishing, the remaining body parts had so many flies on them they looked as though they were moving.

As he waited, Fluke started running through his early thoughts.

The body was always going to be discovered.

He didn't think the victim had been taken there by force either; there were no roads nearby – it was either an almost impossible climb from Embleton Road or a trek along the entire length of the golf course. Dragging someone there seemed unlikely. The victim being *lured* there was the most plausible explanation.

Was it possible the location was more important than the disadvantages it presented? Fluke wasn't ruling anything out yet.

A detective with half his nous would also be thinking 'ritualistic' after taking in the methodical dismemberment. Fluke wasn't so sure though.

He thought this was something different.

Chapter 5

Fluke made Sowerby rest twice more before he finished. By that time it was nearly 9 p.m. and everyone was exhausted and cranky. Sowerby stalked off down the hill and got in his Jag without saying a word. Fluke had taken a call from the Cumberland Infirmary on Sowerby's behalf, confirming a post-mortem suite had been booked for the following day. Hopefully Sowerby would have stopped sulking by then. Fluke didn't like falling out with the pathologist but ultimately the crime scene was his responsibility, and that included the health and safety of everyone working there.

Sowerby knew that; he'd come round.

And he hadn't been the only one suffering from the heat. Fluke had needed rest as well. He'd asked Towler to deputise for him in the early evening, got a lift down to the clubhouse in Wilson's tractor, and went for a drink and something to eat.

Although the course was now closed, the clubhouse remained open. It was full of the police officers and civilian staff who support a murder investigation. Jo Skelton was talking to someone and getting a list of members. You never knew what you'd need.

Fluke ordered a pint of Diet Coke and a bacon sandwich. He wandered through the members' lounge sipping his icy drink while he waited for his food. The wood-panelled walls were covered in photos and boards with the names of club captains. It was clearly a club with a bit of history. Some of the names were good old-fashioned Cumbrian names: Hume, Kirkbride, Thwaites and Lowther. Others such as Smith, Jones, Hendricks,

Watson and Williamson could have come from any corner of the UK.

Fluke had never been a golfer. In fact, the only thing he knew about it was that, unlike most other sports, the object of golf was to play as little golf as possible. The fewer shots the better.

The barman called out his name. He collected his food and called for Wilson the greenkeeper. It was too hot to walk far and he already had a dehydration headache. He wanted a lift.

When the scene was finished to his satisfaction, he issued some early investigative lines and headed home.

He'd considered staying a bit longer, but realised standing in a field with thousands of maggots, millions of flies and several hairy-arsed coppers was no substitute for half a home life. The early stages of a murder investigation never truly finished – you just decided to stop. Bridie never mentioned the hours he put in and the weekends they had to cancel – as a solicitor she knew what the demands of his job were – but she wouldn't be human if she didn't feel put out every now and then. Since he'd been seeing Bridie he had a rule; if he had the chance of going home, he did.

The journey to his cabin would take about an hour. As he drove his mind raced through the gears of a murder investigation. By the time he was turning off B roads onto the dirt tracks that would eventually lead to his cabin, he was in a world of his own. A world of killers and victims. Of clues and red herrings.

He was still ten miles from home and, because his mind was elsewhere, he didn't immediately register the couple standing in the middle of the road. They were both staring at his BMW. He slammed his brakes on. The thick tyres gripped the baked earth and the car skidded to an ungainly stop. One of the pair, a woman, stuck her tongue out and flipped him her middle finger; the second time that had happened today.

At least this time the hand was attached to a body, he thought.

'Bloody hell!' he yelled. He was more shaken than angry.

The cloud of dust the BMW had thrown forward reached the pair. The woman was young, far younger than Fluke had first thought. Dressed head to toe in colourful clothes and carrying a small hemp bag, her dirty hair was braided so heavily he could see her skull. She would probably be pretty if not dressed like a rag-and-bone man.

She gave Fluke and the car the once over.

She said something to the male she was with – another trampy dickhead – who laughed. She offered Fluke a derisory sneer, mouthed 'wanker', and started walking again.

That's all he needed, he thought. A bunch of new age travellers in the area.

Fluke put the car back into gear, and slowly drove up behind them. They made no attempt to get off the road and he couldn't pass them.

Sod it.

He pressed down on the horn and smiled as they both jumped. The woman whipped round and stared.

For a moment Fluke thought he was going to have to get out and do something, although he had no idea what. He doubted showing them his warrant card would be productive. He'd come back the next day and find six of them chained to his house.

Luckily he didn't have to do anything. They clearly decided the man sitting in the metal coffin was beneath them, and stood on the verge giving him Nazi salutes as he inched forward.

'Arseholes,' he muttered, as the BMW crawled past them. When they were no more than scruffy blobs in his rear-view mirror, he picked up his speed again; Bridie and a slowly roasted leg of lamb were waiting for him.

*

Like many people brought up in the Lakes, Fluke didn't always appreciate the scenery. Every now and then someone would visit and he'd be re-enthused by their joyous reactions, but most of the time he looked without seeing.

Except when he turned onto his land. The view of Ullswater. The mountains. The woods. His beautiful Finnish cabin. He'd only been there eighteen months but already couldn't imagine living anywhere else.

He opened the door but the expected smells of lamb and rosemary weren't there. He and Bridie had fallen into the habit of greeting whoever was last back from work with a kiss and a cold drink. Fluke sometimes made sure he was back last just to see her warm smile as she bounded down the front porch to greet him. Usually the room was warm, light-filled. This evening it was cold and dark.

Bridie's car was outside but all the lights were off.

Something was wrong.

Fluke grabbed the nearest thing he could use as a weapon – a small axe he'd been using to chop kindling – and crept into the cabin.

Long-forgotten Northern Ireland training kicked in. He inched into the open-plan living room and, keeping his back to the wall, scanned the corners.

Nothing.

He reached behind him and found the light switch. After a moment's hesitation, he turned it on.

Bridie was in his leather armchair, looking at him. She had taken the duvet from the bedroom and had cocooned herself. Only her head was visible. She'd been crying.

Fluke put the axe on the wooden floor and ran over.

'What's the matter, Bridie?'

She didn't say anything. Instead she pointed at the small coffee table.

Fluke looked across and saw what had upset her.

On the table was a small envelope. Bridie had obviously opened it and the detective in him immediately noticed it had no name or address on it. The item inside the envelope was on the table beside it.

It was a shotgun cartridge.

Chapter 6

The intimidation had begun a few months after Fluke had stolen land from under the nose of a multinational holiday home company. International Luxury Lake Retreats had been holding the Forestry Commission to ransom, assuming no one else would want the land that bordered their own. It was virtually worthless. Steep, heavily wooded and without any form of planning permission, ILLR only wanted it because it had roadside access. As they held out for a lower price, Fluke had nipped in and bought it with the critical illness insurance payout he'd received after being diagnosed with Burkitt's lymphoma.

Fluke had been suffering from PTSD after his recovery from cancer and wanted isolation; the almost inaccessible land had been perfect. He'd imported a Finnish cabin, had it professionally sited and started to find some peace.

ILLR, instead of taking it gracefully, hunkered down with their solicitors. Their opening salvo was to the local authority, and their planning department soon contacted Fluke.

He had no answer to their requests for copies of permission for a residential home; his permission was for a *holiday* home. He ignored the council for as long as he could but they were like mould: slow and persistent. But, just as he was on the verge of caving in and taking the paltry amount ILLR were offering, Bridie Harper-Tarr entered his life.

She was beautiful, complex and a friend of his haematologist. She was also a world-class solicitor, specialising in international law. Not only did she fall for Fluke, she fell for his home.

The council's legal department were outgunned and quickly withdrew. Fluke relaxed. ILLR returned with their own solicitors and battle lines were drawn.

ILLR came back hard. They requested a judicial review – a legal challenge by a private individual or company against a decision made by a public body. It would be heard by a judge and the finding would be final. It would also pass into case law, meaning it could be cited by others in a similar position.

Fluke had been horrified. Bridie had just smiled. 'Means we're winning,' she'd told him.

The legal argument the council had put forward about Fluke only having holiday-home permission had been dealt with by Bridie. It had been retrospectively amended and ILLR seemed to accept the permit was unlikely to be a seam they could mine for legal dissent.

Instead they focused on the cabin itself. Their argument was simple. The law said the cabin in the wood had to be able to be transported fully assembled. Whether this was practical was irrelevant. ILLR complied with the law, Fluke hadn't. All their cabins were transported on lorries, ready built. Fluke's, they argued, had been assembled on site, and was far too big to be transported as it was. The judicial review disclosure papers cited evidence from a wide source of transport experts categorically stating there was no transport system available that could carry Fluke's home.

'We'll wait them out,' Bridie had said.

Judicial reviews take time and are prohibitively expensive for both sides. ILLR were amassing huge legal bills. Fluke hadn't spent a penny. Bridie did it all for free. When she needed outside counsel, she called in favours. It wasn't unusual for strange men and women to suddenly appear at the cabin, stay a day locked in conversation with Bridie, before getting the train back to London.

And then one of her friends, an environmental lawyer who'd visited, handed Fluke a figurative silver bullet: a small wooden box. It looked a bit like a letterbox. There was a narrow slot under a slanted roof.

'Bridie tells me there are bats in these woods,' the solicitor had said.

'Hundreds,' he'd confirmed.

'Put some of these up in your eaves. Game over as far as ILLR are concerned. It's illegal to demolish any structure in this country if bats are nesting in it. Doesn't matter if the building's been constructed correctly or not.'

Fluke had looked at the box in his hand. The answer to all his problems apparently.

In one way the lawyer had been right. It had been the end of his problems. His *legal* problems. ILLR, obviously scared of the huge legal bill without a guaranteed win and recovery of their costs, adopted a more insidious approach.

Harassment.

And that meant a whole heap of new problems.

The first time it had happened, it was a bag of dog shit. Fluke assumed it had been kids, although for the life of him he hadn't been able to think where they could have come from. He was the only person for a mile in each direction. Nothing more happened for a month and he put it out of his mind. Until it happened again.

On a semi-regular basis, Fluke would find something either in his cabin or on his land.

Fluke went to see the managing director of the ILLR resort that bordered his land but it was clear the man knew nothing. If it *was* someone in ILLR, it was someone higher up the food chain.

Until that night, a brace of headless rabbits, their blood soaked into his beautiful wooden porch, had been the worst thing they'd left.

Now with the implied threat of a shotgun cartridge, they had frightened the only woman he'd ever loved. That was unacceptable. It was time to do something about it.

Something they wouldn't expect.

It was time to involve Towler.

Chapter 7

Fluke was still furious when he arrived at FMIT's wing in Carleton Hall, Cumbria Constabulary's headquarters building in Penrith, the next morning. Neither he nor Bridie had slept, and by 3 a.m. they'd given up and played a game of Scrabble. At five they decided they might as well have an early start. Bridie had been, unsurprisingly, quiet at breakfast. They'd eaten in silence.

Fluke was worried. Not about the cartridge – he and Towler would sort that out. No, he was worried about Bridie. While fear would be the rational response for normal people, Bridie wasn't normal. She'd faced down dictators. She'd prosecuted organised crime bosses. Even the dead rabbits hadn't fazed her. She'd actually cooked them. Outside, on the fire pit, in case anyone was watching for their reaction. But last night had been something new. She'd looked genuinely scared.

Jo Skelton was the only person at work when he walked into the incident room. She'd either stayed late or started very early to get it set up. These days she didn't need to be asked. She was the most organised in the team and a natural at making sure the incident room was properly equipped. Fluke knew she'd have also opened a HOLMES 2 account to ensure the chaos of early intelligence was inputted logically. HOLMES was useful but, like most detectives of a certain age, Fluke didn't rely on it. Yes, it could make links and highlight patterns and names that had cropped up, but it couldn't replace intuition and experience.

'What we got, Jo?' he said.

He wasn't expecting much. The investigation was only starting.

'Waiting on an email from tech services, boss. They tell me the fingerprints from both hands are on file. Same person obviously.'

Fluke felt a surge of excitement. Getting an ID this early was a real breakthrough.

'We got a name?'

'Not yet. Problem with the upload last night. They called the IT company out and it should be sorted soon. I'm expecting it anytime.'

'OK. I'm going to get a brew and check my emails. Buzz me as soon as you hear anything. I'll be back when the rest of the lazy buggers bother to show up.'

Skelton raised her eyebrows. It was still only half past six.

Fluke grabbed a black coffee and took it back to his office, turning on his computer as he sat down. He had over forty emails to read. There was one from Detective Superintendent Cameron Chambers asking for an update on the body. Fluke composed a reply reiterating that it was definitely a murder and he was hopeful he'd have an ID today. Quick but polite. He and Chambers had a difficult relationship. Up until Christmas, Fluke had assumed they hated each other but the chief constable had sat him down and explained that Chambers, whenever possible, tried to give him complete autonomy in his investigations. The arrangement worked well. He had free rein to lead his small team as he saw fit and Chambers, technically the officer responsible for major investigations, got the results he needed. Chambers was ambitious but, as the chief had explained, ambition wasn't always a *bad* thing. Just because Fluke had no interest in joining the ACPO ranks didn't mean those who did were arseholes. To keep the truce going, Fluke made a point of keeping him in the loop. Sort of. He didn't tell him everything, but he told him enough.

He skimmed the rest of his emails and decided there was nothing that needed his immediate attention. He leaned back in his chair, sipping his coffee. It was just the right temperature.

A door opened somewhere, something was knocked over and smashed. Someone swore.

Fluke smiled; Towler had arrived.

Matt Towler was the team lunatic. An ex-Para, he was one of nature's sergeants. He'd joined FMIT a few years earlier, when he'd had to cut his army career short to look after a daughter he hadn't known he had. He was the most violent and gentle man Fluke had ever known. He was also Fluke's best friend.

If anyone could help him with someone posting dog shit and shotgun cartridges through his door, it would be him.

Fluke explained what had been happening.

He'd known Towler for over thirty years and could tell when his friend was angry. He could also tell when he was about to go into a rage. His lips went white and his ears reddened.

'And you're only just telling me now?' he said. 'What the fuck, Ave? Abi stays at yours sometimes.'

Shit.

Fluke hadn't considered that.

'We'll be talking about this again,' Towler continued. 'You'd better fucking believe that.'

Fluke believed him. And Fluke also believed he'd have some loose teeth to fix afterwards as well.

'Fair enough,' he said. 'Is there anything we can do? I've spoken to the manager of ILLR and it isn't him.'

Towler snorted. 'Course it isn't him. Some glorified caretaker on twenty grand a year isn't going to give a shit about your land. No, this fucker's someone higher up.'

Fluke nodded.

'We'll stake your place out. Do the main access points. He

won't be coming in by road. Set a trap for the wanker. Break his legs, take him out onto the lake and see if he can still swim.'

Fluke didn't laugh. The same thought had crossed his mind more than once. For the first time in his career, taking the law into his own hands didn't seem abhorrent.

'Whoever it is, they're too clever for that. There's no pattern and the gaps are too big to do a physical stakeout.'

'There's more than one form of stakeout, Ave.'

Fluke knew he was referring to specialist equipment. 'I know, but I can't get that type of stuff, Matt. Wouldn't know where to start looking.'

'You might not know where—'

The phone rang and they both frowned. Fluke answered it and listened.

'We'll have to do this some other time. That was Alan. We're needed in the incident room, the fingerprint results are in. We have a name.'

'Mark Cadden. Thirty-nine years old. Looks like he's a Londoner,' Vaughn told them, handing Fluke and Towler copies of Cadden's Police National Computer printout.

Fluke flicked through the document. It ran to three pages. 'What else we got?'

'That's all. Couple of not-guilty summaries on PND and the odd bit of intel, but otherwise that's it.'

'Bollocks,' Towler said. 'Someone this active has local teams stopping him everywhere he goes. There's got to be intel, even if it was only sightings.'

'I agree,' Vaughn said. 'But there isn't.'

Which was odd.

'Look at these convictions,' Towler said. 'Criminal damage, aggravated trespass, blackmail, arson, malicious communications, harassment, *threats to kill*. Over a period of nearly twenty years. Read me one of those PND not-guilty summaries, Al.'

Vaughn opened up a new page on his computer terminal.

'This is the latest one,' he said. '"Cadden found not guilty of obstructing the clearance of woodland when his solicitor successfully argued that stopping unlawful activity cannot be classified as obstruction. Despite the wood being legally scheduled for clearance, the chainsaw operators were from a different company to the one in the council's petition making the whole activity illegal." West Berkshire Council had to pay Cadden's legal fees.'

'He was an environmental activist then,' said Towler. 'That's all we fucking need. When we get the case summaries for each of these offences, I bet they all relate to animal rights and trespass and other hippy-dippy shite.'

The room went silent as the beginnings of a motive peeked its head above the parapet. The only thing that could be heard was the drip of the filter machine. The smell of coffee brewing made Fluke's stomach growl. He was thirsty. He got up and poured himself a cup. As if he'd broken them all out of a trance, they joined him as one round the machine and refilled their mugs.

'And someone with a record like this doesn't stop either,' Towler continued. 'They go on and on and on. You can't argue them out of their position. They won't compromise. There are no grey areas with them. Have you ever met one? A really committed one? They have nothing. No possessions. No homes. And they don't give a shit. The cause is everything. They can be dangerous. Incredibly dangerous. They might look like tramps but don't let it fool . . .'

Towler faded out as a memory dragged Fluke twelve hours back in time. To his encounter with the two new age travellers the night before.

A coincidence? Probably. Fluke didn't trust coincidences though. They were the lazy man's explanation. He decided not to share the information yet.

It was probably nothing.

Chapter 8

Like mortuaries up and down the country, the one at Carlisle's Cumberland Infirmary had white tiled walls, biohazard posters, sinks and sluices, and an invasive sense of death that the chemical disinfectants could do little to conceal.

With an average of five murders a year, Cumbria didn't need a dedicated forensic post-mortem suite, which meant that rather than being behind a glass screen, the senior investigating officer was in the same room as the pathologist. Fluke preferred it that way. He was charged with finding the victim's killer; why should the impact of the crime be diluted through glass and microphones?

And being up close and personal with the cadaver meant he could see things for himself rather than have them described to him. So he'd attended post-mortems many, many times. Witnessed all their gruesome manifestations. They no longer shocked him, no longer swayed his reason. The post-mortem was a scientific process and it obeyed scientific laws. But more than that, they were a chance for a story to emerge.

A chance for the dead to speak to the living.

So Fluke made sure he always attended the post-mortem.

But he still hated them.

Sowerby was already there. Apart from his gloveless hands, he was suited up, ready to go. Someone had obviously been working hard before he'd arrived. Like an obscene butcher's shop window, the body parts were already laid out on the stainless steel examination table.

An eyeless skull, stripped of all fleshy parts. Clumps of hair. Lopped off limbs and heaps of bones; some white, some still covered with skin, flesh, ligaments and gristle. And other larger, as yet unidentified, body parts.

The parts were laid out in a rough approximation of a human body. Fluke reckoned that about a quarter of the body was still unaccounted for. He made a mental note to expand the search team's area, although he had to accept that some parts would never be recovered. Some would already be scat.

Sowerby looked up as he entered, put down the instrument he was checking and marched up to him. Fluke stopped, not knowing what to expect.

Eventually Sowerby cracked a huge smile. 'You were right, I was wrong. End of the matter?'

He thrust his hand out.

Fluke let out a breath he hadn't realised he'd been holding. He hadn't wanted to fall out with Sowerby but making him rest at the crime scene had been the right thing to do. He grabbed the hand and shook it firmly.

'Already forgotten, Henry,' he said.

'Now to business, Avison.' Sowerby waited while Fluke put on the required protective clothing. 'I've already started my preliminary examination.'

Fluke frowned. 'Oh.'

The PM wasn't supposed to start until the SIO was present.

'Nothing untoward, old chap. I wanted to get the cadaver in the right order on the table. I had to do it myself. John here,' he pointed at the mortuary assistant, 'doesn't know his tibia from his arse bone.'

Sowerby turned to the hapless John who'd picked up a part of what looked like a foot. Sowerby glowered at him.

'If it's wet and not yours, don't touch it!' he snapped. He turned back to Fluke. 'I couldn't help noticing something.'

Fluke had never known Sowerby to offer opinions this early in the process.

'It was hard to tell on the hill yesterday, but with the blood and flies washed off things are a little clearer.'

'How so?' Fluke said.

'Come with me, Avison.' Sowerby started pointing at various parts of the body. 'Do you see here? And here? And here?'

Fluke leaned over. The parts he'd been directed to were all in the area of the upper thigh. He instantly saw what Sowerby was getting at. There were cuts on them all. Some were an inch deep, some less.

Sowerby was walking round the table pointing at more parts of the victim's body.

'And here? At the back of both knees. Another cut. Not deep, but enough to sever the tendons. Another here on the upper arm – again the tendon is severed.'

For ten minutes Fluke was shown round the body, bit by bit.

'I assume these cuts were post-mortem, Henry,' Fluke said. 'Whoever did this wouldn't have had access to anything more than hand tools. There were always going to be some slips.'

'These cuts were *ante*-mortem, Avison.'

He frowned. 'Defensive wounds?' he said. 'They look a bit odd if they are.'

'No, they aren't defensive wounds either,' Sowerby said. 'And if you look at where the injuries are, you'll see that none of the major organs would have been damaged. I've been over the whole body with a magnifying glass. There's not a single stab wound anywhere. Every wound is a slash. I can't give you the exact order.'

'None post-mortem?'

'No. After he was dead the killer cut him up. Jointed him really. It's easier to cut through a joint than sawing through bone.

39

I don't think you're necessarily looking for anyone with specialist butchery skills though.'

'No?'

Sowerby paused before answering, trying to think of something Fluke could relate to. 'When you carve up your Christmas turkey, do you take the legs off at the joint or do you snap the bones?'

'I go through the joint.'

'But you're not a butcher – how do you know how to do that?'

He shrugged. 'Just stick the knife in, I suppose. Avoid the bone and find the path of least resistance.'

'And did you kill this man?' Sowerby didn't wait for an answer. 'My point is that anyone could have done this. Your killer used a hacksaw for the femur,' Sowerby pointed at teeth marks on one of the thigh bones, 'but he snapped the rest of the larger bones.'

There's a profanity in cutting up a dead body, Fluke thought. *It's one thing to murder someone, quite another to destroy their identity completely.*

'But that's not the most interesting thing.'

He moved over to a bench and pointed at an A4 medical outline of the human body, a man with outstretched arms. Sowerby had drawn red marks on the diagram to correspond with the slashes on the body of the victim.

There was a pattern.

A flurry of red marks covered the inner elbows, upper arms, inner thighs and the back of the knees. Fluke picked up the paper. It fluttered slightly in the air conditioning's breeze. He stared without saying a word. For the life of him he couldn't work out which cut had caused death. They all looked superficial.

'What am I seeing, Henry?'

'What weapon do you think was used here?'

Fluke didn't hesitate. 'A knife. And a bloody sharp one at that.'

Sowerby moved back to the examination table and picked up

40

what appeared to be part of the lower thigh. He pointed at the deep cut.

'Back of the leg,' he said.

He pointed just above the back of Fluke's knee. 'The cut went right through the tendons. They all have fancy names but collectively they're the hamstrings.'

Fluke bent over and studied it. Sowerby was right. They were completely severed.

'Now, what's that tell us?' Sowerby said. 'On its own, not a great deal.'

He picked up another part of the body, this time from the opposite side of the table. He laid it next to the one they'd just been looking at.

'But, put the corresponding leg beside it, and what do you see?'

Fluke walked around and looked from different angles. 'It looks like they're the same height on the body. The cut seems uniform throughout. I'd say this was the same cut. Except it can't be.'

'Exactly,' Sowerby said. 'The cuts are the same height but the angles don't work. If they were both horizontal then we might say that someone had run a knife across the back of the victim's legs. One smooth movement. But they're not, they're angled.'

'So they're not the same cut,' Fluke said.

'Yes, they are.' He went back to the table and rearranged the two body parts again. This time he turned them slightly on their sides so the wound was on the top. He bent down and viewed them at eye level. He made some small adjustments before he was satisfied. 'Now tell me what you see, Avison.'

This time Fluke didn't need to look too hard. It was obvious. Despite the two parts being twenty-four inches apart, the cuts matched. He looked down at his own legs. He flexed them at the knee and looked back up at the grisly items. He moved some more until he was satisfied. 'Cut me, Henry.'

Sowerby picked up a large metal ruler, walked over to Fluke, and gently ran it across the back of his legs. It didn't quite work. Fluke moved his legs wider apart.

'Again.'

Sowerby repeated the imaginary slash. Again Fluke wasn't happy. He made a further adjustment, but instead of widening his legs he lifted the front one off the ground and bent it at the knee.

'Try it now.'

He felt the ruler on the back of his knees. He turned round and saw Sowerby smiling.

'That's the one, old chap.'

Fluke straightened up.

'The victim was running away from the killer,' he said.

'Yes,' he replied. 'Now, what else? Tell me what you see.'

Fluke thought about the mechanics of cutting a running man from the rear. He lifted his right hand and drew down an imaginary weapon at the angle of the wounds. He knew what Sowerby was getting at. The weapon had to have been long and it had to have been sharp.

'The killer used a sword,' he said.

Sowerby nodded. 'A long, edged weapon, certainly. Not conclusive, obviously, but there's also some corroborating evidence. How much do you know about medieval combat, Avison?'

'Not much.'

'OK. I'll give you a quick lesson in sword fighting.' He picked up the metal ruler again. 'There are two basic strategies. You either thrust or you cut your opponent.'

'Cut and thrust? Yeah, I've heard of that.'

Sowerby frowned slightly. 'Yes, but that's actually a bit of a misnomer. Weapons weren't really designed to do both. Now common sense tells us that sticking a long sword into the body is bound to be the most effective way of winning a fight. Stick a major organ and it's game over, right?'

Fluke nodded.

'But those who understand sword fighting, who *really* understand it, know different. To get through protective bone, the weapon has to be either heavy enough to smash through' – Sowerby performed a slow-motion swipe at Fluke's head – 'or thin enough to get through small gaps like those between ribs.'

This time he aimed a stab at Fluke's chest.

'The chances of success are small. And even if you do get through to a major organ, your opponent knows they're going to die and goes all out to take you with them. And to thrust you have to get in close. Higher chance of being grabbed or poked with your opponent's weapon.'

Fluke nodded. It made sense. When he'd been in the Marines he'd been taught that kicking someone in the balls during hand-to-hand combat was a bad idea. They might have aching testicles later but right then they'd have enough pain-fuelled adrenaline surging through their system to destroy twenty men.

'The cut, on the other hand, has an elegance to it,' Sowerby continued. 'It won't kill quickly but it's far safer. Anyone who knew what they were doing avoided the major organs initially. Too well protected with armour and bone. Expert sword fighters went for mechanical damage to begin with.'

'Mechanical damage?' Fluke looked back across the table.

'The body's not just a living thing, Avison. It's a masterpiece of engineering. There are hinges and pulleys and valves and all sorts going on in there. The cut across the back of the knees severed the hamstrings. After that he wouldn't have been able to stand.'

Sowerby walked back to the examination table and started pointing at the same bits as before.

This time Fluke tried to think why the killer had chosen each particular cut. A pattern emerged. Most of the cuts were designed to stop limbs working. The back of the thighs would have stopped the victim running. The back of the knees would have brought him to the ground. Slashes to the top of the wrists and to the upper arms would have rendered him unable to lift his arms or close his hands. The killer had systematically and methodically incapacitated him.

'Jesus,' he whispered.

'And that's not all. Can you imagine the skill involved in this?' Sowerby asked. 'The victim's moving, the weapon's moving and the killer's moving. He knew what he was doing.'

Fluke noticed slashes on body parts that didn't have any obvious mechanical significance. 'He missed a couple of times though,' he said. 'Maybe not that much of an expert.'

'No. These were intentional as well, Avison. These cuts opened up major blood vessels. These were the killing cuts.'

The three Ds, he thought. The victim was disabled, he was drained and, finally, he was dismembered.

'And careful when you say "he",' Sowerby said. 'There was no great strength needed here. A woman could just as easily have done this.'

Fluke nodded.

'When I open him up, the cause of death will be a heart attack brought about by blood loss. Manner of death will be the cuts to the femoral artery,' he pointed at the thighs and the corresponding cuts, 'and the axillary artery.' This time he pointed to slashes on the collarbone. 'These cuts, along with the mechanical ones, would have caused him to lose consciousness within two minutes.'

But what a two minutes for anyone to have to live through . . .

As always he was grateful to Sowerby. He'd not once left a post-mortem without a lead. Cumbria wouldn't have that many people trained in medieval combat. He'd start with the historical re-enactment clubs. Take it from there.

'You know what type of sword—'

He didn't get any further. The door to the post-mortem suite burst open. Five men and one woman marched in. A small man held his identification high in front of him as if it were the Olympic torch.

He was short, barely over five feet tall. He wore a beautifully cut suit, a crisp white shirt and his shoes were highly polished. His dark hair was styled and highly gelled, and his subtle tan went all the way up to his hairline. Even though he was in the basement of a hospital, he still wore his designer sunglasses. Obviously a man whose appearance was important to him.

A prick, in other words.

He had a smirk that Fluke wanted to remove with a scalpel; preferably one that had been used to biopsy the anal polyps from a decomposed tramp.

'Sorry, boys,' Fluke said, 'the *Top Gun* auditions aren't until next week. Now if you can just piss off, we have a post-mortem we'd like to—'

Designer Sunglasses didn't wait for Fluke to finish.

'Gentlemen, this will go a lot quicker if you listen carefully.' His smirk didn't falter and he spoke in a thick, but cultured, London accent.

He approached Fluke and handed over a document.

'I'm Detective Chief Inspector John Reyes from the Metropolitan Police,' he said, 'and this post-mortem is finished.'

'Really?' Fluke said.

'Yes, really,' Reyes said. 'You couldn't have known but you've stumbled into one of our active investigations. Please leave all your notes where we can see them. I need everyone to leave. Thank you for all your hard work but this is our case now.'

Chapter 9

Fluke read Reyes's document in silence. It was from the Met's deputy commissioner to the chief constable of Cumbria, ordering him, in the form of a politely worded request, to allow Reyes to take over the investigation.

Fluke didn't get angry. Reyes was an obvious knob, but if it was their ongoing case then it was right that FMIT step aside. Murderers walked free when police forces squabbled.

Sowerby *did* get angry though. It was all Fluke could do to stop the pathologist getting arrested. He was asked for his notes. There weren't any. He was asked for his voice recorder. It hadn't been switched on yet.

'What are your preliminary findings?' Reyes asked.

'Piss off,' was his reply.

'Have you sent anything out for further analysis?'

Sowerby ignored him.

'We hadn't got that far,' Fluke said, as he wondered how they'd got there so quickly. Unless the fingerprint had a marker on it. If someone accessed it, it rang an alarm somewhere.

Reyes said, 'Well, it looks like we're here in the nick of time, gentlemen. Obviously you're a bit out of your depth.'

Fluke ignored the jibe.

'Our own pathologist will do the PM. I suggest you go back to keeping us all safe.'

Fluke had met police officers like Reyes before. Bullying comedians, hiding behind their rank, mistaking arrogance for

46

firm management. But . . . it was their case. The chief had already agreed.

That didn't mean he was prepared to continue taking shit from Tooting's answer to Tom Cruise though.

'Listen, you short-arsed little wanker, Henry here is the best pathologist in the country so pay the man a bit of respect. Now you'll get help from neither of us.'

'Yeah?' Reyes said. 'Good to know. Now, jog on. Be lucky.'

'Come on, Henry,' Fluke said. 'Let's leave them to it.'

As they passed the group of five officers with Reyes, Fluke noticed the female cop's eyes were red-rimmed and puffy. She shrugged at Fluke and mouthed 'sorry'.

So, he thought, *at least one of them had skin in the game.*

In truth, Fluke wasn't surprised something like this had happened. The victim hailed from London and it was likely the Met did have jurisdiction. He had no idea how a murder in Cumbria linked to their investigation and he didn't much care. There was enough work for him to do without him bidding for more. Reyes might be an out-and-out arsehole, but he probably knew what he was doing.

He had a cup of tea with Sowerby in the mortuary office and made sure he'd calmed down before making a few phone calls. He made sure everything would be handed over to the Met when they arrived at HQ. With nothing more to do he decided to go home. He'd booked the whole day for the PM, and now had nothing that needed his immediate attention. He sent Bridie a text explaining he was going to be home early. He didn't have time to put his phone back in his pocket before he got a reply.

'On my way!'

He opened a bottle of red wine as soon as he got in and placed it on the dining table to breathe. He'd been a beer drinker all his life and Bridie had been trying to convert him to the subtleties and nuances of good wine. Every time they went shopping she would patrol the aisles of the supermarket, searching for a bottle that would pair with whatever they were eating that night.

Fluke was prepared to accept other points of view, and he had no problem accepting that people could be passionate and knowledgeable enough about wine to believe it mattered what they drank. Fluke had heard of wine pairing but only in a kind of abstract way; it wasn't something he'd been interested in or something he thought he'd ever do.

But this afternoon he was opening wine. Bridie wanted to talk to him and Fluke knew what it was about.

He'd been an arsehole.

The truth was, the wine was a symptom of what she wanted to talk to him about. She might be able to explain the difference between grapes grown on northern slopes compared to those grown on southern slopes, and she might even know why a soil's acidity produced different flavours, but Fluke didn't care. He didn't like wine. He never had, and despite Bridie's efforts to expose him to it, he doubted he ever would. He suspected he'd been making more than a bit of a fuss about it recently.

He'd been single a long time. He'd had girlfriends when he was younger and partners when he was older. But he'd never lived with anyone before.

As well as the wine, she was also introducing him to a new diet. His morning bacon sandwiches had been replaced by bowel-scouring muesli and his third cup of coffee had turned into orange juice with extra pulp. Curry every night of the week was also a no-no. Pasta was now part of his diet.

He didn't know it was possible to stack the dishwasher incorrectly, and he certainly didn't know there was a wrong way to put the milk back in the fridge . . . But there was apparently.

Little things, big irritations.

His cabin had changed as well. Subtly. Fluke had purposefully kept the open-plan part of the cabin free of clutter. A few comfy seats. Decent television and a Bose sound system. A bookcase and a couple of tables. No ornaments. He wouldn't have described it as minimalist, but it was. One evening he came back from work to see a small bottle on his mantelpiece. It was full of a yellow liquid and had what appeared to be chopsticks sticking out of the open neck. It was called a diffuser, and was supposed to make the cabin smell homely and welcoming. Ha! That was a laugh. He lived in a pine cabin in the middle of a pine forest. His home smelled of pine. Always had, always would. Bridie could bring in an industrial strength blower and blast the cabin with perfume for seven days and it would still smell of pine. He didn't like the look of the strange chopstick vase and, when Bridie wasn't looking, took it down. She didn't say anything but he knew she'd noticed.

The unintended message: this is still my house. He'd felt guilty later that night and put it back, but the next day it had disappeared. Neither of them had mentioned it.

Sleeping in the same bed as Bridie was wonderful. He looked forward to their nights together and loved waking up with her. Loved the tousled look she had in the morning. Loved the little stretches she did before getting out of bed. But he no longer got to decide *when* he got up. Being called 'lazy bones' at seven-thirty on a Sunday morning because Bridie wanted to go walking was something they'd probably need to discuss sometime.

Even when Bridie wasn't there, it changed the way he lived. A month ago she'd been attending a conference in The Hague and was away for a week. Fluke had thought he'd spend his free nights reading, and catching up on some DVD box sets he'd bought but never got round to watching.

When she'd returned, and after they'd made love, she'd playfully asked him how he'd been coping without her. He'd told her he'd been watching *Breaking Bad* and he enthusiastically began extolling its virtues both as a stunning drama and as a show not afraid of having a social commentary. Instead of being interested she'd become withdrawn. Later that night she'd told him that *Breaking Bad* was something she'd wanted to watch. Confused, he'd asked what had stopped her.

So now, *Breaking Bad* was *their* show and, as well as having to start again from the beginning, he wasn't allowed to watch it when she wasn't there.

Again. Little things.

Not that he didn't love her. If anything, he loved her more than he ever had. He loved the way she snuggled up to him on the sofa, how she would fall asleep and make little mewing sounds. He loved the subtle fragrance of her perfume and how she would dab a little on the nape of her neck before they went to bed. He loved her earlobes with the empty holes for earrings she no longer wore, hinting at a past they'd never spoken of. He loved her pale skin and her dark tattoos, peeping from underneath her clothing whenever she stretched for something.

She was funny and she was serious. She was sexy and she was playful. She was more than a match for his intelligence and the conversations they had deep into the night would keep him thinking for days.

They were both getting to an age where incrementalism was no longer an option and he knew he had to commit to the relationship. He *wanted* to commit to the relationship . . .

It was this that Bridie wanted to talk to him about.

She wanted to know if he was still in the relationship. Fluke's job tonight was to convince her he was and to make sure she never felt that doubt again.

His phone beeped and he read the incoming text.

'Fifteen minutes out. Hope you have some energy.'

That sounded promising.

Bridie ignored the wine and sat him down on the sofa. 'We'll talk afterwards,' she said before jumping on him. For five minutes they grappled with each other; exploring each other's bodies through their clothes.

'Bedroom?' he asked hopefully.

'Rug in front of the fire?' she replied.

'Perfect.'

Fluke was struggling with his belt when he heard the worst sound in the world for a man on a promise. The doorbell.

In the silence of the woods, it was deafening.

'Shit,' they said at the same time.

'You'll have to get it,' Fluke said, pointing at his crotch.

'I'm not answering it. What if it's the man with the shotgun cartridge?'

Fluke considered this briefly. 'He's hardly likely to ring the bell.'

Saying that, if it were a member of his team, or another of his few friends, they'd have called first. He didn't like people 'popping in'. He never got strangers knocking on his door. He lived too far off the beaten path.

With all thoughts – and evidence of readiness – of afternoon sex forgotten he approached the door. Quietly. He didn't think it was going to be a masked assassin but he took a deep breath before jerking the door open anyway.

He looked at who was there and blinked in surprise.

'Who is it, Avison?' Bridie asked.

'I have no idea,' he said eventually.

Standing on his porch was the girl in the road from the previous night. The new age traveller. Her companion was standing twenty yards further back in the wood.

He decided one of them should say something. 'Can I help you?'

51

'I'm Jinx,' she said, as if further explanation was unnecessary.

Fluke shrugged – the universally understood sign for 'So what?'

'Mark told me to come here if ever I was in trouble.'

Chapter 10

Fluke breathed a sigh of relief. All that nervous energy and it was the house call equivalent of a wrong number. 'Think you've made a mistake, Jinx. There's no one called Mark here.'

He went to shut the door but she didn't move.

She snorted derisively. 'He said you'd say that.'

Bridie joined him. 'Hello, Jinx, Avison's right. There's no one here by that name. It's just the two of us.'

Her eyes rolled. 'I didn't say Mark was here. I said he *told* me to come here.'

'This isn't a bloody squat,' Fluke snapped.

Bridie touched him gently on the arm and he calmed down.

'What do you mean he told you to come here?' she said. Fluke didn't know anyone who could diffuse tension the way Bridie could.

Unfortunately it worked too well. The young girl burst into tears. The man she was with remained in the shadows. Watching.

Emotional people always made Fluke feel uneasy. This was no exception. The girl looked up. Tears had made tracks in the dirt on her face.

'I . . . I can't find him,' she sobbed.

'You'd better come in,' Bridie said, moving aside before glaring at Fluke when he didn't budge. He relented and the girl stepped past them, looking around as if it were the first time she'd been indoors.

'You coming in?' Fluke said to the man in the shadows.

'Nah, man,' he grinned. 'My job was to make sure she got here. Been walking for two days nearly. Couldn't find this place. Over to you now.'

And with that he was gone.

'Who the hell was he?' he asked, after he'd closed the door.

Jinx's face lit up.

'That's Twist. He's my best friend in all the world. When I said I was coming here he insisted on coming with me.'

'Where's he off to?'

'Oh, he'll be going back home.' She didn't elaborate and Fluke wasn't bothered enough to push it.

'I'll put the kettle on,' he said. He knew Bridie was just about to say the same thing and he didn't want to be the one left alone with her.

The kitchen area of the open-plan room was fifteen yards away from the sofas where Bridie and Jinx were now seated. He relaxed slightly and sneaked a glance at Jinx as he waited for the kettle.

She had piercing blue eyes, as blue as any he'd ever seen. Her hair was heavily dreadlocked and beaded. When she moved her head she sounded like a Newton's Cradle. The *original* colour of her hair was anyone's guess. At the minute it was green, blue and red. He suspected it had been different the week before. If he had to guess, he'd have said she was probably a blonde. She was wearing the same clothes as the night before. Colourful and mis-matched and filthy.

Fluke reckoned she was about thirty, although underneath the grime she could have been younger.

He looked at her dreadlocks again. Could this be connected to the body? He didn't see how but it was a bit of a coincidence.

The whistle sounded and he removed the kettle from the hob. 'Coffee OK for everyone?' he said.

'I don't drink caffeine,' Jinx replied immediately.

'Of course you don't,' he muttered.

'What was that?' Bridie said.

'Nothing. Tea it is then.'

'Tea has caffeine in it,' Jinx said.

Fluke silently counted to three.

'Yeah? Well, tough shit, all I've got is tea or coffee. This isn't Starbucks.'

'Don't be nasty, Avison,' Bridie said. 'I've got some fruit teas I liberated from Belgium a few days ago. They're in my bag. Go and get them. And I don't want coffee either – I'll have a hot water with a slice of lemon, please.'

Her tone didn't invite discussion. Fluke skulked off to find them.

Bloody hippies bolloxing up his sex life . . .

As he was rooting through Bridie's bag, a thought occurred to him. The hand found on the third green. The name on the finger-print database was Mark Cadden.

Mark.

Another coincidence? If it was, they were stacking up.

And he could no longer ignore it.

He would need to tread carefully though. Jinx had said she was in trouble. If her Mark and *his* Mark were one and the same then she might be right. He had a battery of questions.

How did Jinx know Cadden?

Did she know he was dead?

Was she involved?

But as important as those questions were, for now they were being pushed aside by the much more urgent one.

Why would a murder victim he hadn't heard of tell a girl he didn't know to seek him out?

When Fluke returned with the funky-smelling fruit teabags, Bridie and Jinx were talking quietly. If it had been one of her friends he'd have assumed they were talking about him.

Jinx said, a bit too loudly, 'Why would Mark send me to a pig's house?'

Bridie whispered something in her ear and they both looked at him and smiled.

Fluke ignored them and busied himself making the drinks.

OK. So she's calmed down. It was time for him to stop being a tealady and start being a policeman. He knew he should call HQ; tell them there was a possible witness in his house. Let Reyes and the team from the Met come and get her.

But Fluke's curiosity was up.

He wanted answers first. He just didn't know how to get them. Not without revealing what he knew. If they were talking about the same person – and the more Fluke thought about it, he couldn't imagine they weren't – and he mentioned the victim's name, then the first question out of her lips would be: *How do you know him?*

He was on the top of a hill in over forty pieces, Jinx, and they were just the pieces we could find. Yeah, that'd go down well.

Of course, it was possible her Mark and his Mark Cadden weren't the same person. That it actually *was* a coincidence.

Bridie said, 'Avison, do you know anyone called Mark Cadden?'

Maybe not then . . .

Buying some time by bringing the drinks over, he set them down.

'Sorry?' he said.

'Mark Cadden? Do you know him?'

He only had one option. He had to lie. 'No. Why?'

'That's Mark's name,' Jinx said.

It was the first time she'd spoken to him with anything other than contempt. She was staring at him in earnest. He recognised desperation when he saw it. Time to go to work.

'And how do you know Mark?' he said.

The floodgates opened again and Fluke watched helplessly as

Bridie took over once more. She glared at him over the wretched girl in her arms.

Fluke mouthed, 'What did I do?'

'He's her husband.'

'Oh,' he said. 'I'll go and see if we have any biscuits, shall I?'

He ignored Bridie's glare. He wasn't being selfish. Intimate partners carried out the majority of murders, and despite the numbers being heavily skewed towards men killing women, there was a rising number of women killing men. And although the latter was often after the man had subjected them to appalling, prolonged abuse, there was still a small number of women who murdered with little or no motive.

He had to start treating Jinx like a potential suspect.

'I need to make a quick phone call,' he said, after placing a bowl of Grasmere Gingerbread on the table. He left without looking back or giving them a chance to speak.

He turned left out of his cabin and walked to a spot he knew had a good mobile phone signal. He rang HQ and asked to be put through to the duty inspector. It was Kevin Ritchie. Fluke knew and liked him.

He explained what he needed. 'Get me the number for that dickhead chief inspector from the Met, can you, Kevin? I think he said his name was John Reyes.'

Ritchie put him on hold for a minute and Fluke watched the bats flitting in and out of the trees. Gorging themselves on the fat summer bugs. Saving his home from demolition. Ritchie came back to him within a minute with the number. Fluke wrote it on the back of his hand, thanked Ritchie and ended the call.

Fluke paused before dialling. He was loath to give up the case twice in one day but it was out of his hands. Cadden sending his wife to see Fluke should be enough to get him on the investigation anyway. He tapped out the numbers and pressed the green phone icon. The voicemail kicked in immediately. Reyes was either on the phone or had it on permanent voicemail. Probably the latter. Fools like him were arrogant enough to think no one had an automatic right to speak to them. All calls had to be screened first.

Fluke chose to deliberately get his name and rank wrong. Little victories. 'Inspector Reeves, this is DI Fluke. Call me back when you get this, please. It'll be worth your while.'

After leaving his number he went back inside.

'Jinx, look at me.' The change in his tone made both her and Bridie look up. 'Why did Mark tell you to come here?'

She sniffed but answered. 'Mark told me that there were some things happening that were dangerous. If he went missing I was to leave immediately. He said you would help me. That you could be trusted.'

'What dangerous things?' he said. He would think about why Cadden had picked his name out of a hat later.

'He never said.'

'How long have you known him?' Full-on questioning mode now. Don't give them time to recover, just hit them with the next one. It didn't seem to bother her. If anything she looked pleased he was finally interested.

'Nearly a year. He came up with some travellers from London. He was the only one who was nice. We got together one night and haven't been apart since.' She took a breath. 'Until two nights ago.'

One night missing and one night travelling. Two nights. If she was telling the truth, she'd left their camp immediately.

'You said he told you I could be trusted?'

This time she nodded.

'I'm going to need a bit more than that, Jinx. Why did he tell you that? I'm not saying I can't be trusted because I can, but I've never heard of anyone called Mark Cadden.'

'*Can* he be trusted?' Jinx said to Bridie.

Bridie took hold of her hands. 'Implicitly,' she said.

The change in her demeanour was subtle, but it was there. She'd made a decision.

'He said you owed him.'

Fluke frowned. Other than stupid things such as a fiver for the tea fund, he didn't owe anyone anything. He certainly didn't owe anyone anything to the extent a stranger could appear at his door asking for – and apparently expecting – his help.

'Jinx, I don't know him. How can I owe him anything?'

'He says you do.'

This is getting us nowhere, he thought. 'Bridie, a little help here?'

Despite Bridie still being cross with him for deserting her when he'd made his call to Reyes, she stepped up.

'Jinx, if Avison says he doesn't know Mark then I believe him. And maybe you should too. Perhaps Mark got his name wrong.'

Jinx smiled sadly. 'How many Avison Flukes do you think there are in Cumbria?'

'Fair point,' Fluke said. That she knew his name did not go unnoticed.

His phone rang. He looked at the screen. It was an unknown number. Reyes. Good, he could sort this out. Jinx said something to Bridie he couldn't hear.

He pressed accept and said, 'Fluke.'

The reply was the cultured middle-class London accent he already hated. 'Ah, DI Fluke, caught me a cattle rustler, have you?'

Bridie waved her hands to get his attention. He said into the phone, 'One moment, please.'

'Fluke, I haven't got time—'

Fluke covered the speaker with his finger. 'What?'

'Mark gave her something.'

Jinx was searching for something. All manner of items were coming out of the various pockets in her trousers and coat.

59

Wooden pegs, beads, a lump of something that looked suspiciously like cannabis and at least ten pieces of paper. It was these she focused on, picking them up, reading them before throwing them back down in frustration.

Even though his hand was covering the microphone he could hear Reyes shouting. He uncovered it. 'One more minute, please.' He didn't wait for a response.

Jinx picked up what looked like a badly designed flyer for a phrenologist. It was purple with black writing. She read the back of it with fierce concentration.

'Aha!' she said. 'Found it. Mark told me to write something down. Something he said would make you help me.'

Fluke looked at the phone in his hand. He had a higher rank on the other end, no doubt actively thinking of ways he could make his life miserable tomorrow.

'And what's that, Jinx?' he said, feeling nervous for some reason.

'Whiskey. Echo. Foxtrot,' she said.

Three words that would change his life for ever.

Fluke stared at her, uncomprehendingly, not trying to hide his shock. Blood drained from his face. Bridie and Jinx were both staring, startled by the sudden change in him. His subconscious told him he had a chief inspector still hanging on. He had to get rid of him and he had to do it now.

The rules of the game had just changed.

'Sorry, John. Something's just come up. I'll call you tomorrow.' He pressed end as soon as he finished talking.

Bridie got up off the sofa and knelt in front of him.

'Avison, what's wrong? What do those words mean?'

His face set like stone, mouth a grim line, he said to Jinx, 'Where did you hear those words?'

'I told you, Mar—'

'I don't know anyone called Mark fucking Cadden!'

Bridie said softly, 'There's an explanation here, Avison. We just need to find it. Tell me, what do those words mean?'

She passed him his now cold drink and he swallowed it.

'I haven't heard those words for years,' he said eventually.

'What do they mean?' she asked again.

'They're a call sign,' he answered. 'Whiskey Echo Foxtrot was my call sign.'

Chapter 11

Fluke's mind raced. He only knew one Londoner who could have known that particular call sign, and he wasn't called Mark Cadden. He got to his feet and headed in the direction of the bedroom.

Bridie called out. 'Avison, what's wrong?'

He ignored her but heard them both get up and follow him.

Old houses tend to have far more storage than newer ones as builders look for ways to cut costs. His cabin was built for sturdiness and comfort. It was light and airy. Open-plan living and high ceilings. But it didn't have much storage space. Any possession that wasn't going to be damaged by the cold or damp was kept outside in wooden boxes. Things that would be damaged by the weather and things he didn't often need were under his bed, in the smaller second bedroom or on top of his wardrobe.

By the time Bridie and Jinx had joined him, he was on his knees and looking under the bed. There was something he needed to find. A photograph album. It was in a small, cardboard box. A self-assembly job from IKEA. Cheap but perfectly adequate for what he needed. His hand touched warm cardboard and he grunted in satisfaction. He pulled it out.

Fluke threw it on top of the bed, ignoring the dust that marked the cream duvet. He rifled through the box, couldn't find the album he was looking for and, in frustration, upended the contents onto the bed. He looked through it all again, more methodically this time.

He found the album he wanted at the bottom of the pile. He flipped through the pages until he found the photograph he was looking for.

Fluke held it out so Jinx could see it clearly.

'Jinx, is Mark in this photograph?'

It had been taken years before digital cameras. Despite being poorly lit and slightly out of focus, the image it captured was a slice of history. Four young men. All in uniform, heavily armed. Green berets set at jaunty angles. Every one of them grinning. They looked invincible. There was writing on the back.

'"The Brick". West Belfast. Redefining the "Acceptable Level of Violence".'

Nostalgia is a human emotion and one Fluke had little use for. Unlike Towler, whose house looked like a regimental museum, he preferred living in the now and kept few reminders chronicling his past. He didn't have a single photograph of him in his police uniform. He didn't keep press clippings. The big three-page spread in the glossy magazine, after the Dalton Cross case, had been read once and then discarded.

But, although he had nothing on display, he'd never had the inclination to get rid of photographs of his days in the Marines. He didn't know why. Perhaps it was because not everyone in the photograph album had survived their service.

'What's a "brick"?' Bridie said.

'A four-man patrol,' he said. 'Very nimble, extremely close knit. Only used in high-risk urban areas. Ideal for patrolling the roughest parts of Belfast.'

Jinx turned over the photograph and stared at it. Eyes wide and unblinking. Her reaction told him everything he needed to know.

'This was from when he was in the army,' she whispered.

'Not the army,' Fluke murmured. 'The navy. They're Royal Marines Commandos – 42 Commando to be precise.'

Bridie put her arms round the girl.

'Do you have an explanation, Avison? Why do you have a picture of Jinx's husband under your bed?'

Fluke said nothing. He simply took the photograph from Jinx and passed it over to Bridie. 'Look carefully. What do you see?'

She studied it as carefully as if it were a brief for a court case. 'I'm not seeing it.'

Fluke was watching her carefully, waiting for the flash of recognition. When it became apparent that she wasn't getting there on her own, he said, 'Look at that prick at the back. The one with his beret pulled down right over his eyes. The one who thinks he's too cool for school.'

She gasped.

'It's you!'

Fluke smiled grimly. 'Yes. It's me. Avison Fluke. Arrogance personified.'

Bridie studied the photo further. Jinx leaned forward until both their noses were inches from it. They both looked up at the same time.

'You were in Belfast?' Bridie asked. 'You're standing beside Mark Cadden. You must know him?'

Fluke took back the photo and looked at it sadly. 'Yes, Bridie. I was in Belfast,' he said. 'And no, I don't know anyone called Mark Cadden.'

They stared at him. The two of them not understanding.

Make that three of us.

'The man I'm standing next to was called Mark Bishop and he was my best friend.'

'I don't understand,' Jinx said.

They had retired back to the living room, and were settled on the sofa and armchair.

Fluke didn't acknowledge her.

'So you do know him? You were both in Northern Ireland together?' Bridie asked.

Fluke nodded.

'And he was your best friend?'

He nodded again.

'I thought Towler was your best friend.'

It was a fair point. Towler *was* his best friend. Had been since they were young boys.

'He is. But he went one way, I went the other. He joined the Paras; I joined the Marines. We barely saw each other for years. Our leave crossed every now and then but you've got to understand what it's like being in elite units. You're never at home. There's always a tour somewhere and, in those days, tours lasted up to nine months.'

Bridie was silent. Listening to him talk. Exorcising demons she hadn't known existed.

'Bish and I went through Lympstone together.'

'Lympstone?' Jinx was interested despite her obvious concern for her husband.

'It's where the Commando Training Centre is. Thirty-two weeks of hell. I hated it. I was only there to get it out of my system, it was never meant to be a career. But Bish was a natural. He won the King's Badge without even trying. That's the award given to the top recruit in the troop. Huge honour.'

He could feel himself getting emotional and he couldn't afford that. He couldn't tell Jinx her husband was dead. She either already knew or was a material witness. Either way she was involved. And that meant she found out facts when he chose to release them. Not before.

'What happened to him?' Bridie asked.

'We served together for three years. Three great years. We even enjoyed Belfast. It was what we'd trained to do. Getting in among the Provos. Showing them what happens when 42 Commando were in town. We even had calling cards printed.' He smiled at the memory. '"The Boys Are Back in Town". Christ, what a bunch of arseholes we were. Marines and paras should never have served in Belfast. They're basically shock troops, far too aggressive for what was essentially a public order task.'

'What happened to Bish?' Bridie repeated.

'Something terrible happened,' he whispered. He paused. He'd only ever told Towler, and he wasn't about to talk about it now. 'Anyway, we got out safely and the rest of the tour finished without incident. I got back to Plymouth and signed off. I'd had enough.'

'And Mark?' This time it was Jinx asking.

'He tried to stop me but my mind was made up. I'd always planned on being a policeman and it seemed like a good time to get out. We had a bit of a falling out. He was a career marine and couldn't understand why I'd ever want to leave the life.'

'So you didn't hear from him again?' Bridie this time.

'Every now and then. He'd send me postcards from exotic locations. Australia, America, Japan. No words on them but I knew he was trying to make me realise I'd made a mistake. By this time I was already a detective but I suspect he hoped I might get the urge and re-join. Eventually they stopped. I got a get-well card from him when I was in hospital but I've not heard from him since.'

Not until yesterday, he thought.

Jinx cleared her throat. 'OK. So if your Mark Bishop is *my* Mark Cadden, what happened?'

He said nothing.

I have no idea, he thought. *But I will.*

Mark Bishop had been his friend and Fluke was the type of person who didn't make friends easily. He made a decision. An easy one.

Fuck John Reyes. Fuck the Metropolitan Police.

Bish was calling out from beyond the grave, seeking his help. There was a debt to be paid and Fluke wouldn't be found wanting. The Met could keep investigating, but their bluster and hair gel would go down like a cup of cold sick up here. Sooner or later they'd have to come to him. Until they did, he would run a parallel investigation. They might have some of the answers but he had Jinx. She might not know it, but she would be the key to finding whoever killed Bish. To finding out who he'd become and why.

He thought back to the detective who'd accompanied Reyes when they'd stopped the post-mortem. The one who'd been crying.

Perhaps he had an ally?

Standing up, he asked Jinx if he and Bridie could have a word in private. She shrugged, and reached for her cup of what must have been stone-cold fruit tea.

'Do what you want. I'm leaving soon. I wanted answers and all you have is questions.'

Fluke could see she was trembling. She was petrified. He needed to know why. Bridie joined him by the breakfast counter.

'I need her to stay with us for a bit,' he said.

Fluke was prepared for a battle. He needn't have worried.

'Good. If you hadn't suggested it, I was going to. Look at her. She's scared witless.' She called over to Jinx, 'We'd like it if you could stay here tonight, Jinx. Is that OK?'

Although she huffed a little, she fooled neither of them. It was obvious she was relieved she didn't have to go back out on the road.

'Thank you,' she said.

Fluke turned back to Bridie.

'Bish is dead,' he whispered.

She put her hand to her mouth and stifled an escaping gasp. 'Oh, no!'

Fluke nodded; an eye on Jinx, making sure she hadn't heard anything. 'He was the body we found on the golf course yesterday.'

She looked at Jinx then back at Fluke. 'You can't tell her.'

'Not even if I wanted to. She may be in trouble, she may be involved, I don't know yet. But I do know those idiots from the Met won't get close to finding out what's going on, not if they carry on like they did this afternoon. No one up here's going to talk to them. I'm going to have to do this on my own.'

She nodded. 'Well, for what it's worth, for once I think you're probably doing the right . . .' She trailed off. 'What *is* she doing?'

Fluke had taken his eyes off Jinx while he talked to Bridie. He turned to where she was looking. The object of their discussion was busy shedding her final bit of clothing, a T-shirt. She was braless underneath. Fluke stared, mouth gaping, before he realised what he was doing.

Despite the dirt, clothed Jinx had been pretty. Naked she was stunning. Firm breasts, an hourglass figure and long, long legs. She had a small tattoo on her left hip and dirt lines instead of tan lines, but other than that she was unblemished. Fluke couldn't look away.

She was oblivious to the effect she was having.

'What the—?' he growled.

His raised voice caused Jinx to turn. She was clearly comfortable with her body. Fluke felt his face burning in embarrassment.

'What? I'm going for a swim in the lake. I'm dirty and these clothes need washing.'

Fluke turned away. 'Bridie, do something.'

Bridie burst out laughing. 'Jinx, we have a shower and a washing machine. It may be a cabin in the woods but Avison has all the mod cons here. He's not a real caveman.'

'Thanks,' Fluke said.

'Come on. I'll show you where everything is,' Bridie said, walking over to her. 'And put your clothes on, you're going to give Avison a stroke.'

'Great choice of words, Bridie.' Fluke knew he was babbling. He liked to think of himself as a liberal, but if a naked woman was going to be in his front room then it had better be part of a well-hatched plan.

Jinx appeared to have a different idea. She snorted. 'If it's all the same to you, I'd rather bathe in the lake. And I'm not cleaning my clothes with chemicals.'

This was too much for Fluke.

'I don't care what you'd rather do, young lady. In this house we wash indoors, we go to the toilet indoors and we wear bloody clothes.'

Bridie raised an eyebrow.

'When we have company,' he added.

Fluke had seen petulant looks before. Sometimes Towler had to say no to Abi and she could throw tantrums with the best of them. But if she'd been there she'd have happily handed over her crown. Jinx actually stamped her foot in anger.

'Maybe I'll just leave then. I'd rather be on the road than stay with fascists.'

Jinx glared. Fluke glared back. Stalemate. Even Bridie didn't seem to have an answer.

Luckily they were all distracted by a knock on the door. Jinx hastily began dressing. She looked nervous. Despite her bluster she was still scared.

'What is this?' Fluke said. 'Fucking Halloween?'

No one made a move to answer the door. Another knock, this time more urgent. It opened a couple of inches and a familiar voice shouted out.

'You two aren't shagging, are you?'

Towler . . .

'Wait a sec, Matt,' Fluke shouted back. 'We have a guest who isn't quite ready to receive yet.'

'Eh? What's that mean?' He opened the door, walked in and saw the semi-naked Jinx.

Fluke hadn't often seen his sergeant lost for words. He was

a social hand grenade at the best of times, and in awkward situations anything could happen.

He stared at Jinx then turned his attention to Fluke and Bridie. Eventually he shrugged. 'Isn't everyone supposed to have their kit off at an orgy?'

'Come in, Matt,' Bridie said. 'Just a small misunderstanding. We were just sorting it out.'

'Who's this? Another pig?' Jinx said to no one in particular, as she continued dressing. 'Oink, oink,' she added, just in case anyone had missed the point.

Towler looked at Jinx, a bemused expression on his face. 'Who the fuck's this smelly bastard?'

Chapter 12

Towler had brought five trail-cameras, and as an excuse to get him away from Jinx it was perfect. Fluke followed him to his car and they unloaded them.

He talked Fluke through the equipment.

'I got these from a mate of mine. Don't ask me who he is, I won't tell you. They're state-of-the-art camera traps. Fully waterproof, rugged as fuck and self-powered. A single charge of the battery will keep it live for weeks, depending on how much work it has to do.'

Fluke picked up one. They were small; about six inches by three. The front was a tan colour, and had a myriad of sensors and lights surrounding a central lens. All five had a strapping system.

'You've got the perfect environment for them here. Hardly any ground cover but loads of places to conceal them. We'll strap them to some trees and cover the approaches that whoever left that shotgun cartridge is likely to use. We'll make sure one covers the front door and one covers the back just in case we don't get him coming in.'

Together they surveyed the land around the cabin, and selected the trails Fluke's tormentor had most likely used to approach it. They would place three of the cameras on the outer boundaries of his land and, with the natural instincts of elite soldiers, they agreed where they were most likely to capture him. Neither of them thought he'd be stupid enough to drive up the trail that led to the cabin. He was more likely to park off-road and hike through the woods.

'You get badgers round here?' Towler asked.

'And foxes.'

'We'll set them four feet off the ground then, make sure we only get bipeds,' he said. 'You going to tell me what's going on? Who was that in there?'

'She's called Jinx.'

'She's got a fanny like a grizzly bear's armpit.'

If he'd been a normal cop, on a normal team, Fluke would have kept his plans to himself. But he trusted Towler with his life and he was going to need some help anyway. The sooner he brought him and the rest of FMIT inside the better.

'You ever remember me talking about my mate Bish from my days with 42?'

'Mark Bishop? Yeah, I remember him. Didn't we all get pissed in Newcastle one weekend?'

Fluke smiled. He'd forgotten about that. He and Bish had just finished a short tour of Belize, honing jungle warfare skills. The last thing either of them had wanted on their return to the UK was more alcohol, but Towler had a weekend off and insisted they go away somewhere.

'And didn't you piss the hotel bed?' Towler added.

Fluke said nothing. Towler mistook his silence for embarrassment.

'Hey, don't worry, mate. We've all been there. I remember a night in Miami, I'd had that much to drink I actually shat—'

'He's dead, Matt.'

Silence. Towler enjoyed the rivalry between the Paras and the Marines more than anyone, but Fluke knew a dead soldier was a dead brother as far as he was concerned.

'Oh, mate, I'm so sorry. Was it Afghanistan? It's a fucking hellhole over there.'

'He didn't die in Helmand Province, Matt. He died on Cockermouth Golf Course.'

'That was him?' Towler's jaw dropped. 'You're shitting me?'

Fluke didn't answer. He knew Towler wouldn't question the fact. If Fluke said it was so, his sergeant would accept it. He also knew Towler would now go straight into battle mode. Become the ally he needed.

He didn't let Fluke down.

'We have some things to do then,' he said. 'I take it we're ignoring the Met's orders to stay away from the case?'

Fluke nodded.

'And I assume that scarecrow in there is somehow linked to the case?'

'She's his wife,' Fluke confirmed. He spent ten minutes updating Towler on the evening's events.

When Fluke had finished, Towler said, 'I know I only met the man once but he was a hard-core marine. We need to know why he left and why he changed his name. I take it you're not buying this tree-hugging shite?'

'Nope. I'm prepared to believe he was close to Jinx. You've seen her. Scrub the dirt off and she's beautiful. Full of fire too. Scared witless at the minute, but I could see Bish going for that sort.'

Towler frowned. 'But . . . how the hell does he end up with two names? When he joined the Marines his name was Bishop. Had to be, can't join without a legit birth certificate. But now he's on PNC, which is equally rigorous in checking you are who you say you are, as Mark Cadden. He didn't change names via deed poll; Longy would have found that straightaway. It makes no sense. Can't be done.'

Fluke had been thinking about nothing else for the last hour.

'There is one way,' he said quietly.

'Oh?'

'He's a protected witness.'

Even when witness protection involves someone from London, the actual work is usually carried out in police regions, where

73

supposedly the witness would stand a better chance of slipping into anonymity, even though, in Fluke's view, a city, the larger the better, was the best place to hide. Names are changed, people are moved and lives are saved. And more importantly, witnesses can give evidence without fear of reprisals or intimidation. But . . . a lot of witnesses are also criminals, and becoming a protected witness is not a 'do what you want' kind of gig. If a witness, under their new identity, commits a further offence, then they go through the criminal justice system the same as everyone else. And to make sure they're sentenced fairly – which includes previous convictions being taken into account – false criminal records are created on PNC. Different dates, different courts, but similar offences and similar sentences. Close enough to give the judge a flavour of the man or woman they have in the dock, but different enough to ensure they can't be traced via PNC.

Records of protected witnesses are not held on any database, only in secure filing cabinets, which explained why Jiao-long hadn't been able to find him.

It was Bish's false criminal record that PNC spat out when his fingerprint result had been entered. The team from the Met had to be a protected witness team; it was the only thing that made sense. And any team who'd lost their witness wouldn't exactly be flavour of the month. No wonder they'd been so keen to handle it themselves . . .

'We can't hand her over to the Met. We need her,' Towler said. 'We need to find out who he testified against. That's got to be where we start.'

Fluke nodded. He agreed with Towler 100 per cent. If Bish had testified against some heavy-duty criminals then dismembering him would be exactly the type of punishment they would mete out.

'Jinx is staying with me for now,' he said.

'It's a pity I didn't bring live-feed equipment with me. These cameras can be set up with monitors and alarms. If Jinx really is in danger it might have given you an edge.'

Fluke looked round the wood. It was deathly quiet.

'She'll be safe here,' he said. 'No one can find where I actually live without written directions. Satnav won't get you near. It took her two days to find it. Plus no one has any reason to suspect I'm involved.'

Towler seemed happy enough with that. He knew as well as anyone how difficult Fluke's home was to find.

'What's next?'

Ordinarily Fluke would have gathered FMIT together for a brainstorm, or a thought shower, or whatever the politically correct term was that week. From that initial session, theories would be generated, lines of enquiry would be identified. This time he couldn't do anything so overt.

'Keep it to ourselves for now,' he said. 'I'll take tomorrow off and see what Jinx knows. You go back to the team and whisper that we're not done with this case yet.'

'You got a starting point?'

'Nope. But at some point we're going to need to know what the Met know. We'll either have to come clean or find out another way. For now though, we say nothing.'

They had one final walk round to familiarise themselves with where the cameras had been placed before heading back. Fluke didn't plan to tell Bridie about the cameras. No point in bringing up the reason they were needed again. Her reaction to the cartridge was still puzzling him. At least Jinx seemed to have taken her mind off it.

And him.

He was glad the 'talk' had been put on hold again.

Jinx wasn't in the front room when they returned. Bridie was in the kitchen area boiling something in a pan. Fluke instinctively knew it was pasta.

'She's having a shower,' Bridie said.

'About fucking time,' Towler said.

'That's not fair, Matt,' Bridie said. 'She's been on the road for two days and she slept rough last night. Fluke's friend Mark was a bit light on directions apparently.'

Towler grunted non-committedly.

'I'm making us some supper. You're welcome to stay. Jinx is a vegan, you'll not be surprised to know, so it's not something either of you are going to like.'

Unsurprisingly Towler declined.

'Got to get back for Abi, Bridie. Ave, give me a bell when you've decided what to do.' He sniggered as he opened the door. 'Enjoy your tea, mate.'

After he'd gone, Bridie wiped her hands on a tea towel and said, 'I've put clean sheets on the spare bed.'

'It already had clean sheets,' Fluke protested. Sometimes when he was working late he would use the spare room to avoid waking Bridie. Other times when she got so restless it was like sleeping next to a sack full of live goats he'd slip into the next room and try to get a few hours in. Sneak back in before she woke up.

'You've slept in them. At least seven times since they were clean on at the last count. Let's at least pretend we're normal. Clean sheets for guests. And look, the poor thing's exhausted.'

'You think we can get her to stay a bit longer?' he said.

'I'm not sure. She's worried sick about her husband and wants to get back to the camp to see if there's any news. When are you going to tell her?'

'Not yet,' he said firmly. 'What you doing tomorrow? Can you take it off and work on her? I would, but I need to start investigating this thing.'

'Already rang in,' Bridie replied. 'I'm owed loads of time anyway. I'll babysit her tomorrow but I need to be back at work Thursday.'

'Great. Thanks, I owe you one.'

'One?'

'OK. A few hundred.'

Bridie said nothing but returned a rather strange, melancholic smile. He thought back to the talk that the universe seemed determined to prevent happening.

'You OK?' he asked.

She ignored the question. 'Come on, help me set the table.'

Other than Jinx refusing to wear anything underneath the dressing gown she'd borrowed, with the result that her breasts popped out every time she reached for something, dinner was uneventful. The conversation was stilted, and characterised by long silences filled only with the sound of bread being torn, pasta being consumed and hair beads clacking together.

Jinx was clearly shattered and, before she'd finished eating, her eyes began to close. From being the bold young woman who'd paraded naked not two hours earlier, she seemed shy about asking to go to bed. When she started doing a nodding-dog impression, Fluke took charge.

'Jinx, go to bed. We'll talk in the morning.'

For the first time, she looked grateful. She politely took her plate and cup to the sink and stacked them with the other dishes.

The light in the kitchen area was brighter than the rest of the room – halogen spotlights lit the work areas to avoid knife injuries – so Fluke could see her hair colour had changed after being washed. Her dreadlocks had the same consistency as wet rope but he could already see they were a much lighter shade of blonde than he'd originally thought. She still had the coloured strands, and the beads were obviously permanent, but now it looked quirky, not messy. Fluke had been grabbing the odd glance at her when he thought Bridie wasn't looking – he didn't want her to mistake it for an ogle. An innocence radiated from her and, apart from the surliness, which was probably a manifestation of fear, and the extraordinary 'oink' attack on Towler, she seemed nice.

The type of person a perennial white knight like Bish would want to protect.

From what though?

After Jinx left the room, Fluke stood and stretched. 'Leave the dishes, I'll do them in the morning. I'm going outside for a cigar. I need to think.'

Bridie said nothing. She knew it was part of his process.

Fluke opened his homemade humidor and grabbed a dark Dominican Casa Fuente cigar that Jiao-long had brought back from Las Vegas. He snipped the end, grabbed a box of matches and walked outside.

It was still warm and, despite dusk melting into night, the view was breathtaking. It had changed in the short time since he'd been out with Towler. The sky was clear and the moon was full. A pale, rippled mirror image of the white orb stretched across the lake. The silhouette of the riotous, jagged skyline reared above even Fluke's lofty vantage point. It made him feel small and insignificant, but privileged to be part of it nonetheless.

Despite his cabin being less than thirty yards away the tranquillity made Fluke feel as if he were the only person in the world, and he was reminded why he bought the land and built the cabin here. Solitude. He'd never known peace like this before. He glanced at his home and thought about Bridie. Was his need for privacy getting in the way? Was he struggling with being in an adult relationship because he feared losing it? Was he so selfish he didn't want to share his peace with anyone, not even Bridie?

Fluke warmed the end of the cigar before lighting it. Satisfied he had an even burn, he blew out the first thick blue plume into the night air as he contemplated his relationship with the woman he loved. Half-formed thoughts chased each other round his mind. Something had changed over the last few weeks. Nothing tangible, but he could feel her slipping away. Perhaps Bridie needed to see some emotional growth? Some indication that he saw her as more than just a friend. That he now saw himself as one half of two.

As he watched the wisps of smoke curl and dance their way into the night sky, a moth flitted into view and suspended itself against the backdrop of the moon's face. Like an *E.T.* poster, it hung in the air, it's flap-happy flight strangely elegant.

Attracted to a light impossible to reach.

It was a beautiful moment and he instinctively wished Bridie were there to share it. The bat that jinked and glided out of his peripheral vision and into full view didn't care though. It was out to hunt and Fluke watched as its high-pitched echolocation system locked on to its prey. With the tiniest flick of its wings it changed direction and scooped up the moth. A second later the bat had disappeared into the inky-black woods and Fluke was alone again.

The moth's abrupt demise brought Fluke back on message. He needed to think through the events of the last two days.

Unlike cigarettes, which he'd always thought were hasty instruments of addiction rather than pleasure, cigars took time. They were to be savoured, never to be rushed. After a few minutes of quiet smoking, his thoughts began to clear.

It was hard to imagine any other scenario than Bish being lured to his death. Unless he'd been drugged with something, he'd have put up too much of a fight. If Jinx was to be believed – and Fluke did believe her – then Bish had thought there was danger lurking. That meant he would have been wary. The fact that someone managed to slash at him from behind meant he almost certainly knew his killer. Someone he trusted. Or at least someone he didn't believe was a threat.

And if Bish knew his killer, it meant Jinx probably knew them too.

What happened *after* he'd been killed was also confusing.

Although the murder site was on a popular golf course, it

was possible someone was naive enough to think that, in getting scavenging animals involved, dismembering the body would successfully dispose of it.

Fluke hoped the murderer was that stupid.

He didn't think he was going to get that lucky though. Someone had taken their time up there. Without a vice, sawing through bone took effort. Flaying skin and deboning limbs wasn't easy. It was slow and laborious. Sowerby reckoned the killer would've had to stop at least twice to re-sharpen their knife.

You didn't do something like that on a whim. It was planned. The more Fluke gave his thoughts free rein to go where they wanted, the more he agreed with Alan Vaughn. Someone wanted the body found. It was a message.

But to whom?

He turned his attention to who Bish had become. What had happened to make him change his life so much? Having met Jinx, the thought flashed through his mind that Bish had simply been trying to get into her pants. There was a major stumbling block to that, however – two, if you counted the fact she probably didn't wear pants. Bish wasn't a bastard. He'd had a few women when they'd been in the Marines but Fluke had never known him to use subterfuge to get laid.

Fluke considered the few things he knew. As unlikely as it was, Bish had obviously said goodbye to the military and chosen peace. And becoming a new age traveller was the polar opposite of being in one of the world's elite infantry units. Bish had always done things to extremes, but even so it was a bit of a stretch. He'd got married apparently. To a woman who took baths in lakes, didn't drink coffee and didn't eat meat. By any definition, Jinx was a hippy.

He frowned. Bish had gone from being a meat-eating, beer-guzzling lunatic to a beatnik.

Something wasn't right. He needed more information.

Chapter 13

Nothing happened for two days. Reyes didn't ask for assistance. He would though, Fluke was certain of it; they wouldn't get their breakthrough without Jinx, and as she'd agreed to stay at the cabin for now, he knew that hadn't happened. Although he felt guilty knowing Jinx would never get the good news she ached for, it didn't stop him from taking advantage of the situation. He'd started to casually question her. Nothing that was going to raise suspicion. But it was enough to begin finding out what Bish had been doing with his life over the last few years.

As far as Fluke could tell the only thing the Met had managed to achieve since coming to Cumbria was to blag one of the incident rooms at Carleton Hall. They were now FMIT's neighbours. DCI Reyes, in the heart of another force, had lost some of his swagger, but he was steadfastly refusing to ask for help. Jiao-long had offered to monitor their electronic footprint but Fluke had refused. He wasn't prepared to risk anyone's career just yet.

Reyes and his team didn't seem to know where to begin and Fluke knew why. Sleeping in his spare room was their corner-stone, their starting point. He wasn't sharing though, not yet. He owed it to Bish and he owed it to Jinx.

Tonight would be a test. It was the first night Bridie wasn't there in her unofficial role as chaperone. She'd been called down to London and couldn't postpone. Despite their initial antagonism, a half-truce had settled between him and Jinx. Sort of. He was allowed to eat meat, and she was allowed to call him a murderer while he did. It kind of worked.

Arguments about his diet aside, they were getting on as well as could be expected – probably due to a shared, albeit third-hand, history. They would stay up past midnight telling each other stories about Bish. Both of them seeming to delight in shocking the other with the person they knew. Fluke told her about the time Bish had finished some arctic warfare training, and when having a drink in the Norwegian village of Lakselv, he'd fought, and beaten, three military policemen who'd tried to make him leave a bar. As a counterpoint, Jinx told him about the time Bish had chained himself to a tree in a bypass protest. Unwittingly, he'd secured himself directly underneath a crow's nest, and by the time he'd been forcibly removed by the council his hair had so much bird shit in it, it was bleached white.

After these stories, Fluke would shake his head in disbelief. It was almost too much to comprehend. If it weren't for the dreadlocks, and the fact he didn't think Jinx was capable of lying, he wouldn't have believed it.

Fluke stopped at Booths on the way home and bought something for them to eat and, as he wanted to get a running start with the interview, he decided to avoid their regular meat versus vegan showdown by getting himself the only vegetarian dish he had any time for; a thin-crust pizza smothered in mozzarella and fresh green chillies. He knew the cheese on his pizza technically made it un-vegan, but Bridie had got away with putting Parmesan on her pasta the night before so he figured he was on safe ground. He bought Jinx a disgusting-looking nut loaf. He debated whether to buy a bottle of wine but decided it might be weird on their first night alone, and the last thing he needed was Jinx thinking he was coming on to her. He bought organic ginger beer instead.

He arrived back at the cabin around about the time he'd told her he'd be back. As he stepped out of his car the smell of grilled meat hit his nostrils and the back of his throat.

What the hell . . .?

Who was in there with her?

Fluke walked up the steps of the front porch and pushed the door open. Jinx was bent over, dusting the coffee table. She looked up.

'What?' she said. 'I was just dusting.'

She was alone.

Alone and calm. Whereas her demeanour up until then had been as skittish as a cat using a hot frying pan as a shortcut, now she seemed in control. She gave the table a final wipe and stood up.

'I've defrosted some big curly sausage thing from the freezer and grilled it. It's not quite brown so I don't think it's cooked yet. I've not cooked meat before so you'll have to check.'

Fluke said nothing.

'And I've tidied up a bit. You and Bridie are letting me stay here, it's the least I could do.'

'I don't understand,' Fluke said, confused.

She looked directly at him and held his gaze.

'Now Bridie's not here, we can stop playing games. Ask me what you need to know. No pussyfooting around. If something's happened to Mark, or Bish, or whatever he's called, I want to know. I want to help.'

'And the Cumberland sausage?'

'I wanted to get off on the right note tonight. I thought if I cooked you some meat we wouldn't argue about me being vegan.'

He looked down at the salami-free pizza in the bag he was still carrying.

Typical.

Fluke decided to have the peace-sausage for breakfast, and put the pizza and the nut loaf in the oven. Jinx didn't comment on it but he got the impression she knew he'd been planning the same evening.

After the meal he lit a cigar.

'Has anyone told you that you smoke too much?' Jinx asked.

'Frequently,' he replied. 'But I don't listen to bad advice.'

She smiled and let him finish it in peace. When he'd stubbed it out they got down to business.

'Bish told you to come to me if he disappeared?'

Jinx nodded. 'He said something was happening; something serious.'

'So, when he didn't show when he said he would, you came here?'

She nodded again. 'I spoke to Faith and she said I'd better do what he'd said.'

Fluke made a mental note to go back to the name Faith – it hadn't been mentioned before. 'And you've no idea what that "serious" thing was?'

'I asked him but he wouldn't say.'

Fluke made a few notes. If this had been a formal interview he'd have handed it over to Jo Skelton or Alan Vaughn for a while. See if they could tackle it from a different angle and think of something new. Instead he did what he always did when he was trying to break a problem into bite-sized pieces.

He went back to the beginning.

'How long have you been a . . . I don't know what to call you?'

'Traveller's fine.'

'New age traveller?'

'If you prefer.'

'How long have you been a new age traveller?'

'About ten years.'

Fluke jotted it down. Did the simple maths in his head. Bridie had told him she was twenty-five. 'So you started when you were what? Fifteen?'

'Fourteen,' she said. 'So it's been eleven years.'

'What about your parents?'

Fluke had been a cop long enough to know he'd hit something sensitive. Her head dipped. The little he could still see was burning red. She mumbled something unintelligible.

He'd only been digging around for something to do while he thought of an interview strategy. He didn't want to hurt or embarrass her. He should have foreseen the potential for trauma in her childhood.

'Sorry, Jinx. I was being nosey.'

She looked up. Her eyes were glistening. To her credit she didn't turn the potential tears into actual tears by blinking.

'My father was a bad man,' she whispered. 'Very bad. I ran away from home when I was thirteen.'

'He abused you?'

Jinx nodded.

Fluke said nothing. Anything he could say would sound superficial and hollow.

She moved past her parents. 'I lived on the streets in Bristol for a year then met Twist.'

'The man who made sure you got here safely?'

'Yes. We don't have leaders in our group but if we did it would be him. He saw me sleeping rough and invited me to join them. Other than when I went travelling for a year, I've been with the group ever since.'

'Abroad?'

'I'm sorry?'

'You travelled abroad?' If she had, then she'd had a passport. And with a passport came a name.

'Yes, I wanted to do something on my own for a while. Twist got me stabilised before I took off. Thailand, Australia, Nepal, China. Round that part of the world. Then I came back, met up with them again. Been with them since then.'

Fluke made a note. Decided it could wait, and refocused.

'Jinx, I know you've not wanted to answer this before, but I need you to answer it now. What's your real name?'

'Jinx is my real name.'

Fluke sighed. 'Sorry, Jinx, but I work in the real world, and in the real world people have names that are on computers and birth certificates and national insurance registers. Just because someone decides Mildred isn't "rainbow" enough, doesn't mean it disappears from the system.'

She shrugged. 'It's a hard concept to get your head round,' she said. 'We're free, you're not.'

Breathing deeply, Fluke ignored the barb. He didn't feel trapped and he didn't envy the hedonistic lifestyle of the traveller.

Did he?

He looked around his cabin. Noticed the absolute lack of noise. No neighbours for almost a mile. Inaccessible in winter. If he wasn't running from something, why was he here?

No! That was a reaction to the illness.

He was better now though. The cancer was beaten. He was returning to full fitness. Even his blood work was improving.

So why was he still here?

It wasn't as if it was easy. The commute added two hours to his working day, longer in winter. He had to chop firewood to keep warm. The nearest shop was a twenty-minute drive. And a global company had taken umbrage with him because he'd had the audacity to buy something that was for sale.

He thought back to stories of others who'd left the Marines. It wasn't just travellers who turned their backs on society and lived a nomadic lifestyle, lots of marines did too. Backpacking. Ranching in Australia. Trekking in Alaska. Spending their life savings on a boat and sailing the world. Fluke had even heard of one marine who'd bought an uninhabited island somewhere in the Caribbean. Went years on end without seeing anyone.

Fluke took a deep breath of pine-laced fresh air and picked up his pen. Self-reflection could wait. He had one night to do this. Jinx was staring at him, concern all over her face.

'I need your real name.'

'I don't have one.'

A bit of her petulance had returned. Keeping her real name to herself was obviously important. Probably a protective device she'd developed over the years. No real name, no easy way of being traced.

'Look, I may be a bit old-fashioned. I may—'

She snorted, but not unkindly. 'Hardly. You live in the middle of a wood. You have a girlfriend covered in tattoos – who's way out of your league, by the way – and you haven't even reported that someone's posting bullets through your door.'

'Bridie told you about the shotgun cartridge?'

'And other stuff,' she said cryptically. 'She wanted to show you could both be trusted.'

Fluke held her gaze. 'You can. Trust me now. Give me your real name.'

For a second he thought she might refuse. Some new age traveller code-of-honour thing. She shut her eyes before she spoke, as if even the memory was painful.

'Jane. Jane Evans.'

'Date of birth?'

She told him. Fluke asked for her parents' names and their address. She was a bit hazier on the latter; somewhere in Gloucester, but it was enough to go on. He excused himself and went to the kitchen area to text Jiao-long the details. He asked him to search but keep the system footprints down to a minimum. He knew Jiao-long would do more than that; he would be in and out like a ghost. By the time he'd sat back down he'd received a return text. Jiao-long was working late and would do it straightaway.

'When did you meet Bish?' he asked, picking up his notebook again.

'Last summer.'

'Where? In London?'

'No. Up here.'

'Cumbria?'

She nodded. 'He came up with Vane.'

Fluke wrote down the name and underlined it. 'And they came from London?'

'Yes. Came up for the summer. Needed somewhere to stay and wanted to stay off the grid. Vane knew Twist was up here and asked around until he found us.'

'How many were there?'

'Four. Vane was in charge. We didn't get to know the other two at all – they weren't there long and I can't even remember what they were called. All three seemed to do what Vane told them anyway.'

Which was curious. Vane must have been one hell of a leader for Bish to have happily followed him. As a marine, he'd had an anti-authoritarian streak when it came to weak leaders, particularly officers. Hence his relatively low rank compared to his abilities.

'How did you and Bish hook up?'

She didn't answer immediately and her eyes seemed to lose focus. She closed them.

'It wasn't easy,' she said finally.

For the next thirty minutes Jinx talked Fluke through their relationship. From start to finish. Well, the finish as she knew it. Fluke still had one more chapter to add.

The first thing Jinx said was that neither group approved of them spending time together. And given how closely new age travellers identified with the Swinging Sixties, it was rather a strange thing to disapprove of. The frowners were Vane on the London side, and Twist from the resident Cumbrians.

Vane didn't want Bish involved with anyone in Cumbria. They only planned to be there for three months, and the official line was that he didn't want anyone hurt out of a short-lived, doomed romance.

The objections from the Cumbrian corner were equally unlikely. Jinx didn't know what had happened when Twist and Vane had known each other previously, but it was obvious they didn't get on.

When Vane arrived at their camp, Twist told them to piss off. It wasn't until Vane took him away for an hour to talk that he relented. They could stay, but no one was to talk to them. The story was that there was a warrant out for Vane's arrest and lying low in the Lake District suited him fine. Some sort of environmental offence. Jinx had looked a bit shifty when she'd told him that; she obviously didn't believe the cover story either. If she knew more, she'd tell him in her own time.

So, against the camp's will, Vane was allowed to stay. But why was he up here in the first place? Fluke didn't believe for a second it was to evade the law. Cumbria was actually a really shit place to hide. The cities were too small to blend into the background, and new people in villages or towns were instantly the subject of gossip and conjecture. London was a far better place to hide, and given the subculture Vane was part of, he could have evaded the police indefinitely.

There was another reason they were in Cumbria. Had to be.

Jinx and Bish had been careful about seeing each other. Vane seemed to hold some sort of power over Bish, which Fluke was keen to explore later, and although Twist, who was like a father figure to her, hadn't said anything, she could tell he disapproved as well.

Fluke wondered out loud if she thought Twist was jealous.

Even by conventional standards Jinx was a beautiful woman. In a small group she would stand out even more. In everything he investigated, Fluke first looked for the two motives of sex and money. Most of the time there was no need to look for a third.

Jinx openly laughed at the suggestion and Fluke queried why.

'Wait until you see Twist's wife,' she said. 'You think I'm nice looking – Faith could be a supermodel any day she wanted. She's absolutely stunning.'

Faith. Twist. Jinx. Vane. No way these numpties weren't doing Facebook's 'What's My Hippy Name?' quiz.

'Looks aren't everything,' Fluke said.

'Obviously,' she'd agreed, nodding. 'But Faith's also the nicest and brightest woman you'll ever meet. Two Cambridge degrees in the history of art, a masters from Yale and visiting lecturer invites from virtually every major university in the world. Next to Faith, I'm a stupid little girl. No, Twist wasn't jealous. Protective maybe, probably on Faith's say so, but they're the happiest couple I know. And they have a beautiful baby boy.'

'Let me guess. He's called Mist, or Hemlock or something?'

Jinx smiled. 'Sam.'

'So what happened next?' he asked.

'We continued seeing each other.'

Not in the open though. The group leaders had too much influence, and although it was little more than a commune, both Bish and Jinx had to appear to publicly respect their decisions. Fluke, however, was struggling to see how they could carry on any type of secret relationship in a camp full of hippies who spent their days sitting round fires taking mood-altering chemicals. It wasn't so much that everyone would know each other's business, it was more the fact they'd be in each other's line of sight all day. Unless they coordinated going for a shit, he didn't see how they'd get any time together at all . . .

Like an idiot, he expressed this to Jinx.

One severe bollocking later, and Fluke understood a bit more about how new age traveller camps worked. They might not have the basic amenities he took for granted, and they might all be a bit weird, but he now knew that most travellers had jobs. Not one person in camp claimed state benefits. During the day the camp was virtually deserted.

During the spring and summer months, members of the camp worked hard. Some of what they did was unskilled manual labour. Fruit and vegetable picking was a favourite – with an almost unlimited supply of lamb and beef, Cumbria wasn't just England's butcher, it was also one of her larger greengrocers – and someone with few overheads, who was willing to work a hard season in the orchards and fields, could earn money that would comfortably see them through the rest of the year.

But they weren't just limited to manual labour. Some had skills that were commercially attractive. Admittedly, most were in the craft areas, but in a county that held more agricultural shows than any other, there was always a market for their wares. One of them, Jinx told him, practised chainsaw carving and was in demand all summer. Shows, corporate events, weddings; he would take a log and, using only a chainsaw, would turn it into a bear or an owl or a bird. Another man in the camp was a sought-after blacksmith. Modern sculptures were his speciality, but he could turn his hand to repairing things that were too old for manufacturers to still have the spare parts. And in Cumbria, where farm equipment could be generations old, he was never short of work.

Fools, weavers, artists and acrobats, even a solicitor, everyone in the camp had a reason to get out of bed in the morning. But not too early. And they were certainly all back by mid-afternoon. They weren't in the rat race; there was no need to work long hours.

Fluke was beginning to see the attraction.

'Do you work, Jinx?' he asked.

'Sometimes,' she replied. 'I used to make a few things in the camp. Baskets and wooden instruments, that type of thing. I'd get others to sell them for me. I avoid the outside world when I can.'

'So how—?' Fluke started to ask again how she and Bish had managed to spend any time together at all.

'Look,' she interrupted, 'it was really just Vane and Twist who disapproved and they weren't around much during the day.'

Fluke said nothing and she continued.

'Twist's a phrenologist, and this is the time of year when he makes his money. There are a lot of tourists who like that kind of stuff.'

'Phrenologist?'

'He tells people their personality traits by feeling the shape of their skull.'

He stared at her, not sure if she was taking the piss. He decided she wasn't.

'And this works, does it?'

'He makes a small living from it. Spends twenty minutes measuring the client's head before typing up a report on his laptop and emailing it to them. "Pretentious shite," Mark called it.'

Fluke smiled. So, not everything about him had changed.

'Did he say anything to Twist?' Bish was addicted to taking the piss, and Fluke knew murders had been committed for far less.

'Yes. There was tension between the two groups, and Twist and Mark disagreed about me, but they were friends. Mark would tease him and Twist would tell him he just wasn't in tune with his spiritual inner self yet. Bit of fun for them both, I think.'

'So you managed to get some time to yourselves?'

Her eyes sparkled as memories returned. 'Yes. Yes, we did. We started out just going for walks. Long walks where we would talk for hours. We had a meeting place outside of the camp. After about a week we found somewhere sheltered and made love. It was wonderful. Although my father abused me I considered myself a virgin. Mark was so gentle with me.'

Fluke was scribbling notes but his pencil had stopped at the last remark. It remained hovering over his notebook as he considered what he was being told. Not only was it so personal, the last vestiges of the Bish he'd once known were being stripped away.

'We were married on the Hibernal Solstice. There's a pagan in the camp who performed a secret, moonlit ceremony.'

'So, it's not official then?' Fluke said, feeling ashamed as soon as he'd said it.

She looked at him sadly.

'Sorry,' he said.

Jinx smiled. Point made. Move on.

'This Hibernal Solstice, is it the same as the Winter Solstice?' he asked.

Nodding, she said, 'Yes, December the twenty-second. We timed it perfectly. We were pronounced man and wife at three minutes past eleven.'

'Romantic,' Fluke acknowledged. Another question popped into his mind. 'Did anyone find out about the wedding? Twist, or Vane maybe?'

'If they did, they didn't say anything. There was only me and Mark, the person who married us, and my best friend.'

Fluke raised his eyebrows.

'Faith,' she replied to his unspoken question.

'So, what were your long-term plans?' Fluke asked.

Shit! He'd used past tense.

She didn't seem to notice and Fluke breathed out carefully.

'We were going to move away. Mark has some savings and wants to buy a croft in Scotland. One of the smaller islands.'

'You said Vane's group were only up here for the summer? To do what exactly? I doubt they were flogging themselves picking strawberries?'

For the first time since they'd started talking she looked evasive. She looked away. Picked up her drink and gently blew on it. Classic signs of someone not wanting to answer.

'Jinx?'

'I'm not supposed to talk about it.'

Fluke immediately felt a sense of relief. He was finally getting nearer his area of expertise; a reluctant witness. He knew forcing the matter wouldn't work and she needed a break anyway. They both did. It had been quite intense.

'You want some ice cream? I've some in the freezer.'

'Vegan, remember.'

'I think there's some sawdust outside. You want me to go and get you some?'

She stuck out her tongue.

Fluke was about to get up and get his dessert when his phone beeped. He looked at the incoming text. It was from Jiao-long.

Can you call me, boss?

Chapter 14

Fluke excused himself and went outside to call Jiao-long. He picked up on the first ring.

'What you got, Longy?'

Fluke heard paper rustling as Jiao-long started reading.

'Jane Evans. Twenty-five, minor convictions for public order offences. Mostly eco-related. Same type of thing as Mark Cadden actually, but no violence. I take it this is something to do with the case we're not investigating?'

Fluke didn't answer and Jiao-long took the hint.

'Anyway, the family's flagged. If I hadn't used a backdoor I'd have been caught.'

Careful to avoid using the name Jinx, Fluke said, 'The Met are after Jane Evans?'

'No, it's Gloucestershire police who want to speak to her.'

What the . . .?

'What's she done down there, for God's sake?'

'Not her. Her father.'

'He's abused another child?' he blurted out before he could stop himself.

Jiao-long paused. Fluke didn't fill the gap.

'Hardly,' he said after a moment. 'A few weeks ago, he died of a heart attack.'

Fluke walked back into the cabin. He was ashen-faced. Jinx picked up on the change immediately.

'What is it? What's wrong?'

'Jinx, when was the last time you spoke to your family?'

'The group's my family.'

'Your *real* family, Jinx.' Fluke said it in such a way she must have known he was past being nosey.

'I speak to my mother on her birthday. Just to let her know I'm OK.'

'And when's her birthday?'

'September.'

'So you haven't spoken to anyone in your family for ten months?' he said eventually.

Jinx screwed up her face as she thought. 'No. I won't have.'

'And they can't contact you?'

She shook her head.

There really was no other way to break the news. As a police officer he was trained to be direct when delivering bad news. Never leave the family in any doubt that their loved one had died. Avoid using phrases like 'passed away' or 'gone to a better place'. Be compassionate, but be firm.

'Your father's dead, Jinx.'

Ordinarily he would have added something conciliatory but, given that the man had sexually abused her, he had no idea if sympathy was the appropriate response.

A single tear rolled down her cheek. She made no move to wipe it away and Fluke didn't offer her a tissue. It was obviously news. Whether it was bad or not was something she'd have to decide for herself . . .

'What was it? Did he finally have that heart attack?'

Fluke nodded. 'A few weeks ago.'

She said nothing for several moments. Just took in some deep breaths.

'Good,' she said eventually.

*

If Jinx didn't want to grieve, Fluke wasn't going to spend any time waiting. 'Tell me about Vane,' he said.

Her brow furrowed. 'Vane? What does he have to do with anything?'

'Humour me.'

Fluke was convinced he was the key to everything. He wasn't up here simply to avoid a court case; people like Vane thrived on notoriety. They needed it. Most of these eco-warrior types only wanted their egos stroking. In all human subsets, people tried to outdo each other. *Look at me; I'm more hard-core than you. I've been to court more times than you. I'm weirder. I wear stranger clothes than you do. My drugs are stronger than your drugs.*

Fluke reckoned there were probably only half a dozen true activists in the country. The rest did it because it was in vogue, it was the only way they could attract members of the opposite sex, or because they needed something to feel smug about. The question was, what type was Vane? If he were one of the latter, Fluke would have him within twenty-four hours. He'd be showboating somewhere, making sure people knew who he was and what he was doing.

No point having a secret if you couldn't tell everyone.

But if he was the former then something was happening. The something 'serious' Jinx had mentioned. And if Vane was the type of man who could command the respect of Bish, then he was the type of man Fluke planned to be nervous about.

Jinx tore him from his thoughts.

'I don't know a great deal about him. He never mixed with the group, never sat round the communal fire at night. He only spoke to me a few times, and never about why he was up here. The only other person he spoke to was Dan.'

'Dan?'

'The blacksmith I was telling you about before. He was making something for him.'

Fluke's eyebrows rose. 'Oh?'

97

'Yeah. Some sculpture for his parents' thirtieth anniversary. Had the plans already drawn up. Normally Dan doesn't like making things off plans, he prefers working organically when it comes to art, but Vane must have had the money.'

'You ever see what it was?'

'I didn't. Dan's forge is always away from the camp as it's a fire hazard.'

Fluke frowned. He was prepared to acknowledge anyone could enjoy art and anyone could commission it. But anything made by a blacksmith wasn't the type of thing you could put a first-class stamp on and post to Mum. Something wasn't right. But bits of old farm equipment *were* all the rage as garden ornaments in suburbia, so anything was possible. He made a note. Whatever it was, he'd find out later.

He asked a question he already knew the answer to. 'You don't know Vane's surname, do you?'

'No idea.'

'What's he look like?'

'How tall is that idiot friend of yours?'

'Who? Towler? He's not an idiot . . . well . . . not all the time anyway. He's six foot eight, I think.'

'Vane must be about six foot four then, but the same type of build as Mark.'

Fluke grimaced. That was big.

Bish had been stocky. Marines tended to be. Unlike paras, who travelled light and relied on speed and a dependable resupply chain catching them up later, marines carried everything they needed to fight and survive for days at a time. Huge weights carried for huge distances. Something approaching Towler's height but with Bish's build would make Vane a formidable man.

'Hair?' Fluke asked. Jinx wasn't used to describing people, that much was obvious. He was having to drag it out of her a bit at a time.

'Like mine. Dreadlocks.'

'Colour?'

'I think it's ginger,' she said finally.

Fluke wrote it down, underlined it, and added a small question mark beside it. Ginger was a hair colour that stood out. Plus, if Jinx's hair was anything to go by, a good wash changed the colour anyway. He decided to change direction. Getting a working description this way was like trying to snap a coin.

'Is there anything you can tell me? Anything that might help me find him?' Fluke asked.

Jinx's eyes darted towards his and held them in a steel gaze. 'Why do you want to find him?'

Fluke ignored the question. 'Was it Vane that Bish was warning you about, do you think?'

She actually laughed in his face.

Fluke stared. She didn't appear to be concealing anything with her laugh. It seemed genuine. 'I'll take that as a "no", shall I?'

'Vane wouldn't have hurt me. He might have been in charge, he might even have asked Mark not to see me, but when it came down to it he couldn't stop him. Mark knew that. He told me.'

Fluke leaned forward. His instincts were telling him Vane – if he wasn't directly involved – would at least know who was. Was he miles off?

'Told you what?'

She looked shifty again. 'I'm not supposed to say.'

'If you want my help I need to know everything, Jinx. Mistakes are made when intel's incomplete.'

'He told me why they were really up here. Why Vane wouldn't dare touch me.'

'And why was that?' Fluke asked his question as casually as he could, but it was clear to both of them it was a key moment in their discussion. Fluke had led her to the water. Would she take a drink?

'You said earlier you doubted that Vane and Mark were up here picking strawberries. Well, they weren't. And Vane wasn't hiding from the police. They were here to do a job.'

'A job? What job?'

'I have no idea. Mark wouldn't speak about it. Told me not to worry and it would soon be over.'

Fluke said nothing. Jinx filled the silence immediately.

'It was something important though. A package, I think. Mark wasn't directly involved in that though. Vane went off on his own to collect it.'

A package?

'What package?' This was starting to look a little bit too organised. 'It wouldn't be the thing this blacksmith friend of yours was making, would it?'

'God, no. I told you, Dan was making art. I've got no idea what the package was. I'm not the naive child you think I am though. I . . . think it might have been something illegal.'

'Illegal?'

'It might even have been weed.' She looked at him defiantly, as if daring him to challenge her.

'Why'd you think that, Jinx? I thought you didn't know what was in it.'

'I don't. I'm guessing, but you don't go to all the trouble of coming up here and going off in the middle of the night on your own if all you're doing is stealing apples.'

'Fair point.'

'And anyway, it was small enough to fit in his rucksack.'

Fluke listened as she told him how she'd watched Bish talking to Vane one night just before Vane left. When he'd returned, he didn't have the rucksack he'd left with, so maybe he'd hidden it. Fluke asked her to estimate the rucksack's size and, using her hands she described a bag that was more of a knapsack. Hardly conclusive, but certainly indicative of the package's size.

'Why do you think Vane wouldn't stop Mark seeing you? It seems to me that if he had a plan, the fewer people who knew about it the better.'

She paused as if thinking how to phrase her answer. Eventually she settled for, 'Mark told me the job couldn't be done without him. That's why Vane could disapprove all he wanted, he was never going to seriously stop us seeing each other. He couldn't risk Mark leaving. The other two that came up with him had already gone back down south. Mark was the only one left. Vane trusted him.'

Not if he'd been blabbing to his wife he wouldn't, Fluke thought. Perhaps Bish's protected witness status *wasn't* the reason he was killed. Was it because he'd discussed the plan with Jinx? Was operational security something Vane would kill over? Was that why, after realising he'd put them in danger, Bish had given her the run order? If he didn't come back every night she was supposed to leave immediately. It was the closest Fluke had to a theory at the moment. It fitted *some* of the facts. Not all of them.

He reviewed the new information.

There was a mysterious package somewhere in Cumbria.

Vane had had something strange made by a blacksmith.

And a Metropolitan Police Service protected witness team had taken the case from FMIT before they'd even got started. And they hadn't asked for local help. That was either arrogance or – now that he had a bit more information to work with – security related.

Fluke needed more data.

The only person who could help was Chief Inspector John Reyes, and simply asking wasn't going to work.

He considered his other options.

The obvious approach was quid pro quo. Come clean about what he knew in exchange for information. There were a few problems with that though. He couldn't simply say he knew something important. If he did he had a duty to share it. They either wouldn't believe him or, if they did, they'd simply arrest him and keep him locked up until he told them. The law was on their side. But if he shared what he had in an 'I'm trusting you to reciprocate' scenario, he'd get diddly-squat in return. Maybe another smug 'thank you, we'll take it from here'.

Also, he wasn't ready to give up Jinx yet. He would if he thought it would get him nearer to Bish's killer, but he failed to see how Reyes would get more out of her than he had.

He briefly considered approaching the female detective, the one who'd looked like she had something invested in the case. Fluke sensed he might find an ally there. He dismissed it immediately. He had no idea why she appeared more emotionally involved than the others, but he'd worked with women police officers his entire career and knew merit was the only thing that advanced their careers these days. Being in a protected witness unit meant she was tough and resourceful. She might privately think Reyes was the end of a bell, but she'd back him in public. If Fluke approached her she'd tell Reyes immediately.

So, telling them what he knew was out. Telling them he knew something, but wanted something in return, was also out. And he had no one he could approach quietly.

There was only one thing Fluke could do and he got chills just thinking about it.

Fluke needed Reyes to *think* he knew something. He needed to get Reyes so frustrated, so angry with him, the only option he'd have would be to make a deal and bring him inside the investigation.

It was time for Fluke to pick a fight.

Chapter 15

FMIT didn't exactly march in as one, heads held high, heralded by a quartet of trumpets. Rather they arrived at Fluke's cabin in dribs and drabs over the course of two hours. Some of them had been working and had to make excuses, and some had farther to travel. And, other than Towler, most of them hadn't been enough times to drive straight there without getting lost.

Fluke introduced them to Jinx. Towler had already warned them she didn't know her husband was dead, and that Fluke would be referring to him as the 'misper' rather than the victim.

When they'd drunk coffee, and eaten two whole packets of Hobnobs, Fluke began his abridged briefing. Afterwards he said, 'Now you know what Jinx and I know. The problem we have is that when I let slip to Reyes I know more than I'm letting on, the first thing he's going to do is come here looking for Jinx.'

Jo Skelton, the only woman on the team, and by far the most valuable member, started by asking Jinx what she wanted.

Typical, Fluke thought, embarrassed. He'd spent two hours thinking about the issue and hadn't considered asking Jinx once.

'I want to go back to the camp. I shouldn't have left. Mark may be back by now and he'll be worried sick.'

Delicately threading the needle, Fluke explained that if she returned home she'd be arrested immediately. That a team from London were actively looking for her and Mark. Reyes almost certainly had eyes on the camp. Fluke explained there was now a Venn diagram where their interests converged, and for now that meant she had to avoid Reyes. But as a compromise, Fluke promised to get someone out to the camp as soon as possible to check he hadn't returned. It was the very definition of an exercise in futility, but sometimes wasting time was the right thing to do.

They discussed where Jinx could be hidden. Dismissing hotels and B & Bs as being too obvious, they considered whether it was possible for one of them to put her up.

Jiao-long lived in a flat in Carlisle city centre, had an active social life, and was too well known locally to have a live-in guest go unnoticed for long. Towler and Jo Skelton both had young children and couldn't risk bringing danger to their homes. Alan Vaughn was a loner and a weirdo, didn't volunteer, and was never seriously in contention anyway. Sometimes, just sometimes, working with a team of oddballs had disadvantages . . .

A sulky silence settled over FMIT; the problem was simple; their failure to identify a solution was frustrating.

'Of course, there is someone who could help,' Jo Skelton said eventually.

She didn't elaborate and Towler jumped in. 'Well?'

She looked sheepish. 'Forget it,' she said. 'It was a stupid idea.'

In all the time Fluke had known Skelton, she'd never said anything remotely stupid.

'Out with it, Jo. We've exhausted every other option.'

To his surprise, she refused to elaborate.

Fluke decided to help her out. He got up, stretched, and said, 'Jo, come and help me with more coffee. I'll get the cups.'

While they waited for the kettle, Fluke said, 'So, what is it, Jo? What don't you want to say in front of the others?'

Saying the first thing that entered her head wasn't Skelton's style. She was a deep thinker; it was why she was so effective. She didn't get bored; she understood the importance of the less glamorous parts of the job. She would retire as a detective constable, not because of any tactical deficiency, but because that was where she wanted to be. So when she'd said 'Forget it, it was a stupid idea' it was because she wanted to speak to Fluke in private.

'You know that the respect I have for you doesn't depend on whether you're in the room or not, don't you?'

Fluke nodded.

She continued. 'You're the team's moral compass. Some of the things we've done over the years haven't always been by the book. Some of the things haven't even been strictly legal.'

Again Fluke nodded.

'The point is, whatever you've asked us to do, I've not once hesitated. I've not once thought, "Hang on, he's gone too far this time." Not once. And it's rubbed off on us. We do what's right, not what's easy. We don't condone behaviour even when it's easier to look the other way.'

Still Fluke said nothing.

'There is one person who can help. But to ask him would be to give him legitimacy,' she said. 'And he's the last person you want to owe favours to.'

The fog of confusion lifted. There was indeed one man who could help. He even owed Fluke a favour.

Nathaniel Diamond was a criminal anomaly. A ruthless gang leader, he was highly organised and well connected. He ran Cumbria's drugs, massage parlours, prostitutes and loan sharks. Anyone wanting to make money out of crime in the county had to speak to him first, and then pay a percentage. All drugs came through him. He was the wholesaler and anyone who thought they could cut him out of the loop would soon discover he had serious muscle protecting his interests. Alongside his illegal activities, he had legitimate businesses that masked what he did and laundered vast amounts of money. Nothing out of the ordinary. Every large town had someone like that. Some of the larger cities had a few.

What made Nathaniel Diamond different was complex. He

was young, by far the youngest leader of any organised crime family in the UK. He was charismatic, and in a business that didn't value diversity, he was also openly gay. But the most startling thing about him, the thing that made him different from every other thug in the country, was his intellect.

Nathaniel Diamond was a genius. Not just bright. Not just sneaky or cunning. He had an IQ hovering around 180, and that put him in the same kind of group as Stephen Hawking. He'd hidden his intelligence from the police; it suited him to be thought of as just another wannabe gangster. Nothing to see here, folks, move along. Fluke was sure he'd have kept his intelligence hidden indefinitely, but life has a way of forcing things upon people.

Seven months earlier, Fluke had been investigating the murder of a young woman who'd been dumped on a west Cumbrian building site. The investigation had led him to the American, Dalton Cross; a psychopathic contract killer, who'd been hired to protect the reputation of a multi-millionaire in the United States. To get information on the victim, he'd kidnapped, tortured and ultimately murdered Nathaniel Diamond's father. Fluke had brought in Nathaniel, and during the interview he'd had to reveal his intelligence to ensure the focus of the investigation was where it needed to be. It was because of this help that Fluke was finally able to find the killer of Diamond's father.

A few days before Cross was due to be extradited to the States, his cellmate in HMP Durham had thrown 'prison napalm' in his face, stuck a sharpened toothbrush in his neck, and sat on him until he bled out. Although everyone knew Nathaniel Diamond was responsible, he was so far removed from the person who did it, no link could be established.

But by catching his father's killer, and unwittingly affording him the opportunity to exact natural justice, Nathaniel Diamond believed he owed Fluke.

It was time to call that favour in.

Chapter 16

Fluke would have preferred to meet Diamond somewhere neutral, but because of Automatic Number Plate Recognition they couldn't use any vehicle Reyes might find out about later. ANPR stored information, so when Fluke became a target Reyes would eventually know where he'd been and, because the system took photographs, he'd also know who he'd been with. He had no choice, Diamond had to come to the cabin.

'You can't let that fucking nutter know where you live,' Towler had objected.

He was right of course but Fluke was all out of options . . .

They heard Diamond before they saw him. A black Range Rover with tinted windows came into view. It was quickly followed by another. They were both full.

A posse.

The vehicles stopped near the cabin but kept their engines running. Fluke, who'd done some close protection training in the Marines, recognised the tactic. Diamond was being cautious. It was clear he wasn't entirely sure this wasn't some form of elaborate trap.

Fluke and the rest of FMIT made their way off the porch and fanned out in front of the vehicles.

The back door of the second car opened and Nathaniel Diamond stepped out.

A cultured voice wasn't the only thing he'd gained since they'd last met. If Fluke was susceptible to spouting clichés he might have been tempted to say Diamond had gone up in the world. Fluke might not know the difference between a suit tailored on Savile Row to one bought off the peg at Matalan, but he instinctively knew Diamond was expensively and tastefully adorned.

But Fluke hadn't been fooled last time, and he knew better than to take him at face value this time. Then, the shell suits, bling jewellery and shaven head had been a means to an end. He'd looked like a thug, but only because it was the image he'd needed while he established and secured a base of operations to expand upon. It seemed that phase was now complete and, no longer needing the thug image, he'd cast it off like a snake sloughing its skin, emerging as an international businessman ready to expand beyond the borders of Cumbria. A man of his intelligence and ruthlessness was never going to be satisfied being a small-town gangster.

Diamond glanced at Fluke, smiled and casually lifted a hand behind his back. Fluke thought it had been a greeting and was about to respond, but instead the rest of the car doors opened. Nine men alighted and stood behind him. All but one were huge, shaven-headed brutes. All suited and booted, grim and silent. If the situation hadn't been so serious Fluke would have laughed. Diamond was by far the smallest member of the group and the men looked like his backing singers.

For a long minute no one spoke. Even Towler was silent. Out of his peripheral vision, Fluke could see Jinx fidgeting but otherwise everyone was still.

Diamond broke the silence. 'You expecting trouble, Mr Fluke?'

Fluke shrugged and nodded towards the mass of black suits behind him.

'I'm the one taking the risk here,' Diamond said, answering the unspoken question. 'We both know who I am and what I do. And we both know at some point in the future your chief constable will turn to you and your helper monkeys. I'm wondering if he already has?'

Towler tensed up but said nothing. He'd take his lead off Fluke but, even so, he was like a coiled spring.

Fluke shrugged again. Not a great start. And Diamond wasn't that far off the mark. He decided to defuse things.

'How's Mathew?' he asked.

Diamond cocked his head and gave him an appraising look. He must have realised Fluke wanted to move on. That aggression suited neither side.

'He's fine,' he said. 'The photography has taken off recently. He has a collection displaying at the Baltic in Newcastle next month.'

'You'll have to tell me when. I'll go and have a look.'

Fluke wasn't humouring Diamond. When they'd raided his house six months ago, there were several mesmerising black and white stills of Carlisle that had stopped Fluke in his tracks. Mathew had a way of making ugly things beautiful. The castle, Dixon's Chimney, even the hideous millennium bridge, under his lens, gained an ethereal quality that defied their reality.

Diamond appeared to take that as the peace offering it was. He turned to his men. 'Chill out, boys. Enjoy the fresh air. Allow me and Mr Fluke to talk in private.'

All bar one returned to the Range Rovers.

The man who remained had personal bodyguard written all over him. Ex-military and not cheap, if Fluke was any judge. He didn't have the steroid-bulked muscles, neck tattoos and shaven heads the rest favoured, yet he had a confidence that made him stand out. The rest of the men were watching him for instructions. He was clearly in charge of Diamond's security.

'Are you going to introduce me to your friend, Nathaniel?'

Diamond kept a straight face. 'Let's call him Mr Smith.'

Fluke wanted to speak to Diamond on his own. 'OK,

Nathaniel. You might have a Smith, but I have a Towler. Can we assume for now that they cancel each other out? I'm sure they'll enjoy staring at each other for a few minutes while we go and have a little chat?'

'Stay here, Mr Smith,' Diamond said.

No please, no thank you. Smith nodded.

Fluke led Diamond down the path he'd hewn from the side of the hill, all the way to the edge of the lake. It was still holding firm and Fluke felt proud of the work he'd put in. The first outdoorsy thing he'd ever really done.

They stopped at the water's edge and looked out across the lake. There was hardly a whisper in the air and Ullswater was flawlessly still.

'I need you to hide someone for me, Nathaniel. A woman.'

Diamond said nothing and Fluke continued.

'I'm not asking you to do anything illegal.'

'Why me? You're a resourceful man.'

There was no antagonism. Fluke *was* a resourceful man. It was a fair question. One that deserved an honest answer.

'The people who'll come looking for her are well resourced. They'll turn my life upside down and I don't have anywhere or anyone they won't uncover.'

Diamond raised an eyebrow, Roger Moore style. 'And what makes you think I can hide her?'

Fluke didn't want to get into the whole thing about Diamond being at the helm of an expanding criminal empire.

'Because you know where I live,' he said.

Diamond shrugged.

'Don't do that,' Fluke said. 'We're both intelligent men. I called my team a few hours ago, and despite most of them having been here before, they still managed to get lost. Yet you came straight here. Didn't ask for directions or a postcode. Why was that?'

Bending down to pick up a stone, Diamond skimmed it across the water, the glasslike stillness shattering into a thousand ripples.

'Opposition research,' he said finally.

Fluke nodded.

'Who's going to be looking for her?' Diamond asked.

And with that, they got down to business.

Chapter 17

They made their way back to the cabin to find their respective groups doing their best to pretend the other didn't exist. With the exception of Smith, Diamond's men had all retreated to the air-conditioned Range Rovers. They decamped when they saw him return, ready for incoming instructions. Orders really. Smith was leaning against the bonnet of the lead vehicle, chewing on a bit of long grass. The very essence of calm. He had a slight grin on his face and every so often would steal a glance at Towler.

Fluke frowned. Towler was looking agitated and Fluke doubted he would stay still for long. He considered things such as turning the other cheek to be against the spirit of the Parachute Regiment. The fact that someone had brazenly walked into what was, in his eyes at least, a police stronghold, was an insult. Worse still, one of them wasn't even shitting himself.

He did a quick head count and noticed someone was missing. 'Where's Jinx?' he asked.

'Inside, boss. Wanted to make herself useful. She's making bacon sandwiches for everyone.'

That was a turn up. She'd cooked him a Cumberland sausage a short time ago but that was when she wanted him to open up about something. She couldn't have approved of the shaven-headed lunatics that were camped out on his doorstep. So why was she not being . . . well, Jinx?

The answer was obvious. It was because she knew this was how she would get Bish back.

If only she knew.

'Mr Smith, go and help the lady with the food. We'll need to get off soon and she's coming with us,' Diamond said.

If Smith was unhappy with the domestic chore, he didn't show it. He went inside without comment and within a few minutes they were back out carrying trays laden with food and cold drinks. Jinx put a sandwich on a plate and approached Diamond.

'Do you want a bacon sandwich, Mr Diamond?'

Diamond stared. Appraising her. 'Please, call me Nathaniel. And I don't eat meat,' he said eventually.

Fluke winced.

Towler could be relied upon to make tactless comments without any external stimuli at the best of times, but with the heightened emotions they were all experiencing, a herd of mad bulls wouldn't be able to stop him coming out with a 'that's not what I've heard' type of remark.

It was in his DNA.

To Fluke's amazement he settled for a snort.

Diamond barely glanced in Towler's direction. Smith did, but his expression didn't change. If his boss wasn't bothered then he wasn't.

Communal eating, as it has done for millennia, signalled a temporary truce to both real and imagined insults. Despite the intoxicating smell of fried bacon, Fluke was too anxious to eat. Diamond was a vegetarian, and Towler wasn't eating because Smith wasn't or vice versa. But the rest of them tucked in. Jinx had emptied his fridge and freezer judging by the amount of food she was bringing out.

'Where you taking her?' Fluke asked Diamond, careful to keep his voice low.

'Best you don't know,' he said.

Fluke nodded. The further Jinx went into Diamond's world,

the safer she was from his. 'I'm going to need to meet with her though. Soon probably.'

Diamond called out to Smith. 'Get Mr Fluke a few burners, will you? Nothing that's been used before.'

Smith nodded and walked over to the Range Rovers. He appeared to say something to one of the steroid-fuelled chaperones, who retreated to the boot of the rear vehicle. Smith rejoined Fluke and Diamond. He still didn't speak to Fluke. Fluke couldn't decide if he was disciplined or rude. It *was* intimidating though. A very real sense of danger oozed from the pores of the man in front of him.

An uneasy silence settled over the two groups as they waited for the phones. Fluke passed the time watching the man designated to get them. There was something familiar about him. Fluke turned to Towler and raised his eyebrows. Towler smiled, cryptically touched his eye, and went back to staring at Smith. The man rooted about in the boot and found a bag. He opened it, and rooted about again. Taking out a smaller bag he jogged over to the three of them.

It wasn't until he turned that Fluke saw who it was. To say he was surprised was the understatement of the year. Even though he'd read the intelligence briefings he'd never really believed the man now standing in front of him would ever work for Diamond . . .

Steeleye Stan hated the police with a passion. It was in his DNA. Every copper knew this. He'd been a violent child, an even more violent teen and a psychotic young man. A product of his environment, he'd spent time in every institution imaginable. Foster families, children's homes, *secure* children's homes, young offender institutions, prisons, even secure hospitals. Children's services, youth offending services and probation hadn't made a dent in his violence. For a long time he was *the* hired muscle in Cumbria, and was sought after by various gangs for what he could bring: extreme violence.

No one really knew how he lost his eye, although the report from A & E stated there were shards of glass involved. He certainly never told the police what had happened and discharged himself as soon as he'd shaken off the anaesthetic.

He might have lost his depth perception but he didn't lose his brutal propensity for savagery. The assaults and beatings continued. He lost so many prosthetic eyes during the course of his work, he began using steel ball bearings instead. It made him even more menacing and he became a target for every police officer on the force. Stop and search Steeleye Stan just as your shift was about to end, and you'd be guaranteed four hours' overtime as you processed the inevitable arrest.

But like anything it had to end. For Stan it was a combination of natural maturation and the love of a good woman. A good Carlisle lass saw something in him that, to date, no one else had. He settled down and had children – three boys. He didn't want to go to prison any more but he still needed to earn a crust and was bright enough to know that legalised violence, or to use the correct term, door security, was the future. Stan formed a consortium of other like-minded knuckledraggers and together they took over the doors of every pub and club in Carlisle, Cockermouth, Workington, Maryport and Whitehaven. They formed a limited company and went semi-legit. They controlled who went in and who went out, and that included the drug dealers. And it worked. Violence in the night-time economy reduced. Police figures improved. An ironic blind eye was turned. Stan became wealthy. He was being well paid by the pubs and clubs, and he was taking a cut of every Ecstasy tablet sold, every gram of cocaine snorted and every eighth of heroin injected.

And then Nathaniel Diamond appeared.

In less than three weeks Stan's door security company was, in business terms, the subject of a hostile takeover. Nathaniel had his own dealers and his own door business. Stan's bouncers moved across without regret. Nathaniel paid more, and in that business coin was the only currency that mattered, plus the Diamonds had serious muscle behind them. Steeleye Stan's crew used baseball bats, Diamond's used military-grade weapons.

Nobody wanted that fight.

Stan wasn't a stupid man and recognised a fart when he smelled one. He joined Diamond and became one of his key men. Not senior management, but a comfortable mid-level position in the hired muscle part of Diamond's empire.

But in Stan's eyes, Fluke reckoned he'd think that Nathaniel Diamond was no more than a poof who'd ripped him off. A nancy boy who'd hidden behind big brains and an even bigger army of thugs. A man who'd taken away his business and turned him into little more than an errand boy . . .

'Hi, Stan. Remember me?' Towler said. 'Seen any good 3D films lately?' He'd obviously tired of being an observer. He wanted to be an instigator.

It was testament to the discipline Smith and Diamond had instilled in their muscle. A taunt like that would have had Stan bellowing in rage a couple of years ago. Instead he blanked Towler. No indication he'd even heard him.

'There's five in here, Mr Smith,' Steeleye said. 'Four are still in their packaging and the fifth has only been used to do a comms check.'

Smith wordlessly took the bag from the massive gangster before dismissing him with a flick of his hand. Stan turned and jogged back to the car without glancing at any of them.

Fluke frowned. Who the hell was Smith? Even Steeleye was terrified of him. A look in Towler's direction confirmed Fluke wasn't the only one wondering. The big man was looking thoughtful. Probably running through his internal database of ex-special forces turned mercenaries. He hoped someone had secretly snapped a couple of pictures. Smith was someone he wanted intelligence on.

There was no point worrying about it now though. FMIT and Mr Smith would no doubt be getting to know each other in the future, but right now it was reassuring. Jinx would be safe if Smith had anything to do with her security.

Fluke needed to draw things to a close.

'Nathaniel, I don't know where you're taking her, and I think you're right in not telling me, but can I ask that you do one thing? When you leave here, try to avoid as much motorway and A-road as you can. We have ways of tracking you.'

With an enigmatic smile, Diamond said, 'Don't worry, Mr Fluke, these cars are the vehicular equivalent of those five burners you're holding.'

Fluke wasn't even sure if that was possible. Untraceable phones were one thing – you could buy them prepaid and unregistered – but cars? Cars had registration numbers and PNC was linked to the DVLA. The system couldn't be fooled. Cameras on police vehicles, linked directly to on-board computers with a live link to the database, continuously scanned every car they saw. The computer would then alert the officer to any registration that didn't match the car, any stolen vehicle or any outstanding arrest warrant.

Fluke decided the sensible thing to do under the current circumstances was to put it into his 'fuck-it bucket'. He needed to focus on the murder of Bish. If Diamond had a tactical edge with his cars then, for now, Fluke was happy to reap the benefits.

There was nothing left to do. Fluke felt he'd better say one last thing, a reminder that he was still a police officer, despite the strange situation.

'Not one hair on her head, Nathaniel.'

A flash of annoyance darkened Diamond's face. It was subtle and gone in an instant but Fluke, a master of decoding micro-expressions, saw it.

'Goes without saying, Mr Fluke,' he replied, his face a mask again. 'We'll need to do something about her dreadlocks though. She's going to stick out like a turd in a box of truffles where she's going.'

It was testament to the courage Jinx had been showing up until then that this was the first time she'd looked worried.

'Just you hang on now,' she said, her bottom lip set. 'You are *not* cutting my hair.' She crossed her arms in defiance.

Fluke sighed. He could deal with it. Knew he had the skills to turn it around. But he just wanted Diamond off his property. The whole thing had been going on far too long. Diamond could sort out Jinx's hair.

'We'll talk about it in the car,' Diamond said. It wasn't said unkindly but it was said firmly.

Jinx took one last look at Fluke, smiled briefly, picked up her bag and headed to the Range Rovers.

'Let's go,' Smith called out. Instantly there was a flurry of activity as the two groups got ready for the final stage of the meeting.

Departure.

Fluke wasn't taking anything for granted. The hard part was over but the release of tension could make people do strange things. He made sure he knew where Towler was. He could do without him trying to get a parting shot in. He needn't have worried.

'Stay calm, boys and girls. Almost over,' Towler said, taking control of Diamond's withdrawal.

They almost got away with it. Bringing a violent gangster into his backyard without incident.

Almost.

Diamond was in the lead vehicle, and Fluke had started to think about just how much a turd would stand out in a box of truffles, when Steeleye Stan changed the zeitgeist completely.

Maybe it was the humiliation of being visibly scared in front of Smith earlier. Maybe it was just to blow off a bit of steam. And

118

maybe it was nothing more than Stan hating cops so much that he couldn't help himself.

Whatever his reason, he called out to Fluke through the open window of the second vehicle.

'You work for us now, *Detective*.'

It was said with real venom. Although it hadn't been particularly loud Diamond must have heard.

The Range Rovers had only started moving. Both stopped immediately. The passenger door of his Range Rover opened, and Diamond got out. Smith followed him.

The sense of menace that had been palpable since they arrived was ratcheted up another notch. Stan wasn't sneering any more; he knew he'd fucked up. He looked terrified.

Smith beckoned him over with a small tilt of his head. Stan, now visibly shaking, got out of the car and walked over. Smith's voice was quiet but loud enough for everyone to hear. 'What did you say to the detective, Stanley?'

Steeleye mumbled something. Fluke could only hear half of what he was saying, but he caught the words 'owed us', 'filthy bastards' and 'sorry'.

Smith's response was clear and carried over them all. 'You've embarrassed Mr Diamond and you've embarrassed me. Please apologise to Mr Fluke.' The confidence in his voice made it clear he expected his instruction to be carried out immediately.

Steeleye Stan had probably never apologised to anyone in his life, but it was no surprise to anyone when he approached Fluke.

With downcast eyes, the hulking giant apologised in what was little more than a whisper. Fluke didn't think the low volume was anything to do with humiliation. He got the impression fear had dried his throat.

'Satisfied, Mr Fluke?'

Fluke had been struggling to deal with how quickly the situation had turned to shit, and didn't immediately realise Diamond had directed the question at him. He tore his eyes away from the gaze of Stan and looked across at Diamond.

'No harm done,' Fluke said.

'Get back in the car, Stanley,' Smith said.

The terrified giant glanced at Fluke, gratitude written all over his face, before making his way back to the Range Rover.

Fluke breathed out. He felt, rather than saw, Towler do the same.

Smith had his hands in his pockets as Stan walked past him. He took his right hand out and Fluke thought he was going to offer it. A show of no hard feelings. A 'sorry I had to humiliate you in front of the enemy' type of thing.

Fluke could not have been more wrong.

The hand he slipped from his pocket was sheathed in a vicious-looking knuckleduster. A beautifully engineered brass number that belonged in the Museum of Awful Things rather than on someone's hand.

As Stan crept past him, Smith swung his metal-clad fist and smashed it into the giant's face.

The skull contains some of the strongest bones in the body. Given man's capacity for stupidity, and the value of the cargo it protects, it needs to. The dome of the forehead is nearly indestructible. Other bones are equally as tough. Evolution providing the perfect crash helmet.

But not the jaw. The jaw is fragile. The most fragile part of the skull. It's the only moving part in the head. It's also, by far, the most painful bone to break.

Despite being ten yards away, Fluke heard the crunch of bone as Stan's jaw shattered. He saw teeth fly from his mouth. Blood spurted out in great gushes and Stan's perfect white shirt turned wet and crimson in a second. He fell to the ground in stages, like a deckchair being folded by a drunk on Blackpool beach. His head hit the dirt with a sickening thud and the jarring motion caused his ball bearing eye to fall out and roll under the cabin's front porch. Blood continued to spurt out of his mouth. Fluke could see jagged red stumps where his teeth had once been.

Unbelievably he remained conscious, and the scream, rooted in a searing agony, started out as a low, tremulous warbling noise before ending in a long drawn-out whimper. Lying on his side, mewling like a new-born lamb, the lower half of his jaw mutilated, probably beyond repair, Stan began crying.

No one from Diamond's crew made any move to assist him.

No one from FMIT did either.

For a moment the only sounds heard were the distressing gurgling noises Stan was making.

Smith had committed a brutal assault in full view of Fluke and his team. A Section 18 GBH. Five years in prison at the very least.

There was a noise behind Fluke. Towler, of course, was the first to react.

'Boss?' he said through gritted teeth.

Fluke knew Towler wanted the chance of going up against Smith. Had done ever since he'd arrived.

Smith looked unconcerned. Diamond was staring at Fluke.

He wants a reaction. Any reaction. Fluke was in no doubt the assault on Stan had been premeditated.

He was up against a man who was ten steps ahead of everyone most of the time, and in all their previous dealings he had always been a couple of moves ahead of Fluke. There was no way Diamond hadn't thought the assault through before unleashing Smith. No doubt punishment beatings were a normal part of their life, but Fluke was sure they were ordinarily done behind closed doors. To do it in front of a team of cops would usually be a thing of madness. There had to be another reason.

Fluke doubted it was a show of strength. Both sides knew who Diamond was, and what he was capable of. It didn't need a demonstration.

121

But by blatantly committing a crime in front of Fluke, Diamond had given him two choices: arrest Smith, or do nothing. Arresting Smith would be an exercise in futility. Even if they managed it without loss of life or limb, it would result in zero charges being brought against anyone, least of all Diamond. Stan might have just sustained permanent, terrible injuries but he was no grass.

And going the arrest route would also mean Fluke would be back to square one with Jinx.

But doing nothing was going to raise a whole other set of problems. Doing nothing put Fluke in Diamond's pocket.

Diamond had played him.

But, as it was a game, Fluke got to play too. He held out his hand and signalled for Towler to stand down.

Smith spoke – the first person to do so since Towler. 'Stand up, please, Stanley.'

Stan tried to stand, but like a new-born foal, his legs weren't able to support him yet. Smith clicked his teeth, pointed to the rear car and then at the man on the ground. Two men rushed out and picked him up. Using the men as human crutches, Stan faced Smith. His mouth was bleeding steadily and his jaw hung at an unnatural angle. His remaining eye was unfocused.

'We're guests here, Stanley,' Smith said. 'We don't leave litter. Pick up your eye, please. It's under the porch there.'

Stan's humiliation was complete. Every time he bent to pick up his ball-bearing eye he collapsed.

Fluke said nothing. He could feel the team staring at him, willing him to give them the nod. Anything to acknowledge that what was happening wasn't OK.

He stared ahead. Ignored the heart-breaking sound of pain. Every time he was near to caving in, an image of Bish's huge smile popped into his head.

He owed Bish.

He owed Stan nothing.

Stan eventually found his eye. The two men picked him up again, hoisted him onto their shoulders, walked over to the vehicle and dumped him unceremoniously in the boot.

All eyes turned to Fluke. He ignored them, his mind racing.

Diamond spoke. 'Are we all right, Mr Fluke?'

He was silent for ten seconds. Finally he said, 'We're OK, Nathaniel.'

A minute later the Range Rovers had disappeared, and silence descended on the wood once again.

It didn't last for long.

FMIT were looking at Fluke in equal measures of accusation and disappointment. He turned to face them. He wasn't putting up with any shit. Not now. It was his friend, not theirs, in forty different pieces in a fridge in Carlisle. They didn't have the right to judge him. They didn't know the things he knew.

Towler, ever the self-declared spokesman, accepted the gauntlet. 'What the fuck have you just done?'

Fluke walked past him. He picked up the plates Jinx had brought the bacon sandwiches out on. The congealing grease was white and shiny in the failing light. Without turning to look, or even acknowledge them, he walked into his home and shut the door behind him.

He was on his own now.

Perfect.

Alone was exactly where he needed to be.

123

Chapter 18

The moon was shining like a freshly minted coin when Fluke woke the following morning. He got up immediately. The adrenaline that had coursed through his veins during Diamond's visit had exacted its price and he'd gone to bed without eating. Considering what he was about to do, he'd slept surprisingly well.

He was ravenous and knew there was a chance he wouldn't be eating later. A full English was the only way he knew of getting a day's worth of calories in a single sitting. Jinx hadn't left him any bacon, but that didn't matter. He filled two frying pans with a whole ring of Cumberland sausage, Stornoway black pudding, two eggs, tomatoes and hash browns. Four bits of toasted white bread completed his artery-hardening feast. He was glad Bridie was still in London. Her idea of a big breakfast was muesli *and* yoghurt. She'd called last night but Fluke had ignored the phone. He wasn't in the mood to talk to anyone.

He ate outside and watched as the sun washed away the darkness, revealing a light fog that clung desperately to the lake as the air warmed. Within minutes it was gone and Ullswater, in all its early-morning glory, was unveiled. From his seat he could also see part of Helvellyn's deeply gouged craggy eastern side – because of its Celtic name it was, to many, the first and last mountain in England – a reddish hue warming its cold, inanimate stillness. The tension and sense of urgency he'd felt since he'd called Diamond faded away as he breathed in its beauty. Helvellyn didn't care about his worries. It didn't care about time. The mountain's passage on earth was measured in eons rather than days, weeks and years.

His meditative vigil was broken by the sound of distant laughter as the still lake carried the noise of the first tourists of the day. Although they were over on the other side, as far as Fluke was concerned, breakfast was over.

Despite the early hour, Fluke wasn't the first person in the FMIT office. They were all there and it was no coincidence. FMIT usually turned up to work like fun-runners finishing a marathon: in straggles. Fluke and Jo Skelton were usually in first. Towler could turn up anytime within a two-hour window, and Vaughn and Jiao-long were late risers and late finishers. They were all waiting for him.

'What is this? A bloody intervention?'

Towler wasn't going to back down. He never did.

'What happened yesterday was plain wrong,' Towler said. 'You know it, we know it and you better fucking believe Diamond knows it.'

Fluke wasn't ready to share yet but he needed to put this to bed for the time being.

'Yeah? Well, good for him. Seeing as you're the world's foremost authority on Nathaniel Diamond, *Sergeant*, what's he going to do?' Fluke answered his own question before Towler had a chance to respond. 'Squat, that's what. There's dick-all we can do and there's dick-all he can do. So a violent psychopath got his jaw broken in front of us all. So what? He's done far worse to others in his time. Are your egos that big they need to be stroked every day? I made a decision yesterday. You did what you were told then and you'll do what you're told today. End of.'

The outburst stunned them into silence. Mugs of coffee remained halfway to mouths. All eyes were on him. He didn't care.

'Anything else?'

More silence.

'Good. Now I've got things to do this morning. And we have other cases to work on,' he said. 'Sergeant Towler?'

He jumped to his feet and stood ramrod straight. 'Sah!'

Prick.

'Please task the team as per the lines of enquiry we established for the Jensen case. That should stop you sticking your noses in things that no longer concern you.'

Towler returned to his seat without another word. He switched on his desktop computer and started jabbing the keyboard like it was personally responsible. The Jensen case was a bog-standard heist. The forensic evidence collected at the scene would crack it without anyone leaving the office but it would give them something to do. While Fluke poured himself a cup of coffee he could hear the printer warming up. Towler was doing what he was told. If another showdown were planned, it would be later.

As he walked from FMIT's office to his own, he could see them all begin to gather.

Fluke allowed himself a wry smile. If they thought they had something to moan about now, just wait until later . . .

The office that Reyes and his team were parked in was less than fifty yards away. Fluke finished his drink and stuck his head out of the door. He could hear low voices, the rustling of paper and the clack of a keyboard. At least some of them were in. He retrieved a document from his briefcase, took a deep breath to compose himself, and made the short journey.

He knocked on the door and opened it before anyone could object. Reyes was there with two other detectives, one of whom was the woman who'd been crying when they kicked him out of the mortuary. They were crowded round a laptop. As soon as Reyes saw him he closed the lid. Another display of power – you're not important enough to even be in the same room as our intel.

'What do you want, Fluke?' he barked.

'What? Can't the DI from a host force come and see his guests?' Fluke opened his hands in mock subjugation.

Reyes's lips flattened.

'Seriously. What do you want?'

Fluke had been planning for a bit more faux small-talk. It would have helped with his defence later. But no plan survives contact with the enemy and he'd already talked enough to this idiot.

'Got something for you,' he said.

He slid the document he'd brought with him across the table.

Reyes had the decency to look interested. 'What is it?' he asked, glancing at the top page.

'My notes on the crime scene.'

'And why weren't they shared before now? We received assurances everything you had would come our way.'

'Only just finished them.'

Grudgingly, Reyes accepted the explanation. There was little else he could do. Even if he made a formal complaint, he knew it would be ignored. He bit back what was probably going to be a sarcastic retort and said, 'Thank you.'

He opened the lid of the laptop and returned to what he was doing.

'Not a problem,' Fluke said, refusing to take the hint. He pulled up a chair and sat down. 'So, how's it all going?'

Reyes snapped, 'You don't have the security clearance for this, Fluke. I need you to leave.'

Fluke smiled. He actually *did* have the security clearance. In order to speak to Dalton Cross six months ago, MI5 had rushed him through the highest level of clearance possible. It wasn't important. Reyes had just done what Fluke had expected him to do: gob off in front of his colleagues. Never for a minute thinking he was being played.

It was almost too easy . . .

Pretending to accept he'd been put in his place, Fluke said, 'OK, OK. No need for that. The offer of help's still there, obviously, but I'll leave you to it for now. Give me a call if you need anything.'

Snorting, Reyes said, 'Yeah, I wouldn't wait by your phone, Fluke.'

As one they turned back to the laptop.

Dismissed as irrelevant, and even though he was about to drop himself in the shit, Fluke knew he'd enjoy what came next.

'Ha ha, good one. Genuine offer though, Chief Inspector Reyes. We're not glory hunters in FMIT; we'll do whatever we can to help you find out who killed Bish.'

As one, they whipped up their heads, staring at him. Fluke could almost hear their blood boiling. Reyes's mouth opened in disbelief.

Fluke smiled innocently. 'Bye, then,' he said.

He left the room, left his words hanging in the air.

Fluke had expected his phone to ring within five minutes. He was wrong. It was already ringing when he got back to his office.

'Stay where you are.'

A single command and one he wasn't about to ignore. Fluke recognised Reyes on the other end. The bluster was gone – replaced by steel.

The waiting game was one of which Fluke was a master. Letting people stew in the prison of their own lies was a key tool in his investigative armoury. He knew he could outlast a game of nerves with anyone, but he was surprised by Reyes's reaction.

He did nothing.

Two hours passed. Fluke read his emails and issued some instructions to the team about the Jensen case.

The relative humdrum sounds of a busy office environment were interrupted by footsteps and a following tide of silence. More than one person was heading his way, and whoever they were it was enough to make people stop working.

His office door opened without knocking. Fluke had expected Travis 'Action' Jackson, Cumbria's chief constable, to be the man Reyes went to.

He'd planned for that.

But Reyes had been canny; far cannier than Fluke had given him credit for. Why bother going to someone who wasn't on his side? Instead he'd gone to the one person who truly despised him. Someone with the all-consuming type of hatred that only the truly mediocre are capable of. The type of person who'd drive all the way up from Manchester just on the off chance Fluke was in trouble.

A dunce of the first order, and Professional Standards' answer to the question no one had asked.

Alex fucking Fenton.

It didn't matter though; five minutes later Fluke was exactly where he'd planned to be. Carleton Hall, as a headquarters building, didn't have the usual police station facilities, but it did have an interview room.

OK, so the room was usually used to store the Christmas decorations, but that didn't make it any less oppressive. It had everything an interview room needed: a lock on the outside, a supply of electricity on the inside and no natural light. And like any interview room, once that door shut, the isolation covered you like a damp blanket. The effect of helplessness was lessened by two things, however. One: he'd assumed this was where he'd be taken so he was mentally prepared.

And two: there was a polystyrene Santa Claus on the shelf. Hard to worry when Santa's in the room with you.

Fluke settled down for a long wait. So far, so good. Mainly. The 'mistaken' use of a name he had no right to know had worked a treat. Even his isolation from FMIT worked in his favour.

It all added to the illusion of a rogue cop ignoring orders and doing his own thing.

Which was exactly what he was . . .

The one thing he hadn't planned for, though, was Professional Standards. Not this early. He'd hoped Reyes would see sense. That finding out what Fluke knew was preferable to flexing seniority. To jump straight in at the deep end, the deepest end really, smacked of someone with an ego too big for the job. Intelligence was intelligence regardless of where it came from. If you only dealt with people you liked, or those who did what they were told, you'd get nothing done.

It didn't change Fluke's plan, but it did mean he had one more thing to consider as he moved his pieces around the chessboard.

The arrogance of Reyes was staggering though. If he'd even done a bit of basic research he'd have known Fluke couldn't be bullied. That he couldn't be bribed and he was as high in rank as he ever wanted to be. But instead of asking how they could help each other, Reyes had sniffed out Fenton like a rat sniffs out an unguarded turd.

The last time they'd been here, Fenton had Fluke absolutely bang to rights. Caught red-handed forging a letter from his consultant declaring him fit to return to work, Fenton's interview had lasted less than half an hour before Fluke's boss, Cameron Chambers, had stopped the process. The fact that his consultant, Towler, Jiao-long and Bridie had all told bare-faced lies to keep him out of the warm brown stuff was immaterial. Fenton was quite simply one of those men it was a pleasure to fuck over, and Fluke considered it a personal service to the police officers of Cumbria when he'd packed his bags and moved to Manchester.

They only left him alone for an hour; presumably enough time for him to see the error of his ways. When the door opened he was sitting with a bemused expression on his face.

130

Reyes was carrying nothing but a notebook. Fenton followed him in with portable recording equipment.

'Only the two of you, John? Why, we're not even quorate? However will we make any decisions? And Alex, I thought you were still in Manchester. Imagine my delight in finding that you aren't.'

They both ignored him.

Fenton began setting up his equipment. His face was flushed and Fluke could see a small vein pulsing. He was practically wetting himself with excitement. Time to add a pinch of anger to the pot of emotions he was cooking.

'How's Manchester?' he said to his back. 'I bet you've made lots of friends.'

Fenton ignored him but Fluke noticed the tips of his ears had turned red. He plugged in the microphone and set it up on a stand, equidistant between the three of them. He pressed a button and spoke gently.

'We ready?' Reyes asked Fenton. Receiving a nod of confirmation in return, he turned to Fluke. 'Detective Inspector Fluke, this is an interview under caution. You are not under arrest, but anything you say can and will be used in evidence.'

Fluke said nothing.

Reyes continued, 'I only have one question. Where did you hear the name Bish?'

Chapter 19

'Bish bosh? 'Tis the common saying round here.'

It was the third time Fluke had said this and three times really was a charm. Reyes's calm facade didn't so much slip as shatter. Fluke, speaking like he was auditioning for the Royal Shakespeare Company hadn't helped matters . . .

'Bastard!' Reyes shouted.

Fluke grinned. He turned to Fenton and asked, 'We still taping, Alex?'

'No we're not bloody taping! You know we're not bloody taping! Not since you said you wouldn't talk with the machine on,' Fenton shouted.

'Oh, yeah,' he said. 'I forgot about that. That's bish bosh, that is.'

Having them upset and angry was purely tactical, but he would, if pushed, admit to enjoying himself. To his absolute delight, Reyes had even said, 'Don't mug me off, Fluke.'

Reyes tried a different approach. 'I've asked Superintendent Fenton to join me because I'm not sure anyone in Cumbria can demonstrate objectivity where you're concerned,' he said.

'Objective? They have blinkers on. Even the chief constable's in his pocket,' Fenton blurted out.

Reyes frowned.

'This fool can't be objective, John,' Fluke said.

Reyes shrugged. Fenton looked disappointed he hadn't leapt to his immediate defence.

Fluke sighed. 'Fine. But can we please get on with it?'

For the next half an hour they played a game of ping-pong with the word 'Bish'; Reyes insisting Fluke knew a name he shouldn't, and Fluke insisting Reyes had misheard a commonly used Cumbrian saying.

Fluke was prepared to keep the charade going for as long as it took. Reyes would crack and bring him inside the investigation; he had no choice. It was a matter of when, not if.

But Reyes surprised him. He might have lost his temper earlier but he recovered well. Just when Fluke thought he was about to give in, he stopped the interview.

Reyes stood and gathered his notes. He walked to the door and opened it. Almost as an afterthought he turned back round, looked directly at Fluke and said, 'Superintendent Fenton, could you arrest DI Fluke under TACT, please.'

Fluke stared at the closing door Reyes had just walked through. He was gone. He turned to look at Fenton. His grin was back.

TACT. The Terrorism Act. He hadn't thought of that.

Fuck.

Although there was no chance of a charge – not over using the word 'Bish' – being arrested under the Terrorism Act changed the dynamics.

In his worst-case scenario planning, Fluke had thought Reyes might not play fair and would use his power of arrest. He would then have twenty-four hours to question him. That might sound like a long time but Fluke had PACE, the Police and Criminal Evidence Act, on his side. He would be entitled to three meals during that period, outdoor exercise and eight hours of uninterrupted sleep. He could also play his 'I had cancer' card and insist on additional rest periods. Reyes might try to extend the twenty-four hours to thirty-six but he'd be on a loser. Fluke wouldn't have been arrested for a serious crime, only for police obstruction. And anyway, the

133

duty inspector in Carlisle liked him and he was scared shitless of Towler.

Fluke had been on the receiving end of solicitors playing games with PACE since it had been implemented, and knew how frustrated Reyes would get. Twenty-four hours meant three interviews at the most.

But being arrested under TACT was a different matter entirely and Fluke realised the huge error he'd made. By focusing exclusively on involving himself in the murder investigation, he'd forgotten his golden investigative rule: find out how the victim lived, and you'll find out how they died.

Yes, Bish had been murdered, and yes, Bish had been his friend. But he'd also been up here to do a job, and given his criminal record and his association with Vane, Fluke should have at least considered a domestic extremism angle. Animal rights or environmental activism.

But where did the protected witness angle come in? Mark Bishop was now Mark Cadden on PNC and that meant his identity had been officially changed. The only explanation was that Fluke was now interfering in a joint investigation. The protected witness unit and the domestic extremism unit.

The only reason he wasn't letting Reyes have what he wanted was that he and his team had only appeared after Fluke had run Bish's prints. That didn't make a whole lot of sense. If there was an active extremism investigation, they should have already been up here.

The whole thing was giving him a headache.

The other thing giving him a headache was that, under TACT, Reyes now had fourteen days to interview him. Fourteen days was a long time. Long enough for the trail on Bish's killer to go cold.

Fluke had been transferred to a proper police cell in Northern Area Command's headquarters at Durranhill – a flavourless, glass building utterly devoid of character. Apart from letting him know how serious the situation was, a TACT arrest made no sense. They must have known Fluke was stubborn enough to say nothing whether it was one or fourteen days. All it did was extend the amount of time Reyes didn't know what Fluke knew. A fourteen-day detention benefited neither side.

But Fluke was wrong.

Fourteen days did benefit Reyes.

It was long enough for him to manufacture evidence.

The first sign it wasn't all going Fluke's way was Reyes's arrest strategy. Fluke was by no means the most popular inspector in Cumbria, but he still had friends who would do him favours. Not a 'hacksaw in a cake' type of favour, but certainly getting messages out wouldn't be difficult. Reyes correctly assumed that taking him out of Cumbria removed his home-ground advantage.

His watch had been taken from him when he'd been accepted into custody, so when they entered his cell, handcuffed him to the front and bundled him into the back of a windowless police van, he had no idea what the time was.

Although Durranhill was in Carlisle city centre, there were only three roads between the police station and the motorway, and Fluke, having done the journey countless times, recognised the potholes and the noises that led to the southbound lanes of the M6.

Reyes was from London but Fluke doubted he'd be taken all the way down there; the capital was a seven-hour drive from Carlisle. So, if he wasn't going to London, that left only one other possibility: Longsight Police Station in Manchester. It was where high-value prisoners and arrested cops were detained. It also had the added bonus of being Fenton's new stomping ground.

After a couple of hours, the van stopped and Fluke heard muted talking before the sound of a gate opening electronically.

The van moved forward then stopped again. This time the engine was turned off.

Honey. I'm home.

The burst of light Fluke had been expecting when the door was opened didn't materialise. They were inside, in an airlock. Even if he'd had the inclination, escape was impossible. Reyes walked ahead without glancing back. Two uniformed officers handcuffed him to the front again and, without speaking, led him through a dark blue metal door.

Fluke was escorted into the custody suite where he went through the same process he had at Durranhill. The same questions. Full name? Did he understand the reasons for his detention? Did he want to see the doctor? As well as being allowed to keep his watch this time, there was another, more sinister, difference to his previous detention.

At no time was his right to see a solicitor mentioned.

Reyes was being a bully, and intimidatory tactics are always a gamble. When people are pushed their natural instinct is to push back. If Bish's murder didn't have a clock that was counting down from 'golden hour' to 'not a chance of getting solved', Fluke would have tried to enjoy himself.

The custody suite had four corridors of cells leading from it. Three of them had prisoners in. Fluke was led down an empty one; standard practice with arrested cops. He was placed in the end cell and the door shut with a finality he hadn't expected.

The décor was different to any cell he'd been in. Up until then, every one had been alive with graffiti and casual vandalism. From 'five-o can suck my cock' to 'I am innocent', scraped into anything that was softer than the thing they were using to do the scraping. They were often still smeared with blood – or worse. Even when they'd just had one of their regular deep cleans it wasn't long before they were stinking again. The courts didn't seem bothered

136

with criminal damage offences when it came to police cells. It was virtually accepted. If someone smashed up a cell, ripped sinks and toilets from the wall and caused thousands of pounds' worth of damage, the most they got was a fine. If someone smeared blood on the wall, putting the cleaner at risk of contracting hepatitis B, they weren't even charged. 'Emotions were running high', and all the usual bullshit defence solicitors came out with. And Fluke assumed they always came out with it because it worked.

This cell didn't even smell of shit, perhaps a first in British custodial history.

Fluke couldn't smell paint either, but instinctively knew he'd been the first person in since a fresh coat had been applied. It was spotless. It was probably painted after each prisoner to ensure there was no chance of messages being passed on.

Fluke knew the myth of being entitled to a phone call was exactly that – a myth. Under PACE he was allowed to have someone *informed* of his arrest, but it was usually custody staff that did the informing. Under TACT he wasn't even sure he was entitled to that.

He had more chance of finding a one-ended stick than getting a message out to someone. He was completely isolated.

Reyes had been clever. With a fortnight to play with he could leave Fluke alone for days on end. Technically he could leave him for the full fourteen then simply release him without charge. And that was Fluke's fear now; a whole fortnight wasted.

That he'd alienated his team wasn't going to help his cause either. They wouldn't exactly be in the mood to start looking for him. And what about Bridie? She would come home to find the cabin empty.

But panicking, or demanding things he was never going to get, would only play into Reyes's hands. Fluke needed to give the impression of nonchalance. He needed to show he didn't care. And the best way of achieving that was by going to sleep.

Fifteen minutes later he sat up. It was mid-afternoon and Fluke barely slept at night. The idea of a cheeky afternoon nap was absurd.

A nagging bladder gave him other problems.

He knew he was being permanently watched. The cell had three cameras he could see and probably more he couldn't. Although he hadn't been planning to confess his sins through the medium of interpretive dance, a bit of privacy on the toilet would have been nice. Whichever way he positioned himself over the metal bowl, there was still a camera with a great view. But when you've got to go you've got to go. Fluke unbuttoned the paper evidence suit he was wearing and relieved himself. Smiling at the nearest camera the whole time. It was pointless defiance but it made him feel a bit better.

Five minutes later he was bored.

An hour after that he was bored shitless.

Time moved like concrete.

There were no books in his cell and no television, nothing to do but stare at the freshly painted walls. Time stretched beyond all laws of physics. He checked his watch. A minute had passed since he'd last looked an hour ago.

His meals were passed through the Judas door – the sliding metal hatch on the cell door – without comment. So far his main meals had alternated between lasagne and spaghetti. Fluke hated pasta at the best of times, and the soggy, lukewarm microwave dinners they served here did little to change his mind. He refused to eat them and eventually they brought him sandwiches from the canteen.

He was allowed one shower a day and he stretched it out for as long as he could. He was entitled to exercise and they obliged. An hour in a small yard, where he paced back and forth like a trial lawyer. It did little to improve his mood.

The first day dragged but at least he had enough to think about to avoid going crazy.

The second day was worse.

By day three he was so bored he was thinking of trying the lasagne again.

And on day four he was rearrested for conspiracy to supply cocaine, and things got interesting again.

Chapter 20

When the evidence bag containing white powder was placed on the interview room table, Fluke knew he'd won.

Reyes wasn't stupid enough to raise the stakes this high without some, albeit false, corroborating evidence. And when he also found out – and he *would* find out – Fluke had connections with an organised criminal network known to be involved in the supply of drugs, he'd have more than enough to charge him. That there'd be no fingerprints on the cocaine was irrelevant. Fluke was a cop and was therefore forensically aware.

He knew Reyes thought he had him by the short and curlies, and that any sensible person would take whatever deal was coming. He knew Fluke was stubborn – and stubbornness usually trumped common sense – but in the face of overwhelming odds, he'd expect him to comply.

But Fluke knew something Reyes didn't.

Fenton wasn't in the interview room and that meant it was still unofficial. Reyes wanted a deal. He'd wanted Fluke begging to tell him everything he knew about the case. He wanted to win and, more importantly, he wanted Fluke to know he'd lost.

Reyes probably didn't think of himself as corrupt. Planting evidence to get vital intelligence would be an 'end justifying the means' kind of deal. He wouldn't give a shit if he ruined someone's life in the process. Careerists like him had a different kind of morality.

Fluke had no doubt that there would be video evidence of the search of his cabin and the subsequent 'shocking discovery'. Chains of custody for the cocaine would be demonstrated. There'd be everything a jury would need to convict, and everything the press would need to crucify him. Reyes would take the stand and, while crying crocodile tears at having to give evidence against a fellow cop, he'd tell the jury there was no place in the force for corrupt police officers.

And he'd be right. There wasn't.

So, when Fluke 'no commented' every question and instead insisted on seeing his solicitor, Reyes's ever present smirk slipped. It was replaced by doubt.

He knew Reyes didn't really want this going to court. While Fluke was in custody, Reyes was in control. In the uncontrolled environment of the courtroom, with a clever brief telling the jury that 'a crime *had* been committed but not by his client', he knew anything could happen.

Reyes raised his eyebrows in mock concern. 'Really?' he asked, as if he only wanted the best for Fluke. 'OK, I was hoping we could sort this out like men. There's no going back once we involve other people. Your solicitor comes in, and you go to jail. I won't be able to stop that happening.'

He stood up and walked to the door. Slowly. He wanted Fluke to stop him. He opened the cell door and, as if he were giving Fluke one more chance to be sensible, said, 'Are you sure about this, Detective Inspector?' His face now showed the early stages of panic.

Fluke didn't respond. Eventually the door shut.

Less than a minute after being returned to his cell, the custody sergeant asked him if he had a solicitor, or wanted one appointed to him. Fluke asked for Bridie. The man asked him to spell her name.

'Which firm?'

'She's freelance.'

'Phone number?'

'Don't have one.'

The custody sergeant frowned in annoyance. 'But what if we can't get hold of her?'

Fluke said nothing.

'Is there anyone who might know where she is?'

Fluke smiled to himself. It was exactly what he'd wanted. 'Detective Sergeant Matt Towler, Cumbria Force Major Incident Team. He'll know how to get in touch with her.'

He'd purposefully left Bridie's details vague. She was out and about in the UK somewhere. Of course he had her number but Reyes's latest stunt meant he needed to involve Towler.

Towler would do two things. First of all he'd immediately get in touch with Bridie. And second, he'd move heaven and earth to find out what had happened.

Fluke knew both of them would realise he was being set up. They'd also know what he needed from them. Not for a second did he think Towler would use what had happened a few days earlier against him. They had far too much history to ever really fall out.

His breakfast the next day wasn't his usual carton of UHT milk and a small box of cereal. This time a roll and a disposable cup of coffee was passed through the Judas door. He opened the roll suspiciously, half-expecting to see a dog turd. Instead he found bacon, two sausages and a fried egg, smothered in brown sauce. He looked back through the hatch, craned his neck to see down the long corridor, and saw everyone in the custody suite chomping down on the same. They'd obviously been out for a Friday breakfast and, for some reason, had included him.

Fluke thought he knew why; they'd found his solicitor and needed to show they'd been treating him well. An hour later,

Reyes opened the cell door and said, 'OK, you asked for this, remember. Your solicitor's here.'

His eyes were bloodshot. Fluke recognised the look. It was the look of someone who hadn't slept for twenty-four hours.

As an international law solicitor, Bridie was second to none. Fluke had woken in the middle of the night on more than one occasion to find her on the phone, talking quietly to ambassadors and politicians from countries all round the world. And although she wasn't a criminal solicitor, Fluke figured she'd have to have done a bit of everything to get her law degree.

Fluke was led to an interrogation room. The custody sergeant made a big play of turning off all the cameras and recording equipment. Fluke didn't trust the room not to have something still turned on though – Reyes had proved himself to be thoroughly dishonest – so he made a conscious decision to keep the dialogue as non-specific as possible. He was about to ask Bridie to do the same. He needn't have worried.

Bridie didn't want to talk about the injustices of being dragged to Manchester and framed on a trumped-up drugs offence. She had other things on her mind.

'You arsehole!'

Fluke, who'd stood to give her a welcoming hug, let his hands fall to his side. He'd never seen her as angry.

'Bridie—'

She immediately cut him off. 'Don't you Bridie me! How could you? You absolute dickhead! Drugs. In our house—'

This time it was Fluke's turn to interrupt. 'It was planted there! Of course I don't keep drugs in the—'

Like a game of who can butt in the most, she snapped his sentence in half. 'I know they aren't yours! Any sensible person knows that. But you invite these things, Avison, and don't shake your head at me!'

Fluke stopped and sat down, waited for the storm to leave the teacup. Bridie wasn't finished yet, though.

'Yes, you did,' she continued. 'Matt told me what happened. He's not stupid; he knew you wanted to go off on your own to do this. You've got the emotional intelligence of a six-year-old sometimes. Why do you have to go around pissing people off? You must have known there'd be a reaction?'

'As my solicitor, I was rather hoping for something a bit more positive.'

If you can't say something sensible, say something funny, was the ill-advised motto that had got him into trouble his entire life.

He was hoping for a smile but instead got, 'You're seriously misjudging the mood of your audience today.'

'Hey, you're not the one who's been eating horsemeat lasagne for three days.'

She didn't respond. Eventually she couldn't help herself. A smile cracked her face. Only slightly, but it was enough to break the ice.

'You're a dickhead,' she said.

'I know.'

'OK, tell me everything that's happened since I left. And tell me why I have my laptop with me.'

Fluke did.

As he gave his side of the story – lightly touching on the parts that made him look like an idiot, and exaggerating the parts where he thought he came across as heroic – Bridie made notes. She stopped him occasionally, probed for further information, or got Fluke to reword the parts she hadn't understood the first time.

After an hour she closed her pad and said, 'Well, what a pickle you're in.'

'Let me see that computer,' he said. 'Did Jiao-long add a file?'

'I think it was Jiao-long. Matt drove down to Luton last night and collected it from me. I tried to open the file but it's password protected.'

Before he could explain, the door opened and Reyes entered. 'Time's up. We're interviewing in two minutes.'

'Ten more minutes, please. My client has been held for four days and is entitled to speak to his solicitor. Alone.'

'You've got five.'

'This isn't a negotiation, Detective Chief Inspector Reyes. We will either have the full ten minutes requested or I will make a phone call to the IPCC. Your choice.'

There was a bit of muttering and an eventual 'Fine', said as if he hadn't just had his arse kicked.

Fluke turned the computer so it was facing him. He found a file labelled AVISON_FLUKE_IS_A_KNOB – Towler was still angry, obviously – and double clicked. It requested a password.

'Do you know what it is?' Bridie asked.

Fluke grinned. Where Towler was concerned there were only ever two passwords he'd consider. The first was his daughter's name. He knew Towler wouldn't use Abi's name on a work file though. So the other one it was then.

Fluke typed in four letters. P-A-R-A. The file opened.

He turned the computer round so Bridie could see what was on the screen.

She stared.

'But . . . how?' she said.

Now it was formal, Reyes brought Fenton into the interview. Having been mauled by Bridie last time, Fenton didn't look happy to see her, but there was little he could do about it. A scrawny, dark-haired man was also present. His prominent Adam's apple made him look as though he'd swallowed a dorsal fin. Reyes introduced him as Detective Sergeant Marston. Fluke remembered him from the team that crashed the post-mortem. Fluke smiled.

Marston being there was the icing on the cake.

Reyes had clearly decided to get him on the back foot straight-away. Hammer him with circumstantial as well as forensic evidence.

'Why did you ring Nathaniel Diamond five days ago?'

So, Reyes *had* found out about Diamond.

'Who's he?' Fluke asked.

Fenton, the only person in the room who had no idea what was going on, said, 'You know exactly who Diamond is, Fluke. You interviewed him for a rape and murder six months ago.'

'Oh, him.' The cooler he played it, the more Fenton would lose it. 'What about him?'

'Why did you ring him?' Reyes repeated with an audible sigh.

'I wanted to see how he was. His father was murdered earlier this year. I've kept in touch.'

'Do you know he's suspected to be one of the biggest drug sup-pliers in the north of England?'

'I don't work drugs.'

'Fair enough,' Reyes said. 'We'll come back to it later.' He pressed a button on a remote control and a wall-mounted monitor burst into life. He pressed another button and Fluke found him-self watching a video of his own house.

Fenton leaned forward in anticipation. It was obvious he hadn't seen the video yet. He was almost drooling. Reyes pressed the pause button and the screen froze.

'Shall we proceed, Miss Harper-Tarr?'

He's still hoping I'll try to cut a deal, Fluke thought.

Bridie ignored the question and took her small MacBook Air out of her briefcase. They'd kept it out of view until then. It was in sleep mode and, when she opened it, it too burst into life.

'Do you want to confer with your solicitor, DI Fluke? I can give you ten minutes.' He wore a quiet look of desperation.

He's bricking it, Fluke thought. *Good*.

146

'I'm fine.'

Reyes didn't press play. His bluff had been called. It was obvious Fluke should have been more worried than he was. He'd planted evidence and now there was a detective superintendent from Professional Standards in the room. Fluke had gone off-script and there was a world-renowned solicitor with him. Reyes hadn't meant it to get this far, that much was clear.

Bridie wasn't about to help him either. 'Detective Chief Inspector Reyes, you've arrested my client for conspiracy to supply a class-A drug. So far you haven't provided a shred of evidence. Now either shit or get off the pot,' she said.

'Excuse me?'

'Play your fucking video.'

Reyes looked stricken. He tried to get out of it. 'Perhaps we'd better wait. The contents of the bag we found haven't been tested yet. It could be a bag of icing sugar, for all we know.'

Fluke and Bridie said nothing. Fenton looked confused.

'In fact, if I have your client's word that what's in the bag isn't cocaine, I might be prepared to drop the matter,' Reyes said. 'If Detective Inspector Fluke cooperates, of course.'

Getting the charge dropped wasn't what Fluke wanted. He wanted so much more.

'Looked like cocaine to me,' he said.

Reyes looked as if he were about to cry. He'd given Fluke a get-out-of-jail-free card and he'd shoved it back up his arse.

He had no choice but to continue with the charade that even Fenton was now starting to doubt. He pressed play and together they watched the video.

'Do you have an explanation for why a bag of what looks like cocaine was found in your spare room?' Reyes muttered, after it had finished.

'Yes, I have,' Fluke replied calmly. 'It was planted there.'

147

Reyes's laugh was limper than a sock on a washing line. Everyone in the room – even Fenton – knew it was false, but that didn't stop him continuing.

'So, your defence is that I simply happened to have a bag of cocaine in my car and, despite having seventeen years' service, decided to risk it all by planting evidence. Is that what you're saying, Fluke? That's pathetic, even by your standards.'

He looked relieved. He'd probably expected a bit more from Fluke.

'To be fair, Sergeant Adam's apple here actually planted the drugs,' Fluke said. 'Got them from the boot of a grey Ford Galaxy, registration number PY14 EZB, hid the package under his jacket, and then carried it into my house. But as he's your sergeant, working on your instructions presumably, essentially yes, that's exactly what I'm saying. You planted the drugs.'

There was a stunned silence. Reyes's lip trembled. He blinked rapidly and with a bravado that fooled no one said, 'Preposterous, man, how can you possibly know—'

He stopped. Realised what he'd been about to say in front of a superintendent from PSD. Instead he mumbled, 'You can't possibly expect anyone to believe that.'

Fluke turned to Bridie. 'I think I'll let you do the next bit, Bridie.'

With a small cough, she cleared her throat. 'With pleasure.' She turned the Mac so everyone could see it. She didn't press play. Fluke didn't think there'd be any need to.

The three men on the other side of the desk stared at the image on the screen. It was the same as the one on the wall: it was Fluke's home.

'You've shown me yours, Detective Chief Inspector, now let me show you mine,' Bridie said, sweetly.

By telling the custody sergeant that the only way to contact his solicitor was through Towler, Fluke had reached out to his friend

– a request for help he knew wouldn't be refused. Towler would have immediately called Bridie and told her she was needed to get her dickhead boyfriend out of the shit again. More importantly, he would have found out what he'd been arrested for.

Towler would know the evidence had been planted and, as he was the only other person in the world who knew the cabin was now protected by a ring of military-grade surveillance cameras, he'd have known what Fluke needed.

The file Towler had uploaded to Bridie's computer was the edited highlights of Reyes and the rest of his team executing the search warrant.

Fluke suspected Towler had sought Jiao-long's assistance in putting the file together, although whoever had, they'd done a superb job. It was crystal clear and showed the Met turning up in three separate vehicles. Nondescript, bland hire cars, by the look of them.

Ideally, Fluke would have liked to have witnessed someone carrying a bag into his cabin with the word 'Drugs' written on the side. They hadn't been that stupid so he'd had to play an elimination game that would dictate how the rest of his life turned out . . .

Two of the cars involved in the raid had parked right in front of his cabin. The third, a Ford Galaxy, had parked slightly away from them and it was this car Fluke focused on.

Planting evidence was unlikely to have been a team decision. The people who did this type of thing were cautiously paranoid. So Fluke ruled out the three men who exited the lead car; they were all wearing forensic suits and, although it would have been possible to secrete the drugs under them, removing them surreptitiously would have been difficult. The woman was ruled out for the same reason. She was wearing the same forensic suit but was also on the video camera. Her surprise as she narrated was too natural; no one was that good an actor.

That left Reyes and Marston.

It could have been either and Fluke wasn't about to gamble his future on a fifty-fifty. Reyes had exited the second car but wasn't wearing a forensic suit. It was possible he'd planted them. But unlikely.

Not when he had someone like Marston.

Why have a dog and bark yourself?

Fluke had seen sergeants and inspectors like Marston his entire working life. Young and ambitious. Promoted far too early but believing their own press. All they thought about was the next rung on the career ladder and they didn't care who they trampled on to climb up. And they were absolute arse lickers to authority.

Marston fitted this apple-polisher profile perfectly. When Reyes had made snide comments and poor jokes, while the rest of his team had the good grace to look embarrassed, Marston had brayed in sycophantic laughter.

He'd been the driver of the third car and, if it hadn't been suspicious enough that he'd parked away from the others, the fact he was in on the interview was all the confirmation Fluke had needed.

The reactions of Reyes, whose face was now so pale it was almost see-through, and Marston, who looked like he was about to vomit, told him everything he needed to know. Marston had planted the drugs. Reyes had told him to.

The two men stayed silent, waiting for the deathblow. Waiting for Bridie to press play.

Fluke loved psychological games, and twisted the knife in further.

Turning to face Marston, he smiled. 'Unless you were using your own initiative, of course, Sergeant. If you were, then I owe Chief Inspector Reyes an apology.'

Now they had something else to think about. Never mind Bridie and her hovering finger, now they were second-guessing each other . . . Would Reyes try to save his own skin by saying he didn't know anything about it, or would Marston try to get in first and say he'd only been following instructions?

Welcome to Fluke's roulette, boys. You swung the wheel, now you have to wait for the ball to land . . .

Chapter 21

'What's this?' Reyes asked eventually.

Bridie ignored him. Instead, she went back into her briefcase and took out the shotgun cartridge that had been posted through their letterbox. She placed it on the table.

'Do you know what this is, Detective Chief Inspector Reyes?'

Reyes said nothing. He was staring at the cartridge, desperately trying to connect it to the image on her laptop.

'I'm going to take your silence as confirmation that even a slimy city boy like you knows what a shotgun cartridge looks like.'

She picked it up and put it back in her briefcase.

'What it is isn't important actually. What happened because of it is though. You see, I live with the fool to my right here. Now, while I do hear and appreciate your silent commiserations, the fact of the matter remains that I do spend time in this beautiful cabin. And someone is trying to force him out.'

Reyes and Marston stared.

Bridie continued. 'A couple of weeks ago, someone posted this through our letterbox. As you can imagine I wasn't very pleased about it. And the man to my right was furious. Do you know what he did next?'

Despite himself, Reyes shook his head.

'Well, I'll tell you what he didn't do. He didn't go to the police like any normal person would. No, what he did was call the one person in the world who's even more reckless than he is.'

'Hang on!' Fluke protested. Towler was still his best friend.

Bridie waved her hand in frustration. 'You see what I have to put up with, Detective Chief Inspector? He even argues with his own defence solicitor. Anyway, the person Detective Inspector Fluke told was his friend, and fellow police officer, Matt Towler. Have either of you heard of him?'

Reyes and Marston shook their heads. Fenton had met Towler but it hadn't ended well. He said nothing.

'Towler used to be in the SAS or something like that. He has told me but it goes in one ear and out the other, etcetera, etcetera. What he did was call in one of his contacts and, without my knowledge I hasten to add, they set up a load of military camera traps round Detective Inspector Fluke's home. They work off remote sensors or something, and only take pictures or video when something activates them. A bit like external security lights do.'

Reyes was biting his lips. A fine film of sweat had appeared on his forehead. Fenton, as usual, didn't have a clue what was going on.

Bridie turned to Fluke. 'How many cameras did you set up, Avison?'

'Not saying.'

'Well, never mind how many there are. They all seem to be working perfectly as you can see from the image on my computer. And Sergeant Towler took them to a friend who spliced everything together into one nice little movie.'

Fenton was about to burst. 'Now look here, Fluke! I don't know what you're playing at, but unverified footage like this has no place in this investi—'

Bridie, who had an evil streak in her that Fluke found incredibly sexy, almost purred when she clipped his sentence. 'What do you say, John? Shall I press play?'

Chapter 22

Marston looked as though someone had superglued his arse shut; Reyes had the dead-eyed expression of a circus bear. They were beaten, they just didn't know how badly yet.

Fluke waited for Reyes to make a decision. He wasn't out of the woods yet. Fluke didn't believe in Freud's id, ego and superego – humans were way too complex to be pigeonholed so crudely – but if he had, Reyes would have had a fourth psyche all to himself; the super-duper-ego. The trait that allowed him to think he was right even when he knew he was wrong. If he was doing it, it must be right *because* he was doing it.

Beaten look on his face notwithstanding, he was the type of person who might ask Bridie to press play, simply because he didn't know how to back down.

Fluke hadn't breathed for nearly a minute.

Reyes finally elected option B: saving his own arse.

He cleared his throat, turned to Fenton, and said tonelessly, 'Could you leave the room for a minute, please, Alex?'

Fluke carefully breathed out. Relief flooded his body. He turned to Bridie and offered a small smile. She didn't acknowledge him.

Fenton glared at Fluke, furious he'd once again escaped his clutches. He wasn't about to put his career on the line when it came to TACT arrests though. He gathered his papers and left the room.

'Poor chap,' Fluke said.

'Can you give Inspector Fluke and me five minutes as well, please, Sergeant Marston?'

Marston didn't look too happy either. There was still a chance, in his mind at least, that Reyes was going to try to put the whole thing on him. He couldn't argue though.

Fluke and Reyes stared at each other across the table.

'I'm going to need to keep hold of this laptop and also have your guarantee you have no copies before we continue. Agreed?' Reyes said.

Fluke said, 'In your dreams, Reyes.' He turned to Bridie. 'I'll take it from here. See you later?'

Without answering she closed her Mac, gathered her notes and left. She didn't look at Fluke once.

When they were alone, Reyes tried to speak first. 'This is how we're goi—'

Fluke held up his hand.

'Don't, John, just don't. You don't get to dictate terms. Not after what you did.'

'Now listen here, Fluke. My methods may not be to your liking but I have a responsibility you can't possibly fathom.'

Fluke picked up the pad of paper in front of Reyes and began making a list.

'I'm going to need full access to your investigation and I want a liaison officer attached to my team so I don't have to talk to you.'

'I'll find you a liaison officer,' Reyes mumbled.

'Will you bollocks. I'm choosing.'

'But you don't know them!' Reyes protested.

No, I don't, he thought. *But I do know there was someone at the post-mortem who actually looked as though they cared.*

'The woman. I want her.'

For the first time in a while, defiance returned to Reyes.

'You can't,' he said. 'She has a different remit to the rest of the team.'

Ignoring him, Fluke continued. 'And I want a formal approach, from your boss to mine, requesting FMIT involvement.'

'I said, you can't have her.'

'Look, *John*, I'm a happy-go-lucky ray of sunshine most of the time but don't mistake anything I've just said as being fucking negotiable,' Fluke snapped. 'I've written it down so there's no misunderstanding.'

He slid the notepad back across the table. It hit Reyes in the stomach.

'Fluke, you're not listening. I said you can't have her. I'm not just making a point here; it's just not possible to release her. She has to be with my team. Everything else is fine.'

Fluke looked at his watch. 'It's three p.m. I'm going to have a shower then I want my clothes and gear back. It didn't look as though Bridie was going to wait so I'll also need a car with a driver.'

Fluke paused while he did some mental calculations. He could be out of the station in thirty minutes if he got his skates on. It was possible to do Manchester to Penrith in a couple of hours but three hours would be safer, and would also give him a bit of time to catch up on what he'd missed.

'Tell her to be at my office at half past six,' he said. 'And I suppose you'd better tell me her name.'

For a moment Fluke thought he was still going to defy him. Test how hard he was prepared to go.

Finally he relented. 'Koenig. Her name is Zoe Koenig.'

Chapter 23

Fluke got back to Carleton Hall and was immediately summoned to the chief constable's office. Detective Superintendent Cameron Chambers and Assistant Chief (Ops) Michelle Fletcher were there with him. 'Action' Jackson started proceedings by demanding to know why the Met had gone from arresting Fluke for a drugs offence to inviting FMIT into their investigation.

There wasn't a stupid person in the room, and Fluke's claim that Reyes must have had a change of heart fooled no one. It didn't have to, though. All they wanted to know was if there was going to be any comeback, and after Fluke assured them any fallout would be restricted to his vicinity, and his alone, they relaxed. Not even Action wanted a fight with Scotland Yard.

After being dismissed, Fluke made his way to FMIT's wing. At twenty past six it was empty. The news of his release either hadn't made it back or they were still sulking. Towler may have helped him but that was ingrained loyalty; when he was angry it rubbed off on the rest of the team. He didn't intimidate them the same way he did everyone else but he was their sergeant, so had influence nonetheless. Jiao-long took his cues from him as a matter of course anyway – he was still learning how the English behaved, and for some reason had decided Towler was his role model. Alan Vaughn had a deep-seated hatred of bullies and, even taking into account the enormous drag factor of Steeleye Stan's unpleasant personality, what Smith had done was bullying. Plain and simple. He'd picked on a weaker man to make a point.

157

Jo Skelton would be the one to come round first. Fluke had always relied on her to be the team's calming influence. She would see the bigger picture and go beyond her own need for justice. Fluke knew she'd have been mulling it all over, running the angles, and trying to see why, when it had put them all in a terrible position, he'd let Smith go free. She'd know it couldn't just be about Bish.

And if she was as clever as he thought she was, she might even work it out.

A tentative knock on his office door reminded Fluke he was expecting a visitor. Instead of being a dick and saying something such as 'enter' in a deep voice, he got up and opened it.

Zoe Koenig was smaller than he remembered. Her blonde hair was short enough to not get in the way, but long enough to be feminine. Although she was lightly made up, she was no tomboy. Fluke didn't know what you called the shoes she was wearing; they weren't quite heels, and they weren't quite flats. Wedges, he guessed, but wasn't sure. Bridie would have known. Whatever they were called they added a couple of inches, although Fluke got the impression this was more to do with comfort rather than adding height to her small stature.

'Zoe?'

'Yes, sir.' She had a strong voice. No obvious accent but there was a confidence there he liked. Respectful without being an arse licker. He couldn't tell if she resented being dragged away from her team. He'd prefer her to do it with grace but he wouldn't lose sleep if she didn't. There was no indication that she was concerned about the drugs being found in his cabin. If she were a bright copper she'd have known something had been a bit off. Reyes's extraordinary about-turn on Fluke's involvement only had one viable explanation.

'You wanting a brew?' he asked. 'I haven't had one since I got back from my holidays.'

'Lead the way,' she said.

After pouring themselves stewed coffee from the filter machine in FMIT's office, Fluke asked her to take a chair in the open-plan work area.

Fluke perched on the edge of a desk.

'How'd you want to do this, sir?' she asked. 'I've been told to tell you everything. I can give you a quick briefing with a fuller one for the team tomorrow if you want?'

'Yes, to the team briefing tomorrow. No, to the quick briefing now. And it's not "sir", it's "boss" or, if that's not palatable, "Mr Fluke". No, here's what we'll do. I'll tell you what I know and you fill in the gaps. How's that sound?'

'Go for it,' she said.

Blowing on the already lukewarm coffee, he began. 'What you and Reyes couldn't have known, Zoe, is that Mark Bishop was my friend.'

Half an hour later he'd finished. He'd told her he suspected Bish had witnessed, or more likely been involved in, something highly illegal. Enough to get him protected witness status.

She'd questioned him on how he'd found this out and seemed satisfied when he said it was the only explanation for the modified criminal record and legally changed name.

'It's obvious you're the protected witness officer, that's why Reyes didn't want to let you go,' he added. 'It also explains why you were the only one who appeared to be upset at the PM.'

Zoe said nothing but nodded for him to continue.

'The way I figure it, Bish saw something illegal, something big – although running round with those daft hippies it's hard to imagine what. Whatever it was, though, he either had, or was about to, testify against someone. And whoever they are, they went looking for him. I suspect they found and killed him. How am I doing so far?'

159

Refusing to be drawn in, she asked, 'What else?'

'I know protected witnesses get set up with housing and such-like but that was never going to fly with Bish. Suburbia was never going to be for him. I think he either slipped his leash or, more likely, there was a compromise. You probably thought a bunch of new age travellers would be impossible to track down by anyone outside of their crowd. He may or may not have agreed to check in with you periodically, and whether he did is irrelevant. He was a witness and therefore the state had a responsibility to him. A responsibility they spectacularly messed up.'

Still she said nothing.

'And I'm not blaming you, you understand. I knew him. Controlling Bish must have been like herding cats. No, I blame whoever killed him.'

He paused to take a drink of his coffee. So far Zoe hadn't given anything away.

'And so I dropped the name Bish on your lot. Tried to convince your idiot boss I was better in the tent pissing out, etcetera. Instead he locks me up. But I had time to work things through. I don't know what Bish witnessed and I don't know some of the finer details, but other than that I'm confident I've got the basics right. Certainly enough to launch a few lines of enquiry up here anyway.'

Zoe drained her coffee while Fluke waited for his report card.

'You're right, Mr Fluke. The person found behind the tenth green at Cockermouth Golf Club was indeed your friend Mark Bishop.'

Fluke smiled grimly. Sometimes he hated being right.

'But other than that, you're wrong in almost every respect,' she said, with no hint of triumph.

Fluke stared at her open-mouthed.

'Mark Bishop wasn't a protected witness, Mr Fluke, he was an undercover police officer.'

Ah . . .

160

Chapter 24

'Have you heard of the expressions "deep swimmers" and "shallow paddlers"?'

Fluke shook his head. He hadn't. His face had burned for two minutes and then he'd put his mistake behind him. The case deserved his full attention. He could feel stupid later.

Zoe stood as she launched into what was obviously a speech she'd delivered before.

'I'm attached to NDEDIU, the National Domestic Extremism and Disorder Intelligence Unit. We were set up partly as an appeasement to the public, after some high-profile operations came to light.'

'You mean Mark Kennedy?' Fluke didn't live under a stone. He was aware of the undercover officer who'd lived and protested with environmental groups for a number of years. Kennedy had been so immersed in his cover it had later been alleged he'd become an *agent provocateur*, and far from sitting at the back noting what was going on and reporting back to his superiors, he had been right in the thick of it. A high-profile case against six activists collapsed when the revelations came to light, and the Met was sued by any number of women who said they'd been tricked into falling in love with him.

Zoe nodded.

'Not just Kennedy,' she said. 'There were others, some of whom have come to light, many more who haven't. Files that were never transferred onto electronic systems – and never will be if some of the top brass get their way.'

She paused, looked as though she was deciding where to start.

'I was a shallow paddler, Mr Fluke. It's a derogatory term in the unit, meant to imply someone who hasn't the balls or the skills to commit to the task. The truth, as always, is very different. We need the shallow paddlers. Sometimes there's no need to go deep; sometimes all that's needed is a few weeks. But, after my assignment was over, I knew that was it for me. I was honest enough to admit I wasn't a natural. But I wanted to stay with the unit and so I became the next best thing to being an undercover cop; I became a handler.'

That made sense. A handler with field experience would be an asset to any undercover officer.

'I can see you can tell where this is going,' Koenig said. 'Yes, I was Mark's handler, and yes, he was a deep swimmer.'

Fluke had only one question. 'How long?'

Zoe didn't pause. 'Three years. Not the longest – Kennedy did seven – but nowhere near the shortest.'

Three years . . . Fluke didn't even do things he *liked* for that long.

'And being a hairy – that's what we call those who infiltrate environmental and animal extremists – means leaving everything behind. You're given a new identity, a new flat, even a cover job. You have to maintain this identity in a completely hostile environment. There are times when you have to engage in acts of violence to maintain your cover. After a while you can forget who you are.'

Fluke, who lived and breathed every case he worked, could well imagine. A deep swimmer such as Bish would never be able to truly relax. He was living a false life as an undercover officer and was therefore never 'off-duty'.

'Did I read in a briefing note somewhere that UCOs are told they can sleep with targets?'

Zoe nodded. 'They'd be discovered too easily if they couldn't. It's not exactly encouraged but it has to be something they have permission to do. They have to be able to fit in. If that means shagging a hippy or two, or wigging out on LSD, then so be it.'

'That's messed up,' Fluke said.

'It is,' she agreed. 'And that's why they all have handlers. It's a welfare thing more than anything. Even if there's nothing to report they still have to have regular debriefs. It reminds them who they are and why they're doing it. Stops them going native.'

'Let me guess,' he said. 'Bish was a natural.'

He would have been. He'd always been one of those people who just fitted in. It didn't matter where he was, or who he was with, he had a knack for just blending in and making people feel at ease. He might've been a psychotic lunatic – the only other person Fluke had met who was like Towler – but he'd always been able, externally at least, to appear calm.

'Best I've ever seen. Best I've even heard about, to be honest. He could walk that line between follower and leader and that's what the Intelligence Unit is all about now. Gathering intelligence, but also trying to exert influence and make sure some of the more extreme acts are stopped before they can gather momentum. We need them to be the voice of reason sometimes. And Mark was a natural. I wasn't there when he joined the unit, but from what I've heard he wasn't long out of the Royal Marines before our lot snapped him up. He was trained and then held back for the right assignment, they didn't want to waste him on some JAFRA.'

Fluke knew she'd deliberately dropped in the acronym. He took the bait. 'JAFRA?'

'Just Another Far-Right Arsehole,' she said. 'When you have someone as talented as Mark, someone you may only get to use once, you wait until there's a genuine threat.'

'And there was?'

Zoe paused. 'I don't know how you've managed to get this level of clearance so quickly but John's told me to tell you everything. Nevertheless, what I'm about to tell you is highly classified.'

Fluke had higher security clearance than either her or Reyes but he said nothing.

'Four years ago there was chatter. GCHQ picked it up, but by the time they'd analysed it the chatter had been restricted to the UK.'

'You didn't get the source, you mean?'

'A bit unfair. *GCHQ* didn't get the source. By the time it was passed to us, even the UK chatter had stopped.'

She paused and allowed him to digest what she'd just told him. Fluke said nothing. He wasn't ready for questions. He needed more information.

'We didn't get involved straightaway. There was no indication what the threat was. It could have been anything: terrorism, large-scale counterfeiting, a drugs shipment; anything. By the time it was passed from the security services to us, the only thing known was that it involved domestic extremism although we didn't know what the specifics were. But, working on the basis of giving high-est priority to groups with the most dangerous ambitions, we were told to put all our resources into environmental extremists.'

Made sense, Fluke thought. Animal rights activists were com-mitted but tended to restrict their activities to labs and farms. Anything more than that came with military-grade security and would be handled by the MOD. Far-right and far-left extremists, although dangerous, tended to work in isolation. Nothing that couldn't be handled by territorial police forces. There were the Scottish and Welsh nationalists, of course, but they were a bit of a rabble and restricted themselves to setting fire to properties and daubing graffiti.

In their own villages. Knobs.

But eco-terrorism was different. Some of the more commit-ted ones had goals that threatened the national infrastructure and they had an unlimited amount of targets to choose from. Certainly too many to guard against. Factories, power stations, fuel depots, logging companies, mining companies, chemical plants. Virtually nothing was off limits.

Zoe continued. 'There were a few groups we put our resources into. We had to spread ourselves thin because it was getting desperate. We knew it was going to happen but we didn't know what and we didn't know when.'

'And Bish just happened to get lucky, did he? The one group he infiltrated was the group you were after. Bit of a coincidence.' Fluke didn't buy it.

'No. I told you, Mark was being held back. We couldn't just randomly put him somewhere and hope he struck lucky. Mind you, that's what management wanted. Everyone had to be in the field. But Mark refused. He knew his worth and knew we only had one chance of doing it right. He told the chief super he'd walk if he was told to go in blind.'

Fluke smiled. Challenging authority. Didn't sound like Bish at all . . . He was also right. Basic infantry tactics dictated you kept your best units in reserve. Bring your power to a point once a weakness has been identified.

'So one of your UCOs found something, I take it.'

'Yep. By luck actually. There was a small group, no more than four or five men, never been on anyone's radar, never even been identified. Nowhere near a priority. Our woman wasn't with them, she was trying to infiltrate a larger group but she'd met one of them in a pub in London one night. A hanger-on called Russell Bryce. Didn't think anything of it at the time, but later that night one of the group she was with said Bryce had been acting strange. Not enough to raise their suspicions but enough for them to briefly talk about it.'

'Strange, how?'

'Well, according to the group, Russell Bryce was by all accounts a gobshite. No real belief system, moved from one cause to the next depending on what was fashionable. Only in it for

165

the easy pussy.' She said it matter-of-factly. No hint of embarrassment. 'Usually talked about all the things he'd blown up, all the fires he'd started and all the animals he'd set free. Every time they bumped into him there was a list of things he'd been doing. A succession of tall tales. But this time, nothing. In fact, less than nothing; our woman said he'd gone out of his way to say he wasn't doing anything.'

'Pretty thin,' Fluke said.

'Agreed,' she said, nodding. 'But two weeks later he was dead. Found in an east London crack house with a snapped neck.'

'Ah.'

'Ah, indeed.'

'And that's when you deployed Bish.' It was a statement not a question.

She nodded, and pointed at his cup. Fluke offered it up and watched her refill them both.

'And you were his handler?' Fluke said to the back of her head.

There was a small pause before she answered. 'Yes.'

There's something she's not telling me, he thought.

'You're quite young to be a handler, aren't you, Zoe?'

The cups were full but she didn't turn round. Too casually she said, 'Not really, no.'

Gotcha.

'But I'm right in thinking the UCO/handler relationship is a vital one?'

She turned and passed him his drink. 'Absolutely.'

'And with a resource like Bish, possibly their best chance of stopping something awful from happening, I'm going to assume they'd want their best handler with their best UCO?'

'That's me.' Simply said. He didn't doubt it.

There was more to it though. Even if she were their best handler, no senior manager would sign off on someone so young taking the lead. Whether it made tactical sense or not, they'd want someone defensible for when it all went wrong. No, Zoe had been forced on them.

But why? There was really only one explanation.

'He asked for you, didn't he?'

For a moment he thought she was going to deny it, but either the warning about full disclosure from Reyes was having an effect or she could see no harm in telling the truth. She nodded.

'Why?' Fluke said out loud. He held his hand up to stop her answering. 'You're a bonny lass but this is dangerous work. Bish was never so horny he'd put his love life before his actual life. So, if we discount the personal, he had to have had a professional reason for wanting you. And it could only have been one thing.'

Zoe nodded. 'You're right.' She put down her cup carefully. Fixed him with a challenging stare. 'He wanted me there because I was one of the shallow paddlers sent out to generate leads.'

And Fluke knew where she'd been sent. 'You were the one who met Russell Bryce? Spotted his inconsistency?'

Zoe nodded. 'And because I did, he was killed.'

Chapter 25

With that out in the open, the flow of information . . . well, flowed. Zoe filled Fluke in on how the investigation had progressed. Parts he knew from Jinx, other bits were new.

Mark Cadden's legend was one of the finest the unit had ever created but, like all legends, it was essentially a lie. To make it more realistic they'd been pre-emptive. Not only had they given him a criminal record that could be verified by anyone with access to PNC, they'd also gone a step further. PND, the police national intelligence database, had been used to give the cover more credibility. If a bent cop went further than PNC, he'd find the name Mark Cadden had been mentioned in dispatches for more than a few unsolved incidents and not-guilty verdicts. They'd been sneaky though. Knowing that the environmentalists had nearly as good an intelligence system as the police did, they couldn't risk Bish simply taking credit for things he hadn't done. Someone out there would know who'd actually done them. So they invented crimes. They chose arson. Accidental fire reports were subtly changed so the report stated an accelerant had been used. The name Mark Cadden was mentioned on PND as being seen in the vicinity. Nothing actionable.

But enough to hint at the one thing the security services fear above all else – a lone wolf.

The easiest thing would have been to approach the target group; knowing they were down one man with the unfortunate Bryce in a mortuary somewhere. The easiest thing but also the wrong thing.

Instead, Bish had integrated himself into a group that had nothing to do with them. As a natural leader, within a month he was deciding which pub they drank in and which demos they went to. Acting on intelligence, like a shark circling a drowning man, Bish's group slowly neared the target group.

After Bryce had drawn attention to the group's statement of inactivity, they'd clearly decided they'd better get back out to some actual protesting while they planned whatever it was they were planning.

And one demo proved irresistible to every eco group in London. To not attend would have been too suspicious. One of the few remaining green belts had been re-designated as brown and was being developed. The subsequent protest had attracted limited support, but when one particularly committed man chained himself to a tree, and an ill-advised council went to court and secured an order to forcibly remove him, the shit hit the fan.

It was the proverbial red rag. Every anti in London was incensed at the shabby treatment of this visionary activist. They converged en masse. Bish took his group there in the hope the late Russell Bryce's group would also show up for appearances' sake.

They did.

And the whole thing got out of hand.

'The Territorial Support Group showed up, mob-handed,' Zoe said. 'There were scuffles and before long a fully fledged riot had broken out. On our instructions, TSG staged an attempt to arrest the group's leader – the man we now know as Vane. The plan was, Mark would help him get away, see if he could ingratiate himself.'

Fluke nodded. Smart move. In the chaos of a TSG-controlled riot, friendships could be forged. It had been the same on Belfast's Falls Road when the petrol bombs had turned the night sky orange.

'I'm sensing a "but" though.'

'One of Vane's group completely wigged out,' she said. 'Attacked one of the arresting officers with a railroad spike. As soon as that happened it didn't matter what their orders had been, all bets were off. TSG went for a hard arrest. Vane and his friends were grabbed and were in the process of getting a right kicking when Bish took his chance.'

She went on to describe how Bish had fought TSG and managed to get Vane away. He'd got a broken nose in the process but said it was worth it. And because Bish was a natural at knowing when to back off, he made sure Vane was safe and then left. No names, no pack drill.

'"He has to come to me," Bish said. Reckoned the only way it would work was if Vane approached him, not the other way round.'

'Risky,' Fluke said.

'He was right though. Within twenty-four hours we noticed the name Mark Cadden had been searched on both PNC and PND. Someone was checking him out. Three days later Vane called on him. How he found him we don't know, but to find a hippy – albeit a make-believe one – in a sea of hippies within three days means he had connections somewhere.'

Fluke wanted her to spin ahead three years. The history lesson was interesting but it could wait, and he said as much.

She frowned but did as he asked.

'A few months ago I met Bish for a debrief. He was starting to make progress. He confirmed there was a plan although he didn't know the what, when or where. The other thing we'd asked him to do was to find out Vane's name, and that was—'

'What! You don't even know who he is yet? How's that even possible?'

'It's because we're all incompetent arseholes, obviously,' she snapped.

Fluke raised his hands in appeasement. It had been an insensitive remark.

'I'll rephrase. I find it surprising someone like Vane isn't known to the authorities.'

Calming down as quickly as she'd flared up, she said, 'The man's a fucking ghost. We've tried everything. Mark got his fingerprints within a week. Nothing. He got a DNA sample the week after. Again, nothing.'

'So, he's not been arrested recently?' Fluke asked.

'Most likely never.' After a moment she added, 'You seem to know a bit more about Vane than I've told you, Mr Fluke. Almost as if it's not the first time you've heard the name. Isn't it about time this information sharing actually lived up to its name? How about some reciprocation?'

Ignoring her, Fluke said, 'What else?'

Realising she wasn't getting anything just yet, she continued. 'Mark thought Vane was getting instructions, help and funds from an outside body. He was simply too well organised to be doing this on his own. Mark had a theory he was actually working for someone. I was supposed to meet him this week in Ulverston. His next debrief wasn't for a month but he'd got a short message to me saying he had news.'

'And now he's dead,' Fluke finished for her.

She looked down. It had hit her hard, that much was obvious.

Fluke didn't have time for sympathy yet. 'Theories?'

She looked back up and this time the anger was back in her eyes. 'I have more than a theory. I fucking know.'

The venom in her voice took Fluke by surprise. For the first time, there was hate.

'The last time we met, Mark told me he'd fallen in love with some new age slag called Jinx, had some weird pagan wedding, and was claiming he was now a married man,' she said, before adding through gritted teeth, 'As if that fucking nonsense counts for anything in the real world.' She stopped and composed herself. After a moment she continued. 'OK, not ideal

171

but not a drama. Could even work in his favour if he played it right.'

'I sense another "but" coming,' Fluke said. He was interested in her description of Jinx. There was something more than professional resentment there and, not for the first time, he wondered if Zoe had told him everything.

'Yeah, a big one. I hadn't known Mark that long so couldn't tell if he was the type of man who'd throw everything away for a woman. I didn't—'

'He wasn't,' Fluke confirmed.

'Well, whatever he *had* been like, he wasn't thinking clearly last time we met. After telling me he was married to this Jinx, he told me he was going to come clean to her. Tell her he was a cop.'

'Shit,' Fluke whispered. *Not good Bish. Not good at all.*

Zoe saw the change in his expression. 'I can see you've skipped ahead to the last few pages. I asked him not to disclose he was a UCO, I begged him, I even ordered him, but he was adamant.'

Her shoulders slumped as she recounted her efforts to stop him throwing away his career and, as it turned out, his life.

'I am one hundred per cent convinced that Mark did exactly what he said he was going to do,' she said. 'He told her and, either intentionally or unintentionally, she told Vane.'

Keeping his expression neutral, Fluke nodded. At some point he'd been expecting to bring Jinx in, let her tell the story she'd told him. But now he had to mentally reverse as he processed the new information.

Zoe's team were clearly fixated on Jinx being the person who'd exposed Bish. When she'd arrived at Fluke's she was scared, but not for herself. She'd wanted to find Bish and got upset every time she thought about him being missing. It wasn't the reaction of someone who felt betrayed. He wasn't so rigid in his thinking that he didn't think it was impossible Jinx was the world's best actress, but sometimes there was no choice but to

172

go with his gut, and his gut was telling him Jinx hadn't known Bish was a cop.

And the other thing that didn't feel right was Bish himself. He loved his country. There wasn't a thing he wouldn't do for it. He might have wanted to tell his new wife, and would have resented being denied permission, but Fluke would have been surprised if he'd actually gone through with it.

So offering Jinx up as a sacrificial hippy to NDEDIU didn't feel right. Not just yet anyway. He needed to speak to her, and that meant either bringing Zoe inside FMIT's tent or finding a way to exclude her without raising suspicions.

Fluke elected for the latter. For now, he would trust only those he knew. He came to a decision.

'You want to know how I knew about the man you call Mark and I call Bish?'

She nodded.

'A few days ago Jinx turned up at my house. Bish had told her to go to mine if she was ever in trouble.'

Zoe's eyes widened. It was clear she hadn't expected him to have known about Jinx, never mind have met with her.

Continuing, Fluke said, 'She was dropped off by another traveller called Twist. She stayed a while then left.'

It wasn't an outright lie, but it was hardly full disclosure. Fluke tried to move on before she focused on how long Jinx had stayed.

'We talked about Mark.'

'Where'd she go?'

This time Fluke didn't have to lie. 'I have no idea.'

Zoe nodded again. He couldn't tell whether she believed him or not. 'Why had Mark told her to go to you though?'

Fluke stood up. 'I think it's time I met the rest of your team, Zoe.'

Chapter 26

Fluke looked across at the assembled ranks of the National Domestic Extremism and Disorder Intelligence Unit. They were wearing different degrees of contempt. Only Zoe had anything approaching a friendly expression.

The previous night, after finishing with Zoe, he'd gone home and written up all the new information. It was clear he knew more than Reyes. They had the background but Fluke had the current intel.

Saying as much hadn't exactly endeared him to Reyes and his team though. Even after he'd told them most of what he knew – he had omitted the part about Jinx staying at his cabin – it was clear they still bought the 'Bish told Jinx – Jinx told Vane – Vane killed Bish' theory.

They were so obsessed with the idea – and because tunnel vision is fatal in detective work – they'd managed to lose what should have been the primary focus of their investigation: that someone was out there planning a terrorist act. Fluke had arguably an even more personal reason for wanting Bish's killer doing life with a forty-year tariff but, after hearing from Zoe, he knew his responsibility was to Cumbria now. His personal vendetta would have to wait.

'Do you have any idea what Vane's up to?' Fluke said, ignoring the filthy looks he was getting. The resentment of idiots was something he suffered on a daily basis.

'We don't,' Reyes admitted.

'I assume you think he's up here to train?'

'We do. It wouldn't be the first time,' Reyes said, referring to the 21 July bombers who'd trained in Cumbria.

'But you don't think the target is up here?'

'We don't,' Reyes said. 'I know you're going to say Cumbria's a target-rich environment but that's bullshit. You *do* have BAE and Sellafield, but both of those are so well protected we've ruled them out.'

Fluke said nothing.

Reyes carried on. 'That's not to say we haven't been thorough. They've both been told to increase their security status to their highest rating, which they have. And even if Vane and his chums did manage to infiltrate one of them, the damage they could do is minimal. The locations for these places are chosen for a reason. Sparsely populated so there's no real impact if something goes bang and, as we know there's an eco angle, it's hardly going to involve damaging the environment – which both BAE and Sellafield would do.'

It made sense. It really did. But Fluke didn't know for sure, and until he did he'd work on the assumption that Cumbria *was* the target.

'OK then,' he said. 'Zoe tells me there was chatter about a terrorist attack. An undercover officer of yours is the second person to be killed because of it, and I've just told you that your target is assembling devices and receiving packages up here. And when you raid their camp he's nowhere to be seen.'

'You think you can do better?' Reyes said.

'I do actually.'

'Then tell us how; we're all ears, I'm sure.'

'When your pipes are blocked you call for a plumber,' Fluke said.

Reyes frowned. 'I'm not follow—'

'What I mean is, you might know how to investigate extremism, but *I* know how to investigate murder.'

Fifteen minutes later, Fluke was on the road. He wanted to see the camp for himself, and he wanted Zoe with him in case there was information she hadn't told him yet. She hadn't been on the camp raid and was keen to accompany him. Reyes, happy to see the back of him, agreed.

'I want to get a feel for what the atmosphere's like. See if anyone looks nervous when we show up. Shake the tree a bit; see what falls out.'

Zoe nodded. 'I wouldn't mind dropping in on the blacksmith as well.'

Fluke grunted. They might not be seeing eye-to-eye on Jinx just yet, but on this they were as one. He was just as curious as she was to find out what he'd made for Vane.

She looked glad to be out of the office and she wasn't the only one; he felt as though he'd been indoors for weeks, not days. He opened the driver's window and took some deep breaths. The weather had cooled to a more manageable temperature. The gauge on his dash said it was twenty-one degrees.

'Where is Muncaster anyway?' she asked.

The grounds of Muncaster Castle were where most of Jinx's friends were working during the summer, and their camp was in a small wood on some private land belonging to the estate. It was obviously a mutually beneficial arrangement. Cheap labour for free digs.

He pointed at the map in the passenger footwell. 'Page seventy.'

She made no effort to pick up the battered *AA Road Atlas*. 'Is it near Windermere?'

Fluke smiled. Virtually everyone had been to the Lake District. With over fifteen million visitors a year, it was the nation's favourite tourist destination. But the vast majority of people stayed within the National Park. Grasmere, Windermere and Ambleside. As soon as the signs for Keswick were only visible in the rear-view mirror most tourists got lost. He told her about holidays in West Cumbria. About trips to the castle, birds of prey exhibits, mazes and rides on La'al Ratty – one of the few working minimum gauge railways in the UK.

'Why's it called . . . La'al Ratty?'

'Not got a scooby. Whatever the reason, though, it's a bit of a tourist magnet,' he said. He wasn't an expert on the Ravenglass & Eskdale Railway and hadn't been on it since he'd been old enough to tell his mum and dad he didn't want to go any more. 'It's just a steam engine. You sit on it and then get off. Tourists get their picture taken with the driver.'

She took out her phone instead. 'Says Muncaster hire a fool every year,' she said.

Fluke grunted. It didn't surprise him.

'They seem to have year-round events,' she added. 'It's the chilli fair this week.'

'Hopefully there'll be one or two still in camp,' Fluke said, remembering what Jinx had said about most of them having jobs.

'Might even find that deceitful bitch,' she said.

Fluke glanced at her. She was staring straight ahead, her white lips were flattened together and her nostrils flared.

Any thoughts Fluke might have had about coming clean about Jinx disappeared.

The conversation was stilted for the next twenty minutes, but Zoe eventually lightened up. Before long she was telling him all about Reyes. It was clear she was conflicted. She admired his tenacity but despaired at his stubbornness. The more she spoke, the more Fluke recognised attributes that he himself possessed, although Reyes had a defect that allowed him to cross the line. Their component parts might be the same, but they were fundamentally different animals.

As they passed Sellafield, the nuclear waste processing plant, there was a natural lull in the conversation. It seemed implausible,

177

but unless he was planning an all-out assault on BAE's heavily defended submarine base in Barrow-in-Furness, Sellafield was the only target in Cumbria worth hitting. If it wasn't Sellafield, then Reyes was right: Cumbria was just a staging post.

Fluke pulled into Muncaster Castle car park and turned off the engine. 'They should be within walking distance of here,' he said, unbuckling his seatbelt and getting out. He arched his back and stretched. It had been a long journey.

Jinx had told him the camp was near the car park and Fluke scanned the horizon, shielding his eyes from the sun, to get his bearings. The wood was about half a mile from the car park. He thought he could see tell-tale tendrils of smoke drifting up through the thick, green trees.

Fluke looked at Zoe's feet and grunted in satisfaction. She was wearing outside shoes. He could always tell if he was going to get on with a cop or not by what they wore on their feet. He walked to the back of the car park and began climbing over the wooden fence. He turned back. Zoe was standing there – a bemused expression on her face.

'Come on,' he said. 'This way.'

Chapter 27

If Fluke had thought about what Jinx's camp might look like once, he'd thought about it a hundred times. And despite Jinx's representations, he'd got it all wrong. He'd expected drab and battered camper vans; rusting buckets of shit held together by paint and dirt. Hippies sleeping under bits of old tarpaulin, corrugated iron and filthy second-hand tents. He'd expected it to be smelly. He'd expected it to resemble a refugee camp.

What he found was something quite different.

It was spotless for a start. Clean and fresh smelling. Despite being outside, Fluke felt as though he should wipe his feet.

There were about twenty-five vehicles of varying descriptions. One or two of the vans Fluke had expected to see were there, but they all looked roadworthy. There were no tents, although there were a couple of yurts. There was even an old American school bus.

What surprised Fluke the most though was the number of elaborately decorated horse-drawn carriages. Beautiful things. Brightly coloured and intricately carved; they were works of art.

Fluke had the feeling he'd stepped back in time and place.

The smell of pine and freshly baked bread mingled and made a heady bouquet. Smoke-blackened Dutch ovens hung from tripods over small cooking fires. Their flames danced across the dark trunks in the dappled shade of the wood. From the mouthwatering smells emanating from some of them, it was clear that not everyone was as rigidly committed to the cause of veganism as Jinx.

As well as the colours and smells there were any number of other distractions. Musical instruments by the dozen were leaning against trees and vehicles. A staggering array of craft equipment was on display. Some, such as a kiln and a potter's wheel, Fluke recognised, others he had no earthly clue what they could be for. Some had people working them, others lay still and unused. A small number of tourists had wandered over and were looking at the baskets and dreamcatchers that were stacked beside the inevitable sign that said 'handmade'.

Fluke smiled. Neoliberal hippies.

The camp's occupants were clones of Jinx. In their efforts to look different, they'd ended up looking the same. Heavily dyed clothes and a variety of silly hats. Fluke estimated more than half of them had dreadlocks.

Still, it wasn't an aggressive look and, although he was almost certainly viewed as establishment, he didn't feel threatened. To be fair, it was hard to feel intimidated by a woman wearing a green ballgown and a top hat.

Some were gathered in small groups quietly chatting. Others worked, and some just enjoyed the late afternoon sun. One was quietly strumming an old-looking guitar and mumbling to himself as he tried to learn a song. Children played.

A different pace to the life he led emanated from the wood. There was no sense of urgency, no raised voices. It was nice. There was no other way to describe it.

'Jesus, will you look at the state of these fucking zoobs?' Zoe muttered. 'Stinking, work-shy bastards.'

Despite Zoe's city-girl cynicism, Fluke was fascinated by what he was seeing and could have explored the camp for hours. He was therefore glad when a vaguely familiar voice called out from within one of the carriages.

'Mr Fluke! I was wondering when we'd see a proper policeman round here.'

180

It was Twist. The man who'd walked Jinx to his cabin.

Fluke turned in the direction of the voice. Like a tortoise peering out of its shell, a scraggly head popped out of a carriage door. The hair was a different colour to the last time he'd seen it but Fluke wouldn't have expected anything else. After all, Jinx had managed to change the colour of hers while staying at Fluke's and she'd not once left the cabin.

'Hello, Twist, nice to see you again,' Fluke said.

'How's Jinx?'

'Fine as far as I know,' he said, ignoring Zoe's scowl. 'She didn't come back here then?'

'Nah, man,' Twist said. 'Didn't really expect her to. She was fair shook up, you know what I mean?'

Fluke nodded.

A floppy-eared spaniel came bounding out of the carriage, its tail wagging so fast it was almost a blur. Twist shouted it back, and for a moment, it seemed to have two conflicting demands. Half of it tried to turn and obey its master and the other half wanted to carry on and see who the strangers were. In the end, his master's voice triumphed. The spaniel turned on its heels and, tail between its legs, walked back to where Twist was now standing.

'Sorry about that,' he said. 'He sometimes bites people he doesn't know.'

Fluke had never seen a dog that looked less likely to bite than Twist's spaniel, but he said nothing. His dog, his rules.

Zoe coughed politely. Fluke took the hint.

'Twist, this is Zoe Koenig. She's another police officer, from the Met. We're trying to find Mark Cadden,' he said.

Twist said nothing. There was a noise from further within his caravan but he didn't look round to see what it was. A woman's head appeared at his side.

It could only be Twist's wife, Faith.

Jinx's description hadn't come close to doing her credit. She

181

was quite possibly the most beautiful woman Fluke had ever seen. She was wearing no makeup and her hair was styled in the new age traveller way of thick, heavily beaded dreadlocks, but whereas Twist's and Jinx's were dyed a multitude of garish colours, Faith's hair was a corn-yellow blonde and unspoiled. She was wearing a man's plaid shirt and a pair of black and white combat trousers. She had the kind of look that fashion designers would kill for. Tall and willowy and with flawless skin, she could have easily commanded a seven-figure salary on the catwalk. She didn't say anything immediately and a small look of confusion flashed across her face.

Without turning his head, Twist said, 'Mr Fluke, may I introduce my wife, Faith?'

'Oh, you're the policeman Twist told me about?' A smile lit up her face. She offered her hand.

For a moment Fluke was lost for words. Just looking at her made him think he was being unfaithful to Bridie. He took her hand. It was warm and dry. He shook it once and let go. Zoe did the same. Twist looked on, amused; he was obviously familiar with people's first reactions to his wife.

'We were expecting you, Mr Fluke. Those London cops came in mob-handed and left with nothing. It was only a matter of time before someone who knew what they were doing showed up.'

Fluke glanced across at Zoe but she wasn't biting. She hadn't been part of the raid and Fluke was getting the feeling she was happy enough not to be associated with Reyes and his gang of idiots right now.

'Twist's right,' Faith said. 'Anything we can do to help, we just want them back. They're such a lovely couple. Jinx is just about as sweet as it's possible to get and Mark has finally found some peace.' She filled a cast-iron kettle with water from a plastic container and hung it from a tripod over the fire. 'I'm making tea. Can I offer you both a cup?'

'Yes, please,' Fluke said.

As they sat round the small log fire waiting for the kettle, Faith asked what they were hoping to find.

'I just wanted to see where they were living,' Fluke said. 'Get a feel for what their lives were like.'

Faith nodded. 'They didn't live together, Mr Fluke. Heaven knows why, but Vane didn't want it. It was funny, Mark didn't strike me as the submissive type but he did everything Vane asked him to.'

Fluke knew why: he'd been making himself indispensable. He changed the subject before Faith said something. She didn't strike him as stupid.

'Jinx's caravan is over there,' Faith continued. 'The police who were here a couple of days ago searched it, though; I doubt they missed anything although you're welcome to have a look. And you can look at the ground where Mark's tent used to be. The police took everything he owned.'

Fluke glanced at Zoe. Why hadn't he been told?

She shrugged. 'There was nothing.'

'I also wanted to speak to your resident blacksmith,' Fluke said. 'The one who made that thing for Vane.'

'Dan's at the castle,' Faith said. 'He does his blacksmith displays in the grounds. Makes a few things in real time and sells them to the tourists.'

'Did he speak to the police who were here earlier?'

'Not to my knowledge,' Faith said. 'Twist?'

Twist had been poking about in the fire with a small branch. 'Nah, man. Dan was at the castle when they came. They looked in his van but he had his trailer with him obviously.'

'Why obviously?' Zoe asked.

'It has all his gear in. It's too heavy to lug over every day so he leaves it there most of the time.'

A noise came from their caravan. Faith said, 'That's our son, Sam. He's having a nap.'

'He must enjoy it round here,' Fluke said.

'We all do,' Faith said. She waved her arms around them. 'How can you not enjoy this? I've nothing against living in a house but I need my freedom. I wouldn't want Sam to have to live in the middle of a city. Unless he chooses to later, of course.'

She was frighteningly convincing and Fluke had that uneasy feeling that comes when you realise you're a bit of a hypocrite. He'd given away large parts of his life in exchange for the daily grind of work, traffic and bills. The freedom and the lifestyle that came with detaching from modern society was alluring.

Faith asked them how they took their tea and they settled into silence as the domestic task of making hot drinks took place.

'I take it there's been no sign of Vane either?' Fluke asked, after he'd been passed a white tin mug full of sweet, black tea. There was no harm asking about him. For all he knew, Vane could be fast asleep three tents down.

Twist shook his head. 'Not seen him since the night Mark disappeared.'

Silence settled over them again as they sipped their drinks. Fluke surreptitiously looked at Twist and Faith. They were a strange couple. Not exactly opposites but certainly different. Twist was outgoing, never without a smile, and irrepressible. Like a hippy version of Towler, there was nothing he didn't seem to enjoy doing. Faith, on the other hand, seemed sensible. Happy, but certainly grounded. Fluke got the impression that Twist would be homeless and penniless inside a week if Faith wasn't there. She would be the one who made sure their few bills were paid on time, that their son had clean clothes to wear and they had food on their table.

It was a universal law that people tended to end up with partners of visual equity. As a rule of thumb, unless money or power was involved, ugly people didn't end up with good-looking people, and while Twist wasn't exactly a hobbit, he wasn't in the same league as Faith.

Unless phrenology brought in a seven-figure salary, Fluke couldn't see how they'd got together. It was true some women get together with men – and vice versa – because they know they'll hold the balance of power in the relationship, but Fluke didn't think that was the case here. There was genuine affection. They were constantly touching each other, and when one of them spoke the other paid full attention. They seemed delighted with each other's company. It didn't seem to be an act; it looked like the real thing.

Then again, Fluke mused, they were hippies. For all he knew, Twist could be the catch of the century.

'You come here every year?' Fluke asked.

'The castle likes us,' Faith said. 'We provide all their entertainment needs. Fire breathers, acrobats, sword swallowers. Did you know the resident Muncaster fool has come from this group for the last six years?'

Fluke couldn't imagine where else they'd get one from but said nothing.

'And then there's all the craft we supply. Dan is just one of the group working up there. So we're allowed to stay here for free. The arrangement suits us both. We're even talking about having a resident camp here to help out the castle during the off-peak season.'

Fluke raised his eyebrows. 'Doesn't that go against the traveller spirit?'

Laughing, Faith said, 'You've hit the nail on the head, Mr Fluke. Having a permanent camp has its advantages, of course, but no one wants to give up their freedom.'

With the conversation now reduced to small talk, Fluke stood up and stretched. 'Can we look at Jinx's caravan now?'

Twist frowned when a small voice cried, 'Momma!'

Faith looked back into the carriage. 'Twist will have to show you. Sam needs me,' she said.

He jumped to his feet. 'Follow me.'

Fluke said goodbye to Faith and felt melancholic as she retreated into her home. He hoped he would see her again.

Following Twist across the camp, they were first shown a bare patch of earth, which he told them was where Bish had pitched his tent. Faith had been right. Zoe's colleagues had taken everything. There wasn't even a tent peg left. As they made their way across to Jinx's caravan, Twist gave them a running commentary on how the camp functioned. Although he wanted to see the blacksmith before it got dark, Fluke found himself listening – Twist's enthusiasm was infectious. He was telling them about how the camp recycled their greywater to help grow crops when Fluke noticed Zoe wasn't with him.

She was still at the patch of earth where Bish's tent had been pitched. Fluke stopped listening to Twist and refocused his attention.

Zoe's shoulders were shaking and she was surreptitiously trying to hide the tears rolling down her cheeks. Fluke could be the gentleman and leave her alone until she had composed herself, or he could try to find out what was happening.

She was so focused on her grief she didn't notice him arrive by her side. She jumped slightly when she saw him.

'You were more to him than just his handler, weren't you, Zoe?'

Silently she nodded.

'You loved him, didn't you?'

Again she nodded.

Fluke asked the question. The one that had bugged him since he'd seen her crying at the post-mortem.

'And was it reciprocated?'

This time she turned to face him, her eyes blazing with ferocity.

'I was his fiancée,' she snarled, 'until that bitch stole him from me . . .'

Chapter 28

Jinx's caravan was smaller than Twist and Faith's. Almost a mini caravan. It was wooden and painted a light shade of blue. What he initially thought were mud spatters running up the sides, and along the trim, were in fact delicately painted flowers. Whoever had construed the idea had painted a thin band of green running all the way around the base, and it was from this the flowers grew. And it wasn't just flowers, Fluke noticed as he bent down to have a closer look. Birds were flying in the sky, as were vibrantly coloured butterflies. He marvelled at the skill of the artist.

'Who painted this?'

'Jinx,' Twist replied. 'The caravan was a right state when she bought it. We all told her it was a bad deal but she fell in love as soon as she saw it. Wouldn't take no for an answer.'

That fitted with the little Fluke knew of her. Stubborn but passionate.

'Course, we have any number of expert wood carvers here, so it was soon fixed up. She spent the best part of a year painting it. Everything you see was something she'd seen on her travels.'

Jinx clearly lived her life outside. The inside was only just big enough to sleep in and keep a few possessions dry. It was a primitive way of living but Fluke suspected it was liberating. He doubted she'd ever get shotgun cartridges posted through her front door.

Of course, the illusion of idyllic life was slightly tempered by the police tape and sealed paper lock. Fluke removed his keyring from his pocket and selected a small multi-functional tool.

Opening a blade, he slit the seal on the door. It didn't have a lock. Fluke opened it.

The light in the wood was still bright enough for Fluke to see all the way into the caravan. It was empty. Stripped bare.

Frowning he turned to Zoe. 'This your lot's work?' he said, quiet enough so Twist couldn't hear.

She nodded. 'She's a suspect.'

Fluke said nothing. In his mind, Jinx was just as much a victim as Bish.

'We were looking for Mark's notebook. We knew he kept one although no one ever saw it.'

'And what about Jinx's stuff?'

'Nothing. Mainly clothes, if you can call the fucking rags she wore clothes, and some other weird shit. Incense burners, that kind of thing. They took it all anyway.'

Fluke sighed. Although it hadn't been a wasted trip – he'd found out a bit more about Zoe's relationship with Bish – the traveller's camp had been a bust. And Zoe's antagonism towards a woman she'd never met was beginning to grate.

He stepped into the caravan anyway. Five minutes later he was satisfied. Reyes might be a prick but his team had completed a thorough search. Jinx hadn't struck him as the type of person who put much store in possessions. She'd had next to nothing when she had stayed with them. Just her iPod and a small sack containing one change of clothes.

'Now what?' Zoe asked.

'Now we go and see the blacksmith.'

Muncaster Castle combined everything Fluke both loved and hated about Cumbria. The ancestral home of the Pennington family was a stunning building with parts of it dating back to the thirteenth century. It had unrivalled grounds and was set in an unspoiled part of the county. It didn't have the same issues the areas in the National Park did. Properties in towns such as Keswick, Grasmere and Ambleside were now so expensive the younger generation could no longer afford to live there. And when that happens, towns die. Local trade dries up and towns have no choice but to compete for tourist money. Instead of quaint local businesses, towns in the National Park become overrun with outdoor survival stores, fudge shops and, to service the night-time economy, fun pubs and takeaways. And yet another hurdle is put before any locals wanting to return to the place of their birth; their home towns are no longer pleasant places to live. They become seasonal – either packed with tourists or deserted.

Being so far from the Lake District National Park, Muncaster Castle had so far managed to avoid that trap. But they still needed the tourists' money to survive. Fluke was no historian, but he did wonder what Gamel de Pennington – the first Pennington to live on the site – would have made of the World Owl Centre (the finest collection of owls in the world!), the Meadowvole Maze (where you might not get lost but you could get eaten!) and the Heron Happy Hour. Fluke was always wary of activities that came with exclamation marks. He was prepared to accept that these massive homes needed money to keep them going, and therefore they had to diversify, but did Muncaster Castle really need a Japanese *and* a Himalayan garden?

Even the name irritated him. Castle? In his opinion, a real castle had a moat and dungeons, and a bloody past. It didn't matter how many turrets they stuck on the roof – Muncaster Castle was, and always would be, a stately home. It had windows instead of arrow slits. It had ornate stonework. It hosted parties, not battles. Unlike Fluke's own beloved, albeit extremely ugly, Carlisle Castle – which looked as though it could have once been a medieval borstal – Muncaster looked as if children armed with snowballs could take it.

Fluke and Zoe crossed the road, showed their badges to a man

189

in a ticket booth, and entered the castle grounds. Twist, there as their guide, didn't need to pay either.

The grounds were huge and sprawling. Despite it being too late for their world-famous rhododendrons and azaleas, tourists were exploring the gardens as far as the eye could see.

It was worse than he remembered. Laughter, music and the general buzz of large numbers of humans having fun. The noise assaulted his ears.

Fortunately, Twist forged a path through the thick crowd and they were soon where they needed to be.

For obvious reasons, the blacksmith display was sited away from the main gardens. It had a large area all to itself; flammable tents and small children didn't mix well with hot forges. It was cordoned off with heavy rope and a female traveller was inside making sure nobody encroached. The crowd was quiet, and in Fluke's experience that usually meant something interesting was happening.

The blacksmith was wearing leather trousers laced up at the sides. Flame resistant, Fluke was willing to bet. He was wearing a heavy, brown leather apron and thick leather gauntlets – far thicker than the ones the falconers had been wearing at the owl sanctuary they'd just walked past. He was bare chested and heavily muscled.

Unlike everyone else they'd met from the camp, he had short hair. Shorn almost. He was tattoo free, and when he turned to quench a white-hot bit of metal they could see that, apart from one ridiculously long, thin rope of dreadlocked beard hanging from his chin like a rat's dirty tail, he was clean-shaven.

Fluke and Zoe watched him finish his demonstration. It involved taking everyday bits of scrap metal and gradually turning them into the theme of the day: owls. Ones he had presumably completed earlier were lined up near the edge of the safety rope with price tags tied to them. They ranged from thirty pounds for the smaller owls, to three or four hundred for the bigger ones.

Every one had 'sold' written on them in red felt-tip pen. Business appeared to be booming. Either that, or they were remaking *Jason and the Argonauts* nearby.

While they waited for him to finish, Twist left their side and started acting the goat. Before long a portion of the blacksmith's crowd had wandered off to the new attraction. He seemed to be doing a cross between acrobatics and village idiot. Still, the crowd seemed happy enough. Soon they were putting coins in the hat he'd put on the grass.

Fluke turned back to the blacksmith. He was undoubtedly a huge talent. He was repeatedly striking a lump hammer against his anvil as if it were no more than a child's toy. The iron shrieked in protest and, ignoring the sparks that bounced off his bare chest, he worked it hard.

When he was satisfied the iron was how he wanted it, he carried it to the almost complete sculpture and attached it. Taking a smaller hammer he gently tapped the new piece a few times until it was secure. Fluke had watched him make a wing. The blacksmith stood back and eyed the finished piece. Eventually, he nodded at the female traveller who picked it up and put it with the others. A scramble of tourists immediately crowded her with wallets and purses out.

The blacksmith threw his tools into a canvas holdall and picked up a bottle of water. The crowd, realising he'd finished, applauded enthusiastically.

Taking this as their cue, Fluke and Zoe ducked underneath the rope and marched over. The female traveller rushed over to stop them – the forge was still glowing dangerously – but Zoe stopped her with a well-timed flash of her warrant card. It was a bit too *Sweeney* for Fluke, but it worked.

The blacksmith was wiping the sweat and muck from his face and upper torso when he noticed them approach. He put down the towel he'd been using and waited.

Fluke wanted to lead so spoke before they arrived. 'Dan?'

He nodded. 'Dan Malloy.'

He reached out and shook both their hands. His grip was firm and his hands were heavily calloused.

'I'm DI Fluke from Cumbria Constabulary and this is DC Zoe Koenig from the Metropolitan Police. I understand you were out when some of *Zoe's* colleagues came to your camp a few days ago?' He emphasised Zoe's name to put some distance between himself and the raid.

'I was hardly "out",' he said. 'I've been working these grounds every day for months. Start at eleven and finish when the crowds die down at about six. On that day I was setting up a new display area so I had my trailer across with me. They were gone by the time I got back so, yes, I missed the police officers from London when they came if that's what you meant?'

'It is,' Fluke said.

Dan said nothing and Fluke realised he hadn't actually asked him a question. 'Do you mind if we have a quick chat?'

He shrugged. 'Fire away.'

When Fluke finished, he was no further forward. Dan had merely corroborated what they already knew. Vane and his group had joined theirs shortly after they'd arrived for the summer season at Muncaster. Yes, he knew Jinx well, and yes, he approved of her relationship with the man he knew as Mark Cadden. He didn't know why Vane had been set against it. And no, he didn't know where either Vane or Mark were.

Zoe – in danger of becoming predictably monotonous – asked him if he knew where Jinx was. Dan cast a glance at Fluke before shaking his head. Twist had obviously told the camp where he'd taken her that night. So, for the second time in an hour, Fluke had to do his whole 'Don't worry, Zoe knows' thing. Dan nodded, but added nothing.

Fluke asked a few more questions without gaining anything. He didn't consider the time wasted though, and was happy that those he'd spoken to seemed to be telling the truth. Jinx, Twist, Faith and now Dan had all said the same thing and he'd heard enough bullshit in his career to know it hadn't been rehearsed.

He couldn't think of anything else to ask. Zoe grabbed her chance. 'What can you tell me about Jinx?'

Despite his rising anger, Fluke waited for Dan to answer.

'What's to tell? One of the nicest girls you'll ever meet. Innocent, but not shy and withdrawn like some are. Twist found her homeless in Bristol a few years back. She was almost feral when he and Faith took her in. Now she's the absolute epitome of everything we stand for.'

That obviously didn't fit Zoe's internal narrative. She pouted and didn't follow up with anything. Fluke decided he'd better say something or they'd look weird.

'How so?'

Dan swept his arm all around. 'Take a look at this. It's beautiful and we get to live here. And not just here, when the season's over we'll move to Cornwall or Scotland or London or . . . you get the picture. Thing is, we're free. Completely untied. Jinx embodies that spirit totally. Gives herself completely to the lifestyle. When Twist found her, and she decided that travelling was what she wanted to do, she went back home. Once. Picked up her passport and what little cash she had, said goodbye to her mother, and backpacked for a year. When that was out of her system she found the group again and bought that little caravan she lives in. She makes craft goods, baskets, dreamcatchers, that type of thing. Doesn't sell a lot, but enough for her to pay her way. Never asks for anything but is the first to muck in when needed.'

Zoe snorted. 'She's sounds manipulative.'

'You haven't met her,' Dan said. 'If you had you wouldn't say that.'

A simple statement but all the more powerful for its brevity, and one Fluke agreed with entirely. Zoe needed to get past it. She was beginning to get in the way; if she continued harassing witnesses, Reyes could have her back.

'Tell me about this thing Vane asked you to make,' Fluke said.

'Ah,' Dan sighed. 'A rare commission.'

Fluke waited for him to elaborate.

'He said it was for his parents' garden but that was bullshit. It was like nothing I'd ever seen before. Complex pieces, clamps, exact measurements – the works.'

'And you could make something like that?'

'I'm a metalsmith. Give me a forge and an anvil and there's nothing that idiot could show me that I couldn't make.'

Fluke put 'idiot' in the filing cabinet in his head, ready to be retrieved later. It looked as though Dan hadn't warmed to Vane. 'Was he there the whole time?'

Dan shook his head. 'He left me detailed blueprints so he didn't need to check in or anything, if that's what you mean?'

'He left blueprints of the sculpture?'

He nodded. 'He took them back when I'd finished though. Said he wanted the sculpture to be bespoke.'

'And what type of sculpture was it?'

'Let's not kid ourselves, Detective Inspector, it was a device. I may work in the sun a lot but I'm nobody's fool.'

'Any ideas what it was for?'

Dan shook his head. 'Nope. Bloody detailed plans though. Exact specifications, measurements, the lot.'

It was more than they'd had before. Certainly more than Jinx had been able to give them. But really, they still didn't know anything. A thought occurred to him. Dan didn't seem to like Vane. Perhaps he hadn't done exactly as Vane asked.

'And did you?'

'Did I what?' Dan replied.

'Give him the plans back?'

'Of course. He was the customer.'

Fluke maintained eye contact.

Dan grinned. 'Although I might have taken a photograph or two.'

Excitement flooded Fluke's system. Finally, something seemed to be going their way.

'Of?'

'Oh, I don't know. Of the device; assembled and unassembled. Of the blueprints, of the designer's notes . . .'

'And these photos are safe, I take it?' Fluke said.

'On my laptop, back at the camp. And, just in case he thought I might try something like that, I uploaded it to the cloud. As long as you don't mind wading through a load of metal owls, it should all be there. I'll give you the password. If you come back to camp with me I can show you before you go.'

As they walked back through the thinning crowds, Dan told them how Vane had upset the natural synergy in the camp.

'He had too much anger. It never manifested as anything physical, but you could tell. He didn't mix. Ever. And that's quite an achievement in a close-knit group like ours. I mean, one of his group *married* one of ours we were together so much.'

Fluke winced as he waited for a snide remark from Zoe. Nothing. He glanced at her and saw tears in her eyes again. His attitude softened. She was going through the wringer.

Something occurred to Fluke. 'These plans, did Vane understand them? Do you think he wrote them?'

Dan laughed. 'You're joking, aren't you? He didn't have a clue what they meant. Even when I gave him the finished product he had to check it for an hour to make sure it matched.'

'No way of telling who drew them up, I suppose?'

'Nope. If it was a blueprint of a building or something, someone might be able to recognise one architect's style over another. But it doesn't work like that for tools.'

'Fair enough,' Fluke said.

The fact Vane didn't understand them though – and Fluke was happy to accept Dan's interpretation of events – added another layer to the puzzle.

There were two obvious possibilities. Either he had commissioned someone to design the device, just as he had commissioned someone to build it, or he was working for someone else, and that thought scared Fluke. Most detectives went through their whole career without ever bumping into an über-villain. It was entirely possible he was about to go up against two in just six months . . .

It was testament to their relaxed lifestyle that no one in the camp had moved since they'd left. Those weaving were still weaving, those cooking were still stirring their Dutch ovens and the groups chatting still hadn't run out of things to talk about.

Fluke smiled. If this had been a police station, by now, three people would have been promoted, two would have retired and one would have been suspended.

Dan climbed into his van, popped back out with a laptop and powered it up. They waited while it whirred and clunked its way to a home screen.

Finding the right folder, Dan brought up a photograph of the blueprint. What was it though? That was the real head-scratcher.

The first thing that went through Fluke's head was that it looked like a plough and a bear trap's bastard love child. No wonder it had needed to be commissioned. Something this weird couldn't be picked up at B & Q.

It was a hollow rectangle; a steampunk picture frame with attitude. Two plough-like fixtures were attached to the shorter sides. The same sides also had what looked like clamps fixed to them, four on each; eight in total. The longer sides weren't as thick. Fluke thought they were probably there to connect the shorter, sturdier sides. Maybe keep it stable when it was assembled. The clamps and the plough-like fixtures were all adjustable.

To Fluke, with a military background, it looked a bit like the shaped-charge frames that special forces used to breach walls, windows and doors. But they were designed to be portable. This thing was heavy. Too heavy to carry and *far* too heavy to attach to a window frame. It might have adjustable clamps, but they weren't *magic* adjustable clamps . . .

It was meant to be attached to *something*, though, that much was clear. Probably something on the ground judging by the weight of it. It also looked as though it could bear the weight of something big.

There were measurements – all in millimetres – attributed to each and every part of . . . whatever it was. In his head, Fluke converted the millimetres to something a bit more manageable. The wider sides measured just under a metre and a half, and the smaller sides were half a metre.

There were numerous other parts, and they were detailed in both the assembled and unassembled state, but essentially it was just an iron frame with bits attached to it. Very simple, extremely ominous.

The three of them stared at the image. After a few minutes, Dan pressed a button and the next one came up. It was the back of the blueprint and was a costing spreadsheet. There were columns for parts, quantities and projected prices. It was blank.

Dan shrugged. 'It's a standard template. They all have prices on the back. Useless for this though. Each bit had to be handcrafted.'

Fluke frowned although he didn't know why.

Dan brought up photographs of the device being made. He'd photographed each piece from several angles, including at least one with a ruler to show its size. Fluke was impressed. A forensic photographer couldn't have chronicled it better. Finally there were a dozen photographs of the assembled device.

If Fluke was confused by the blueprint, he was completely stumped by the finished piece. His early view of a frame for a shaped-charge hadn't been far off. It clearly *wasn't* a frame for a shaped-charge, but that was what it looked like. Also, he doubted any frame special forces used would have had ploughs on the side . . .

There was no point standing there guessing though. Zoe would send a copy to someone in her team – he couldn't exclude Reyes from something this important – and he'd send the same file to Jiao-long. Collectively, they'd have enough resources to work out what it was, and what it was for. Fluke gave Dan an email address.

'I'll need to tether my phone to the computer,' Dan said. 'One of the drawbacks of living in a wood – there's no wi-fi.'

While he waited, Fluke's thoughts drifted to the back of the blueprint. Something had bothered him about it. He asked Dan to bring it up again. Zoe leaned forward and stared but it was clear she didn't see anything. Dan glanced once – he'd seen it before – and went back to trying to get a signal.

Fluke stared at the costing spreadsheet, willing it to reveal something. Anything. But it seemed a normal enough document. The first column was headed 'Unit Part Number', the second was 'Quantity', and the rest all related to pricing. The final one was headed 'Total Unit Cost €/£'.

He instantly knew that this was the column that had clicked his interest button. The designer had used an English language template.

So why was the euro sign before the pound sign?

If it was a European form, then fair enough. Cost in sterling would be an afterthought. But this was a template for English-speaking designers and engineers.

Of course, Fluke didn't know anything about engineering. Costing things in euros might be the norm now.

But what if it wasn't the norm?

What if this particular template was for the one country in the Eurozone whose official language was English?

Ireland.

Fluke stood up straight and stretched his back. He'd keep this to himself for now. Didn't want to feed Reyes an excuse to quote national security just yet. Not until he knew more.

But if he was right . . . well, then they were in a whole new ball game. Because somewhere out in the ether was a lunatic with a strange device designed in one of the few countries that was actually good at terrorism.

The official 'Troubles' might be over, but Fluke wondered if his were just beginning.

Dan said, 'Sorted. The file should be with those addresses soon.'

He closed his laptop and Fluke saw the lid for the first time. It had a film company's promotional sticker on the back. A swords-and-sandals epic that had passed Fluke by.

Dan noticed him looking.

'A present,' he said. 'I did some work for them. Made some replica swords and all I got was that lousy sticker. Well, that and fifteen grand.'

Fluke whistled. 'You're that good?'

'I don't think it's a case of being particularly good. More a case of there's hardly any of us left.'

'Blacksmiths?' Fluke knew some of the older trades were dying out, but surely in Cumbria a blacksmith would always have work?

'Not blacksmith, Mr Fluke. *Blade*smith. It's a dying art. I spent three years at Durham University studying ancient and medieval weapons, and the techniques used to make them. And, because government tax breaks mean more films are now being made in the UK, it's quite lucrative.'

Dan continued talking but Fluke had stopped listening. In his mind he was back in the post-mortem suite and his exchange with Sowerby.

'*The killer used a sword.*'

'*A long, edged weapon, certainly.*'

'Dan,' Fluke said slowly, being careful not to raise his voice, 'do you have any of these swords here now?'

Zoe stiffened.

'I do, actually,' he said, frowning. 'In my trailer back at the castle. Half-a-dozen scimitars I made for a prop company. They haven't collected them yet.' He looked concerned. 'What's this about?'

Fluke turned to Zoe. 'Ring Reyes and tell him what he missed, will you? It'll be better coming from you. I'll get SOCO up here; they'll need to impound the trailer. We'll walk back into the castle grounds and you can stay with the trailer until they arrive.'

She nodded. 'Where will you be going?'

Fluke ignored her and turned to the now worried blacksmith-bladesmith.

'Dan,' he said. 'You're going to have to come with me.'

Chapter 29

Fluke didn't believe Dan was their killer. The big blacksmith had walked Fluke back to his trailer, unlocked it and confirmed that none of his swords were missing. The murder weapon could well be in there.

SOCO would take the swords back to the lab and swab them for blood. That would take some time though, and in the meantime Fluke needed to make sure Dan didn't go anywhere. The safest way to do that was to make an arrest. It would also give Dan some legal protection if Reyes took the path of least resistance and tried to pin the whole thing on him. Reyes seemed like the type of cop who'd charge a man he knew to be innocent if it meant he could save face.

Fluke didn't want to be there for the next part. There was going to be a lot of huffing and puffing and very little progress. A thought occurred to him as he considered how easy it had been for the London team – all professional police officers – to miss a potentially vital lead.

He was now convinced that Bish had found a way to surreptitiously store information – his memory had been notoriously poor, and the fact that Reyes and his team had been looking for a notebook confirmed it hadn't improved over the years. And if Dan had taught them anything, it was how easy it was to store information electronically these days.

Reyes had taken both Bish's and Jinx's possessions and subjected them to a detailed search. They'd found nothing, and Fluke was prepared to accept that he probably wouldn't fare any better.

But there was still one thing left to search. Something Reyes didn't even know about. Something small, electronic and more than capable of storing vast quantities of information. Photographs. Videos even.

Jinx's iPod.

Taking Zoe with him was an obvious no-no but Fluke wasn't stupid enough to go alone either. Nathaniel Diamond was doing Fluke a favour but it was only because he expected something in return. When he refused, an 'exciting incident' could occur.

And when exciting incidents happened, Fluke only wanted one person at his side.

Towler.

Who, other than the occasional 'Good morning, sir' – and like all squaddies, Towler could make the honorific 'sir' sound very much like 'arsehole' – wasn't speaking to him. Other than Jiao-long, none of FMIT were.

Not a problem; he knew something they didn't.

Fluke had a final word with Zoe, made sure she knew what she was doing, and, after dropping Dan off at Workington Police headquarters, he drove back to HQ.

Despite it now being early evening, none of FMIT had gone home. A break, even in a case they had little to do with, was still a break. Fluke helped himself to some coffee and grabbed an unguarded sandwich.

Towler was pretending he hadn't seen him. Alan Vaughn probably *hadn't* seen him, and Jiao-long had nodded and gone back to whatever it was he was doing. Jo Skelton winked and smiled. Fluke smiled back and nodded towards FMIT's door. She got up and closed it.

'Right, dickheads. Listen to me. This bollocks stops now . . .'

Silence.

Towler broke it. 'You owe us an explanation, *sir*.'

He was right. He did. But it would be better coming from them.

'Anyone?' Fluke asked.

More silence.

He sighed. 'Jo, you play chess. Talk everyone through the basic tactics.'

She shrugged, thought about the question for a moment, and said, 'Essentially it's a combination of setting and springing traps. Making sacrifices for strategic gain . . .' She trailed off and stared at him. 'Oh, you've got to be kidding me?'

Everyone but Fluke looked at her.

'You came up with that?' she asked Fluke. 'How long did it take you?'

'Before he hit the ground.'

She paused a moment. 'You're a freak of nature. You know that, don't you?'

This time it was Fluke's turn to shrug.

Towler had had enough. 'Can you two stop wiping each other's arses and tell me what the fuck's going on?'

Fluke liked Jo Skelton for many reasons. She had down-to-earth common sense, dogged tenacity when everyone else was getting bored, and her attitude to her family was laudable. But the thing about Jo Skelton he found most impressive was her lateral thinking. He'd lost count of the times it had been her who'd come up with the theory that led to a new line of enquiry. But even Fluke was surprised by how quickly she'd worked out what he was up to this time.

'You tell them, Jo,' Fluke said.

She smiled. 'The boss is going to recruit Steeleye Stan . . .'

*

As Steeleye had lain screaming on the ground, and while the rest of the team had been gunning for action, Fluke had realised Diamond had made a mistake. Smith had obviously been working to Diamond's instructions when he'd carried out the assault and Fluke knew why. Diamond had wanted to force Fluke into ignoring a crime.

FMIT's reaction had been perfect. A mixture of humiliation and impotence. Just as Diamond had no doubt predicted. They had their pride, and watching Smith drive off unscathed had hurt them deeply. It was a natural reaction. When someone makes you feel powerless, humiliation is a very human emotion.

But FMIT weren't the only ones to be humiliated that day.

Steeleye Stan had once run a criminal enterprise that brought him an annual six-figure income. And now he was no more than a lackey; someone who'd been used to make a point – even if that point meant he'd never chew properly again.

Steeleye Stan hated the police with a ferocity that was frightening.

But Fluke was willing to bet there was someone he hated even more now. When the time came to take down Nathaniel Diamond, Fluke might already have an asset in play . . .

Fluke rang the pre-programmed number in the burner phone. Diamond answered with his trademark sardonic drawl.

'About time,' he said. 'Any longer and I was going to have to put her to work.'

'I need to see her.'

'I'll ring with an address tomorrow morning,' he replied, and hung up. The whole thing had taken less than ten seconds.

'We're on,' Fluke told his team.

There was nothing else to do so Fluke drove home. He hadn't seen Bridie since he'd been released from custody – she'd returned to

London after getting him released but had been due back that afternoon. Fluke was hoping they could have an early night and see if they could get back on track. He stopped at the off-licence and spent twenty pounds on a bottle of red wine; about eighteen more than he was comfortable with.

But Bridie wasn't in the mood to talk or drink; she wasn't well. She had a bad back and was so hot all the doors and windows were open. To avoid filling the house with moths and bugs, all the lights were off. It was summer flu, she told him. She asked for a glass of cold water and then went to bed without another word. Fluke closed the cabin down and retired to the spare room. It still smelled of Jinx, and the thought made him even more despondent.

He knew their relationship was on the way out. He no longer knew what Bridie wanted – although, whatever it was, it didn't seem to involve him. If his thoughts hadn't kept drifting back to the investigation he'd have cried.

Fluke got a text from Jiao-long first thing in the morning. One of the swords in Dan's trailer had come back positive for Bish's blood. It seemed they had their murder weapon. Fluke didn't see how it could help them right now but it was another box ticked off. Vane's prints had also been found on the sword so Dan wasn't being treated as a suspect. That might change, though, if they couldn't find Vane. Reyes was the type of cop who'd find an accessory scapegoat if the murderer evaded justice for long.

So he left for work with barely a word to Bridie. He'd taken her a cup of tea but she'd waved him away and run to the toilet where she vomited noisily. Fluke knew he should take the day off – if he was serious about trying to save their relationship, then taking time to tend to his sick girlfriend was the ideal opportunity to show it – but she wouldn't hear of it. Waved him away and got angry when he protested.

'Just leave me alone, Avison!'

Fluke hadn't put any real thought into where Diamond might be hiding her. It was hard to imagine her fitting in anywhere but the camp at Muncaster. She wouldn't be on one of the estates Diamond controlled; there was far too much police surveillance. That pretty much ruled out Carlisle and most of the towns in West Cumbria. Likewise the quiet villages would be out; strangers were noticed, became a source of gossip. Fluke would have bet she was either in Barrow or out of county.

So, when Diamond had called with the address, it had surprised him. He'd been to it several times before.

Lime House – known by those who'd worked there as 'Slime' – used to be Cumbria Probation Service's headquarters building. Five miles from Carlisle in the village of Wetheral, it had been a grand old building overlooking the village green and war memorial. Cumbria Probation had owned the property until it became a luxury they could no longer afford. They handed it back to the Ministry of Justice and looked for somewhere smaller.

When Fluke had worked in the Public Protection Unit – the department that managed Cumbria's sexual and violent offenders – he'd attended multi-agency meetings at Lime House. He hadn't been back since the MoJ had sold it at a dubiously low price to a developer.

When he turned into Wetheral and saw the new Lime House he winced. What had once been a beautiful, red sandstone building was now covered in glass and chrome. Ugly windows stuck out of the roof like warts. Garish doors had been added – beautiful windows had been removed. The developer had managed to lose all the building's charm and turn it into something from *Footballers' Wives*.

Fluke turned up the drive and parked at the rear. He'd often eaten his lunch out there when meetings stretched on. There'd been a lovely lawn and an apple orchard.

'Fuck a duck,' Towler said.

Indeed.

The lawn and orchard had been replaced by the world's smallest housing estate. Six houses were crammed into what had been a place to sit, relax and think about rapists and psychopaths. They exited the car and stared at what remained of another piece of Cumbria's heritage. Fluke realised how lucky he was to live where he did. Until they invented anti-gravity houses, no one was encroaching on his wood just yet.

'Come on,' Fluke said. 'Let's go and see her.'

Looking at the paper in his hand, he walked up to the door and looked for the name he'd been given. Mr Proctor. He pressed the intercom.

A man answered. 'Yep.' Curt. Direct.

'Fluke.' Two could play at that game.

The door clicked open. They climbed a flight of stairs and found the right apartment. They didn't need to knock. A man Fluke didn't know opened the door and let them in. He didn't follow them in. He'd clearly been told to leave them alone.

If Fluke hadn't known it was Jinx, he wouldn't have recognised her. The transformation from the hippiest of hippies to modern young woman was complete. She'd have fitted into any professional environment. The eclectic garments she had worn had been replaced by a smart trouser suit. The matted dreadlocks had disappeared, replaced by a short, trendy style. The blonde hair was now chestnut and, unbelievably, she was wearing makeup.

But any thoughts she was happy with her new appearance were put to bed by her expression. It was a mixture of acute embarrassment and a scowl that would have shamed an emo.

Fluke flashed Towler a look that said 'keep your mouth shut'. Now wasn't the time to take the piss.

The room they were in screamed taste and money. Stripped

wooden floors, stark white walls and minimal furnishings. A few black and white photos hung from the wall and Fluke instantly recognised the style. He'd be amazed if Mathew, Nathaniel Diamond's partner, hadn't taken them.

Was this apartment a safe house, or the apartment of a close friend or family member? Maybe Nathaniel and Mathew's second home. Their country retreat. Fluke had too many questions and no time to ask them. He put it in a new drawer in the filing cabinet in his head and labelled it, 'Taking Down Nathaniel Diamond: A Fool's Errand'.

Towler was looking around the room. Fluke watched as he picked up a thin, chrome reading lamp and checked the base for something. He turned to Fluke and shrugged.

'Dunno, boss. It could be. No way to tell without proper search equipment.'

What Towler was telling him, without being explicit in front of Jinx, was that he didn't know if anyone was listening. Fluke couldn't see any reason why they would be, but it was a nice day and there was no point risking it.

'Fancy a walk, Jinx?'

The way she bounced off the sofa told him all he needed to know. She might look like a stockbroker but at heart she was still an outside girl.

Chapter 30

Even by modern standards, the Wetheral Viaduct was a breathtaking piece of engineering. Six hundred feet long and a hundred feet in the air, it had been built in the 1830s to carry the Newcastle & Carlisle Railway Company's trains across the River Eden. Like Lime House, it was made of red sandstone. It had five arches, and two of the pillars were in the river. It was an imposing structure. A wooden pedestrian footbridge was fixed to the side; accessed by walking through Wetheral Station and over the cast-iron bridge, which they did.

Jinx seemed to have a head for heights so they walked along the footbridge until they reached the middle. They looked down at the River Eden and along the valley beyond. The view was spectacular. The water shimmered. Birds swooped in and out of the riverbank catching insects. Swans and ducks glided underneath the bridge. A lone angler tried his luck with the sly trout the river was famous for.

Fluke ignored it all. He turned to Jinx and lied to her. 'We haven't been able to find Mark yet, I'm afraid.'

Jinx nodded. She turned to face him. 'Do you think he's dead?' she said.

This was the first time she'd explicitly asked the question. She'd hinted and skirted around it before, but a few days on her own must have focused her thinking.

Fluke didn't want to lie so he elected for more carefully worded sins of omission. He was getting good at it.

'I don't know what's happened. But I need your help to find out.'

Her face scrunched in confusion. Fluke had never met anyone as easy to read. If he hadn't spent so much time with her he'd have sworn it was all an act. No one was that innocent.

'I've told you everything,' she said.

'I know you have, Jinx, I know you have. But I need to ask you a question.'

She looked at him blankly.

'Did Mark give you your iPod?'

'No, I bought it. Why?'

A feeling of defeat crept up his spine. Fluke was on a precipice – if the iPod contained nothing, then he had nothing. He had run out of things he could do. Reyes might get lucky working out the purpose of the device but *he* had nothing left to add.

Jinx lifted his self-pity comfort-blanket. 'I got it after I sold my first dreamcatcher. Mark said I should get something special as a keepsake. He picked it out for me. He's so thoughtful.'

Fluke breathed out a sigh of relief.

'Can I see it?' he said. He didn't want to spook her.

She opened her bag and started searching.

While Fluke waited for her to retrieve it, he watched her surreptitiously. She suited her new look. She was a beautiful woman. She'd occasionally reach up to where her dreadlocks had once been – he'd have loved to have been a fly on the wall when Diamond told her they had to come off – and Fluke was reminded that she had played with them when she was nervous or concentrating.

Jinx found the iPod and handed it over without a word.

'I'm going to have to take this away with me. I need to look at it properly.'

'Could it help you find Mark?'

'It could help us find out what happened to Mark, yes,' he replied.

She nodded, and he put it in his pocket.

Fluke turned to Towler. 'Matt, can you take her back to Slime? Get the car and pick me up at the station. I need to think what to do next.'

Jinx scowled. 'Why can't I go home? What if Mark comes back and I'm not there? Won't he just worry about me?'

'You're going to have to bear with me, Jinx. I need you to stay here just a bit longer.'

She didn't look angry; she looked like someone who didn't understand what was going on.

'Come on, Jinx,' Towler said softly. 'Let's go and get a brew in the Posting Pot. If the boss lends me a tenner I might even stretch to a bit of cake as well.'

Fluke knew the big man was warming to her. The Posting Pot was the local coffee shop. It overlooked the village green and was well known for cakes, sandwiches and artisan coffees and teas. He reached into his wallet and handed over a twenty-pound note.

'I want change,' he said.

'No chance,' Towler said, winking at Jinx.

Fluke didn't watch Towler lead Jinx away, but he could hear them talking. Towler was trying to make amends for past transgressions.

'And how about I teach you some moves? Just in case someone tries to harm you. Not promising you'll be the next Karate Kid, but I can show you how to twist a man's balls so hard they'll swell up like a pair of mangos.'

Fluke didn't hear her reply but Towler laughed at whatever it was she'd said.

Fluke hadn't needed time to think. He'd wanted to have a first forensic look at the iPod, and because he didn't know what he was going to find, he didn't want to do it with Jinx there. He knew his way around Apple products more than he'd care to admit. He was a self-confessed technophobe but enjoyed the benefits of an iPhone, and knew an iPod Touch was essentially the same machine. One could make calls, the other couldn't.

Opening up the email icon he went straight for the obvious. An account that wasn't hers. One of the oldest, and still the best, ways of concealing information was having a shared account and leaving information in a draft email.

Nothing.

Not only was there no additional email account, there was no email account at all.

Another, less secure, method would be the photo album. It was possible Bish had simply taken photos of anything he fancied the look of, including some handwritten notes, which could then be destroyed.

Fluke opened it up.

There were hundreds, possibly thousands, of photos. She'd already shown him and Bridie some, of course, but he hadn't had the inclination to look at more than a dozen. There were none of Bish anyway.

He opened the first few. They were in reverse chronological order. The newest one was of the war memorial at Wetheral. Jinx must have taken it recently. Fluke scrolled back further. They were all as he remembered; the camp and life on the road. Things she and the others had made. He flicked through about fifty before closing it. They'd need to be properly analysed but he doubted there was anything there. The iPod wasn't password protected so anyone could have looked. Bish wouldn't have been that careless.

Fluke did a bit of mental reversing. He'd assumed that when he opened the album there would be photos of everyone and everything. There were. Hundreds of them. But the others, the ones he'd also expected to see, were conspicuous by their absence.

Because what was the one thing he knew they liked?

Each other.

212

And from what he'd seen so far, the pictures in the iPod's photo album were far from intimate . . .

Where were the ones of them in the altogether? In the buff. Nude. Starkers. Wouldn't two people, as madly in love as Jinx professed they were, be snapping away at each other all day and night? Of course they would. And only an idiot kept dick-pics where anyone could see them . . .

But these days you didn't have to have them where any pervert could scroll through them. Fluke knew you could download apps that acted as digital safes. Somewhere secure to store your risqué photographs. They were password protected even if the device they were on wasn't. And, of course, the app let you put in anything you wanted; you weren't restricted to naughty, 'bound-to-end-up-on-the-internet-eventually' photographs and videos.

You could upload other photographs. *Classified* photos. You could make notes and photograph those notes.

You could be the key witness in your own murder investigation . . .

Fluke searched for an app that looked like a vault. Jinx didn't have many and the apps she did have were weird ones like the lunar clock. Nothing that looked remotely like a secure photo album.

It didn't matter though. Some of the more sophisticated apps were designed to look like something else. You could even pro-gramme them to open and be something else if the right password wasn't used. A secure photo vault could also act as an alarm clock, a game – virtually anything.

And when you had a bit of electronic bullshit that was doing your nut in, you didn't persevere with it.

You just gave it to Jiao-long.

Chapter 31

By the time Jiao-long arrived at Carleton Hall, the iPod had been round everyone in the room. They all seemed to have their own methods of hiding stuff on their phones. Fluke found it all a bit disturbing. He must be old fashioned; there wasn't anything on his phone worth hiding.

Reyes hadn't objected when Fluke said Jiao-long was going to run the tech. He'd asked Fluke where the iPod had come from and had accepted a weak explanation. 'Someone in the camp was looking after it for Jinx' wasn't a great lie, but it allowed everyone to save face.

Jiao-long was on a day off, but had driven straight in. He walked into the massed ranks of FMIT and NDEDIU without showing concern.

Fluke told the Beijing detective that he suspected Bish had been using the iPod to hide things. Jiao-long began flicking through it.

Reyes turned to Fluke. 'We'll give him a day then send it to our lab in—'

'Found it,' Jiao-long said.

Instead of explaining, Jiao-long removed a black lead from his bag, attached one end to the iPod and the other to one of the sixty-inch monitors on the incident-room wall. The iPod's home screen flickered into view. Everyone made space so they could see.

'This icon here,' Jiao-long said, pointing to the top right of the monitor, 'the one looking like a calculator, isn't. It's a vault.' He pressed the icon on the iPod and the monitor changed into a calculator. 'It will do calculations but, and this is the clever part, if you press the multiply, percentage and division signs at the same time' – he pressed them – 'this happens.'

Another screen appeared. This one had four boxes.

'It's a secure vault to store photographs and videos. Very sneaky. And it still needs a four-number password.'

'Can you hack it, Longy?' Towler asked.

Jiao-long paused a moment. 'I probably have some software that can crack it faster than the stuff IT use. I'll go and get my laptop. Shouldn't take long.'

Fluke looked at Towler and smiled. His sergeant blinked a couple of times then smiled back.

'No need, Longy,' Fluke said. 'I know what the number is. Type in nine – four – six – five.'

Jiao-long entered the numbers and the app opened. A menu appeared. Fluke could have chosen to keep it to himself, but he thought he'd used up all the goodwill he was going to get with Reyes and his team.

'Any of your lot ever served, John?'

Reyes shook his head. 'No.'

Fluke turned to Towler. 'You want to talk them through it, Matt?'

'They'll be the last four digits of his regimental number. Like police badge numbers, they're used to tell people apart when they have the same surname. It's not too bad in the regiments the boss and I served in. Bootnecks and Paras recruit from all over the UK so there's a good selection of surnames. But you serve in the Welsh Guards and see what happens when you shout for Guardsman Jones. Half the fucking battalion comes running. So it'll be, "Jones 2345" or "Evans 6789". Only way it works. Your "last four" are imprinted on you for ever. The boss'll have known Mark Bishop's just as well as he'd have known his own.'

Reyes seemed satisfied that Fluke hadn't been withholding even more information. He turned to Jiao-long and asked him to open the vault's contents.

'Hold on a minute, Longy,' Fluke said.

'Problem?' Reyes asked.

'Yes,' Fluke said. 'This was my friend. If all there is in there is dirty pictures then it's going to be a closed set. You can have one person in the room while we scan them for anything embarrassing.'

'Fair enough,' Reyes said. 'I'll stay.'

Fluke nodded. 'That goes for you lot too,' he said to FMIT. 'Longy, you need to stay, but otherwise you can all wait outside.'

When the room was clear, Jiao-long pressed a couple of buttons and brought up a gallery of pictures. He pressed the slideshow icon. Each picture remained on the monitor for approximately ten seconds. Jiao-long fiddled about in preferences and it speeded up. The next one stayed there for barely three seconds.

The first few were all of camp life. Bish was in some but not many. He was probably taking the pictures. Most of them were of Jinx with other camp members. She was rarely in the centre of the photographs though.

'Look at that,' Fluke said, pointing at the wall monitor. 'Although Jinx is in all these photos, the focus is really the other person. He's been using Jinx as cover to get pictures of everyone in the camp. Very clever.'

Reyes nodded in agreement.

After about thirty photos the atmosphere changed. Gone were the happy faces. The poses for the camera. The showing off. Instead there were pictures that had clearly been taken surreptitiously. They weren't brilliant quality. Jiao-long changed the setting so they were on the screen longer. They viewed them one after the other without anything too obvious appearing.

A photo appeared and Reyes shouted, 'Stop!'

The screen froze.

It was a murky picture of three men standing together. Two of the men were listening to the third man. He stood a good six inches above them both. It looked like Bish had been holding the iPod by his side and hoping for the best when he took the pictures. The two men talking to the taller one were frustratingly indistinct – despite not having much directional control over his photographs, it was clear who was the focus of his attention.

'That's Vane, DI Fluke,' Reyes said. 'First name unknown. Last name unknown. Purpose unknown.'

Fluke stared at the man they suspected of being Bish's killer.

Not only was Vane tall, even on camera he had gravitas. There was no doubt he was in charge. Some people were leaders, some weren't. Fluke was a leader. He knew that to be true just as much as he knew Cameron Chambers and John Reyes weren't; they were managers.

Vane was dressed the same as everyone else in the camp: a scruffy, nondescript top and a pair of combat trousers. His hair was long and had the obligatory dreadlocks. His face was covered in dense stubble.

'And the other two?'

'No idea,' Reyes said. 'Mark never got their real names but he said they were unimportant, little more than hangers on. Vane was the only one who knew what was going on.'

'Let's see the rest, Longy,' Fluke said. The photo of Bish's probable killer was unnerving him.

Jiao-long restarted the slideshow. The next picture appeared.

'Stop!' This time it was Fluke shouting.

The photo on screen was of the device in its unassembled state. It must have been taken after Vane had secured delivery, as it was in an open-sided khaki canvas bag – the kind used for large tents. It was tied tightly at one end but the other end was unfastened. If Fluke had to guess, he'd say Bish had been the one to unfasten it. Fluke could only admire his balls. Working undercover was one thing; to risk his life taking pictures such as this was another thing entirely. For a second Fluke wondered if Bish had been caught in the act, before realising they wouldn't be looking at the photos now if he had.

It would have been a revelation a day ago, but the photo was nowhere near as detailed as the ones Dan had taken.

'We've seen this already. Move on, Longy,' Fluke said.

Bish had clearly had just the one opportunity to photograph the device, as the next photos were all of camp residents.

Until they got to the last photograph there was nothing else of interest.

But the last one changed everything.

Chapter 32

Bish *had* found a way of taking and hiding his notes and observations. He'd utilised the iPod's default Notes app – a simple word-processing app that allowed the user to make multiple notes on any subject they wanted. Combined with the iPod's screenshot function and the vault app, Bish had been able to protect his notes as well as his photographs.

Fluke knew the note on the wall monitor was no longer in the iPod's Notes app – it had been one of the first places he'd checked while standing on the viaduct bridge. Bish had obviously written his note, taken a screenshot, then copied the screenshot to the vault app. He'd then deleted both the note and the original screenshot in the photo album. Simple but flawless.

Fluke stared open mouthed at the note on the screen. His heart was racing.

The notes were in bullet point form. The first three were useful.

- Vane – real name Kevin Hendricks?
- Thermos sized package received by V.
- Dan's metal thing now functional. V won't say what it's for. Package and device now both hidden.

They'd likely never know how Bish got Vane's name but, however he did, it was gold. With a name came intelligence and with intelligence came a profile. And profiles led to sexy police

219

terminology such as modus operandi. The real name of the killer is usually everything.

But not this time. This time Bish had one more surprise left.

Fluke read the fourth bullet point and gasped. He reread it. It wasn't possible. *Couldn't* be possible. He broke out into a shuddering cold sweat.

The last bullet point was the game changer to end all game changers.

- Must've misheard V earlier. Overheard him on phone and he said the word 'Choreographer'. Can't be surely? Will pass on to Z anyway.

Fluke shouted for Towler. He came in and read the note. His jaw dropped when he read the last bullet point.

'Holy fucking shit,' he said.

'It can't be, Matt,' Fluke said. 'It can't be.'

'Holy fucking shit,' Towler said again.

By now everyone was back in the room. No one was looking at the screen. All eyes were on Fluke and Towler.

'You know Kevin Hendricks?' Reyes asked.

Fluke and Towler shook their heads at the same time.

'Not a fucking scooby, mate,' Towler said. He was shaken enough to forget his rank. Reyes ignored him.

Fluke was about to say something similar, but a small yet powerful voice inside his head stopped him. Kevin Hendricks? Had he heard that name recently? It was ringing bells but not loudly enough to point him anywhere useful. It was a common name and he read lots of briefings and intelligence reports. It was probably on one of those. If the name had already cropped up in the investigation, HOLMES would make the connection. Still, he had a feeling the name Kevin Hendricks would be a pea under his mattress for a while . . .

Reyes continued. 'The Choreographer then? What's that?'

Fluke reached for a drink and drained his cold coffee. He looked Reyes in the eye and held his gaze. He was about to say something stupid but he needed him to take it seriously.

'John, there's no other way of saying this. The Choreographer is a ghost.'

Chapter 33

Belfast, Northern Ireland

The bullet missed Fluke's head by no more than an inch. He heard, rather than saw it punch into the brightly coloured mural to his left. Before the round's sonic boom cracked the air, he was already on the pavement scrabbling for cover. As the last man in the four-man brick, he saw his fellow marines do exactly the same.

The shot had come from over his shoulder and, despite adrenaline flooding his body, he was savvy enough to change direction and crawl to the only cover immediately available from a sniper in that direction. The road. The high kerb afforded some protection. Not much though. If the sniper knew what he was doing, Fluke was a clichéd sitting duck. He pushed his head as far into the kerb as it would go. Luckily there was a drain, which meant a natural dip in the road. He was fairly certain that from where the sniper was, a head shot was out. He looked down the length of his body. Plenty of other organs were still exposed though. Some of his favourite organs in fact . . .

Ten yards ahead of him, Bish was radioing HQ to tell them they were under fire. 'Zero, Whiskey Echo Foxtrot. Contact. Wait, out.'

There was excitement in his voice but he remained calm.

HQ was always called 'Zero'. 'Whiskey Echo Foxtrot' was the brick's own call-sign and 'contact' meant they'd come under effective enemy fire. 'Wait' meant further information would come when available, and 'out' was Bish signing off. There would be nothing more until the situation became clearer. Fluke knew their 'contact' meant the Quick Reaction Force, commonly called the QRF, would be scrambled back at HQ, and they'd be sprinting to their Saracen six-wheeled armoured personnel carriers. They'd be desperate to help their friends, but even if they set off now they'd be a while. And they couldn't leave base until a full sit-rep was radioed in. Fluke could hear Bish back on the radio telling Zero what they knew so far.

'Pinned down by a sniper,' he shouted, high on adrenaline, 'no idea where the fucker is!' Radio protocols weren't always followed in the middle of hot contacts. Bish listened to Zero's reply before snapping, 'Up my fucking arse, you REMF bastard! Out!'

Fluke didn't want to know what was up Bish's arse but REMF was military slang for Rear Echelon Motherfucker. For Bish's sake, he hoped Zero was someone with a sense of humour. He'd done the right thing though; the officer on duty shouldn't be pressing soldiers under fire for details they couldn't possibly know yet. If they were going to get out of this, everyone needed to stay calm and allow their training and drills to take over, and that included headquarters.

Fluke reckoned it would be at least a minute before they had a grip of the situation. Best guess was the QRF were ten minutes away. More than enough time for the sniper to pick one or more of them off.

Or worse, turn him into a one-bollocked man.

He swivelled on the road, and risked a glance behind him. The bullet had taken a chunk out of the knee of some rebel hero painted on the wall. Despite his pounding heart and rasping breath, he started to laugh. The IRA had just kneecapped one of their own.

The brick commander, Lance Corporal Noel Holten, had leapt into a garden and was taking cover behind a red brick wall. Bish was the most fortunate. The first bang had happened just as he was walking past a postbox. An Armalite – the IRA's sniper rifle of choice – with its accurate but piss-weak 5.56-mm rounds, wouldn't get through all that cast iron.

The fourth marine in the brick was even more exposed than Fluke. Bereft of cover, he zigzagged across the road and joined him in the gutter.

'All right, Flukey?' the marine grinned at him. 'Good 'ere, innit?' He was called Tommo and looked as scared as Fluke felt. 'We gonna send something back?'

Fluke shook his head as much as the drain cover would allow. 'No idea where he is, Tommo. Bish or the boss'll have to spot him for us. I'm keeping my fucking head down until then.'

For a moment he thought Tommo was going to disagree. But eventually he grinned. 'You're fucking right, mate,' he said. He twisted and shouted to Bish and Holten, 'Get a fucking move on, you two!'

'You two shagging in the gutter?' Bish shouted back. 'Dirty bastards.'

Fluke and Tommo looked at each other and rolled their eyes. Nothing was sacred in the Marines; everything had a piss-taking value.

For a few seconds the only sound was their heavy breathing, but that didn't last long. Another shot rang out. It zipped off the road. Fluke pushed himself further into the kerb.

'Fucking hurry up!' he yelled. 'We're sitting fucking ducks out here!'

The name and numbers on Tommo's dog-tags were clearly visible through his sweat-soaked T-shirt. Fluke knew his would be the same.

'What's the fucking rush?' Bish said.

Despite the flippancy, Fluke knew Bish and Holten would be desperately searching for the target. Tommo grinned at him. They were Royal Marines and they were pinned down by a sniper on the Falls Road. It didn't get more exciting. Fluke grinned back.

In some Catholic areas of West Belfast, attacks on soldiers were something to look forward to. A bit of light entertainment in an otherwise dreary existence. On the Falls Road, if residents weren't actual IRA, they were IRA sympathisers. Before long, Fluke could hear rebel songs being chanted behind curtains. He ignored them. Royal Marines were despised on the Falls Road, and insults had been a feature of every day of his tour. To be honest, Fluke didn't blame them. They'd behaved just as bad. The first patrols of their four-month tour involved introducing the faces of every known player to the butts of their SLRs. Knock them about a bit; let them know real soldiers were now on their estates and shit wasn't going to be taken. On every thug they rolled, a calling card was stuck to their forehead with a drawing pin. 'The Boys Are Back in Town' it said.

And they were.

And now they were lying with their heads in a shitty gutter, listening to rounds ping off the road, as the sniper adjusted his distance.

Payback was a bitch.

The shooting stopped. The sniper had either fucked off, was *pretending* to have fucked off, or was reloading. There was no way to know.

The IRA only ever fired on armed soldiers when there was an obstacle between the patrol and the sniper. A dual-carriageway, the Lagan Canal, a gap in a street; anything to slow down the inevitable response and make their withdrawal easier. It was what made them so dangerous. The Marines were constantly evolving their tactics but so were they. The IRA only had to be lucky once; the Marines had to be lucky every time. But, as their colonel had said before they left Plymouth, 'The harder we train, the luckier we'll be.'

Fluke risked a glance at where he thought the shot had come from. He saw a gap between two semi-detached houses. The sniper had almost certainly used it as cover and fired from at least two streets away. If he was still there, they were too exposed. If he'd disappeared into the warren of West Belfast then they needed to start getting cordons and roadblocks arranged. Fluke glanced at Bish and the brick commander. Both were desperately scanning the area. They needed the sniper's location.

Another shot pinged into the already scarred pavement. It left a deep gouge. Fluke pushed himself further into the drain's dip.

They'd been in the same place for too long now. One of the more successful tactics of the IRA was to set up a kill zone. Pin a patrol in an area of their choosing, so someone closer could throw a grenade or an IED.

They had to move. Start to reclaim the initiative.

The brick commander had obviously come to the same conclusion. Using hand signals he instructed them to get ready to move. Without thinking, Fluke checked his ammunition pouches to make sure they hadn't opened during the dive to the ground.

'Wait!' the brick commander shouted.

Fluke clung to the kerb again, wondering why the move order had been cancelled. He tilted his face up, and saw why. An old lady, oblivious to the four marines, was walking into the middle of them.

She was holding a letter and walking towards Bish's postbox. The brick commander's indecision was obvious. She was heading right into the kill zone and the IRA weren't squeamish about sacrificing civilians . . .

She walked with a stoop and was pushing a tartan-patterned trolley. Despite the heat she was well wrapped up. She was wearing a headscarf, a large overcoat and gloves. Fluke was only wearing a thin smock, and he'd been sweating since seven o'clock that morning.

The old woman paused and reached into her trolley. Probably had another letter in there.

Oh well, better to ask for forgiveness than permission, Fluke thought. If the brick commander wasn't going to do anything, he would. He leapt up and ran to the old woman. His brick commander screamed at him but Fluke ignored him. If he reached her he could shepherd her into a nearby doorway. At least she'd be safer than they were.

Ten yards away and the situation changed dramatically. The old woman looked at Fluke and grinned. Her hands came up from the trolley and in each one she was holding a grenade.

Time stopped for Fluke. There was no flashing image of his life, no regrets about lost love. Just a sense that he'd seriously fucked up.

'Die, you fucking Brit bastard!' came the guttural shout.

In that split second, one that would wake him up screaming for years to come, Fluke knew two things. It was no old woman holding the grenades, and he was about to die.

He desperately tried to swing his SLR into a firing position, but the barrel was too long and the arc too great. He wasn't going to make it. He shut his eyes and waited.

Boom!

For the second time in as many minutes, Fluke felt a bullet zip past his head. He opened his eyes and saw the old woman/young man staring sightlessly at him, a third eye in the middle of his forehead. Like a felled tree, the IRA man toppled backwards and hit the pavement with a sickening thud. It didn't matter; he'd been dead as soon as the bullet hit him. His grenades dropped on the pavement beside him. Fluke was about to yell for everyone to take cover when he noticed the pins were still in. They were harmless.

Fluke heard footsteps behind him and turned. The brick commander hit him across the side of the head.

'What the fuck did you think you were doing?' he screamed. 'Arsehole! Now, get into some fucking cover and wait for the QRF. Ours are all busy so we're getting the Queen's Lancashire

Regiment's. You're a Royal Marine, fucking act like one. That sniper's still out there somewhere and I don't want to tell them northern bastards we've been too busy hiding to fucking look for him. And Bish,' he added, 'fucking well done. At least someone was concentrating.'

Fluke didn't move. The sniper would be long gone. The whole plan had been to pin them down then take them out with a grenade. He stood on the road looking down at the dead man. Footsteps from behind caused him to turn again.

'Fuckin' hell, mate, what a shot that was. Had to aim right over your shoulder. No one else had a line of sight on him.' He bent down to look at the corpse. Blood and brains were spilling out of his skull and onto the pavement. 'Bang! Right in the fuckin' 'ead!'

Fluke said nothing.

'You OK?' his friend asked, but got no response. The sirens of the QRF could be heard in the distance. They were less than a minute away. Because grenades had been used, the QRF would now be coming to their location rather than the sniper's. Explosive devices had to be secured as quickly as possible. Northern Ireland protocol.

'Poor bastard,' Fluke said eventually. What made someone dress up as a woman to try to get close to some of the most highly trained soldiers in the world. It didn't make sense. Even if he'd managed to throw the grenades, it was doubtful he would have killed more than one of them. They all had cover of some sort. The only person in any real danger had been Fluke, and that was only because he'd messed up. As plans went it was a stupid one.

'Fuck it,' Bish said. 'We'll be laughing about this tonight.'

'You think so?' Fluke wasn't so sure. This was the first time he'd seen a corpse and he felt as though he shouldn't be looking at it. This was someone's son, someone's brother.

This whole operation was bothering him. He went through the sequence of events. Tried to see it from the IRA's angle. They were on a patrol. They'd been shot at and took the only available cover. The sniper hadn't hit any of them and now Fluke was wondering if that had been intentional. If he'd tagged any of them they'd have ignored their Yellow Cards and shot the shit out of anything that moved. They'd have also bugged out sharpish. No point staying pinned down if you were being picked off. And it would've been anyone's guess which direction they'd have headed. Probably through the front door of the first house. No way of knowing.

If the purpose was just to keep them in the same place, the sniper wouldn't have wanted to hit any of them. He'd have just kept them there with the occasional shot.

Just like he had done . . .

Pinning them down in a prearranged kill zone was professional. A buffoon dressed as an old woman – who hadn't even known grenades had to be unpinned – not so much. It made no sense. They were missing something.

He ignored what had happened and concentrated on what was *yet* to happen. The throaty growls of the QRF Saracens could be heard as they closed on their location; belting through the streets on the most direct route they could take. Supporting stranded patrols and securing explosives was exactly what the QRF was for.

I wonder if the person behind all this knew that? Fluke thought. Because if they'd wanted a Saracen in this location, at this time, they'd done everything right. But why would they? The IRA had nothing that would dent the heavily armoured wheeled vehicles, and there was no intelligence to suggest that they were getting anywhere near.

And it wasn't even their Saracen. The Royal Marines' QRFs were all on the other side of the city – the brick commander had told them that not five minutes ago.

Fluke shouted across to Bish who was still looking through the telescopic sights on his SLR, scanning windows and rooftops for

229

the sniper. He turned at the sound of Fluke's voice and raised his eyebrows. 'What's up?'

He went straight back to scoping out the skyline.

'Radio Zero for me, would you? Find out why our QRF isn't free.'

Without taking his eyes from the task, he reached down with one hand and pressed the button pinned to his lapel. 'Zero, sit-rep on our own QRF vehicles, please.' The radio he was using had a throat mic so he didn't have to lower his rifle. Bish was wearing a one-earpiece headset so Fluke didn't hear the reply. Bish listened and frowned. 'Say again, over.'

Bish took his hand off the mic button and called out to Fluke. 'Three bomb threats, mate. All called in within a fifteen-minute period. Our QRFs are all on crowd control.'

'Cheers.' Fluke crouched down behind a garden wall and thought about the ambush. Whoever had planned it must have known that there was more than one regiment operating in Belfast. It was common knowledge. And the Queen's Lancashire Regiment, hailing from towns such as Blackburn and Burnley, were hardly shrinking violets. It was a tough regiment, and although they were having a hard tour, they weren't shirking it. Fluke knew they'd be here as quickly as they could and they wouldn't hesitate to put themselves in harm's way to get the marines out of trouble.

But they had a long journey and their most direct route would be to come in from the other end of the Falls Road.

The derelict end.

Where no civilians lived.

The purpose of the ambush became clear.

Fluke leapt over the low wall and sprinted to Bish. The brick commander moved to cut him off. He grabbed him by the arm.

'Fluke, I'm not telling you again. Get behind some fucking cover!'

Fluke tried to jerk himself free but Holten had him in a vice-like grip.

'We're not the fucking targets!' he screamed. 'It's not us! It's the fucking QRF they want!'

The brick commander let Fluke go, stared at him for a moment and then said, 'Oh, shit!' He turned to Bish and shouted, 'Bishop, get a fucking halt on them! Tell them the route might not be safe!'

Bish reached up to his lapel again and pressed the mic button.

And just as he did, the air pressure changed. It was followed by the inevitable crump of an explosion and the all too familiar screams.

They were too late.

Chapter 34

'They opened up the Saracen like a can of beans. There were eight boys from the Queen's Lancashire Regiment in the back, plus the driver and the vehicle commander. Four of them died and two never walked again.'

Fluke told his story to a silent room. If anyone had questions, they were waiting until he'd finished. He stopped and looked round. Everyone was staring at him. Even Towler, who'd heard the story many times before.

'The man with the grenades?' a member from the London contingent asked.

'Terminally ill fanatic,' Fluke said. 'To the best of my knowledge, it was the only time the IRA ever used a suicide bomber. He was only there to make sure the Saracen came to our location from the direction they wanted.'

Zoe was frowning. 'But what was the point of it all? I mean, why bother going to all that trouble to set a bomb off? Surely there were easier ways to kill British soldiers?'

'That's enough, Zoe!' Reyes snapped. The first time he'd spoken for a while.

But she was like a dog with a bone and Fluke knew why. She wanted to know how this related to the name on Bish's list. She was going to ask another question and he could see Reyes getting angry.

He held his hand up to placate him.

'She's right, John. An IRA cell, disguised as council workers,

232

had dug up the road and buried a pipe bomb the day before. It had a shaped-charge we'd never encountered before and it was in a part of the Falls we didn't go.'

'But how does all that relate to Mark's note?' She gestured towards the wall monitor to emphasise her point.

Fluke told them what MI5, and 42 Commando's own intelligence, had concluded. 'The killing of soldiers wasn't the IRA's main objective that day. What they really wanted was to show we weren't safe in our little armoured trucks any more. We had to change all our protocols mid-tour, and after six months' prep, I might add. The Saracens all had to be retrofitted with additional armour to reflect the new threat. And during that time, with no armoured QRFs available for operational support, patrolling was kept to a bare minimum. More troops had to be deployed and that meant units were withdrawn from their NATO bases in Germany. From our annoyed allies to the Prime Minister, no one was impressed by what happened that day.'

Fluke paused, and refilled his cup. He might not like them, but he had to admit the team from the Met had some good coffee. He breathed in the rich, smoky aroma.

No one, including the remaining members of FMIT, had taken their eyes off Fluke as he'd refilled his mug. He sat back down and continued.

'MI5 hit their snouts hard. We hit ours harder. Four boys from Skelmersdale had died and we felt responsible. We didn't fuck about. Everyone was brought in. And eventually a name started to appear.'

'The Choreographer?' Zoe asked.

Fluke nodded. 'The Choreographer.'

Like Moriarty in Arthur Conan Doyle's Victorian London, it began as a rumour – easily dismissed and easily forgotten. But with everyone saying the same thing, some of them after having bones broken – the marines were not gentle souls – people began to pay attention.

'The Choreographer was supposed to be an IRA strategist of unequalled brilliance,' Fluke said. 'Never missed, and played the long game. Wasn't interested in killing for killing's sake. When he planned something it had serious knock-on effects; a change in tactics, a backlash in public opinion. He wanted the Brits out of Northern Ireland. Period.'

He drained yet another cup of Reyes's fine coffee.

'The name came up enough times for an inquiry to be launched. It was undertaken quietly and only a select few in the MoD were allowed to read it. When it was viewed as favourable, an executive summary was circulated more widely. It concluded the IRA had just got lucky that day. Nothing more. A perfect storm created the ideal environment. The vehicle commander was demoted. He shouldn't have driven up that end of the Falls, despite SOPs stating that when there were unsecured explosives the most direct route had to be taken.'

'And?' Skelton asked. Fluke knew she was asking if the Choreographer was real.

'Propaganda. Top brass wanted nothing to do with an IRA bogeyman. And to be fair, some of his supposed operations were so far-fetched it did seem like all their successes, no matter how lucky, were attributed to him. There was a blue-on-blue contact – a patrol of Grenadier Guards shot at a patrol of the Devon and Dorsets. Total screw up, something to do with wrong radio frequencies. Regardless of the reasons, a soldier from Taunton was shot in the ankle. The IRA claimed it was the work of the Choreographer. Total bollocks, of course, and because of things like that we all came to believe the report had got it right: that the Choreographer didn't exist.'

'What did you think, boss?'

'An IRA mastermind? Luring squaddies into increasingly

complex and cunning traps? I didn't think so then and I don't think so now.'

'But Mark—' Zoe interrupted.

'Got it wrong,' Fluke snapped. 'This isn't an international conspiracy we're investigating here. John, if your lot want to chase rumours, be my guest.'

Reyes, however, didn't want to consider a puppet-master called the Choreographer was behind it all either. A man called Vane was his suspect and he now had a name. Kevin Hendricks. Jiao-long had already checked PNC and PND, but without a date of birth or an address the computer had churned out hundreds of names. HOLMES confirmed the name hadn't come up in the investigation yet either. The net was tightening though. Fluke would contribute to the hunt by tasking Jo Skelton, Alan Vaughn and Jiao-long to help Reyes and his team.

He and Towler had something else to do.

Chapter 35

Fluke's first task was to go and see Dan the blacksmith-cum-blade-smith. He couldn't really spare the time, and should have delegated the task to someone else, but he felt responsible.

Dan had never been a suspect in Fluke's eyes. At best, he was a person of interest. Although one of his swords did have Bish's blood on it, no one seriously thought he was involved. Not even Reyes; he still had his eyes on the double prize of Vane and Jinx. Vane was their killer; Jinx his accessory.

The murder weapon also had a number of other prints on it, one of which was a match for the ones Bish had lifted from Vane some time ago. Convicting him was looking more and more like a slam-dunk.

Catching him though . . .

Dan was still in the cells at West Area Headquarters in Workington, an hour away from Carleton Hall. Speed was of the essence so Fluke put his foot down and sped along the A66 as fast as his BMW would let him. Towler hung on to the over-head handle as Fluke navigated some of the steeper bends. Luckily most of the road was either fairly straight or dual-carriageway and he shaved twenty minutes off the journey. Towler had rung ahead and warned traffic that a dark blue BMW might be passing them at over a hundred miles an hour and it wasn't to be pulled.

The car park was full so Fluke pulled up right outside the door. He turned to Towler and said, 'Stay here. If some wanker wants the car moved, move it. I'll be ten minutes, max.'

Fluke was back in eight. Dan was in tow. They shook hands and Fluke climbed back into the driver's seat. The window was already down. Fluke leaned out. 'Sorry again, Dan. A car will be along soon to take you back to Muncaster.' He removed his wallet, extracted a cheap card and handed it through the window. 'You can get me on this number – day or night.'

Dan, his ever-present smile still etched on his face, took it, shook Fluke's hand and walked over to a bench to sit in the sun and wait.

'That seemed to go well?' Towler had turned in his seat to watch Dan as Fluke wheel spun out of the car park.

'Better than we could reasonably expect,' Fluke said.

Towler looked at his watch. 'What time's the plane?'

There were twenty-two Newcastle to Belfast flights each week, and they were booked on the first available one; a budget airline leaving at ten-to-three in the afternoon.

Fluke had only half-lied to Jo Skelton earlier. When he'd been in Northern Ireland he *had* bought the official version; the Choreographer was nothing more than IRA scaremongering – the make-believe hero of a disenfranchised people. A bit like Robin Hood had been. He'd been a young marine and believed his country would do right by him. The best part of twenty years later, and after countless government scandals, he now knew that this was rarely the case. The country did what was best for the country. Correction, he thought. The country did what was best for the people *running* the country. Old Etonians, Old Harrovians, Old Paedonians, self-entitled idiots obsessed with the past and frightened of anything not directly designed for them.

Now he was older and wiser – and with the blueprint already pointing at an Irish connection – he wasn't so keen to dismiss the Choreographer. Not this time. Not when his friend had died

237

getting the name. He was also reminded that the full report had never been made public, only the executive summary. And executive summaries could say something different to the body of the main report. Selective interpretation here, dismissal of key findings there, and the summary could say what you wanted it to say. Fluke knew this as he'd done it himself when he'd investigated cops who'd stepped over the line but hadn't deserved to lose their jobs.

Fluke knew MI5 should be informed. They still had eyes and ears in Belfast. They had databases even Jiao-long couldn't get into. They were the best agency for a job with an Irish connection. But if he did, Fluke knew the case would be taken from Reyes and they'd never hear anything about it again. MI5 was not known for playing well with others and he'd put too much time in the case to give it up now.

Anyway, so what if he didn't have their resources, their databases, their long-term experience of running covert ops in Northern Ireland?

He had Towler.

And Towler was worth his weight in gold. He'd worked in Belfast at least three times and knew all the players. Knew who was a hard-core militant and who'd only ever been in it for the money and the girls. Now the Troubles were officially over, some of the latter might be open to talking.

Especially if the price was right.

They arrived at Newcastle Airport half an hour before departure. As they were supposed to check in an hour before their flight, it meant they were late. Abandoning Fluke's car in short-term parking, they ran through the small airport until they reached their gate.

As neither of them had luggage they were through quickly. The plane had stopped loading but the flight attendant reopened the gate when they flashed their warrant badges.

Towler looked at his watch. 'Ten minutes to take off, fifty-five minute flight – excellent, I'm getting my head down for an hour.' Within a minute he was snoring.

Fluke, who had never been able to sleep while sitting upright, settled down to think through his next moves. There were long odds on them finding out anything useful in Belfast but he needed to keep going and, for now at least, tracking down Vane was a computer search job – not a 'boots on the ground' job. At least this way he felt he was moving forwards.

And he was still getting jaggy splinters from the name Kevin Hendricks. It sounded familiar but he didn't know why. It was a common enough name but Fluke was irritated he couldn't shake the feeling.

Zoe Koenig popped into his mind. She'd clearly loved Bish. It may well have been reciprocated. Bish used to discard women without putting much thought into how he did it. Letting them down gently hadn't been a major strength of his. Was it possible she'd done something stupid when she'd found out he'd got married? Of course it was possible, he thought. Murders had been committed for far less.

He dismissed Dan as a suspect completely. For the sword-maker to actually kill someone with a sword he'd made, then keep said sword, un-sanitised, in his own trailer, was either the world's biggest double bluff or proof he'd had nothing to do with it. Fluke, trained by the best to detect lies, had seen nothing in Dan's micro-expressions to indicate any form of deceit.

Jinx was even more of an outside bet; longer odds than Dan and Zoe put together. She was just too innocent. Just too in love with Bish. And to spend days and nights in the same house as the man investigating the murder she'd just committed – that was even more implausible than Dan keeping hold of the murder weapon.

All roads led to Vane.

He was the perfect suspect; means, motive and opportunity.

He was well resourced. He looked physically capable. It was possible he'd discovered Bish was an undercover cop and, because of the group dynamics, his opportunities would have been endless.

The 'fasten seatbelts' sign pinged. He looked across at Towler. His shirt was wet from the accumulated drool seeping from his open mouth.

'Unbelievable,' he said.

The last time Fluke had been in Belfast someone had shot at him. Back then it had been the most dangerous city in Europe and, although that dubious crown may have passed to Moscow or Sofia, it still wasn't exactly safe. The 1998 Good Friday Agreement might have been the beginning of the end of terrorism in Northern Ireland, but the organisations left behind had been big machines. It was naive to think they could be stopped with the signing of a bit of paper. The idealists did, of course. They got the best political settlement they could, then laid down their arms and rebuilt their lives. But there was also the faction nobody talked about, the ones who had only ever been in it for the money and the status. For them, the Good Friday Agreement had been a disaster. Analogue thugs in a digital age, they turned to what they knew: crime. With an effective infrastructure already in place, they became successful. Drugs, kidnappings and extortion proved to be far more profitable than pipe bombs and assassinations. They became organised criminal gangs, dangerous and heavily armed, ready to protect their interests and themselves.

Fluke was taking no chances. He wanted in and out. And, although the flights didn't allow for a one-day visit, he intended to be on the first available commuter plane the day after.

Even Towler was quiet when they left the airport and got in a taxi. Fluke had completed two tours of Belfast. Towler had done three. Or to be precise, he'd told Fluke about three. It was possible he'd also been there doing jobs he couldn't tell him about. Towler took his special forces days seriously and only ever spoke about them in broad brushstrokes.

'You gonna let me lead, boss?' Towler asked. 'I know someone who'll give us a pointer on the man we need to find.'

Fluke raised his eyebrows.

'McGinty's the man we're eventually after. Bit of a legend in Belfast. Took money snitching on both sides and came out without a scratch. We assumed he had the names of every top player written down somewhere, ready to go to the Det if anything ever happened to him.'

Fluke grunted. He knew of McGinty, although 42 Commando had never had dealings with him. But having a sealed envelope ready to be posted to 14 Intelligence Company – the specialist reconnaissance unit known as the 'Det' – made sense. It was as good a way as any of ensuring your safety. The IRA particularly believed that the Brits weren't above sending out their own death squads, so a sense of self-preservation kicked in among their upper echelons when it came to McGinty.

'Got no idea where he is though,' Towler added.

Suitcases. That was Fluke's overriding thought as the taxi drove them into the heart of the city. More than the swanky new restaurants, the upmarket boutiques and the modern art sculptures – it was the sight of people dragging wheeled suitcases behind them that stood out as the biggest indicator of the transformation the city centre had been through since Good Friday. Belfast was now a tourist destination.

Before the agreement, visitors only came to Belfast if they absolutely had to. Even residents of the city rarely ventured out after dark – it was simply far too intimidating. Checkpoints, soldiers and fortified police stations had not induced the sense of security they were there for.

Now people felt safe enough to come out and have a drink,

have a meal, take in a movie. It was good to see and Fluke felt a stirring of pride at the small role he'd played in ensuring enough people lived long enough to get to the peace table.

However, as the taxi left the new and shiny city centre and travelled into the residential areas, Fluke could see that violence hadn't left the city completely.

As they drove through Catholic streets adorned with tricolour flags and IRA murals, and Protestant streets with the red, white and blue kerbs and their own 'King Billy' murals, a sense of familiarity settled upon him. There were more memorial gardens and peace walls than he remembered, but this was the Belfast he knew.

There was tension on these streets; a nervous energy Fluke hadn't felt since the last time he'd sprinted out of the gates of 42 Commando's heavily fortified base. He was under no illusions that doing an 'off the books' job like this was foolish and, in all probability, pointless. The actual Irish connection was tenuous at best. What did they have really? The name of an IRA strategist who MI5 themselves had ruled didn't exist, and a blueprint that had prices in euros before sterling. It was pretty weak.

Fluke wondered if racing to Belfast had less to do with finding this Irish connection and more to do with reconnecting with his dead friend. This had been the last time they'd been on tour together, the last time they'd been really close. When Fluke had been ill, Bish had sent him a get-well card, along with a number to ring, but at the time he'd been too self-absorbed to respond, and up until a few days ago, he hadn't given the card a moment's thought. Now he wished he'd picked up the telephone . . .

He caught himself and smiled. Long periods of introspection weren't his style. It was the Jinx factor. Making him re-evaluate everything. He wondered if it was time to make some big changes. A bit more focus on getting the work–life balance might not be a bad start. He'd speak to Towler when this was finished. His work life never seemed to encroach on his home life.

As if he knew he was being thought about, Towler interrupted his musing. 'Just here, mate,' he said to the taxi driver.

The car pulled up next to an Aldi a few hundred yards away from the Falls Road. Fluke didn't need an explanation. First rule of not drawing attention to yourself in Belfast – fit in. And what said 'I belong here' more than a blue and yellow shopping bag filled with bananas and cheap German lager?

After purchasing enough to fill a bag each they made their way to the Falls Road, each of them holding an open can of lager. Fluke pretended to drink his. Towler pretended to pretend.

The Falls, as it was known locally, had resisted a lot of Belfast's gentrification. There were none of the fancy restaurants and boutiques that were situated just a few hundred yards away. The vibe running through this part of the city was less like that of a thriving modern city and more like a forgotten ex-Soviet bloc town.

Terraced houses rubbed shoulders with the kind of businesses found all over the UK's deprived areas: bookmakers, off-licences, payday-loan companies and pubs. At least the Falls had resisted the city council's efforts to tone down the colour scheme. It had been a feature of Belfast for pubs to be as colourful on the outside as they were drab on the inside. Catholic landlords, bragging to their Protestant counterparts; look at our drinking holes, imagine the wealth, imagine the community spirit we have. And, in truth, it worked. It alleviated some of the inherent grimness that had soaked into the very fabric of one of the most infamous roads in Europe.

Murals still adorned any wall that offered a decent-sized canvas. Locals walked past, immune to their undoubted charms. Fluke and Towler, trying their best to blend in, did the same. They walked past the leisure centre that looked like a job centre, and the job centre that looked like a prison. They barely glanced at the spectacular mural of Bobby Sands – the hunger-striker whose death resulted in a massive increase in IRA funding activity, a boost to membership and an escalation in terrorist activity.

But when Fluke saw *his* mural – the one he'd been patrolling past all those years ago – he couldn't help himself. He approached it, touched the warm brick building and the brightly coloured paint. It was still as vivid now as it had been twenty years ago. The knee of the terrorist was pockmarked where the bullet that had missed his head had struck the wall. It had since been coloured in – the mural was clearly more important than commemorating the opening shot in one of the IRA's bloodiest victories.

The mural depicted three 'volunteers'. Two had – for that era anyway – unfashionably short hair. One of them wore a sleeveless jumper, an atrocity both sides of the political divide were glad to leave behind in the eighties. Two of them were kneeling, their rifles pointing skywards.

The third volunteer was standing and had the more traditional long hair. His rifle was raised above his head in a victory salute. Above him was the ever-present tri-coloured flag, waving in an imaginary breeze. Some murals, like this one, were superb street art and, despite them all portraying him as the enemy, Fluke fully supported the commission that protected them. Murals were a part of Belfast's story. To forget your history is to repeat it.

'Boss,' Towler said, quietly but firmly, 'we need to move on, people are looking.'

Fluke took one last look and joined his friend on the pavement. Towler was looking pensive, nervous even. And Fluke knew why. The Marines might have made the front pages with their notorious calling cards, but the Parachute Regiment's narrative in Belfast was even more fractured than theirs.

He picked up his carrier bag and turned to Towler. 'Come on then, what we waiting for? Where's this pub?'

*

O'Dowd's Bar had been a notorious Provo bar in the seventies and eighties. Fluke could remember patrolling past it when they were unlucky enough to be given the Falls. The spotters would tell the drunks inside that a brick of marines were on their way, and by the time they were anywhere near they had all piled outside – chanting rebel songs and hurling pints of piss. Although it had been better to turn the other cheek, Royal Marines weren't brilliant at that and there'd been some infamous scraps – enjoyed by both sides – in the car park of O'Dowd's. Despite that, Fluke had not once been inside.

Towler had, although he wouldn't say why or when.

O'Dowd's was still painted shamrock green, although this time it didn't seem to be throwing down the gauntlet like it had all those years ago. Then it had been a filthy Provo drinking pit, now it was iconic . . .

Despite their history with the bar, neither of them hesitated. They walked in as if they drank there every night.

Fluke needn't have worried. Inside, the bar was modern and clean. Light wooden floors, red-brick walls and framed photographs of sports teams Fluke couldn't identify. Probably Celtic; it might have tidied itself up but it was still a Catholic bar.

An array of Guinness pumps, standing guardsman straight, protected the barman. A staggering array of spirits was arranged on the shelf behind, and the optics above.

O'Dowd's was virtually empty. Too late for the after-work drinkers and too early for the evening revellers. Towler walked up to the highly polished wooden bar, caught the eye of the barman and said, 'Two, please, mate.' He held up his fingers, victory in Europe style, to emphasise the number.

If you wanted anything other than Guinness in this part of Belfast, then you had to be specific. Otherwise you simply said how many pints you wanted. No one in Belfast drank halves.

The barman nodded, didn't comment on Towler's English accent, and started the eight-minute process of pouring their pints.

While they waited they turned their backs to the bar, leaned against the brass rail, and surveyed the few people in. Mainly hard-core drinkers, quiet men sitting on their own, not inviting conversation.

'You recognise anyone?' Fluke asked, speaking quietly but not making a play about it.

'Nope,' Towler replied. 'But I will.'

They were on their second pint when the door opened and a man shuffled in. He walked with a limp, was wearing a thick coat despite the warm weather, and had one of the worst combovers Fluke had ever seen. A right Bobby Charlton.

'Gotcha, ya little bastard,' Towler said immediately.

The man saw Towler and did an almost comical double take. His brain was saying turn round, but his legs, that were so used to approaching the bar they didn't know how not to, kept walking forwards, almost causing him to fall. After a struggle, he approached the bar, and ignoring them both completely, signalled a pint from the barman. He was even more economic with his order than Towler had been. He didn't even speak, just lifted his hand and waited to be acknowledged. Satisfied, he turned to survey the bar in the same fashion as Fluke and Towler. He rubbed his eyes as though tired.

'Judging by the way you're limping, it would appear you didn't get off scot free then?' Towler said.

The man glared at him.

'Ach, fuck off. I might be a gimp but you're still a Brit bastard.' He spoke with a thick Belfast accent; the peace process couldn't tame some things. His glare turned into an apologetic smile and, as his mouth opened, Fluke saw teeth that Shergar would have been proud of. Blunted and chipped yellow-brown pegs, each one in with a chance of winning the 'Most Disgusting Tooth in the Mouth' award.

The two men briefly touched hands. Not really a shake. It was clear they weren't friends. But they weren't enemies either.

'What brings ye to the Fair Isle then, Mr Towler?' the man said. 'Ye can't still be with them red-devil bastards?'

Fluke flinched and caught his breath. The situation merited a calm and thoughtful response. Insulting Towler's Parachute Regiment would bring about a reaction. Fluke carefully put down his half-finished pint and prepared to do something. In a few seconds it would be either fight or flight. There was no way to tell yet.

But to Fluke's amazement, Towler roared with laughter. Fluke breathed out again, managed a weak smile and picked up his drink. He looked at the inky, black liquid. He found he didn't want to finish it.

'Ave, meet Lawrence McGinty,' Towler said.

Chapter 36

'*The* McGinty? The one we're after?'

Fluke felt stupid as soon as he'd said it. Why would Towler have bothered introducing him to a different McGinty? He covered his embarrassment by draining the rest of his now warm drink. He ordered three more for them. McGinty had yet to be served his first, but he didn't turn down Fluke's offer of a free pint of the black stuff.

McGinty reached out to do the same 'shake/not shake' handshake he'd done with Towler. His hand was dry and leathery.

'The very same,' he said. 'Now, who might ye be? I have an eye for the faces and I've not seen yours before.' He studied him. 'Or have I?' he murmured. He lapsed into silence and searched the dregs of his memory. 'Ye weren't with four-two, were ye? One of them Brit thugs with the clever little cards and the silly green hats?'

Fluke said nothing. It had seemed funny at the time. Made them think they were the big men. People to be feared. Now it just seemed petty.

'Aye, ye were. Your face tells me everything. You can't hide anything from old McGinty.'

Luckily Fluke didn't have to answer.

'Ye mind if we sit down, lads?' McGinty said. 'This warm weather plays havoc with my knee. The barman's a grand lad, so he is; he'll bring our drinks over.'

He didn't wait for an answer, just limped over to a horseshoe-shaped booth with high wooden walls and green leather seats. He edged into the middle, his back to the window, and waited for Fluke and Towler to take seats either side of him. Fluke introduced himself.

They made small talk as they waited for their drinks. After the obligatory eight minutes, the barman walked over with a tray and put four pints of Guinness on the table. Fluke's round and McGinty's first.

McGinty took a deep drink of his first pint, wiped his lips with the back of his sleeve, and said, 'Now, what can I do for ye both? McGinty's out of the intelligence business. I keep my mouth shut these days.' He pronounced mouth 'maith'.

'We need to know two things, Lawrence,' Towler said.

McGinty's eyebrows rose. Towler took that as tacit permission to continue. 'One, does the Choreographer really exist? And two, if he does, what's he planning for the mainland?'

It was clear that of all the things McGinty might have thought they wanted, this wasn't even close. He picked up his drink and sank it in one. He picked up the second pint and drank half. He was spooked.

'What makes ye think I'd tell ye that?'

Towler paused, then said, 'Because I'm asking nicely.'

'Aye, that'd be right. Ye didn't always though, did ye? I remember them red-devil thugs smashing up this bar and any other place an honest Catholic stopped off for a drink on the way home from a hard day's work.'

Snorting, Towler said, 'Piss off, McGinty, you're no more Catholic than I am, and you've not worked a day in your life. The only reason we started in this bar is because you're a creature of habit. I know you'll drink on the Falls for a bit then head on over to the Shankhill. See what's happening on both sides. And this posh city-centre bollocks is fooling no one; Belfast still has two sides and you're still playing them both.'

McGinty shrugged. 'Aye, well, I'm still not telling ye. You see this limp? The new boys don't fear the Det any more. There *is* no more Det. Everything I had on the top boys was forgiven by that fecking agreement. McGinty's insurance policy was cancelled, and some of the boys decided it would be better if one of my knee-caps was drilled out with a masonry bit. A warning not to get up to my old tricks.'

'Bet that hurt,' Towler said, ever the master of the understatement.

McGinty said nothing.

'We're not going until you tell us something, Lawrence. A man, this man's friend, was chopped to pieces because of what's happening over there. And the Choreographer's name has come up. But we were told it was just a rumour; a scare tactic put out by IRA Command. A way to make us think there was method to their madness. Claiming lucky victories were planned to the last detail.'

Still McGinty said nothing. Fluke had the feeling he was a man tormented. He risked sitting in a wheelchair for the rest of his life if he said anything. But, on the other hand, he was a natural gossip. And gossips hate keeping secrets.

Towler might be FMIT's resident meathead, the brawn to Fluke's brain, but he was not stupid. Not at all. When needed, he could be as subtle as anyone else in the team. He displayed that quality now.

'We don't want to see you get hurt again, Lawrence. Too many people have been hurt during this case already. You won't know, but this idiot' – he pointed at Fluke – 'got himself sent to prison for a week just to get involved in the investigation. That's how important we think it is.'

Silence is sometimes more effective than the most probing question. Towler added nothing. Waited for McGinty to fill the void. All four pint glasses were empty – stained with an off-white froth. No one moved to replenish them.

Ten seconds passed. Twenty. He's not going to say anything, Fluke thought.

McGinty moved in his seat. Decision made. 'This didn't come from me, ye hear?' He stopped until they both nodded. He didn't continue.

Fluke frowned. Nodding in acquiescence wasn't going to cut it. McGinty had no reason to trust either of them. And when you're gambling with your last kneecap, trust becomes very important.

'We hear you, Lawrence,' he said. 'And if you want a bit of reassurance, I can tell you that the reason we're here is that we already have the Belfast connection.'

It was an exaggeration, but Fluke hoped it would give McGinty the reassurance he needed. It worked. That the information could have come from someone else seemed to settle him down.

'Do I have a story for you boys, then. Best not to tell it on a dry mouth though, eh?'

He pointed at the empty Guinness glasses. Fluke obliged and went to the bar.

'The Choreographer existed all right. That's the first thing you need to know,' McGinty said, after Fluke had returned. 'At the height of it, in the eighties, the Catholic boys were getting a feckin' pounding. The mainland bombing campaign had cut off their fundraising in the States, and the Loyalists and the security services had had some successes.'

Fluke and Towler both nodded. This was a part of history they knew well. They'd sat through tedious lectures before every tour. As if telling a bunch of young paras and marines all about William of Orange was going to make a blind bit of difference to how they behaved when they got over there.

The barman brought their pints over and they all took a drink.

McGinty wiped his lips and continued.

'What they needed was a strategist. Someone who could actually plan things. Something a bit different to the usual shootings

251

and car bombs. It was her idea to target British soldiers in main-land Europe. Make nowhere safe for them.'

Fluke was about to nod in agreement. The shooting of off-duty soldiers at a ferry port in France had changed army life in Germany. It was no longer a place to feel safe. Made it a pain in the arse to go on leave as well. All that flashed through his mind before the mind-blowing part of what McGinty had just said forced its way to the front of his mind.

'What do you mean, "her"?' he said.

McGinty had obviously slipped 'her' in for dramatic effect; the privilege of the gossip, Fluke supposed.

He grinned delightedly. 'Didn't know that, did ye?'

Both Fluke and Towler shook their heads. 'No, we did not,' Towler said.

'Aye, a grand woman by all accounts. Wasn't a terrorist as such. Had a proper job. I think she may have been a teacher or some-thing like that. No one ever really knew.'

The Choreographer's real? thought Fluke. Although he'd been prepared for it, he was stunned nonetheless. And he wasn't a typical Provo; tattoos, alcoholism and vitriolic views – *she* was a woman.

Fluke deleted all his preconceptions.

A woman changed things. A woman wouldn't have felt obliged to get involved with the 'who has the biggest dick in the IRA' shenanigans. When the men were getting pissed and talk-ing about taking on the Paras, she could sit quietly and actually think about how to do it. And a woman – especially a respect-able woman – could walk among the security services untouched. Observing them. Looking for their weaknesses. Fluke didn't doubt McGinty was telling the truth. When he thought about it, the Choreographer *had* to be a woman.

'So what happened?' Fluke asked.

'Happened?' McGinty replied. 'Nothing happened. Way I heard it, she thought the Good Friday Agreement was as much as they were going to get. Saw it as a victory and packed up. She was never in it for anything more than a fair settlement.'

So why start up again now? As far as Fluke knew, the peace agreement hadn't been cancelled. Protestants were still the majority in Northern Ireland, but only just. Their numbers were declining and Catholic numbers were growing. It wouldn't be long before the Catholics were in the majority and then the chance of real and lasting change would be within their grasp. A unified Ireland was no longer just a nice dream.

Something else had happened. And Fluke knew McGinty knew. The Irishman had been eyeing him with a sly look. Probably seeing how long he could drag it out; how much Guinness he could cadge.

Dragging out gossip for alcohol was one thing, but he didn't have all day. Reyes was in Cumbria without adult supervision.

'McGinty, get on with it, will you?' he said. 'You know what I want to know. Why's she back in business now?'

McGinty was about to say something smart. Fluke could see him gearing up for it. Towler slammed his glass down on the table. He couldn't have been looking properly though, as he accidentally caught one of McGinty's fingers.

McGinty yelped.

A couple of drinkers looked across. Towler stared and they soon returned to their Guinness and *Racing Post*s.

'Apologies, Lawrence,' Towler said, as if he hadn't just crushed the man's pinkie finger. 'You were just about to tell us what's changed.'

Through watering eyes, McGinty said, 'Jeez, lads. Violence isn't the answer any more. Haven't you heard, we negotiate these days?'

'What do you want?' Fluke asked.

McGinty's eyes sharpened. 'I want your word that this didn't come from me.'

'Done,' Fluke said.

'And I want fifty pounds.'

Fluke stared. Fifty quid. Was he kidding? The Guinness they'd drunk between them nearly came to that. Way to dream big, McGinty. He reached into his pocket, took out three twenties, and threw them on the table.

'Sixty for cash?'

McGinty might have been getting on in years, he may have had the worst teeth in Belfast, but when there was money on the table he could fair shift. In the blink of an eye it had disappeared.

'Talk,' Towler said.

'You got any children, Mr Fluke?'

That hit its mark. It was one of the things cancer had taken from him: the chance to have children. The chemo had made him sterile.

'No, I haven't,' he said.

He was about to add that Towler had a daughter but thought better of it. Towler didn't readily offer up information like that.

'The Choreographer had a son.'

Had. Fluke said nothing. There was nothing to say. Towler kept quiet too. This was motivation. She blamed someone for his death. Whether her son had been an IRA volunteer, the innocent victim of an atrocity or, even worse, killed by the security forces, the motives of the Choreographer were now clear: she wanted revenge. It didn't explain the gap, but grief affected everyone differently. Stewing on something for twenty years before deciding to do something was more than believable.

A thought crossed Fluke's mind. Bish had shot and killed a young man in the ambush. Was it possible he'd been her son? Was this no more than a simple tale of revenge? It was a motive, he supposed. It didn't explain what Vane was up to though . . .

'Was he a volunteer?' Towler asked.

McGinty stared. Not comprehending. 'Who?' he said finally.

This time it was Fluke and Towler's turn to look mystified. Fluke spoke first. 'Her son.'

Understanding dawned on McGinty's face. 'No, you misunderstand. The Choreographer was just a wee lassie during the Troubles. In her early twenties, I heard.' He paused and looked thoughtful. 'Imagine sending men to their deaths at that age. What would that do to someone?' He shook his head as if clearing the thought. 'She was in the most successful ASU the Provos had. An Active Service Unit you lot never even knew about. And when you heard the whispers you ignored them rather than believe there was someone out there better than ye.'

'So her son couldn't have been more than a toddler then,' Fluke said. He couldn't remember a specific incident of a small child being killed in Northern Ireland but there was bound to have been one. More than one probably. Bombs weren't fussy, and indiscriminate killing had been a perennial feature of one of the dirtiest wars ever fought.

'Try a little wee taddie swimming in his daddy's bollocks,' McGinty said. 'The boy wasn't born until later. Much, much later. Long after she'd given up the gun. Died about five years ago.'

Fluke's mind was turning into spaghetti. If it wasn't a death attributed to the Troubles, which he could accept as motivation, then what was it? Sectarian violence still happened and it was entirely possible one of the splinter groups that were still beavering away with a fight no one wanted had missed their target and hit a child. But he hadn't heard about it and, in any case, what would that have to do with Bish or with Cumbria?

'How did he die?'

McGinty picked up his empty pint glass and looked wistfully into the bottom.

'Now we're getting to the nub of it, aren't we?' he said. 'He died of a brain tumour, so he did.'

Prickles settled in the pit of Fluke's stomach. He thought he knew where this might be going. In any other country in the world, a woman could blame her child dying of cancer on bad genes, a doctor's misdiagnosis, even an insurance company's refusal to fund treatment.

But in Ireland there's another option. A thing. A *faceless* thing. A monstrosity.

Fluke only needed one more question to get confirmation. 'Where did she live?'

'Are ye fecking joking me!' McGinty exploded. 'You gave me sixty pounds not six fecking hundred! Anyway, I don't know exactly.'

Fluke frowned. Fair enough. McGinty was taking a risk just sitting there.

'All right, McGinty. You don't have to tell me the town, not even the county. But just tell me one thing. Did she live on the west coast or the east?'

McGinty turned to Towler. He jerked his thumb in Fluke's direction.

'Your man there, he knows what this is about.'

He turned back to face him, nodded, and confirmed Fluke's new nightmare.

'The east coast, Mr Fluke.'

Chapter 37

Sellafield is the biggest nuclear site in western Europe. It is the biggest nuclear waste depository in the *universe*. To Cumbria, and its bid to live up to its self-penned reputation as the Energy Coast, Sellafield is vital. A major source of income and employment; a model business, fully integrated into the community.

To the Irish, it's a reeking turd that threatens their very existence.

Their view is that Sellafield – with its dated operating practices and documented radioactive leaks – is a Chernobyl waiting to happen. In 2002, the Irish government, fearing a 9/11-style attack on Sellafield, issued every home in Ireland with iodine tablets, they fear the place that much. They remain in permanent litigation against the UK authorities, trying everything to force its closure. Radioactive waste getting into the Irish Sea would have a devastating and long-lasting socioeconomic impact on Ireland. The health problems would last for generations.

The British government cited study after study proving emphatically that previous leaks into the Irish Sea, while regrettable, posed no health risk to the people of Cumbria, south-west Scotland and beyond. The Irish said, 'Yeah? Well, you would say that.'

You'd have to be living in a teapot not to know that when cancer is diagnosed, a significant percentage of the Irish population blame Sellafield.

And Fluke didn't live in a teapot.

He lived in the real world. And the phrase, 'their perception is their reality' had never been so relevant. If the Choreographer believed Sellafield caused her son's cancer, then Sellafield *did* cause her son's cancer . . .

Fluke had attended countless security visits to Sellafield. On each one the message had been the same: these visits are precautionary, the site is safe. Fair enough, but every time they told him he wasn't needed, he wondered: *So why am I here then?*

A few years ago, a team of scientists conducted risk assessments on a plethora of scenarios ranging from minor equipment failures to catastrophic, end-of-days events such as meteorite strikes.

Again, fair enough. It was right to complete risk assessments. As a senior officer in FMIT, Fluke did them all the time. However, when he thought about Sellafield, it had never been the threat of meteors that kept him awake at night.

It was terrorism.

It didn't matter if it was a 9/11-style attack or just an idiot with Semtex in his underpants; in his mind, Sellafield was nowhere near as safe as their executive team made out. It couldn't be. When fanatics are involved, there is *always* a risk.

Now the Irish connection was confirmed, Fluke wasn't looking much further than the parcel being a bomb. The device could be anything. As a bespoke piece of engineering it was virtually impossible to work out what it was for. They'd even sent it to Imperial College London – the best engineering university in the UK – for their views, and they'd come back with the engineering equivalent of 'not a clue, mate'. No one knew what it was for. But, given the IRA's expertise with explosives, the most likely explanation now was that it was going to be used to secure a bomb to something.

The target was Sellafield. That was a no-brainer. And that meant it couldn't be Fluke's pet project any more. He'd called

Reyes as soon as they'd left O'Dowd's. The Londoner had been sceptical at first, but a call to MI5 had confirmed that Fluke hadn't been lying about McGinty and his prior value to the security services. If McGinty said something was true then it probably was. MI5 were interested, but also knew local police were best equipped to handle the investigation at this late stage. They were on standby if needed but otherwise would keep a watching brief. Reyes promised to call the CNC – the Civil Nuclear Constabulary – immediately.

Fluke rang Cameron Chambers and repeated what he knew. Chambers rang him back within the hour and told him that although they were now on their highest possible alert, it was clear they didn't think a bomb would have much impact. The site was too secure, and the really nasty stuff was either in impregnable bunkers or in parts of the compound an army wouldn't be able to breach. A lone bomber, however well-resourced and motivated, wasn't a credible threat.

But their highest alert level *did* mean that only core staff could get in. Contractors and non-essential staff were being turned away. If Vane had blagged a temporary job, an unlikely scenario given the vetting required just to clean the toilets, he wasn't getting in through the front gate.

As an added precaution, the remote operations centre in the civic centre in Carlisle had been opened and staffed. Chambers had sent a gold command-trained chief inspector to assist them.

Fluke was still uneasy. Although they were up against a grieving mother, about as unpredictable an animal as there was, senseless destruction hadn't been the Choreographer's style. She wasn't squeamish – the Falls Road ambush proved that – but Fluke thought her more of a change agent than a pedlar of mindless violence. There was no doubt that a deliberate act of sabotage, resulting in a significant leak, would seriously threaten the future of the plant. But it would also damage Ireland and that would be psychotic.

And Fluke didn't think she was psychotic.

McGinty had told them that he'd heard about the plan to shut Sellafield at least four years ago. So either she'd taken that long to think of something – which Fluke doubted – or whatever it was she was doing, it had taken four years of planning.

Fluke had first-hand experience of what the Choreographer could do when she didn't have long to prepare; thinking about what she might be able to do in four years brought about a cold sweat.

But, to a large extent, it was no longer his problem. Towler had asked him what was next. Fluke told him he was going home. They'd achieved what they'd set out to do. They'd identified the threat. Vane was in the mist and would either get caught trying to get into Sellafield, or he wouldn't bother trying when he saw the increased security.

Chapter 38

Bridie was cooking when he stepped through the door and the aroma of tomato and basil told him he was eating pasta tonight. He sighed quietly and removed his shoes. Cooking a healthy meal he hated was passive-aggressive behaviour in his opinion. He vowed to say nothing.

To his surprise though, the pasta was for her. He was having curry. In the oven was a takeaway lamb vindaloo, onion pilau and a Peshwari naan to mop it all up. And the frosted pint glass on the table meant he wouldn't need to pretend to like wine tonight. He checked the fridge. Four bottles of the Carlisle Brewing Company's Spun Gold were chilling on the top shelf.

He went to kiss her; with him being in Belfast and her being in London, they hadn't seen each other for a couple of days. She accepted one on the mouth but there was no real warmth to it. Her puffed up eyes were circled by dark rings. She didn't look well at all and, thinking back, she hadn't done for a few weeks. Had she been lying about having a summer flu? It would explain the change in their relationship. Serious illness is second only to debt as the main cause of divorce.

Was the dinner to soften the blow?

They ate their meal in silence. Not uncomfortable silence, but Fluke knew there was something coming up behind it. He only drank one bottle of the Spun Gold. He could barely match Bridie's intellect when sober; he'd have no chance through an alcoholic haze. Bridie was drinking sparkling water. She obviously felt the same.

After they'd washed the dishes they retired to the open-plan living room. Fluke sat first and Bridie chose a different seat. She grabbed the remote but didn't switch on the TV. She was making sure there were no distractions.

She faced him. Her eyes were red and glistening. She looked scared. 'Avison, there's something we need to talk—'

His phone rang.

For a moment he stared at it. It was a number he didn't recognise, an eleven-digit mobile. He knew he should press the red 'refuse' call button. Knew that Bridie needed him to press the red button.

But he also knew he'd be unable to.

You had to *choose* to get a work–life balance. If you were passive, the police took everything. They didn't want detectives putting their families first; they wanted detectives who'd work eighty hours a week for forty hours' pay. With successive governments slashing police funding it was the only way the system worked. Fluke knew this but played along anyway. People rang his number because they knew it would be answered.

To refuse the call would be to refuse who he was.

He mouthed 'Sorry'. Noticed the disappointed look on her face. 'Fluke,' he said.

'Mr Fluke, it's Dan. From Muncaster.'

'Hello, Dan. Is everything OK?'

'It's Vane, Mr Fluke. He's just called me.'

Chapter 39

Fluke arranged to meet FMIT at West Area Headquarters. It was the nearest large police station to the Muncaster site.

As was always the case, he arrived last. Although Vaughn lived farther away, he had better roads. Fluke was on dirt tracks and single-file country lanes for a large part of his journey.

'No Reyes?' Jo Skelton asked him as soon as he walked through the briefing-room door.

He shook his head.

'I want this done properly,' he said.

Dan had told Fluke that the device needed amending. Vane wanted longer handles on the clamps. Dan reckoned it would make it easier to undo. Quick release, in other words.

Fluke told the team what he knew before adding the kicker.

'And he's coming to collect tomorrow,' he said. 'So, by nine o'clock tonight we need a plan.'

The basis of the operation was settled within the hour. They needed someone in the camp working undercover. Fluke could almost taste the irony.

Fluke had a rule. The women on his team were either detectives or they weren't. If they couldn't do the job physically, he wasn't interested in employing them. Jo Skelton had been with him for years and she'd not once let him down. They were only going to be able to put one person in the camp and, although Vane was as dangerous as they came, she should have been in contention. She immediately volunteered.

Fluke said no.

It wasn't on the basis of capability, he explained – he'd seen her fighting thugs with the best of them – but on the basis she was the only regular earner in her family. If she got hurt on an unofficial op, she wouldn't get compensation or an enhanced pension.

He ruled out Jiao-long on the grounds of ethnicity. Fluke was sure, somewhere in the country, there must be a Chinese new age traveller, but there wouldn't be one in Muncaster tomorrow. He took it better than Skelton, who'd called him a sexist arsehole.

He couldn't go himself – he'd already been to the camp and they all knew him. He might as well go in uniform and have blues and twos flashing at the same time.

Alan Vaughn, even when off duty, looked like a Liberal Democrat MP. No way would he fit in. To pinch Nathaniel Diamond's phrase, Vaughn would stick out like a turd in a box of truffles.

That left Towler, and Fluke had the same problem he'd had with Skelton. He was the only earner in his family. However, he could live with that; Towler hadn't served anywhere near as long as Skelton, so his pension wasn't as much to risk, he already received a special forces pension and, sexist or not, he was far less likely to get injured.

The real problem was that Towler was the last person you'd choose to go undercover in a new age traveller camp.

He was being unusually quiet. Fluke knew why. On the one hand, there was the chance of a scrap with someone who people thought of as a handy fighter. A dangerous man. A killer. On the other hand, the team would laugh at him.

Off-duty, he wore the para uniform of jeans, desert boots and a maroon T-shirt adorned with 'Death From Above', 'These Colours Don't Run' or just the 3 Para insignia. It was either that or his work suit. All he'd really done when he left the army was swap one disciplined institution for another.

'I don't wanna go undercover with a bunch of fucking hippies,' he said.

'They're not hippies, they're new age travellers,' Skelton said.

'They've got long hair and don't have jobs. They're hippies.'

'They *do* have jobs.'

'Being a juggler isn't a real fucking job.'

And so on.

Despite his reticence, Fluke had no choice.

'Matt, you're doing it,' he said. 'Go home and get a pair of your old combats. It's the type of thing they wear so you should fit right in.'

'I'll stay.'

'Go. I need you there by five a.m. tomorrow.'

'OK. But I'm not wearing anything stupid.'

'Go,' Fluke repeated.

Grumbling, he left the room.

Fluke waited for the door to close. He turned back to the team. 'Right, no way will that fool fit in with just a pair of combat trousers. We're going to need a bit more.'

'I've got an old pair of boots I use when I work outside,' Vaughn offered. 'Old Doc Martens, red leather. They should fit Matt, I think we're the same size.'

'Really?' Skelton said.

'You not noticed how small his feet are?'

'Sure it's not yours that are disproportionately massive?'

'Doc Martens are perfect, Alan,' Fluke said.

Boots sorted.

Trousers sorted.

They still needed a jacket. And it couldn't be military. Apart from the fact all of Towler's old smocks still had airborne wings stitched on them, too much camouflage gear was going to scare off Vane.

They tossed it around for an hour, but the only idea with legs seemed to be knocking up an owner of one of the town's myriad charity shops and hoping for something big, scruffy and colourful.

Jo Skelton raised her hand.

'I may have something,' she said. 'You remember two years ago when I took you all to the Theatre by the Lake to see Tom?'

Fluke nodded. He did indeed remember. It was another addition to FMIT's catalogue of infamous nights out. Skelton's choice for FMIT Friday – the monthly piss-up they all took turns to arrange – was to go and see her husband who was in the orchestra pit for a musical. The evening had been memorable for two reasons: first, the show had actually been really good and, second, during the Keswick pub-crawl that followed, Towler had got drunk and vomited on a dwarf.

'Do you remember what Tom was wearing?' she asked.

Ah.

Now that Skelton mentioned it, there *was* something else memorable about that night.

An evil grin crept across his face.

'I'll give you a million pounds if you let me tell him,' Alan Vaughn said.

Chapter 40

'Not a fucking chance!' Towler shouted. 'No fucking way I'm wearing that thing.'

It was three in the morning and FMIT had reconvened at Workington nick. Towler had brought in his combat trousers, Vaughn had his old Doc Martens and Skelton had brought the jacket Tom had worn.

Towler liked the boots. Doc Martens were iconic and cool. He'd had Doc Martens when he and Fluke had been punks all those years ago. But he wasn't happy with the jacket. Not one bit.

Vaughn, who was smiling for the first time in as long as Fluke could remember, wasn't helping.

'I don't know what you're moaning about, Matt,' he said. 'It's an army coat. Thought it would be right up your—'

'Go fuck yourself, Alan.'

'Will you at least try it on? It might not even fit,' Jo Skelton said, trying unsuccessfully to keep a straight face.

'Course it'll fucking fit.'

Fluke let him get it out of his system.

He was wearing it, even if he had to be ordered to. And, as a bit of misdirection, the coat was perfect. Every photo of cops who'd infiltrated activists had them looking exactly the same. Straggly beards, dirty clothes, the odd silly hat. Fluke had never seen a photograph of a cop wearing anything like the coat Skelton had brought in. He looked round the team. They all had their phones out. He knew as soon as Towler put it on they'd be snapping photographs.

He'd have to stop them posting on social media until the op was over though – the last thing he needed was #RidiculousLookingUndercoverCop trending on Twitter . . .

Looking at his watch, Fluke said, 'Right, fun's over. You lot, stop winding him up. And Matt, put the coat on.'

Towler had his faults. He was boisterous, he was stubborn and he was a handful when drunk, but he wasn't insubordinate. He pulled on the coat. As Fluke predicted, every member of FMIT took a happy snap. In deference to his friend, Fluke kept his phone in his pocket.

He'd get someone to email him one later.

'I don't even like the fucking Beatles,' Towler said when he'd finished doing up the buttons.

In a long and illustrious career, the Beatles' concept album, *Sgt. Pepper's Lonely Hearts Club Band*, is considered their seminal achievement. With iconic songs such as 'Lucy in the Sky with Diamonds', even Fluke, who only really listened to punk, knew of it.

It also had one of the most widely recognised album covers in the history of rock. It won awards. It won critical acclaim. It featured a host of celebrities, both dead and alive, standing behind the four Beatles who were all dressed in garish, mock-military uniforms, fashioned loosely on the Napoleonic era.

Jiao-long studied the picture he'd just googled.

'At least she didn't bring the hat,' he said.

More laughing.

Towler turned to Skelton. 'Why did Tom have to have this one? George Harrison couldn't pour piss out of a shoe if the instructions were on the heel. Why couldn't he have been Lennon? I'd have been fine with Lennon.'

Jiao-long, who was still looking at his phone snorted. 'Liar.'

'And another thing, why's it have to be so long? It looks like I'm auditioning for fucking *Trumpton*.'

The coat almost reached his knees. It was a lurid, almost lumi-nous red, an alarming, trip-inducing colour. The buttons were oversized and glittery. The epaulettes stuck out so far it looked like Towler had wings.

It was hideous, it was tasteless, and it was utterly perfect for what they wanted.

'Look at me, Matt,' Skelton said. As soon as he did, she snapped a picture. Towler lunged for her phone but she was too quick. 'Excellent. I'm getting this put on T-shirts. Who wants one?'

Fluke stuck his hands up. 'And a small one for Abi, Jo,' he said.

'Arsehole,' Towler said.

'Stop being a drama queen, Matt – you'll be able to take it off when you get there. Topless seems to be the order of the day.'

'Yeah?' said Towler, perking up slightly.

'Well, only the men,' Fluke said.

'What do the women wear?'

'Ballgowns and top hats,' Fluke muttered.

Skelton giggled.

'What was that?' Towler said.

'Nothing,' he said.

Chapter 41

The plan was simple. Towler would be mic'd up, and would wander into the camp at first light. He'd claim to be a traveller looking for work. Other than Dan – who Fluke had phoned to warn – no one in the camp had seen Towler before.

He'd worked undercover in Northern Ireland so Fluke wasn't worried about Towler's safety, but the chances of an unknown man spooking Vane were real. He was taking a risk going back to a camp he knew the police had raided. His antenna would be up.

The rest of them would be in an unmarked van in the car park. Fluke had got a cop to drive past in their personal car: he said there were vehicles there now so a van wasn't going to stick out. They'd wait in the back while Towler gave them a running commentary. When he'd confirmed Vane was in situ they would rush the camp and make the arrest.

Simple.

Fluke was worried.

Simple plans seemed the best on paper. KISS – Keep It Simple, Stupid – was an acronym drummed into all SIOs, but sometimes plans needed that extra bit of finesse. They needed contingencies. This had been put together so hastily, none of that had been possible. Doing it under the nose of Reyes had made it even harder. And Fluke was very aware that no plan survives contact with the enemy . . .

Despite his concerns, he began feeling the familiar surge of adrenaline. The calm before the inevitable storm. He loved this.

He forgot about his problems with Bridie. He forgot about the idiot who'd posted a shotgun cartridge through his door. He forgot about Reyes, and the fact that he was putting his career on the line. Again.

The only thing that mattered was the hunt.

Five hours later and he'd remembered why he delegated stakeouts now that he was the boss. They were boring. The four of them were crammed in the back of the van and despite it only being 9 a.m. it was already ridiculously hot. They were drinking their body weight in water. The planning may have been hasty, but it had included bringing plenty of fluids. Vaughn had been in charge of that, and while he'd brought water for everyone, his idea of pop didn't include regular brands like Coke or Sprite, but did include a massive, unbranded bottle of a suspicious-looking lime drink. Fluke couldn't imagine anyone but Vaughn buying a drink like that. It was too big to fit in anything but a commercial fridge, you nearly broke your wrist trying to lift the thing, and it was by far the fizziest liquid he'd ever drunk.

To alleviate the boredom – and to take their minds off their nagging bladders – they listened to Towler's running commentary. They could hear everything he said, but at such short notice the logistics of getting him an earpiece small enough to avoid detection had been insurmountable. They could hear him but he couldn't hear them.

And Towler was thoroughly enjoying himself. It was as if he was the first visitor to an alien world and he'd been allowed to describe everything to the eager listeners back home. They'd heard him wander in and introduce himself to the first person he saw. Told them he was looking for work and somewhere to kip for a couple of nights. They had no idea who it was he spoke to, but when Towler said 'Nice one, ta,' they assumed he'd at least been offered a cup of tea or something.

When Fluke had been at the camp he'd seen a cohesive, self-sustaining community. People with a different idea about how to live their lives.

Towler obviously saw something different.

'Fuck me, you should see the clip of this one. He's carrying a trombone.'

Two minutes later.

'No way, there's a woman wearing nothing but a poncho. When it flaps open I can see her fan . . . wait a minute, what the hell's he . . . that's not right, surely . . . it fucking is, you know. There's a man wearing a *wizard's hat*. A fucking wizard's hat!'

His brew must have arrived.

'Cheers, mate. Got any milk? . . . No, ta.' A pause. 'He's just offered me goat's milk.' Another pause. 'I can't see any goats round here . . . There are a lot of dogs though . . . I bet I've just been offered dog's milk.'

And every time a gem like that came through, they all strained, desperate not to laugh out loud. He was sure Towler was acting the fool on purpose. Revenge for the coat.

'Hang on, who's this?' Another pause. In the van they all tensed.

'Stand down, it's not him.'

They relaxed.

And so it went on.

By midday even Towler was floundering. He started asking them questions, despite not being able to get an answer.

'What drinks did Alan get?'

'You want this coat back, Jo? I reckon some of these weirdos would take it off your hands.'

They were able to get out of the van when the tourists started to arrive, so at least they could relieve themselves. Out in the sunshine, their cramps disappeared and their sweaty clothes dried out. A burger van had set up in a nearby layby – for those who didn't want to pay Muncaster Castle's inflated prices no doubt – and Fluke bought everyone breakfast. Afterwards, they leaned against the van, enjoying the sun, letting their meal digest.

Unaware of Fluke's decision, Towler kept up his running commentary. 'How's the van? Hot in there, is it? I bet you're all sweating your . . .'

He didn't finish. Fluke looked up. They all did.

Towler whispered urgently. 'I have Vane in my sight. No play, Vane's here.'

No play. Military terminology used during exercises to let listeners know when something, normally an accident, was real and not part of manoeuvres.

They made their way across the car park, careful not to draw attention to themselves. They hopped the fence, and hugging the treeline, headed to the camp.

'I still have Vane,' Towler. 'IC1 male. Wearing cut-off denims and a combat jacket – I swear that'd better not be a para smock – and a pair of blue trainers. He's just knocked on Dan's trailer . . . Dan's opened the door, they're talking.'

Fluke subconsciously put a spurt on. Dan wasn't trained in this type of thing. He could give the game away without even knowing. Vane would be suspicious of everyone.

'I still have him,' Towler said. 'Still talking to Dan. He's taken a bit of paper from his pocket. They're both looking at it. Dan's nodding. Must be a new blueprint.'

Fluke kept walking. So far, so good.

'Shit!' Towler said. 'Dan's glanced at me. Fucking bollocks, now Vane's looking at me.'

Silence.

'Oh shite, where the fuck are you lot? This is about to get real!' Towler shouted, all semblance of cover blown. 'Shit! Shit! Shit! He's just twatted Dan! He's heading my way! He's heading my

273

way! Boss, what do you want me to do? He's got one of Dan's fucking swords.'

Fluke was already sprinting, and by the time Towler had shouted about the sword they were already in the camp. Fluke stopped, eyes acclimatising to the gloom of the wood. He spotted Towler immediately. He hadn't taken the red coat off and was hard to miss. He was standing about ten yards away from Vane, who was holding a cutlass type of sword out in front of him.

He was the same height as Towler but had at least a three-stone advantage. His hair was wild and with the cutlass he resembled a pirate.

They were circling each other warily. Neither standing still long enough to allow the other to make them dizzy. Both men were silent.

'Vane!' Fluke shouted. 'It's over.'

Vane didn't look; he was concentrating on Towler. He was standing with perfect balance and Fluke knew this wasn't the first sword he'd held. Fluke knew he'd taken down Bish with something similar.

Towler said, 'Boss, what do you want me to do?'

The two men kept circling each other.

His limited options raced through his mind. Towler wanted to have a go and he could let him. Vane had a sword but Towler had skills and he was fearless. He dismissed it though – he'd already lost one friend to this murdering bastard.

They could swamp him. Dive on him at the same time, overpower him with sheer weight of numbers. Fluke dismissed that too. He would have no way of controlling what happened. One or all of them could get hurt.

There was really only one decision he could make. He knew it was right as he didn't want to do it – the hardest decision was invariably the right one.

'Let him go, Matt.'

'Say again?' Towler said, his eyes fixed on Vane.

'Let him go. We'll get him some other time. He won't get far.'

Towler said nothing. Fluke knew this was hard for him. Retreating wasn't in his nature.

'Boss, I ever tell you what I think about the Royal Marines?' he said.

'Frequently,' Fluke said.

'What I *really* think about the Royal Marines?'

To be honest, he didn't think Towler ever had.

Towler continued. 'What I think of the Royal Marines is what the rest of the Parachute Regiment thinks, whether we admit it or not.'

'Yeah, craphats, bootnecks, I get it, Matt. Now let him go.'

'Elite soldiers,' he said. 'The Royal Marines are elite soldiers. Paras and marines are the *only* elite soldiers outside of special forces. We're a different kind of animal to everyone else.'

Keeping his voice as calm as he could, Fluke said, 'That's nice, Matt, but we have to let him go.'

'Fuck that,' Towler said. 'You kill a marine, you may as well have killed a para.'

Vane frowned. He glanced at Fluke. Only for a second but it was enough.

Moving faster than any man had a right to move, Towler darted inside the sword's reach. Vane swung, but only managed to hit him with the handle. Towler launched a flurry of uppercuts. There was no visible injury, but they must have been effective as Vane dropped the sword. He touched his side briefly, winced, then took up a martial arts stance. He looked annoyed, not scared.

But he didn't know Towler.

Vane swung a giant fist. Towler swayed back and the punch moved harmlessly past his nose. Vane tried again. Same result. He spun and tried a roundhouse kick. If he'd connected he'd have broken Towler's spine. But Towler was too quick and was well out of his reach.

Fluke knew he had to let the fight play out now. To stop it risked Towler's life. To join in risked *everyone's* life.

For a moment there was a pause in the action as they continued to circle each other. Vane was panting, Towler wasn't. Eventually they came full circle. Towler was near enough to the sword to pick it up. He did.

He then lobbed it gently to Vane.

'Here you are, mate,' he said. 'Have your girly sword back.'

Vane frowned but caught it.

He really should have let it bounce off him.

Because as soon as his arms were raised, Towler was inside his reach. He didn't check his momentum, but drove his head forward in a ferocious headbutt. The dome of his forehead – that solid arch of bone – crunched into Vane's nose and crushed it flat. Twin spurts of blood arced in the air.

Vane gurgled once, collapsed and passed out.

Towler loomed over him.

'Twat,' he said. He turned to Fluke. 'Can I take this fucking coat off now?'

Chapter 42

With his fingerprint matching those on the murder weapon, and with solid physical evidence, they had enough to charge Vane with the murder of Mark Bishop, as well as the attempted murder of Towler. Reyes was working on the murder of the activist, Russell Bryce, in London but it wouldn't form part of the immediate investigation.

It was two days before Vane was well enough to be interviewed. Reyes had insisted on going first, but for the first time in his life Fluke was happy to hide behind the rulebook.

'Sorry, John,' Fluke said, making it abundantly clear he was anything but, 'you can't interview Vane. You're too senior in rank.'

Reyes said nothing. He knew Fluke was right.

A ruling under the Police and Criminal Evidence Act meant that criminals could now claim intimidation if a rank of chief inspector or above was present during an interview. Anything they said could be ruled inadmissible.

'I want one of my men in on it though,' Reyes said.

'Not a problem,' Fluke said. It wasn't an unreasonable request.

Fluke had interviewed hundreds of criminals – murderers, rapists, paedophiles, even a case of fabricated illness – but he'd never interviewed a terrorist.

It was possible, although his age was against him, that Vane was ex-IRA. Fluke suspected the Choreographer wouldn't have used her own people though; the chance of them being on an MI5 watch-list was too high. Fluke reckoned she'd found a committed and competent extremist on the mainland, and provided logistics, funding and strategic direction.

The interview room was Fluke's arena and the detective constable from Reyes's team was under strict instructions. Say nothing, do nothing. He was there to observe, nothing more.

Fluke went through the basics. Names of those in attendance. Confirmation Vane was refusing a solicitor. That type of thing. When he'd finished, he said nothing, simply stared at the man who'd killed his friend.

His broken nose had been reset. A metal cast covered it. The cheekbone fracture was uncomplicated and would heal naturally. The blow to his nose had caused two black eyes. They had swollen to slits.

He was in a white, police-issue tracksuit. It contrasted starkly with the earthy tones of his skin. He looked exhausted. Fluke didn't care. He hadn't requested time to sleep so there was no legal reason to give him any.

'Now, before we start, would you prefer to be called Vane . . . or Kevin Hendricks?'

Vane frowned. 'Call me whatever you want.'

'Who's the Choreographer?' Fluke asked. No point leading with his chin. Get a jab in with a surprise question. Keep him off balance.

The fatigue left Vane's eyes. It was replaced by shock.

Fluke pressed his small advantage.

'You really think it's that easy to shut down Sellafield? A billion-pound facility? If it was, it'd have been tried years ago.'

Vane stared. Said nothing.

But Fluke hadn't finished. Some interviews required a slow drip feed of the facts. Others, like this one, needed a steamroller. Blast the suspect with everything. Disorientate him. Make him think you know everything and their only option is to deal.

'When did you find out Mark Cadden was an undercover policeman?'

Vane laughed.

'Mark wasn't a cop,' he said. 'If he was he'd be in here with you.'

Fluke studied him. Vane was calm. Good liars often were.

'OK then, where is he?' he continued. 'Bring him in. You can't, can you? Mark's in the wind. You know what he did before he became a traveller? He was a Royal Marine. Means you'll never find him.'

Vane was controlling the interview. Fluke needed to regroup. Hit him with a few more facts.

'We know you commissioned Dan to make a device. We know you also received a thermos-sized package – in all probability explosives. We know you are working under the instructions of an ex-IRA strategist called the Choreographer, and that your goal is to take Sellafield offline in retaliation for her son dying of cancer.'

Vane stared at Fluke.

Eventually he spoke, and when he did Fluke was stunned.

'The thermos. The one I *found* and was keeping safe. It's not full of explosives so you're not going to need the bomb squad; you're going to need a cancer-pedlar from that place you're all so proud of. If you go to this address' – he picked up Fluke's pen and wrote it down – 'along with my garden ornament, you'll find a canister containing a small amount of AGR fuel waste.'

'And what the hell is AGR waste?'

Vane told him.

He really wished he hadn't.

Chapter 43

Fluke stopped the interview. He needed confirmation on what Vane had told him. AGR waste didn't sound like the type of thing you sprinkled on your cornflakes but he needed confirmation it was as bad as Vane had said it was. He didn't want to be the cop who shut down Sellafield because someone had stolen the equivalent of red diesel. Whatever it was, though, it needed recovering.

And he also needed time to think. Why had Vane given up the flask so easily? He must have known it would be used as evidence against him. The 'I found it' defence Vane had started in the interview room was paper thin.

Fluke left the room and called Chambers.

'AGR fuel?' Chambers barked. 'You sure that's what he said?'

'AGR fuel *waste*,' Fluke said. 'And I'm pretty sure, sir.'

He had told Chambers what Vane had said, and where the flask was supposed to be. The superintendent hadn't balked. He'd taken control of the situation immediately. He also seemed to know what AGR waste was.

'No way he confused it with something else?' he asked.

'Don't think so, sir,' Fluke said. 'Why, what's AGR waste?'

'The AGR stands for Advanced Gas-cooled Reactor,' Chambers said. 'AGR fuel is the nasty stuff that powers our nuclear plants. It's in rod form though . . .' Chambers paused before speaking again. 'Unless, and I'm dredging my memory here, he's managed to get hold of some of the dissolved waste. He'd be able to get that into a flask.'

Fluke didn't respond.

'Well, you're aware that Sellafield processes all the spent nuclear fuel in the UK?' Chambers said.

'Vaguely,' he said.

'Sellafield takes this waste and puts it through their Thermal Oxide Reprocessing Plant. Most of it can be recycled as—'

'Thermal Oxide Repro . . . Do you mean the Thorp plant, boss?'

'I do. Thorp does all the UK's, and a fair bit of foreign, reprocessing. I'm dumbing it down a bit, but basically they receive the transport flasks, remove the fuel underwater, then store it in ponds until it cools.'

'It's hot?'

'Figure of speech. Really it means until the radiation has reduced to a safer level.'

'Then what?'

'Then it goes into another process where it's chopped up into small pieces and dropped into some chemicals, which dissolves it. The uranium and plutonium is recovered and either goes into secure long-term storage or it's recycled into more AGR fuel.'

'So when Vane says the flask contains waste, what exactly does he mean?'

'I've no idea, but pretty much any by-product of the process is considered nuclear waste. It could be anything. The flasks that the rods are transported to Sellafield in have to be cleaned out and that waste is considered dangerous. The ponds where they remove the rods from the flasks contain dangerous levels of radiation. The ponds they store it in while they cool it down, the dissolving plant – I could go on. There are so many processes involved, a determined person could easily get hold of a small amount of AGR waste.'

281

'That's not good,' Fluke said.

Although he'd never really believed all the press and hyperbole about how safe Sellafield's was, he'd never really considered how many ways there actually were to circumnavigate their security. Like all security, it relied on the honour system: it was only effective when the staff didn't actively sabotage it from the inside.

They knew about Vane but there could be others they didn't know about. If the plan had been in operation for a number of years, it was entirely possible someone involved in the plan had got a job at a nuclear plant somewhere. Possibly Sellafield itself . . . Fluke was willing to bet that, like all jobs, the dirty and more dangerous ones – and the reprocessing of radiated fuel would fit that description – wouldn't attract much competition.

'Assuming he has some of this waste then, boss, what the hell do we think he had planned for it?' Fluke said.

Chambers said nothing and Fluke's anxieties ratcheted up a notch.

'Sir?'

It was as if Fluke hadn't spoken. When Chambers eventually replied, it sounded as if he was speaking from a different country his voice was so distant. 'If this man has what he says he has, then we need to get it back and we need to get it back now.'

Silence.

Fluke said, 'Towler and I will do it, sir. We've handled explosives in Northern Ireland. We know not to touch things we're not equipped to deal with.'

Whatever nightmare Chambers was in, he snapped out of it. He dismissed Fluke's offer. 'You're not near enough and it's nuclear waste, Avison. Sellafield have people trained for exactly this. I'll get them there immediately.'

With the recovery of the flask being managed by people who knew what they were doing, Fluke decided he'd better eat. He found Towler, still sporting a bruise on his forehead, in the canteen having a brew. Together they made their way up the hill to Superfish, the chippy all Workington cops used.

Fluke was in the middle of a cod or haddock deliberation when his phone rang. He glanced at the caller ID. It was Chambers.

The sound wasn't great. It sounded like he was driving. The message was clear though.

'Fluke,' he shouted, 'get back in with Vane. That address was empty. I need to know if he's been yanking our pissers or whether, God forbid, something's happened to it.'

'Empty?'

'That's what I said, Fluke. There was a mild radiation reading on the Geiger counter but nothing conclusive.'

'Do I tell Reyes?'

'Fuck Reyes!' Chambers said, still shouting. 'If that bastard had told us what was going on a bit earlier we could have stopped this!'

'On it now, sir,' Fluke said.

At least the run back to the station was downhill.

After half an hour Fluke was convinced Vane hadn't lied to them. Fluke wished he had. If he'd lied to them then all they'd done was made fools of themselves. And the police were good at that. Most of the time they didn't need assistance.

He rang Chambers and told him the bad news. Vane *had* had a flask of radioactive waste but if it wasn't at the address he'd given them he didn't have a clue where it was. He'd seemed genuinely confused.

'Sweat the bastard!' Chambers said. 'Throw the book at him. Tell him that because the victim was an undercover cop, who we believe had been identified to him, we will be asking the CPS for a whole life sentence. See if that makes him a bit more chatty.'

Fluke was about to protest. They weren't ready to discuss the

283

murder but he realised Chambers needed him to bring this one home. Time to do what he was told for once.

'I'll get it done, boss.'

Despite the clinical nature of the post-mortem photographs, Fluke could feel himself getting upset again. The body parts, washed and set against an evidence ruler, were his friend. He was reminded, if he needed reminding, why he'd put himself through so much shit in the last few days. It had only ever really been about catching his killer.

And now he was sitting in front of him. Chambers could worry about the AGR waste. He had a murder confession to get.

Fluke placed each photograph face down on the table. Vane had been offered a solicitor but he'd declined again. He was watching Fluke with interest. When he had fifteen of the worst ones on the table he looked up.

'You still say Mark Cadden isn't an undercover cop?'

Vane snorted in response.

'You're right,' Fluke said, noticing the slight shift in Vane's expression. He turned over the pictures one at a time, making sure Vane had seen each one before he revealed the next. 'Mark Cadden *was* an undercover cop. Now he's the evidence in his own murder.'

That got a reaction. Not the one Fluke had been hoping for, but any reaction was better than the confidence Vane had been showing up until then. His eyes widened as it dawned on him what Fluke was getting at.

He sat bolt upright in the hard plastic chair. 'This is bullshit!'

Fluke ignored him. 'We have the murder weapon and your fingerprints are on it.'

Vane stared.

'One of Dan's swords,' Fluke said.

'One of Dan's . . .'

Vane picked up one of the photographs, the one that was a knee or an elbow. Something with a hinge anyway. He studied it. Put it down. Picked up another.

'You aren't pinning this on me,' he said eventually.

Fluke said nothing.

'I'm telling the truth, Mr Fluke,' he said. 'Even if I'd known Mark was a cop I wouldn't have hurt him.'

'And the sword?' Fluke said. He was getting no satisfaction from this.

'I picked some up to look at when Dan was making that sculpture for me. I'm interested in swords. Always have been. Dan can confirm this.'

Fluke didn't see any deception in his micro-expressions. Vane had to be Bish's killer – the evidence was compelling – but he was making a convincing fist of his denials.

Filling the silence, Vane continued. He seemed to have been thinking things through.

'I'm not the man you want, Mr Fluke, and if my flask has disappeared then there's another player in this that neither of us are aware of.'

Vane's use of the term 'player' sparked a thought. The Choreographer's operations had never been reckless. Was it possible she had contingencies in case her plan was discovered? Contingencies to make sure dangerous nuclear waste wasn't left lying around for anyone to open. Was it possible Vane had been told to give it up if he was caught? The more Fluke thought about it, the more he thought it likely. Vane had claimed he'd found it – he had to think about self-preservation after all – but as soon as Fluke had revealed they knew enough to make sure he wouldn't get bail, he'd immediately given it up. Or tried to anyway.

The wheels within wheels were giving Fluke a headache. Just what the hell was going on?

'Where was he found?' Vane said.

'I'm sorry?'

'Mark. Where was he found?'

If he'd committed the murder he already knew where and if he hadn't then he might be able to help. There was no reason not to tell him.

'Near Cockermouth. On the golf course.'

Vane put his hands through his unkempt hair. 'I've no links to Cockermouth. It's not somewhere I know well. I certainly don't know where the golf course is.'

Fluke reopened his file and took out some photographs. This time of the crime scene. The impact of the pale, dry grass stained with dark blood didn't lessen the more Fluke saw them. Not with this case. He placed them in front of Vane and allowed him to peruse them.

His increasing uncertainty regarding Vane's involvement was a problem – they had no other suspects. Not one. He needed to get back out into the field. Because, if it wasn't Vane, it was someone else. And every minute Fluke spent inside was a minute wasted. Vane wasn't going anywhere – they still had him on the attempted murder of Towler – and the conspiracy to commit terrorism wasn't going away any time soon either.

He began packing up. Vane had to be given an eight-hour break now anyway. He was about to ask for the photographs back, but paused.

Vane was staring at one of them.

He was frowning. He rifled through the rest until he found another. He put the two together.

Fluke could see they were both shots of the wider crime scene. Most had been of individual pieces of the body, but a few had been taken from farther away. The context photographs, Fluke called them.

'What is it?' he said.

Vane ignored him. He searched through the thick sheaf once

more. Found another one, this time taken from a height. Fluke remembered the SOCO guy climbing a portable stepladder to take it. The photo showed the body parts and how they'd been dispersed.

In what was probably the most bizarre change of direction in the history of police interviews, Vane eventually said, 'I used to love nature documentaries, Mr Fluke.'

On the basis that he had to have a point, Fluke allowed him to continue.

'A couple of years ago there was one that was really special. It was called the *Human Planet*. Did you see it?'

Fluke said he hadn't.

'John Hurt narrated it and each episode focused on—'

'Where are we going with this, Vane?' There was only so much he was prepared to put up with.

Ignoring him, Vane continued. 'Each episode focused on different parts of the planet and how humans have adapted to live there. There was an episode about people who live in jungles. Others were about people who lived on the ocean or in deserts, that type of thing.'

'Get there quicker, Vane.'

'One of the episodes was about people who make mountains their home. Real mountains, not the foothills we have here. There was a bit about Mongolians hunting with golden eagles, and another bit about catching giant bats.'

Fluke folded his arms and stared. 'I won't tell you again.'

Vane ignored him. 'One of the scenes – the key scene of the episode really – took place in Tibet.' He cleared his throat. 'You ever heard of a body breaker, Mr Fluke?'

Fluke shook his head.

'In Tibet, which is basically on the side of a mountain, there are no easy ways to dispose of the dead.'

Fluke stiffened.

'It's too rocky to dig graves, and because there are hardly any trees, there's no fuel for cremations. But this isn't a problem, you see, because, as most Tibetans are Buddhists, they believe the corpse is just an empty vessel. There's no need to preserve or honour it. The body's spirit leaves at the point of death.'

Fluke said nothing.

'So they practise something called a sky burial, and that's where the body breakers come in. The corpse is taken up a mountain, placed on a flat rock and ritually dissected.'

Vane paused. Fluke stared at him, mesmerised.

'It's then fed to the wild animals. Vultures flock and take the smaller pieces – scavenging animals take the bigger bits.'

He picked up the photo taken from the stepladder.

'Now, correct me if I'm wrong, Mr Fluke, but doesn't this scene look exactly like the one I've just described?'

It was easy to dismiss. It was a ridiculous idea. Preposterous to the extreme. And yet Fluke knew that it was exactly what had happened. Despite the warm room, he shivered.

He knew who'd killed Bish.

And it wasn't Vane.

'I don't suppose anyone who's cropped up in your investigation has been to Tibet?' Vane continued. 'Because if they have, it may be that as well as killing Mark, they're also the ones who stole my flask.'

Fluke shook his head. He didn't know anyone who'd been to Tibet but that didn't matter. Because he was willing to bet that if they practised sky burials, then it was practised in the neighbouring countries too. As long as it was mountainous and predominantly Buddhist.

His geography was awful, but even he knew what that part of the world looked like; it was basically an enormous lump of granite. He might not know of anyone who had been to Tibet but he certainly knew of someone who'd spent time in the country next door.

288

And that person also had a motive. Even more of a motive than Vane.

And, as if they were daring him to find out, that very same person had even told him they'd spent time in Nepal.

Chapter 44

Seven months earlier, unaware he was actually an American contract killer, Fluke had shared coffee with Dalton Cross. It seemed in this case he'd gone one step further and invited the murderer into his home.

Jinx.

Get past the 'little-lost-girl' act, and her duplicitousness was obvious. The appalling childhood she'd had with her father. Sexually abused, unable to trust the one man who was supposed to keep her safe. She runs and finds Twist, a sweet affable hippy. He takes her in and shows her friendship but he's unable to show her the love she craves. Not with Faith at his side. And then she meets Bish and he must have felt like the freshest breath of air anyone had ever sucked into their lungs. Funny, loyal to a fault and ferocious in defending his friends. She'd have fallen for him hard.

And Bish falls for her too. Two lovers, both damaged, both seeking redemption in a world that, until then, had only spat at them. A chance for peace and a life.

But Bish has a secret. He knows it will destroy her but he has to tell her anyway. He asks permission to tell her. Permission was denied. But Bish had always treated orders as suggestions. He tells her anyway.

Fluke imagined her rage.

How could it have been anything different?

Another betrayal by a man she should have been able to trust.

It explained the one part of the murder Fluke hadn't been able to get his head round. Bish knew Vane was dangerous. Even if he'd thought there was a genuine reason to go to Cockermouth Golf Club, he'd have been hyper vigilant. He certainly wouldn't have turned his back on him.

But add another variable to the mix – going there with his wife, for instance, maybe on the promise of some alfresco fun – and he'd have been an easy target. Sowerby had told him the first cut was to hobble him – the tendons at the backs of his legs. Ex-commando or not, after that he'd have been helpless.

She'd probably planned to tell Vane that Bish was a UCO. Tell him he had to flee so he would unwittingly take the blame for Bish's murder. But when she returned to the camp, Vane had already disappeared. What was she to do next? Go and get herself an alibi, that's what. Go and see Bish's friend – just like she'd been told to do – make him believe she was the innocent victim in it all. See what happens. Find out what the police knew.

And he'd fallen for it, hook, line and fucking sinker.

And now that Vane was caught, and her alibi was starting to unravel, she only had one thing left.

She would complete Vane's work.

Not for any moral cause – although the closure of Sellafield was probably on every hippie's Christmas list – but if she could dishonour Bish's memory by finishing what he'd dedicated his life to trying to prevent, it would be the ultimate payback.

A big 'fuck you' to every man who'd betrayed her.

As soon as the truth dawned on Fluke, he grabbed Towler and they sprinted to his BMW. Within two minutes he was out of Workington and, with a police high-speed pursuit vehicle as an escort, was touching ninety miles an hour along the A595.

They took the Carlisle bypass and were soon on the M6 heading south. At junction 42 the pursuit vehicle turned off its blues and twos. Wetheral was a country village and Fluke didn't want the noise of the siren carrying up the river and into Lime House.

They parked outside the nearby Fantails Restaurant this time. No point warning her they were there. He tried to call Diamond but it went straight to voicemail.

Fluke would have preferred to get a message to the man looking after Jinx, warn him they were coming in and might not be knocking, but he didn't have the luxury of time.

He still hadn't decided on the best approach: the 'knock and wait' or the 'smash and grab'. He didn't need to ask what Towler's preference was, and in any other circumstance it would be the correct choice. But neither of them had dealt with radioactive nuclear waste before and that changed things.

They turned the corner on the landing and saw that the decision had been taken out of their hands.

The door was wide open.

In a village such as Wetheral you might leave your door unlocked during the day, but never wide open. Carlisle was just five miles away. Doors were shut unless you were expecting guests. Fluke didn't need to be C. Auguste Dupin to smell a long-tailed rodent.

After slipping on latex gloves, Fluke stepped inside. Towler followed, careful to take the same route – if this was now a crime scene they wanted to disturb as little evidence as possible.

Fluke saw the blood before he saw the body. The pool had followed the natural grain in the wooden floor and spread into the corridor. He bent down to look. It was dark and congealed. Whatever had happened had occurred a while ago.

He stepped into the living room and was lucky not to trip over the corpse.

Diamond's house-sitter was dead.

His throat had been sliced through to the bone.

The corpse's grey complexion, sunken eyes and cold skin showed they'd missed Jinx by hours, not minutes.

Fluke sighed. He'd been hoping he was wrong about this.

'Call it in, Matt,' he said. 'And remind SOCO they need to be trained in hazmat.'

He began a rudimentary search for the flask. He knew it wouldn't be there but he didn't want to tell Chambers he hadn't looked.

Nothing. The place was minimalist, so there were few hiding places.

To his credit Chambers didn't shout or moan. Nor did he ask how they knew to look for Jinx in Wetheral – that was a conversation for later, Fluke suspected. He simply told him to get back to HQ. They needed to regroup. Begin the search for Jinx.

'I'll get uniform to secure the scene then go and have another crack at Vane, sir. Now we know who has the flask, and that she's probably trying to finish what he started, he might tell me more of the original plan.'

That wasn't the only reason he wanted to head back west. Instinctively he knew that whatever was going to happen would occur there. HQ was too far away from where he needed to be.

'I'd ordinarily agree with you, Avison, but that idiot Reyes has him. I don't know where he is now, just that it's not Cumbria.'

Shit.

'I'll base myself in the west anyway though, sir. Makes sense.'

'Not to me it doesn't. You're my best DI and I need you managing the hunt from HQ. Towler can head it up in the field.'

'OK, sir. We'll come back in.'

He pressed end call, then dialled Zoe. They hadn't left on particularly good speaking terms but he was sure she would do the right thing if pressed.

The dial tone kept going. Eventually voicemail kicked in and Fluke left a message for her to call him back. She either would or she wouldn't. In the meantime, he had a decision to make.

Towler came back into the living room. 'What did the boss say?'

'He wants us to go back out west,' he lied. 'See if we can sniff out some leads. We'll go back to Muncaster and speak to some of the travellers. See if any of them can point us in her direction.'

They arrived just as the storm that had been threatening for the last hour finally broke. It was monsoon-like and reminded Fluke of the rains he'd seen on a tour of Belize. Wet and hot. Prickly heat weather. They decided to wait it out rather than get drenched for the sake of it.

An impressive rainbow appeared above the castle and Towler began singing the colours of the rainbow song under his breath. Unless his musical tastes had changed from punk to nursery rhymes, it must have been something he and Abi had been doing recently. Fluke glanced at him, irritated. He hated doing nothing when it felt like he should be doing something.

'Sorry,' Towler said.

As he turned the engine back on to clear the fogged-up windscreen, Fluke waved his apology away. A man practising a song for his daughter shouldn't have to apologise. They sat for a few more minutes. The rain slowed and tourists began to appear; the plethora of umbrellas made Muncaster Castle car park look like a Chinese festival.

Towler was the world's most easily bored man. If he couldn't entertain himself through normal means he'd try to annoy whoever he was with. Anything to get a reaction.

He finished the rainbow song and started on 'Baa Baa Black Sheep'. Fluke ignored him. Letting him see he was getting to you was the worst thing you could do. The familiar words washed over him.

He smiled. If you can't beat 'em . . . He opened his mouth and joined in for the last line of the rhyme.

'And one for the little boy who lived down the lane!' they both yelled, grinning at each other.

'Incey Wincy Spider' came next, complete with all the hand gestures. Towler stopped when he saw Fluke's expression.

Much later, whenever anyone asked where Fluke had drawn his inspiration, he always lied. He never once admitted it was through singing nursery rhymes with Towler.

But listening to 'Baa Baa Black Sheep' had sparked a memory. Initially it had simply been the word sheep. It had made him think of Cockermouth Golf Course. He'd seen pictures in the clubhouse, and knew that although they now owned all of the land the course was on, they hadn't always. They used to rent half of it from a local farmer. And that farmer had used it to graze his sheep. So, in addition to narrow fairways, high winds and grass bunkers, the first few holes going out and the last few going back had the additional obstacles of live animals and sheep shit to contend with. The greens, in agreement with Farmer Awkward, had been guarded by low wire fences pulsing with electricity.

So what? Most of Cumbria had sheep on it. If it didn't, the fells would soon be covered in woodland. The mention of sheep alone hadn't got his neurones juiced up. He'd delved deeper into his mind, searching for that most elusive thing: subconscious memory.

Black sheep.

That was it. The black sheep of the family. The odd one out.

He didn't know anything about Vane's childhood – no one did yet – but he'd be willing to bet he was also a black sheep.

The only thing they knew about him was that his real name might be Kevin Hendricks. Bish had somehow found that out. Jiao-long hadn't turned up anything on his trawl of the internet and agency databases. There were plenty of Kevin Hendrickses, obviously, but none that matched Vane.

But because of the nursery rhyme, for a few seconds, he'd had Cockermouth Golf Club *and* the name Kevin Hendricks swirling around in his mind together.

Hendricks and Cockermouth.

Cockermouth and Hendricks.

Confused thoughts finally cleared.

He snapped bolt upright. Looked at Towler, and said, 'Fancy a drive?'

Fluke knew where he'd seen the name before . . .

296

Chapter 45

In Cumbria, there are places so high that the people who live there are always the first to know when it rains. One such place is the Shap Summit. A bleak wilderness on the top of nowhere, constantly soaked in mist and misery, where the only things that live there are loners and Herdwick sheep.

Another place is Cockermouth Golf Course. When it rains there, sensible golfers run for cover. It's either that or get swept off the top of the fell. This time they'd even had lightning so when Fluke arrived the course was empty. The clubhouse was full. It was hot, steaming, and packed.

A glassy-eyed drunk, wearing tailored shorts, knee-length socks and a sneer that was going to earn him a fat lip if he carried on looking at Towler like that, approached them.

'I'm sorry, gentlemen, this is a *private* golf club. You're going to have to leave. As you can see, we only have room for members today. The storm, you see?'

He turned to some of his friends and smirked.

'If it's lager you're after, there are pubs in Cockermouth that *may* serve you.' He emphasised the *may* as if there were no guarantees.

Fluke was tolerant of snobs. As a senior police officer he had to be. Every day brought one more snooty bastard thinking he had the right to preferential treatment. If he'd heard one halfwit tell him their council tax paid his wages, he'd heard a thousand. So he ignored the man.

Towler frowned. He wasn't used to dealing with snobs. He always preferred mixing with the lower end of the social spectrum. Fluke recognised the frown and it wasn't good. He was about to calm his friend, tell him he should go and wait in the car, when the idiot in the shorts decided to speak again.

'Don't let the door hit you on the way out, chaps.' He laughed at his own joke. His friends, more attuned to the mental weather change, didn't join in.

Fluke upgraded the man from 'idiot at risk of getting a fat lip' to 'man who deserves everything he gets'.

Before he could do anything, Towler spoke.

'You know something, boss, that rain hasn't half made the floor slippery. I'll have to be careful with these wet shoes on.'

The man looked down. 'It's a carpet, you idiot!'

In an exaggerated movement that fooled no one, but would be a perfectly defensible position in court, Towler's right leg shot out and caught 'idiot in shorts' on the shin.

'Argh!' He grabbed his leg and started hopping.

'Whoops-a-daisy,' Towler said.

He reached out and pretended to help. Hidden to all but Fluke, he gave the man a quick knuckle jab to the throat.

'Oh, look at that, sir, the rain appears to have given you a nasty cough.' He helped now 'struggling-for-breath man' to his feet and looked him in the eye. 'If I were you I'd go to the changing room; you look as though you're about to be sick.'

The man looked for help but found none. His behaviour, or Towler's reaction to his behaviour, had lost him all support.

'Go and sit down, Duncan,' someone said.

Duncan glared at Towler and hobbled out of the bar.

The man who'd just spoken said, 'Sorry about that, gents. This *is* a private club, but it's not a rich one. Members of the public are always welcome. Now, can I get you both a drink? I'm Robin, the club captain.'

After showing Robin his warrant card, Fluke explained he was there to have a look round.

'Of course.'

Fluke walked slowly round the clubhouse. They were quickly the centre of attention. He asked a man to move, so he could sit in the same seat as he had last time. He looked around and saw nothing that grabbed his attention.

He tried to remember what he'd done. He'd read a report, if he remembered correctly. He'd also waited for Wilson's tractor to take him back up to the crime scene.

Diet Coke. He'd had a Diet Coke from the bar. A Diet Coke and a bacon sandwich. Fluke got up and walked to the bar. Found a seat near where he thought he'd sat last time. He looked around. There was plenty to see. Trophies. Engraved plaques. Framed pictures. Nothing with Kevin Hendricks on it though.

Had he imagined it? He didn't think he had but he couldn't be sure.

He put his head in his hands and tried to think. What had he done while he waited for the bacon to cook? Had he stayed by the bar talking to the barman? No, he hadn't. The barman was also the short-order cook, so he'd been in the back.

He hadn't sat and waited though. He'd been too restless. Too much going through his head to sit still for any length of time. So, he'd had another wander. Taken in some of the club's memorabilia.

Fluke retraced his steps, trying to drown out the noise. Accumulated tat filled the shelves and bookcases, no doubt stuff they were incredibly proud of. He settled in front of the boards that displayed the names of club captains, and saw it immediately. It was on the Junior Captains' board.

K. Hendricks. Junior Club Captain. 2000/01.

He beckoned Robin over and pointed at the board.

'Would this be Kevin Hendricks?'

Shaking his head, Robin said, 'I've not lived here that long.' He gestured over to the barman; a grizzled man in his sixties wearing a Jennings Brewery polo shirt. 'Jeff here has been around longer than anyone.'

'I remember you,' Jeff said after Fluke walked over. 'You were here when that body was found.'

'And you made me a bacon sandwich.'

Jeff nodded. 'I did, aye.'

'Tell me about K. Hendricks. Would his first name be Kevin?'

Jeff stared at him for longer than was comfortable.

He sighed. 'I've been waiting for a day like this. You'd better come into the back, Mr Fluke.'

Chapter 46

'There's been men farming these fells for centuries, Mr Fluke,' Jeff said, as soon as they were seated in the small office. 'And they'll tell you that, every now and then, what looks like the perfect ram will be born. Looks like it'll be able to tup the entire flock. Enough piss and vinegar to make the sheepdogs pregnant.'

Fluke said nothing. Cumbrians gave up their information in their own way.

'But the farmers who know their stuff also know when things aren't right. I've known farmers who'll take a rock to what looks like the perfect ram. Stove its head in right there on the fell. Bad meat. Don't want it anywhere near their bloodline. Don't even want it going to auction and infecting someone else's.'

'And Kevin was bad meat?'

Jeff snorted. 'He was a talented golfer – good at everything he did, to be fair to the lad – but it came too easy to him, know what I'm saying?'

Fluke did. If things weren't hard fought for, they weren't valued. Direct-entry cops were a good example – no real understanding of the privileged position they were in.

'He could have made county if he'd wanted, but he was obsessed with becoming the youngest Junior Captain we'd had. That was all he cared about. There was another young chap – a better golfer, a nicer kid, who was a shoe-in though. But . . . Kevin kicked and screamed, and young Ben, who I guess didn't want the hassle, stood down. Let Kev have a free run at it.'

'So he got it?' Fluke asked.

'That he did. And was he grateful to Ben for stepping aside?'

'I guess not,' Fluke replied.

Jeff hesitated before continuing. 'It was only a rumour – and Kev's parents made it clear that anyone repeating it would see the inside of a slander court – but I heard that young Ben was found on the tenth green, not far from where your victim was found, unconscious and bleeding. He never said what happened, but we all knew. His generosity had made Kev look bad, and for him that was unforgiveable.'

'What happened?'

'Nothing. Ben's parents didn't go to the police. Kev did his year as captain, although he lost interest in it immediately. As soon as his name went on the board.'

'Where do his parents live?'

Background on Vane would be useful. It might even help them locate Jinx. It was clear she'd been observing him far more closely than anyone had realised. She'd known where the flask and the device had been stored and that meant she'd been following him. And if Vane had gone somewhere else as well – some hidey-hole from his childhood – Jinx could well be laying up there. He knew the area; she didn't.

For the first time Jeff looked shifty. 'I don't know.'

Sometimes the best way to get information wasn't always the direct way. Sometimes you had to tease it out. Fluke shot Towler a warning glance. This wasn't to turn into an interrogation.

'Would it surprise you to know that Kevin was involved in that body we found?'

'Wouldn't surprise me at all, Detective. And you know why?'

Fluke shook his head.

'Because he's done it before.'

Both their heads snapped up.

'What are you talking about, Jeff? There's nothing on any of our systems,' said Towler.

Jeff ignored him. 'He had a sister called Jenni. From what I hear she was a lovely girl. Wasn't into golf so wasn't round here much. Brilliant student by all accounts. Straight A grades at sixth form, and accepted into Columbia University in Manhattan on a full scholarship.'

Despite the heat and humidity, Fluke suddenly felt cold.

'Now, of course, Kevin didn't like that. Didn't like having any attention being taken away from him. Spent hours and hours in the bar here drinking his Cokes and holding court. Told anyone who'd listen what an easy school it was to get into. That she'd cheated. That she'd been sleeping with her teachers. Anything and everything to belittle what was a remarkable achievement. I heard he demanded that his parents stop her going. Threatened them. But by then even they'd had enough.'

He stopped talking, reached for a bottle of vodka and poured himself half a mug. His hands were visibly shaking. 'I don't even like to think about this, never mind talk about it.'

'We need to know, Jeff.'

'The night before she was due to go, she went out in Cockermouth with her friends. Sort of a leaving do.' He drained his mug. Looked at them. 'She never made it back. The official version was that she'd got so drunk, she slipped and fell into the Derwent.'

Fluke vaguely remembered the story. It had been investigated by detectives in the west and ruled accidental.

'And the unofficial version?'

Jeff shrugged.

'You don't think it was an accident?' Fluke asked.

'I *know* it wasn't.'

A bold statement. Fluke wondered if Jeff needed to put it through his 'fact, opinion or guess' exercise.

'How?' Fluke asked.

Jeff poured himself another vodka. Drained it in one go.

'Because he told me.'

Fluke sat still, stunned. 'He told you?'

'Close as I am to you now. "Old Jeff," he said – that was what the cheeky little bastard called me despite me asking him not to – "Old Jeff, am I evil?" he asks. "No, Master Hendricks, of course not," I says, "Why'd you ask?"'

'And what did he reply, Jeff?' Fluke already knew the answer.

'"Because I killed my sister," he says. Clear as day. Just comes out with it. To this day I don't know why. Only thing I can think of is he wanted it known. Why do it if you can't tell anyone?'

So there it was. Vane had killed before. Long before he became an activist, he'd drowned his sister in a jealous rage. He might not be their number-one suspect in the murder of Mark Bishop, but he was a killer nonetheless. Russell Bryce and Jenni Hendricks. History has a way of catching up with people.

That aside, it was time for Fluke to force the issue. 'Jeff, I know his parents must have been through hell, and I know you think you're protecting them, but I really do need their address. Even a phone number will do.'

Jeff looked at Fluke strangely. He reached for the vodka bottle again but Towler stopped him with a gentle, but firm, grasp.

'Jeff,' Fluke said, 'people have died. His parents may be the only lead we have left.'

He stared at Fluke and there were tears in his eyes.

'They were my friends, Detective. No one deserves what they went through. Can you blame them for disappearing? Kev went off with those long-haired louts and they were left with a big house and a dead daughter.'

'They didn't tell him where they'd moved to?'

Jeff shook his head. 'They told me, but I was sworn to secrecy. They were scared. It was only a matter of time before he came for them. He held grudges over the smallest things.'

'The address, Jeff?'

Chapter 47

The rain had made the steering light and the cornering dodgy but Fluke was in a hurry. They'd left Cockermouth immediately, and sped along the A66 until they reached the motorway. Conventional wisdom told Fluke that junction 36, the Barrow-in-Furness turn-off, was another thirty minutes away. He intended to get there in twenty. The address Jeff had given them was in the delightfully named hamlet of Stank. Neither of them had heard of it, but a quick check on Google showed it was a couple of minutes outside Barrow.

Fluke's mind was a washing machine – spinning and swirling. He'd been convinced that Vane was their killer. Arrested him on that basis. But he'd denied it during interview and Fluke didn't think he'd been lying. And overwhelming evidence now suggested it was Jinx, not Vane, who'd killed Bish. She'd certainly killed her minder and disappeared. Now there was disturbing information suggesting that Vane was every bit the sociopath they'd originally thought he was. He didn't know what to make of it any more . . .

He turned to Towler. 'Any of this make any sense to you?'

Stank was little more than a road with a few houses on either side. The very definition of the middle of nowhere.

They exited the car. 'Rigghazel Cottage we're looking for,' Fluke said, consulting his notes. 'You take the left and I'll take the right.'

After two hundred yards, Towler found it.

It was a small cottage, nestled in a clump of birch trees. From the road it could barely be seen. A wooden sign indicated they were in the right place. The car was fine where it was so they walked up the dry track that led to the front door.

It might have been small, but the cottage was immaculate. Honeysuckle competed with dark green ivy for the sun's attention on the whitewashed walls. Purple foxgloves were in full bloom, and butterflies and bees were taking full advantage. The black door was wooden with a highly polished brass knocker. Fluke had already lifted it to announce their presence when they heard voices coming from the back. Setting it back gently on the striking plate, they made their way round the side of the cottage.

A man in his sixties was on his hands and knees, trowel in hand, digging up weeds then passing them up to a similarly aged woman holding a bucket. A small fire of wood, weeds and other garden waste had been built but not lit. They were engrossed in their work and didn't notice the two detectives watching them.

Fluke coughed and noted their reaction: a quickly stifled flash of fear. He showed them his warrant card. Towler did the same.

The man groaned as he got to his feet. His trousers were stained green at the knees. He retrieved a handkerchief from his rear pocket and wiped his forehead and the back of his neck.

He gave them a resigned look. 'What's he done this time?'

Five minutes later they were seated in the garden munching on homemade jam tarts and drinking hot tea, courtesy of Mrs Hendricks.

'So, he's calling himself Vane now, is he?' Mr Hendricks asked, after Fluke had told them all he could.

Fluke nodded. He'd half expected that one, or both, of them would at least try to stick up for their son. The clichéd 'our Kevin would never do such a thing'. The fact that neither questioned anything told him Jeff hadn't been exaggerating what type of child

Vane had been. No wonder they ran. At some point you have to think of yourself . . .

'This is a nice place,' Fluke said. He didn't want to dredge up the past but he needed information. Instinct told him they'd talk, but they'd have to be coaxed.

Mr Hendricks grunted. 'You obviously didn't see our town-house in Cockermouth, Mr Fluke. The only thing this place has going for it is that Kevin doesn't know where it is. Not that he hasn't tried to find us.'

Fluke said nothing. Towler took another tart and ate it in two bites.

Mrs Hendricks took over. 'Do you think we're bad people, Mr Fluke?'

Shaking his head, Fluke said, 'I know you're not. From what I gather, Kevin made your lives a living hell.'

She shrugged. 'Our lives didn't matter. It was obvious he was going to walk down a different path to the rest of us, but we had to stay strong for Jenni. We knew he hated her. We tried to protect her from him as much as we could, but you know what girls are like; wouldn't hear a bad word said against her little brother.'

Fluke, whose two younger sisters had covered up many of the scrapes he and Towler had got into as kids, fully understood.

'Did he ever tell her he didn't like her?'

She snorted. 'No, he didn't, Mr Fluke. Kevin was more of a direct action kind of boy. Everything she valued either went missing or got destroyed. We told her but she didn't believe us.'

'She couldn't see it?' Fluke asked. Blood ties made people blind sometimes.

'Not even when he killed his own dog,' she replied.

Towler – whose daughter had a young springer spaniel and had therefore turned into a dog lover overnight – stiffened. 'What?' he said.

'He had a Border collie. One of the farmer's sons he knew

had been giving them away after one of their sheepdogs had got itself pregnant. And to be fair he loved that dog. Possibly the only thing he ever has. Went everywhere with it. But no one else was allowed to touch it, you understand? We couldn't feed it, stroke it or take it for walks. He didn't want it paying attention to anyone but himself.'

'And someone did?'

'Jenni just thought he was being silly. She'd been feeding him little treats when Kevin wasn't in, taking him for short walks along the river, that kind of thing. Well, of course, one day she came in from sixth form and the stupid dog raced to the door to greet her.'

Fluke whistled softly.

Mrs Hendricks nodded. 'Exactly. He didn't say anything at the time and Jenni thought she'd been right all along. That we'd been overreacting.'

Neither of them said anything.

'He took a cricket bat to it, Mr Fluke. Left its body in the boot of the new car we'd bought her for passing her driving test. Jenni blamed herself. She was that type of girl.'

'We took him to see a child psychiatrist. Paid to go private; didn't want him carrying the stigma of mental illness around with him for the rest of his life.'

'And?' Fluke asked.

'Histrionic personality disorder,' she said.

Fluke frowned. As a cop, he knew most of the common disorders but this was a new one on him.

'It means Kevin gets uneasy when he's not the centre of attention. And that can manifest in a number of ways. Anger towards those who are the centre of attention and extreme changes to his physical appearance are just two off the top of my head.'

'Hence the long hair and dreadlocks,' Fluke said.

'Most definitely,' she replied. 'There's no medication for histrionic personality disorder. Long-term psychotherapy is the only way to treat it. We were willing to pay, of course, but it came to nothing. Kevin attended one session and never returned. Said we were idiots and there was nothing wrong with him.'

Mr Hendricks, who'd seemed happy to let his wife speak, said, 'Do you know what he told the psychiatrist when he was asked what his childhood dream had been?'

Fluke shook his head.

'He'd said he wanted to be a unicorn.'

'Sounds like the type of thing Abi might say,' Towler said.

'So he could stab people with his head,' Mr Hendricks added.

Towler frowned. 'Maybe not.'

Fluke had a sip of his tea. Mentally regrouped. How did you rationally discuss the irrational? He knew that mental ill health took many forms, just as he also knew there was never just a medical solution. Some eminently treatable conditions went untreated because some people *enjoyed* their conditions. They enjoyed what it allowed them to do. They chose not to be treated. Medication was refused. Therapeutic sessions weren't attended. The rush from the freedom their conditions gave them was unparalleled.

Mrs Hendricks put down her cup. Her eyes were red and glistening. 'He seemed to lose interest in Jenni when he joined the golf club though. We thought it might have blown over.'

There was a sniffle from his right and Fluke knew Mr Hendricks was crying. He allowed him to keep his dignity and didn't turn to look.

'When she got her scholarship to Columbia,' she continued, 'we begged her to take it but she was unsure. She didn't want to leave England and she had an offer from Oxford anyway. But we could both see the storm brewing. Kevin might have been good at sports, but academically he wasn't in the same league as Jenni. Her being out of the country for three years might have allowed him to mature a bit. He tried to stop it, of course. Tried everything. Threats, emotional blackmail, that type of thing. But we stood firm and for once Jenni seemed to see through him. He even destroyed her passport and made a call to the American embassy saying she was a drug user. Nothing worked. She was going.'

Mr Hendricks wasn't bothering to hide the fact he was crying now. Mrs Hendricks's eyes were moist and Fluke, knowing what was coming, cursed his job. Some things were better left in the past.

'He left it until the last damned day!' she snarled. 'When I'm feeling particularly uncharitable, I think it was to give us hope. He wanted us to think he was going to let her have a normal life.'

There was no need to relive the drowning of their daughter and Fluke purposefully jumped ahead in their chronology. 'What was he like afterwards?'

'Honestly? It was as if nothing had happened. The day of the funeral he played golf and got a takeaway. The day after he demanded to be driven to Newcastle to get a new putter.'

'And the jealousy?'

'For a while it seemed to settle down. He continued being the spoilt little child he'd always been. We spent a fortune on him. Anything to keep him happy really. Any time someone did something new, he had to do it as well, only he had to have the newer, more expensive kit. His room still looks like a sporting goods store.'

'His room?'

'Oh, yes. We wouldn't dare mess about with his room.'

'But . . . he's never lived here,' Fluke said.

'Well, not his *actual* room, obviously. For our peace of mind we recreated his Cockermouth bedroom. Even used the same wallpaper.'

'Why?'

'Because, Mr Fluke, when Kevin finds us – and he *will* find us – he'll expect it to be exactly as he likes it.'

*

Vane's bedroom looked exactly like that of every other adolescent male. It had posters on the wall, CDs in racks and action figurines on shelves.

But when you knew the background, it took on a more sinister tone. The sporting trophies for golf were fine. The ones for fencing were not. Fluke picked up a thin sword from the stand it was on, and looked at Mrs Hendricks.

'His épée, Mr Fluke. Strictly speaking he should have started with a foil – that's the standard beginner's sword – but Kev wouldn't have it. Liam at school had a foil, so Kev had to have the next sword up. It was another sport he excelled at but, as soon as he replaced Liam on the county team, he gave it up.'

Fluke and Towler exchanged glances, very aware of the sword's significance. It was possible that they had been right all along – Vane had killed Bish. Or at least taught Jinx how to do it. He hadn't killed Diamond's minder though; that had been Jinx. Were they working together? Was it possible Vane had recruited her when she'd told him about Bish being an undercover cop? But if they *were* working together, why give up the location of the package?

Except of course, he hadn't. He'd given them an address. Had them chasing their arses for a bit. What he'd *actually* done was give Jinx time to disappear.

It didn't explain why Vane had mentioned Tibet and the sky burial though. Although he was unlikely to know Jinx had told Fluke she'd been to Nepal, why even risk it? Unless he was hoping she'd do the deed then disappear for good. Take the blame for everything. Allow Vane to walk. Although, from what the Hendricks were saying, he didn't like to share the spotlight. None of what he'd learned over the last few hours made sense.

Also, why would the Choreographer work with someone this unstable. It seemed the more they uncovered, the less they knew.

Fluke put down the sword – because whatever its fancy name, it *was* just a sword – and continued looking. Anything that could

311

point to something that might explain where he'd been hiding before Towler had headbutted him. An old photograph, a letter, anything. Something.

Jinx was following his plan and she wouldn't be able to hide without help. He'd had the local knowledge, not her.

He looked around and frowned. For a room with so many memories there were no photographs. Fluke said as much.

'We have them in scrapbooks, Mr Fluke. He likes things neat. He sends us newspaper clippings. Some environmental nonsense he'd been up to that made page seven of some local rag. He even includes instructions as to which section it was to go in. We've carried on getting them as we still have a redirect on our mail.'

'Can I see them, Mrs Hendricks?' he said.

She nodded, and left to get them. Mr Hendricks remained and the silence was getting awkward.

Towler picked up a small model train. 'I used to have these when I was a lad. Bit bigger than this one though.'

Mr Hendricks perked up slightly. 'Another of my failed attempts at father–son bonding, Sergeant Towler. I had trains when I was a boy, thought if I could get him into them, it might help him find some peace. I bought him that one. It's valuable but he didn't care. Never played with it once. It's N gauge. Twice as small as the popular Double-O you'd have had?'

Towler nodded.

'Would that be to the same scale as La'al Ratty?' Fluke asked. It was more to keep the old man's mind off what they'd discussed earlier than any burning desire to understand the intricacies of model railway gauges. La'al Ratty was the only train he'd ever been on for pleasure.

Shaking his head, Mr Hendricks said, 'La'al Ratty is fifteen inches minimum gauge. Standard gauge, the one our trains run on, is actually three and three-quarters times the size.'

Fluke nodded. He didn't know what else to do.

'Here, I'll show you,' Hendricks said, taking a book from his son's bookcase.

His ordeal should have been halted by the return of Mrs Hendricks, clutching a stack of photo albums. Fluke moved to go to her, but Mr Hendricks grabbed his arm and held him fast.

'You see, Inspector, most people don't realise that the history of steam engines and the progress of human advancement are inextricably linked.'

Towler grinned.

Towler sat with Mrs Hendricks and looked through the photographs. Fluke tried to follow what they were talking about but Mr Hendricks simply talked louder every time he turned his head. Eventually he gave up. Towler was more than capable of reviewing the photo albums for anything useful.

Not satisfied with an oral history of the railway, Hendricks was now on how model trains had developed. If he'd been asked to repeat a single thing he'd been told, Fluke would have struggled. He looked at the small train Towler had picked up earlier. It was far smaller than the ones Towler used to have. To him it looked to be the same scale as La'al Ratty, but he had no doubt Hendricks was right; it was almost a quarter of the size of the train tracks found across Britain. He turned it in his hands and idly did the maths. It was something to do.

Fifteen inches and it was a quarter of the size of normal railway tracks. That made them sixty inches across. Roughly. Hendricks had said they were actually closer to three and three-quarters bigger. So about fifty-six inches. About four and a half feet.

At school Fluke had been taught the metric system, although he had a working knowledge of imperial measures and, like most people his age, used a mixture of both in his daily life. Some measurements, such as the Fahrenheit and Celsius scales of temperature, he mixed and matched without even realising. The temperature outside was still in the mid-eighties Fahrenheit, but come winter he'd be shivering and measuring how cold it was by comparing it to zero degrees Celsius. If someone told him how hot it was in Celsius, or how cold it was in Fahrenheit, he wouldn't know whether to wear a jumper or a thong.

Fluke could visualise four and a half feet, although he didn't know how that translated to centimetres. As Hendricks started on how La'al Ratty had more in common with Indian than European railways, he took his iPhone out, swiped it on and found an imperial to metric conversion site.

He typed fifty-six inches in the imperial column and pressed calculate.

The answer popped up on the screen and Fluke froze.

He knew what the Choreographer was planning.

Chapter 48

There are 2.54 centimetres in an inch, and 56 inches meant that Fluke was looking at 142 centimetres on his phone.

Just under a metre and a half . . .

The two largest pieces on Vane's device were just under a metre and a half.

Towler and Fluke had both instinctively thought the device was a frame for a shaped-charge; it was the right shape and the right size. It also fitted given the context of an established IRA connection. Their only question had been which part of Sellafield had Vane been planning to blow up.

But the Choreographer didn't work like that. She wasn't interested in bangs and lots of noise for the sake of it. She was a change agent, not a mindless vandal.

The device on the blueprint had clamps. They'd assumed it was to fix it vertically to a window or doorframe. They'd never considered it might be designed to sit on top of something.

Like a railway track.

This was how she was going to bring down Sellafield. By attacking the infrastructure that allowed it to function. Almost everything Sellafield processed came by rail. The roads were simply too dangerous.

And, as soon as he understood the real target, Fluke knew what the plan was in its entirety. All the little bits, all the confusion, made sense.

The Choreographer planned to derail a train.

A nuclear train.

The plough-like bits on the device were designed to lift its wheels off the track. It only needed to work for a fraction of a second. That would be enough; the weight and unstoppable momentum of the train would ensure the rest followed.

But simply derailing a train wouldn't be enough. The AGR fuel flasks were designed to stand up to a train wreck. It would be a spectacular own goal if all the derailment achieved was to prove just how safe transporting radioactive material by rail was.

Enter the stolen AGR fuel waste.

In the carnage of a train crash, who would notice a solitary man emptying the package among the wreckage?

And then, to complete the illusion of an accident, the re-designed fast-release clamps would be utilised, and the device would be spirited away. The world would think a train had come off the tracks, and that the flasks weren't as indestructible as advertised. Without really putting anyone or anything at risk, the Choreographer would have created the perfect illusion of an environmental crisis. The train driver might end up with some cuts and bruises but it was unlikely anyone else would get hurt.

There'd be a public outcry. Parliament would shut down Sellafield until a full investigation could take place. It might never reopen.

The Choreographer would have won and no one would have been any the wiser.

'Boss, you've got to see this,' Towler said urgently, breaking into his thoughts. Hendricks was still waffling on about something but the sergeant's tone had caused him to trail off and quieten.

'Not now, Matt.' Fluke needed to think. He didn't know when the plan was due to go down. His gut told him Vane would have carried it out in the dark – far less chance of being seen – but that didn't mean Jinx would. She'd become unhinged and that meant logic was a distant second to vengeance.

'Boss!'

Fluke waved him away. What else did he need to do? He and Towler had better get back on the road. He knew the main Sellafield routes. The isolated parts of the journey were all in the west of the county. That's where he needed to be next.

'For fuck's sake, boss! Will you look at these bloody photographs?' Towler almost hit him in the face with one of the albums.

Irritated, he looked down at the grinning face. He stared and sat down on the bed. He gasped as he turned the pages over, each photo or newspaper clipping increasing his desire to see the next.

They were shocking.

'We couldn't have known, boss,' Towler said. 'How could we?'

As everything fell into place, Fluke continued to go through the photograph albums. The pictures were all of Kevin Hendricks in his younger days. Smiling. Scowling. Looking happy, looking sullen. Some were family pictures and some were clippings of sporting achievements. The later clippings were taken at environmental protests or in some traveller camp or at a festival. Posing with a golf club and a trophy or chained to a tree. At a concert or sitting round a fire. They detailed the journey he, and his family, had been through. He was front and centre in every one – even in photographs where the subject was his sister or someone else. Whoever had been behind the camera had obviously learned – probably the hard way – that Kevin had to be the focus of the camera's eye.

But in every photograph, the face looking back at him wasn't the man they knew as Vane.

It was Twist.

The smiling Twist in the traveller camp was a different man to the sullen boy staring back at him but there was no question it was him. Kevin Hendricks. The boy who'd killed his sister in a jealous rage. Whose histrionic personality disorder made him irrational and attention-seeking.

And it wasn't as if the clues hadn't been staring Fluke in the face. The way he'd stopped him touching his dog at the campsite. The way he'd frowned when his son said 'Momma'. The way he'd tried to take attention away from Dan's blacksmith display. The fact he didn't want Bish – who'd owned every room he'd ever stepped in – getting together with Jinx. Didn't want him stealing the heart of a woman who'd looked up to him for as long as she'd known him. He had Faith, so wouldn't want her romantically, but his 'centre of attention' addiction meant no other man could be part of her life. So he'd have hated Bish. Probably Jinx too.

And then the final insult – he discovers Vane has a well-funded plan to commit the most audacious environmental strike in the history of activism. How could he not be angry? What a kick in the spuds that must have been for him. In his eyes, he was *the* activist – he even had the newspaper clippings. It should have been *him* the Choreographer approached. Not Vane.

The solution?

Kill Bish.

Frame Vane.

Two birds, one stone; all his histrionic boxes ticked.

There was only one thing left to do.

Derail the train.

But Twist would have no intention of taking the blame for it. That's why Jinx was with him. She'd betrayed him by running off with Bish and she needed to be punished too.

Of course, for Jinx to take the blame, she'd have to die at the derailment site . . . She trusted Twist completely – certainly enough to ring and tell him where she was – and probably would right up until the moment he killed her.

Towler had already gone outside. He was on the phone, although Fluke had no idea who he was calling. Time was a luxury Fluke didn't have right now. He needed to do several things.

318

He still hadn't called anyone to make sure all the trains going in and out of Sellafield were stopped. No, scratch that – he needed to make sure every train in the *country* carrying nuclear waste was stopped. Fluke had no idea how these things worked but there had to be a system to warn all drivers of potential danger on the tracks. Fallen trees, landslides, people wanting to commit suicide, the wrong kind of leaves . . .

Before he did anything though, he needed to ring it in.

Chambers didn't ask questions when Fluke told him what he'd discovered and the conversation lasted less than a minute. Chambers was so flustered he even forgot to reprimand Fluke for ignoring his order to go back to HQ.

Just to be sure, Fluke rang a contact at Sellafield and asked to be put through to the police there. He got lucky; instead of a pompous arsehole determined to prove the Civil Nuclear Constabulary were the same as the territorial forces, he got a sergeant with a bucket load of common sense. He didn't ask for proof – he wouldn't press any panic buttons without checking Fluke was who he said he was – but he took all the details and promised to act on it.

Job two was to start the search for Twist. And that was far more difficult. Stopping every nuclear train in the country? Simple, one or two phone calls. Finding a hate-filled lunatic and a naive hostage in the second largest county in England was a different matter entirely. They'd both made living off the grid an art form.

He rang Vaughn and sent him up to the camp to speak to Faith. She had to be in the dark about all of this but might know some of Twist's favourite haunts. He asked Jo Skelton to email him a map of nuclear waste routes. He tasked Jiao-long with working on likely places for a derailment. The Choreographer wouldn't want casualties so when the train came off the tracks it wouldn't be anything dramatic. The weaker the crash the better.

Look how unsafe this all is. Even this small derailment was enough for a spill . . .

It would be somewhere rural. Setting up and removing the device would have to be done without anyone observing it. There could be no hint of sabotage. If you farted in Ambleside thirty tourists would smell what you'd eaten for breakfast, but there were parts of Cumbria, particularly in the west of the county, where you could stage the Quidditch World Cup and be confident no one would be any the wiser.

It would be like looking for a needle in a big pile of needles.

Of course, there was one person who could help narrow the search.

Unfortunately, that person had everything to lose by telling him.

Vane.

Chapter 49

It was a nice idea but there was no way Fluke could make it happen. Even if he had the time, Reyes had ghosted Vane out of Cumbria. Fluke knew he'd either be at some obscure London station or HMP Belmarsh.

Vane was gone.

The next time he'd see the light of day would be in the dock of the Old Bailey.

They said their goodbyes to the Hendrickses and got back on the road. Getting in touch with Vane might be a dead end but there had been some good news. Chambers had called to tell him that all trains going to Sellafield were fitted with something called GSM-R – an acronym for a wireless communication system called 'Global System for Mobile Communications – Railway' – and the message to stop all trains carrying nuclear material had been given. As a backup, the controller had a red button he could press that would stop all trains in any particular area. The button for the north-west of England had been hit immediately, and now every train was stationary with no chance of moving any time soon. Fluke had winced at the thought of all those commuters. Couldn't be helped though.

With one less thing to worry about, Fluke put his mind to gathering information. Network Rail were out scouring the tracks, searching for anything untoward. They might get lucky, but Fluke wasn't holding his breath.

The incoming tone sounded and Jiao-long's details came up on the dashboard display. Fluke pressed receive.

'Longy, tell me you've got news.'

'I'm sorry, boss. I can probably narrow it down to under a hundred locations but there's no one place that stands out.'

'Bend,' Towler said.

'What's that?' Fluke asked.

'It'll be on a bend,' Towler said. 'Think about it. The original plan had to look like an accident. He had three options. He stages something on the track like a stone, he stages broken rails or he stages human error.'

'So why not just put an actual stone on the track, or physically damage the rails yourself?' Fluke finished for him.

'Exactly. So he uses human error – which is even scarier really. Every fucker out there doing dull, repetitive tasks will believe someone is capable of taking a shortcut.'

'And everyone will understand it's also something you can't eliminate,' Fluke said. Bored humans take shortcuts. It's what they do.

'So, if I'm a train driver, what's the one shortcut I have?' Towler asked. 'Can't exactly take a sneaky left and drive through a residential area.'

'Speed,' Jiao-long said through the speakers.

'Exactly right. Excessive speed's the only way a driver can shorten a journey. You'd simulate the driver taking a corner too quickly. That's how I'd do it anyway.'

It made sense. They were looking for a bend in the track somewhere rural.

'Longy, email me a list of locations and triage the ones on bends.'

He was about to add that he should send the list to Chambers, but withheld at the last minute. Chambers's priority was the recovery of the AGR fuel. He'd deploy everyone he had and Fluke didn't want that. Twist would be spooked and Jinx would die. The only way this ended well was if Fluke talked to Twist alone.

Going into his call history, Fluke found another number. It was probably a waste of time but nothing ventured, and so on.

There was no answer. The younger generation never had their phones out of their hands, so calls were either answered on the first ring or not at all. He let it ring while he thought of who to call next.

A voice came over the car speaker system. 'Hello?'

For a second he was so surprised he forgot to answer.

Towler dived in. 'Who the fuck's this?' He'd never mastered tact.

'You rang me, dickhead.'

'Zoe. It's Avison,' Fluke said.

There was a sharp intake of breath. 'You!' she hissed.

'Me,' Fluke said.

'You fucking knew where she was all along! That's why you knew to go to that house in Wetheral – you were hiding her.'

Fluke didn't have time for this. He would face the consequences of hiding Jinx later; right now he needed answers.

'Yep, I get it. Avison bad, Zoe good. I haven't got time for a rerun of which team are the biggest dickheads.'

'They are,' Towler said without hesitation.

Fluke shook his head for him to be quiet. 'We've got something,' he said.

Silence. An angry silence if there was such a thing.

'I'm listening,' she said eventually.

'Bish's killer. It wasn't Jinx.'

Silence.

'Fuck off, Fluke,' she said finally. 'I know you still feel sorry for Mark's pet but I'm not buying it. That man was opened up like a Christmas turkey and if she's capable of that, she's more than capable of killing an undercover police—'

'It was Twist, Zoe. He's the one who killed Bish. He killed that man in Wetheral as well.'

'Twist? That fucking clown!' she snapped. 'What you trying to pull here? Vane and that bitch were in it together. I don't actually know who killed Mark, but they're both going down for it. John was right, you've been so far out of your depth on this investigation you've been drowning. Just leave it be. I'm not interested in any more of your theories.'

'We've just been to see Kevin Hendricks's parents,' he said.

'When?' she said. 'We've not been told about this.'

Fluke carried on. 'And Kevin Hendricks is Twist, not Vane. And he's a bloody nutter, Zoe. He was diagnosed with something called histrionic personality disorder when he was a child. In all probability he killed his sister as well.'

'And his dog,' Towler added.

'And his dog,' he confirmed. 'His parents are in hiding from him.'

'So how did you—'

'Doesn't matter how we found them. We just did.'

'But Bish told Jinx he was a cop. She told Vane.' There was a little less certainty in her voice.

'Twist's mother and father said he had to be the centre of attention – we both saw what he was like at the camp. I think he got so angry at Bish, and so jealous of Vane, he was prepared to kill one and frame the other. And now he's planning to derail a train—'

'What? How do you kno—'

'Don't worry, they've been stopped,' he interrupted. 'We're now on a full-scale search for them both. We think he's planning to leave her body at the scene and walk away scot-free. Even when he realises the train isn't coming he'll still have to kill her. He'll probably stage a fall or an accident with the AGR fuel.'

A pause.

'It's a nice story.'

Fluke needed more. The magnitude of the favour he wanted meant Zoe would need to be sure it would help nail Bish's killer.

'There's one more thing,' he said.

'I'm listening.'

'He represented the county as a fencer. We've seen his swords and his trophies.'

Fluke had read the Met's post-mortem report. It echoed what Sowerby had said. Zoe was fully aware Bish had been killed with a long-bladed weapon.

'But the only way I can prove Twist killed Bish is if I catch Twist in the act,' he added.

Without Twist, all they'd end up with would be a dead suspect, no corroboration and a team from London with no interest in the truth. Jinx would forever be remembered as a failed terrorist.

Bish's killer would walk free.

'What do you need?' Zoe said at last.

What Fluke needed was for Vane to have a mobile phone put in his hand. Zoe had argued it was impossible. That Vane was heavily guarded and was being interviewed almost constantly. So far he'd said nothing.

In the end she promised to do what she could. Fluke wasn't holding his breath.

To his enormous surprise she rang back almost immediately.

'They're taking a break for food. You have ten minutes max and you're on speakerphone. If I think you've been bullshitting me I'll end the call. You're on now. Go.'

Thanking her would have to wait. Ten minutes wasn't long. Fluke held a finger to his lips. He needed Towler to keep quiet. The last thing he needed was Vane clamming up because the man who'd nutted him unconscious was listening.

'Vane, it's Detective Inspector Fluke. I'm not going to insult your intelligence by asking for a confession – that's not why I'm ringing. DC Koenig tells me I have no more than ten minutes so I'm going to tell you a story. And that prick Reyes – I'm sorry, Zoe, but he is – doesn't know what I'm about to tell you . . .'

For five minutes Fluke laid out his theory. Vane had been planning – under supervision – to attack the nuclear railway infrastructure. He explained how it was supposed to have been done. He told him that he suspected Twist had killed Bish. That Twist had Jinx somewhere and, in his mind at least, he was going to become a legend while framing his enemies at the same time. The fact every nuclear train in the country was stationary was irrelevant right now. Twist didn't know that.

Vane wasn't about to incriminate himself though. He had no motivation to do so.

'Nice story, Detective Inspector,' he said. 'Why are you telling me though? I'm the innocent party in all this. All I did was find something dangerous and keep it from falling into the hands of children. And getting an ornament made for my parents' garden isn't a crime either.'

'You attacked me with a sword.' Towler never could keep his mouth shut.

'No. I defended myself against a lunatic wearing fancy dress. Again, no law broken.'

'Fuck off,' Towler muttered. He turned to Fluke and whispered, 'See, I told you I looked like a knob.'

'You don't care that he ruined everything for you?' Fluke said. 'A plan, years in the making, gone because some attention-seeking twat wasn't getting to play. That doesn't bother you?'

The resulting pause told them it did. The silence that followed the pause told Fluke it still wasn't enough for him to fall on his sword. Vane was all about self-preservation now.

It was going nowhere and Fluke was running out of time. There was no incentive for him to say anything. Was there a way for Vane to give up the information *without* incriminating himself then?

'You know you'll go down for the murder of Mark Bishop, don't you?' Fluke said.

'You've just told me Twist did it. You think I'm stupid?'

'I don't, Vane. But do you know who I do think is stupid? Chief Inspector John Reyes, that's who. He doesn't care about my theory because, until we get hold of Twist, that's all it is – an unproven theory.'

Silence. At least he'd got his attention.

Fluke pressed his advantage. 'You'll have your day in court where you can try your circumstantial evidence defence against a confirmed terrorist plot. You can even try your "I like swords that's why my prints were on them", but I wouldn't recommend it. I leave this call with nothing, and you spend the rest of your life in a jail cell. Simple as that.'

Fluke didn't mention he knew he'd almost certainly killed Russell Bryce – the murder that Zoe uncovered all those years ago. Vane would have to take his chances with that.

More silence. He was listening.

But was he thinking?

He reinforced his position. 'Reyes thinks you killed Mark Bishop because Jinx told you he was an undercover police officer.'

'She didn't.'

'Doesn't matter. I've seen the briefing notes. In the last contact Mark had with his handler, he told her he was going to come clean to his new wife. There is no evidence to suggest he didn't do exactly that. If Twist kills Jinx, she won't be able to confirm or deny it.' He was stating the obvious, but sometimes the obvious needed to be stated.

Towler wanted in. Sometimes he was insightful. 'Don't forget, matey. You attacked me with a sword—'

'I've already said it was because you were dress—'

'A jury will see that as competence with the murder weapon though,' Towler cut in.

'He's right, Vane,' Fluke said. 'Now weigh this up and do it quickly. Reyes has physical evidence tying you to the murder of an undercover police officer. He can also prove you have both competence with the murder weapon and a violent disposition. You had the motive – Jinx told you Bish was a cop.' Fluke paused. Allowed time for Vane to digest the information. 'Now, you've met Reyes, how hard do you think he'll look for an alternative explanation?'

'Vane,' Zoe said, finally getting on board with what they were trying to do, 'I can confirm that John has already asked the CPS to press the judge for a whole-life tariff for Mark's murder. He's saying that you knew he was a police officer and the murder was premeditated.'

'Do you know what a whole-life tariff means, Vane?' Fluke asked. 'You might not; they're not often handed out. It means you never become eligible for parole. You *will* die in prison.'

No hesitation this time. 'What do you want?'

'This plan that existed – the one you had nothing to do with – it relied on secrecy, yes?' Fluke said.

A small pause.

'That would be a reasonable assumption,' Vane said carefully.

'We think the location will be isolated, and my good friend Matt here seems to think it may be on a bend so it might appear the driver had been speeding before he derailed.'

'Plausible,' Vane said.

We'll call that a yes then, Fluke thought.

But where though? How could Vane tell him without incriminating himself? Zoe would *have* to use whatever he said as evidence at his trial. Fluke looked at the car's clock. His ten minutes were up. He looked across at Towler who shrugged.

Fluke stared out of the window, searching for inspiration. Something, anything, that would allow Vane to talk. The sun was low in the sky. It was another beautiful evening. They'd been spoilt recently. If this case ever finished, he made a mental note to stop off at a deli somewhere and get some snacks. He and Bridie could take a boat out and eat on the lake. He'd always wanted to do that with her. If she was even there when he got home.

A picnic . . .

He wondered. Could it be so simple? Over the speakerphone he could hear noise.

'Vane, it's a beautiful evening out here and I'm sorry you can't see it. It's a shame you couldn't help us.'

Towler stared at him. He had no doubt Zoe would also be wondering what he was playing at.

He continued. 'So, I'm going to go and find somewhere to watch this sunset. Maybe share a bottle of wine and a picnic with my lady friend.'

Towler was still looking at him blankly but knew enough not to interrupt. Fluke asked his question.

The question . . .

'The thing is, at this time of year the Lake District is packed with tourists, and neither Bridie nor I like crowds. You seem to know the area well. Is there anywhere nice you can recommend?' Fluke asked. He paused then added, 'Perhaps somewhere a bit off the beaten *track*?'

There was the sound of a door opening. Someone shouting, 'What the hell's going on?'

'Vane! Now or never!' Fluke shouted over the noise. 'Can you recommend somewhere?'

A lingering pause.

'I can actually, Detective Inspector . . .'

Chapter 50

Vane's suggestion for a 'picnic' was an isolated stretch of train track in West Cumbria. It was located between Parton and Harrington, just outside the fishing town of Whitehaven.

As they drove there, Fluke rang Jiao-long and told him to email a satellite image to his phone. They discussed how to handle the situation. Fluke was convinced the softly-softly approach was best. Try to talk Twist down. Towler thought they should sneak up and bash him on the head with a rock.

A 'ting' from his phone told him Jiao-long's satellite image was in. There was only one bend in the track between Parton and Harrington and it was incredibly isolated. There were no roads. Fluke suspected Vane had planned to bring Bish into the plan at the last minute; get some muscle for the final push. Twist would be carrying the huge metal device on his own. Even in its disassembled state that would be a Herculean task. He would also have a flask full of bollock-rotting nuclear waste and – because he'd slit the throat of her minder – a now struggling Jinx to contend with. No way was Twist using the bend that Vane had selected. It was too far away. He'd have to choose somewhere else.

They compared the image with Fluke's road map. Realistically there was only one option: Foundry Road. Due to the much more modern A595 it was rarely used, but it still served as the coastal route between Harrington and Parton. It ran parallel to the train track, and despite it being almost five miles long, there was only one point that looked to be both accessible and isolated. Just before the outrider buildings leading into Parton, the road and the railway track both hugged the rugged coastline and were less than ten yards apart. There was even a bit of hard standing nearby that Twist could use to park whatever he was driving. With the sea on one side and what looked like dense shrub on the other, the chances of being observed would be zero.

Twist wouldn't have access to the same quality images they had but he'd surely arrive at the same conclusion by simply driving the road. He didn't even need the bend – only privacy. To have Jinx assume posthumous responsibility, the device *and* her corpse would need to be left in situ. The illusion of an accident didn't suit Twist's needs.

This was about settling scores . . .

Jiao-long told them the nuclear waste train would have been due to pass that part of the track in an hour. They had to find him by then; Twist would get suspicious if the train didn't arrive.

Rather than travel in the same direction Twist probably had, Fluke decided to drive to Parton and approach from the opposite end. He turned into the village, found Foundry Road, and turned right towards Harrington. If he were right, Twist should be less than a mile away.

The traffic was non-existent, so Fluke was able to crawl without causing a tailback. It wasn't long before they saw the hard-standing area they'd identified earlier. A ragged-looking van was parked there. Fluke sped up and drove past. As soon as they were out of sight he parked. He and Towler walked back to the hard standing.

The van was an old VW camper, and although Fluke didn't recognise it from the camp, it was the type of thing at least some of the travellers drove. He knew that they were considered classics but he doubted this one was worth anything. It was rusted beyond the help of even the most ardent restoration specialist.

It was empty.

Towler touched the bonnet. 'Engine's cold,' he said.

'Let's go for a walk then,' Fluke said.

The satellite image hadn't done justice to the long grass or the dense patchwork of ground shrubs. It would be easy for Twist to hide from them and observe their approach. If Jinx was dead, or incapacitated, then she'd be easily hidden as well.

But the device couldn't. It wasn't the type of thing that could be fitted in seconds. It would take time to set up properly. Fluke glanced at his watch and figured he had about fifteen minutes before the train would have been due. No other trains had been scheduled to pass beforehand. Common sense suggested the device would already be on the track. And wherever the device was, Twist would be nearby.

Fluke was an ex-marine, and Towler was an ex-para; they both knew how to move quietly and basic infantry hand signals were second nature. They patrolled silently along the side of the track, their eyes peeled.

After ten minutes of cautious searching, Fluke was ready to concede he'd been wrong. With Twist not having the same goal as Vane, it appeared he'd taken the device, and Jinx, to a different location entirely. He could be absolutely anywhere. The VW must belong to someone else. Probably a surfer.

Shit.

Although every available cop and railway employee was out searching, Fluke had been desperately hoping it would be him who found Twist. He was Jinx's best chance of surviving.

Towler, slightly ahead of him, dropped to his knees. Without turning he raised his hand. The signal for stop.

Fluke froze.

Towler placed the palm of his hand flat on his head.

Come to me.

Fluke approached silently. Towler pointed along the track to where the device could clearly be seen.

Despite it being nearly thirty yards away, Fluke could see that it fitted perfectly. He was almost tempted to ring Dan and congratulate him. The two longer arms spanned the track; their only purpose to give support and add rigidity. It was the snowplough parts on the shorter arms that were for the actual derailment. They had a gradual slope and started at the same height as the rail. But over the course of eighteen inches they gained six inches in height. They also had a slight curve. The train's wheels would start at the lower end then gently ride up and off the track. The natural speed of the train would ensure that it left the track with little more than a bump. By the time the driver realised, he would be fifty yards too late.

Fluke looked for the device's owner but Twist was nowhere to be seen.

Chapter 51

Fluke stood still. If the marines had taught him anything, it was to take as much time as you could in tactical situations. Neither he nor Towler were in any rush to approach the device. Not because it was dangerous – it wasn't – but because Twist would almost certainly be watching it.

From where though?

He was spoilt for choice. The coastal geography offered an abundance of places to stay out of sight. Long grass, natural dips and elevations, even some holes. Someone could easily observe the track and remain hidden. There was also noise cover: gulls screeched, the sea did its thing and a breeze moved the grass. Even smell – a much under-utilised part of detecting – was nullified on the coast, the rich salty fragrance more than enough to mask the scent of a human.

They approached it slowly. Scanned both sides of the track. Twist wasn't there.

'He'll have seen us and legged it, mate,' Towler said. 'Jinx will turn up, don't worry.'

Fluke grunted non-committally. He looked down at the device. It had a strange beauty. Simple yet deadly. He could admire it later though. Now, he just wanted it off the track. Get the trains moving again; they'd been at a standstill for over two hours and counting. He put on a pair of latex gloves and undid the clamps. It was testament to Dan that, as secure as the device was, it released immediately.

'Take this back to the car, Matt. Wear gloves, it'll probably have prints on. I'll ring Chambers and tell him the device is secure. I'll also ask him to get his search teams here. Twist's got to be around here somewhere; he's on foot.'

He reached for his phone, called headquarters and brought his boss up to speed. Chambers said he would get the north-west trains running again, although any carrying nuclear waste would remain grounded until Twist was in custody and the AGR waste secured. Chambers also arranged for teams to be diverted to the Whitehaven area and Fluke promised to be his man on the ground. He and Towler would coordinate the search.

Fluke sat down on the grassy bank and looked out to sea. The sea breeze cooled the sweat on his brow. A lone fishing trawler – one of the two hundred that used Whitehaven port – chugged its way out to sea. The cod season was behind them, of course. Most of the bigger specimens had migrated to colder, Scandinavian waters. He idly wondered what they were fishing for.

The cod season was behind them . . .

Something dawned on him.

The train would have been coming from Workington. Which was behind him.

A thought popped into his head. *If I'm derailing a train, I want to be upstream when it comes off.* Otherwise you risk becoming the filling in a thousand-tonne sandwich . . .

Twist hadn't fled at all.

He was behind him.

Fluke turned.

A voice called out from the thick grass.

'How'd you find us?'

Twist was holding Jinx in a restraint move. She looked to be in pain. He had a knife to her throat. It had already nicked her and the blood was running freely. Superficial, but it showed intent.

335

As well as Jinx's fresh red blood, the knife was also dark red where the blade met the handle. The blood of Diamond's minder.

In his other hand Twist held the deadly flask.

Fluke looked round for Towler but he was still out of sight.

'Glad to see you again, Twist. What's happening here?'

Nice and calm. No drama.

Yet.

He approached Twist, stopped when he was ten yards away. Didn't want Twist to think he was planning to rush him.

The lid of the flask – which looked like a steel thermos but probably wasn't – was at an angle. It looked like it had been unscrewed but left on.

Twist gave him the same smile he'd flashed when he'd dropped off Jinx all those days ago. The face of an innocent man. A cheeky rascal of a grin, and despite the situation – flask in one hand, hostage in the other – he appeared confused by Fluke's presence. As if nothing that was happening there was worthy of his time. He could have been sucked in by that look of innocence. He knew many had in the past.

But this time Fluke looked beyond the smile, and into his eyes. They belonged to a madman.

A strange expression crept across Twist's face. Fluke knew he was building a narrative, one that explained everything. And, as he was about as spoiled and deranged as it was possible to be, he would expect it to be believed.

'Seems like you owe me one, Detective Inspector.'

As opening gambits went, it wasn't bad.

Fluke ignored it.

'You all right, Jinx?' he asked.

She tried to nod but Twist tightened his grip around her throat. Her face went purple. The knife drew a little more blood.

'NO!' Twist screamed, the noise shattering the tranquillity. 'You should be asking if *I'm* OK, not this fucking bitch!'

'Are *you* OK, Twist?' he asked calmly. He'd play along for now.

'Yes! And I'm a hero. I stopped her before she could do it.'

'Do what, Twist?'

His voice turned into a whine. 'You know,' he said. 'I *know* you know.'

'Tell me anyway.'

'She killed Mark. Chopped him up with a sword then fed him to the foxes. Just like she was taught in Nepal. She killed that man in Wetheral as well. Slit his throat. I saw her,' he said, before adding, 'She kept following Vane around too. Found out all his plans. But I stopped her!'

The look on Jinx's face confirmed Twist had already told her Bish was dead. There was no shock there. Just dull resignation. Fluke doubted he would have been gentle with the news. He'd have been as vindictive as he could. Told her she was going to take the blame for his murder. That her legacy would be that she was the woman who'd dismembered her husband.

Fluke had seen enough. He needed to be proactive. He would ease Jinx's pain. Let her know he knew exactly what was going on. It would have the added benefit of destabilising Twist.

He nodded. 'That man in Wetheral, the one Jinx killed, is that his blood on the knife? Did you disarm her, Twist?'

'I did, yes!' A look of relief flashed across his face. 'I told you, I'm a hero. Wait until Faith hears what I've done! Do you think I'll be in the papers? I bet I will be!'

'So her fingerprints will be on the knife then?' Fluke said.

A wild look. A panicked response. 'She was wearing gloves. Those yellow ones ladies wear when they do the dishes. Yes,' he said, getting into the lie, 'she took them off and threw them away.'

'Where? We'll go and look for them. We have search teams who can find things much smaller than a pair of gloves.'

'I . . . I can't remember . . . She burnt them!'

337

'Where, Twist? There's always something to recover. If we want her to go to prison, we're going to need that evidence.'

Twist tilted his head as if trying to will up a credible answer. Time to remind him just who it was he had in his grip.

'Jinx hasn't done anything to you. She's your friend. Remember?'

A confused look replaced the innocent one he'd been trying to effect. Obviously this wasn't part of his script.

'No! No! No! She did it all. Ask my mum and dad, I'm a good boy. A credit to them. Twist is nice, everyone says so!'

'We have spoken to your parents . . . Kevin.'

His shock was immediate. He quickly moved into a full tantrum.

'WHY WON'T YOU BELIEVE ME!' His voice shook with fury. 'She did it, not me! I stopped her!' Tears streamed down his face. 'And my parents don't know anything! I didn't kill my dog and I didn't kill my sister. Jinx did that too! Where do they live? It's against the law to hide from your son.'

'He's fucking losing it, mate,' Towler whispered.

He had crept up silently and now stood at Fluke's shoulder. Normally Towler would have just come up behind the target and, depending on who was looking, either restrained them or belted them over the head with something hard. A hostage and some radioactive waste changed things though. Their best option was still to talk Twist down, but they were on a clock; Chambers's search teams would be arriving soon.

'Jinx didn't know you when your sister died, Twist,' Fluke said gently. Relaxing and soothing. Nothing more than two friends talking. 'She was living in Bristol. You found her there, remember?'

'You did it then!' He blinked as if realising what he said. 'No. It wasn't you and it wasn't Jinx. It was someone else then! I haven't killed anyone.'

'Why did Mark have to die, Twist?'

While he was unbalanced it was perhaps the only chance he

338

had to get answers. As soon as they got him back to the station, any solicitor worth his salt would hit the mental capacity defence hard. They'd tell him to shut up while they looked for a tame psychiatrist.

'Was he stealing Jinx from you?'

Fluke kept saying her name, reminded Twist who she was.

'Ha! You think I care about her?'

'The woman whose throat you have a knife to? Yes, I think you care about Jinx. I think you care about her a great deal.' The lie slipped out easily. Twist didn't care about anyone but Twist. 'Did Mark need punishing for something?'

He gripped the knife harder but it moved no closer to Jinx's throat.

'You shouldn't say things like that. It's not nice. I'll . . . I'll sue you for . . . telling lies about me! Yes, that's what I'll do.'

He was irrational but at least he was talking. And while he was, Jinx wasn't in any immediate danger. Short of a sniper, he had no way of getting her away from Twist anyway. Talking was all he had – Twist still had that flask.

'Was it because of Vane? Was he taking over the camp? Your camp?'

That got a reaction.

At the mention of Vane's name, Twist's lunacy ramped up another notch.

'Him!' he hissed. 'He spoilt everything! Why did he have to come? With his stupid plan. I could have had a plan like that if I'd wanted. A better plan. Mine would've worked. I wouldn't have been caught like him. Ha, what an idiot Vane is. Sitting in his police cell while I'm free. Who's the top man in camp? Not stupid Vane. Everyone knows that now.'

'You killed Mark to get rid of Vane then?' Fluke asked gently. It was a reason, he supposed. A messed-up reason but he'd heard worse.

339

'And because he got married to Jinx without my permission!' he shouted. His movements had become jerky. The knife nicked Jinx's throat again. She gasped but Twist didn't notice. He was too absorbed in his own narrative.

The end was near. Fluke had seen it countless times. Eventually criminals cave in to overwhelming evidence and it all comes out. All their motivations, all their neuroses and petty grievances.

'He must have put up quite a fight?' Play to his ego. The man's an idiot. Bish had been ambushed and slaughtered. There had been no fight, but that wouldn't fit with what Twist wanted everyone to think.

'He was a soldier, you know. I'd told him we needed to go and meet one of Jinx's friends up at the golf course. Said it was about her mum. Jinx still likes her mum. When we got up there he pulled a sword on me. Said that Jinx could never love him as much as she loved me. Said he was going to chop me up and "disappear me".'

'Did you have a sword as well?' Fluke asked, allowing him to run with his fantasy.

Twist laughed manically. 'I didn't need a sword! Just my bare hands. He tried to kill me, but he was the one who ended up dead. He was the one chopped into little pieces, not me! Turns out *I'm* the real soldier.'

It was a confession, he supposed. Fluke didn't say anything for a moment and Twist took the time to compose himself. It must have dawned on him what he'd just said.

'Ha! That was a good joke! You believed everything I said. You're not allowed to remember that because I was joking. Jinx did it, not me. That's the bit you have to write down in your notebooks.'

And so on.

Despite having turned into a ranting, panting lunatic, Twist still had a firm grip on the flask. The knife at Jinx's throat also remained steady. He couldn't move anywhere though, and while Fluke kept his distance they remained in a standoff.

Twist obviously thought he needed to do something. He flipped off the flask's lid. The lid fell to the ground and Fluke watched it land.

And there's a bit of ground that will have to be fenced off for thirty years, he thought.

'What's your plan here, Twist? You don't want to get any of that stuff on you. Radiation poisoning is a slow and painful death. Just look at the bloke in London that the Russians killed.'

In his peripheral vision he saw Towler move. The big man wouldn't risk Jinx's life, no matter how reckless Twist was being, but he clearly had something on his mind.

'Jinx, do you remember me?' he said.

Jinx nodded slightly.

'Don't you speak to her!' Twist shrieked.

Towler ignored him. 'Do you remember what we practised? When we got back to the apartment in Wetheral?'

'What did you practise?' Twist spun Jinx round so he could look at her face. 'I demand to know what you practised! You don't keep secrets from me! Ever!'

Jinx was staring so hard at Towler, her eyes were nearly popping out of their sockets.

Despite the utter chaos, Towler's voice remained even. 'Do you think you could do that now?'

She shook her head. Terrified.

'Yes. Yes, you can,' Towler said. 'Just do that one thing for me then we can all go home.'

'What!' Twist screamed.

Towler raised his voice. It wasn't a shout. It was a command. 'Do it now, Jinx.'

It was over in a matter of seconds, but Fluke knew the sequence of events that followed would be etched in his memory for ever.

As Twist launched another obscenity-filled tirade about secrets, Jinx's free hand reached down and grabbed his groin. Twist's face changed. 'What are you doing?' Unbelievably, he said, 'Stop it, I'm married!'

Jinx grabbed Twist's testicles through his loose flannel trousers and, before he realised what was happening, she'd wrenched down with a sickening jerk. Twist screamed and let her go. Jinx sprinted to Towler.

Fluke watched as Twist slowly collapsed to the ground. As he opened his mouth and screamed in anger, the elbow of his flask arm bounced when it hit the ground. Foul-looking liquid spewed in the air like the world's smallest geyser.

And hit Twist in the face.

In his eyes and in his mouth.

'Get her out of here!' Fluke screamed.

Towler didn't hesitate. He grabbed Jinx, hoisted her over his shoulder and sprinted down the track.

Fluke took a couple of steps back. He didn't know what to do. He certainly couldn't offer any assistance.

Twist staggered to his knees, groaned, then vomited. Fluke doubted it would be enough to act as a stomach wash. He was a dead man. After spitting to clear his mouth, Twist stood up. He looked down at the empty flask and realised what he'd just swallowed.

'Nooooo!' he wailed.

He got to his feet and lurched towards Fluke.

He backed off. Twist was now a walking, talking, biohazard.

'You did this!' he cried. 'Help me! Get it off me! You have to get it off me!'

The poison in his eyes meant Twist could barely see. Arms outstretched he continued to move towards Fluke.

For a moment, his base instincts almost took over. He considered picking up a rock and, as if it were a coconut at the county fair, hurling it at Twist's head. Ethical positions on police brutality go out of the window when a radioactive man is chasing you.

Fluke looked down at the sandy ground. There was nothing he could use anyway.

Fluke backed up at the same speed that Twist was walking towards him, maintained the ten-yard gap. He risked a glance over his shoulder. They were now dangerously close to some houses.

He needed to draw Twist away from them.

The beach. Like most West Cumbrian beaches, it was rocky rather than sandy. If he could lure Twist there, there was bound to be something he could use to disable him.

Slowly, he backed up onto the track, careful not to fall. Twist followed, stumbling.

A noise registered. More of a feeling. *A vibration*.

There was a train coming. But how? They'd only just released them. The next train due was the one carrying nuclear waste, but that had been stopped at least an hour away from where they were now. It was also still locked down, according to Chambers. Fluke looked over Twist's shoulder and saw nothing. No train approached.

He didn't understand. The track was humming now.

Oh shit!

He'd told Chambers to start the trains running again. Said it was safe now the device was off the track. And although the nuclear train was still stuck in a siding somewhere, there would have been plenty of commuter trains waiting in the nearby Whitehaven station. The two o'clock, delayed for hours, would have left as soon as Chambers had given the release order . . .

Fluke didn't hesitate. He stepped over the track just as the train rounded the bend and came into view. Put himself on the rocky beach side.

Twist was still on the other side of the track, a confused expression on his face. He didn't see the train, until the horn blasted. He jerked round, his confusion turning to hate as he realised Fluke would soon be safe.

The train was about to become an insurmountable barrier. By the time it passed, Fluke could be away.

He didn't hesitate. He hurled himself in Fluke's direction. Tried to dive across the track and beat the train. His all-consuming desire to hurt overriding all sense of self-preservation.

He almost made it.

He *should* have made it.

But, in his madness, Twist had forgotten one thing. Fluke had stepped over the track; he was jumping.

And the ground on his side was sandy.

As he leapt, the ground beneath his feet gave way and he fell, spread-eagled, across the train track. Like a drowning man he clutched at the rail nearest Fluke and tried to pull himself across.

He had nowhere near enough time.

The two o'clock from Whitehaven loomed, brakes screeching.

Twist looked at Fluke in desperation.

He cried out, 'I'm sorry!'

And then the train passed over him.

There were four carriages and by the time they'd passed, and the train had come to a halt, Towler had returned. He was holding one of the device's metal struts like a baseball bat.

'She's in the car, boss,' he said. 'What the fuck's happened here? Where's Twist?'

Fluke couldn't speak. He pointed at the red mess on the tracks. Towler walked up the embankment. Fluke joined him.

Towler looked down. 'Oh, man. His fucking head's come off.'

And he was right. It had.

Chapter 52

In less than five seconds, the train had managed to do what must have taken Twist hours: it had dismembered a body. Not only had it removed Twist's head, his arms and legs had been neatly amputated too. There wasn't much blood. Twist had been killed instantly.

Fluke waited with Twist's headless torso until help – including specialist help from Sellafield – arrived. The train had stopped three hundred yards up the track and he told Towler to manage the crowd of terrified commuters. With a voice a parade-ground sergeant major would have been proud of, he yelled at them until they got back on the train. They were in for another long wait – one of Twist's arms had managed to mangle itself in the front wheel.

When support arrived and the scene had been handed over, Fluke walked back to the car. He wanted to check Jinx was OK. She had probably heard the screams and would be wondering what had happened. She got out when she saw him approach.

'Is everyone OK?' she asked anxiously.

He didn't even bother trying to answer that, just shrugged.

'Is it true Mark is dead?' Jinx said. Her tone made it clear she knew he was.

'I'm sorry,' Fluke said. 'He was my best friend but he was your husband. I can't imagine how you feel.'

'I didn't know Twist was like that.'

Fluke said nothing.

'Is he OK? Has Sergeant Towler arrested him?'

He couldn't duck this one. 'Twist is dead. He was hit by the train.'

'Oh,' she said. 'And are you both OK? What happened to that horrible stuff? You didn't get any on you, did you?'

Fluke shook his head.

'That's good,' she said. She sounded genuinely relieved. 'I would have hated it if something had happened to you. You've been so kind to me and you have so much to look forward to.'

Fluke nodded.

Wait . . . what?

And then she said the thing that would change Fluke's life for ever.

'You're going to be a great dad, Avison . . .'

Fluke didn't remember the journey home. He couldn't believe how blind he'd been. The clues had been everywhere.

Her refusal to drink alcohol. Vomiting in the morning. The reduction in her coffee intake. 'The talk' he'd selfishly put off. Even her overreaction to the shotgun cartridge through the door made sense now. She didn't think the cabin was safe but it wasn't her she'd been scared for.

Agonisingly he'd had to go back to headquarters first. There'd been a nuclear incident and a criminal had died while he'd been trying to arrest him.

There was paperwork.

The radioactive AGR fuel waste had hardly touched the ground. Virtually all of it had stayed on, and in, Twist. There was some near the track where he'd thrown the flask lid but, as an environmental disaster, it would have about the same impact as a fart in a wind tunnel. Twist's remains, the flask, and the lid had been bagged and taken away. After two hours, and a thorough scrubbing, the train had been allowed to continue its journey. The commuters had been less than happy.

There'd be an investigation. He'd handled parts of the case badly and he'd be punished. Lightly. He might have defied almost everyone, but ultimately a disaster had been averted and a murderer had been caught. It would be bad, but no worse than anything else he'd done. Because of the planted drugs, Reyes couldn't complain about him. When Fluke was ready, he would have a think about what to do about the corrupt cop. Half of him said do nothing. Someone in London – someone ambitious – who owed him, might be useful one day. You collect sources wherever you can.

Thoughts of Reyes and Zoe, of Twist, of Jinx and Dan, drifted away.

As unlikely as it seemed, particularly considering the testicle-destroying chemotherapy he'd had, he was going to be a father.

A father . . .

It was a concept so alien, he didn't even know how to begin processing it. He was about to bring a child into the world. No, scratch that. He was about to bring a child into *his* world.

He had a lot to think about. Perhaps the job wasn't for him any more . . .

He would soon see Bridie. He wanted to hug the mother of his unborn child and tell her everything was going to be OK. That he might be scared, but he'd never been more ready for anything in his life.

He turned on to his drive and let out a sigh of relief. Bridie's car was still there. He parked beside her.

Fluke glanced through the rear windows of her car as he walked past. She'd only just got back; her suitcases were still on the back seat. She hadn't had time to unpack. There'd be time for that later. He'd stopped off and picked up some flowers, a card and some chocolates. He'd even found some alcohol-free wine.

He wanted the full 'new father' experience. The highs, the lows, the worries. Everything. And part of the experience was enjoying it from day one and he intended to start now.

347

He opened the door, a huge smile splitting his face. He wanted her to know he knew.

Fluke froze.

Bridie was watching television. Her face was grim. She glanced up when he approached. No kind words. His smile went unreturned.

'Watch this,' she said.

There was no emotion in her voice. She pressed play and the screen started moving. There was no sound. Of course there was no sound. It was the feed from the trail cameras. Fluke recognised the scene immediately. Smith was about to 'knuckledust' Steeleye Stan.

And he was right in the middle of the screen. Standing there. Doing nothing.

Stan fell to the floor and Bridie pressed pause.

'This here, Avison,' she pointed at a small dark object on the screen, 'is why I'm leaving. A man you once told me is the most dangerous person in Cumbria comes to our home and someone gets punched in the face so hard HIS FUCKING EYE COMES OUT!'

Now wasn't the time to tell her it was actually a ball bearing, and these days Stan's eye socket was so loose it fell out when he sneezed. It wasn't the point. He said nothing.

'Judging by the flowers, you've finally picked up on the fact that us two screw-ups are having a baby. And as I'm not supposed to be able to get pregnant, and you're not supposed to be able to *get* anyone pregnant, the child growing in me has to be the most stubborn baby in the history of the world. But before we get on to how the hell it happened, let's just recap the last six months, shall we? Afterwards you can tell me if you think you're safe to be around.'

'Bridie, let me—'

'Six months ago you take on an armed, international contract killer with nothing more than a torch. And when you finally find him, what do you do? Run away? Hide? No, Avison Fluke, spurred on by the thought of what Towler would say, no doubt, tries to run him over while being shot at.'

'I *did* run him over,' Fluke protested.

She ignored him. 'Let's spin forwards, shall we? A few weeks ago, someone posted a shotgun cartridge through our door.'

'I'm doing something about that,' he said. 'That's what the cameras are for.' He may as well have said nothing. This was a rehearsed speech by a renowned lawyer. He'd have been better off shouting 'objection'.

'A few days later – caught on film by one of your stupid cameras – one of the most violent things I've ever witnessed happens. Right on our doorstep. And you invited them all here. Why? Because you didn't want to hand over a witness.'

Now was obviously not the time to tell her about his cunning plan to recruit Stan. Fluke let her vent.

'Next on the list of things that can only happen to you: a bent policeman plants drugs under your bed. Where anyone could find them. Where a *baby* could have found them.'

'They were in a bag in the wardrobe,' he protested. 'A baby couldn't have undone the zip. Their fingers aren't strong enough.'

'Piss off, Avison. That's not the point and you know it.'

An uneasy silence settled over them. Fluke walked over and sat next to her. He turned off the TV; the sight of Stan, writhing around on the ground, wasn't helping his case one bit.

She calmed down. Spoke rationally. 'I can cope with bringing up a child in all this isolation. It's manageable. I get that you'll sometimes have to dart off with no notice. And I can even cope with your stubbornness. I love you. It's who you are.'

'But?' he said.

'You're not safe to be around, Avison. Trouble will always find you.'

He said nothing. He couldn't argue. He agreed with her. It

had been less than four hours since a man got decapitated right in front of him.

She looked at him and her eyes were red and glistening. 'I thought it was OK. It *was* OK.'

'But?' he said again.

'But now it isn't. Not with a baby. This is the only chance I'll have and I can't take any risks.'

She looked him in the eye, reached across and touched his arm.

'I have to leave you, Avison,' she said.

Chapter 53

Fluke begged. He made promises. He even offered to sell the cabin and move back to civilisation. All to no avail. Her mind was set in granite. The needs of their baby came first. *Their* needs came a distant second.

The luggage in her car had been her ready to leave. At least she'd done him the courtesy of telling him face-to-face. She was gone within half an hour and refused to say where.

Bridie's friend, and his haematologist, Leah Cooper, rang the following day to see if he was OK. She was concerned, although not concerned enough to tell him where Bridie was. She knew all about the pregnancy. Had been advising her – although she was very clear she'd left the relationship side of it alone. Her role had been medical advice only. Towler came round with some beers but Fluke wasn't in the mood. He rang Chambers and, without telling him why, booked some leave.

A couple of days later, he drove Jinx down to meet Bish's parents. It had been emotional and draining. Jinx was going to stay with them for a while. They had a lot to talk about. And then – with her father now out of the picture – she was going to go and see her mother. Rebuild some bridges.

Fluke was happy for her.

The evening was warm and oily, the air heavy and lubricated. Fluke was outside, wave after wave of self-pity washing over him. It was a process he knew well. It was the same as when he'd been diagnosed with Burkitt's. Life was unfair. Shit happens. But why did it always have to happen to him?

Eventually though – and because he was a reasonable man – he began to see it from Bridie's perspective. She was right. Danger *would* always follow him while he did this job.

If he wanted her – and the baby – back, serious changes would have to be made.

Changes like leaving the police altogether.

He knew he couldn't be a deskbound officer; the temptation to get involved would be too great. He would need a complete break.

Some things were worth the sacrifice though. He would call Chambers tomorrow. It was the only way.

He was thinking about what he could do for a living when his mobile rang.

An unknown number. He pressed receive.

'Hello?'

'Good evening, Avison.'

A woman. A woman with a slight Irish accent.

Surely not?

'Who is this?' he asked.

'You know who I am. Well, you know of me. Mr McGinty has quite a big mouth.'

'Is he OK?' Despite the mess his own life was in, he didn't wish harm on the man.

'He's fine. McGinty's always fine. No, this is just a courtesy call. And to tell you it's over. I won't be trying again.'

'Am I supposed to believe you?'

'Yes, Avison,' she laughed. 'And you do. I know you know about me. I also know that we have a connection from the old days. It would be rude of me to try again.'

Fluke said nothing. The Choreographer was on the other end of the line and there was nothing he could do about it. She'd be using an untraceable phone. She hadn't stayed under the radar this long by making such basic errors in security.

And anyway, he was now starting to understand what it was like to be a parent. He'd only known he was going to be a father for a few days, and he already knew he'd kill to protect his child.

But would he kill to *avenge* his child?

He hoped he never had to find out.

Fluke got the impression she just wanted to talk.

'Tell me about your son,' he said finally.

It was later that night the case came full circle.

He'd thought the colour green had been the consistent feature of the case. The Emerald Isle. Twist's jealousy. Royal Marines. Eco-extremism.

And although it might have been the most obvious feature, it wasn't the most important one.

Bridie had left him to protect their unborn baby.

The Choreographer had tried to bring down Sellafield to avenge her dead child.

Mothers.

This case had always been about mothers.

Chapter 54

What do you do when you've married a monster? A man filled with a seething hatred. A man who can never be happy. Someone who holds grudges and sabotages the dreams of others. Someone dangerous . . .

He charms his way into your life. With a cheeky grin and boyish good looks he steals your heart. He believes in the same things you do. He's fun. He's the breath of fresh air you've always looked for.

By the time you find out what he's really like, it's too late.

You're married.

You're pregnant.

And for someone who has to be the centre of attention, a baby isn't a blessing, it's a threat. Someone like that could very well kill a child . . .

What do you do?

You get rid of the danger, of course.

But how?

The authorities can't help; he'd ignore any court mandate. You can't do it yourself; you can't risk your son growing up without his mother.

And then a miracle happens. Someone tells you a secret. A secret you can use against the monster. You plan carefully.

You know the monster has a self-destruct button. You press it for him.

You manipulate him with tales of others' achievements and betrayals. Exploit his insecurities. Hint at how it can all go away.

Vane is why he's unhappy. *He* should be the man in this camp, not Vane. Vane has no right to be there. Vane is showing you disrespect. It's his fault.

You sit back and wait . . .

Fluke didn't take anyone with him this time.

Faith greeted him coolly. He was the man who was responsible for her husband's death after all. He'd expected no less.

Fluke knew it was an act.

She offered him tea. Fluke ignored her.

'Was it worth it?' he asked. Blunt and to the point.

She stared. Knew he knew. Knew he couldn't do anything. She held her son close. Kissed the top of his head. Said nothing.

'I'm assuming you knew Mark was a cop? He'd have told you his secret before he told Jinx. He'd have wanted to see if you thought it was a good idea or not.'

She hugged her son tight. Looked at him with those beautiful, sad eyes.

'And finding out was the catalyst for your plan. With an undercover cop in the camp, you could get rid of Twist for good. You just needed him to kill Vane. Or at least die in the attempt.'

Fluke paused to gauge how he was doing. Her expression remained neutral but her eyes told him he was right.

'Of course, you'd need any subsequent investigation to head Twist's way, so you lied to Bish, told him Vane's real name was Kevin Hendricks. You gave him Twist's so that when the investigation began, and as soon as we traced his parents, we'd know he was a killer. How am I doing so far?'

More silence. She was watching him carefully. Evaluating something. She cleared her throat.

'My husband had three sides, Mr Fluke,' she said. 'The quiet and sweet side I fell in love with. The fun and daft side everyone else fell in love with. And the side you never wanted to see.'

Fluke didn't interrupt. He wasn't going to hear a confession, but he might get a measure of understanding.

He wanted someone to take responsibility.

'I know you saw his face when Sam said "Momma". Can you imagine how he reacted when he said it for the *first* time? He was enraged. Threatened me. Threatened Sam. He punched him, Mr Fluke. My husband punched our baby.'

'There are people who could have helped,' he said. It sounded weak.

'Against Twist? No, there aren't. Even if they managed to get a restraining order or something, he was so crazy he would have killed us both. He'd have convinced himself he was justified in doing so. I knew him. You didn't. Anyway, I don't know what you're talking about.'

Fluke nodded as if he'd expected as much.

'People died, Faith.'

She nodded. 'I'm sorry. I really am. I loved Mark, I really did. And he was perfect for Jinx.'

'Then why—'

'You still don't understand Twist, do you? He hated Vane. He was constantly following him around, trying to find out what he was up to. But when it came down to it, he was also terrified of him. Absolutely petrified. Too scared to do what he wanted to do.'

'And that's why he killed Bish instead?'

She lingered before answering. 'No. I don't think it was. I think killing Mark, and blaming Jinx, was my punishment for Sam's first word.'

Jesus . . .

It made sense. From Twist's distorted view of the world it really did make sense. Even if he'd had the guts to go after the man he blamed for everything, Vane would have been suspicious of everyone. No way does he get lured anywhere by anyone. Bish, on the other hand, trying to gain the approval of the man Jinx looked up

356

to more than anyone else . . . Well, Bish would have been easy to lure up there. And as Faith had just said, in his eyes, they'd all betrayed him. Jinx, Bish, even Faith. Of course they all needed punishing . . .

Faith hadn't wanted Bish dead but he was dead all the same. Twist might have been the weapon, but she'd pulled the trigger. How had she ever expected to control someone as reckless? It was culpable homicide.

Unprovable in any court in the land.

But once the terrible deed had been done, she had to make sure Twist still took the blame. She'd told Jinx to run to Fluke's cabin. Told Twist to go with her. Made sure he knew what Twist looked like.

And then she'd have watched. Grown frustrated as the investigation kept leading them to Vane. Someone else died. She could do nothing. She could say nothing.

She could only wait.

And if he hadn't forced himself into the investigation her plan wouldn't have worked. Twist would have got away with murder. Faith and her child would still have been at risk.

And all that time he thought he'd been working for Bish . . .

Unbelievable.

'People died,' Fluke repeated eventually.

'My son didn't.'

And that was it. The only argument she had. The only argument she needed.

Fluke turned his back and left.

Chapter 55

Fluke walked down to the lake for a cigar. He wouldn't be sharing his suspicions about Faith. Let others worry about that. As far as he was concerned, the case was as closed as it was ever going to be. Was it ideal? No, of course it wasn't. But he had to move on. Bish would understand.

He turned his attention to his unborn child.

The shock of losing Bridie was still raw but he had no intention of turning into 'weird stalker man'. If she needed some time to herself, then he wasn't going to trace her.

Tonight would be his last as a policeman.

He planned to hand in his resignation tomorrow. Take leave instead of working his notice. It wasn't a knee-jerk reaction. He wanted to be a part of his child's life and it was a sacrifice he was happy to make. It might not make any difference to how Bridie was thinking but he didn't want to die wondering.

His thoughts were interrupted by the distant sound of sirens. Someone, somewhere, wasn't having a good day. Probably a drunken tourist. Too much sun and too much beer. Never a good combination.

His mobile rang.

Another unknown number. He pressed receive.

'Mr Fluke! How the devil are you? You've closed your case, I gather?'

It was Nathaniel Diamond. No doubt calling to talk to him about reparations for his dead employee. Well, tough shit. Fluke wasn't in the mood to be blackmailed.

'Nathaniel,' he said, 'what do you want?'

'Jinx told me about the trouble you're having with your neighbours. What naughty people. Posting shotgun cartridges through the door of my dear friend, Avison Fluke.'

Fluke said nothing.

'Can I hear sirens?'

He shivered. Acid settled in his stomach like concrete.

'What have you done, Nathaniel?' he said, dreading the answer.

'Not me, Avison. You. Distraught at losing that nice lady of yours, you took it out on the neighbouring campsite's manager. The man you believed had posted shotgun cartridges through your door. You weren't thinking straight though. If you had been, you wouldn't have used your own knife to stab him. And you wouldn't have dragged him down to the shore of your lake.'

Fluke gripped the phone hard. If it had been anyone else, he'd have assumed Diamond was bluffing. But he remembered Mr Smith going into his cabin to help Jinx with the bacon sandwiches. He'd thought it strange at the time; that his lieutenant had been given an errand like that. It didn't seem strange now though; Smith had stolen one of his kitchen knives. Diamond probably didn't know what, if anything, he'd use it for at that point. Just wanted it in case the need arose.

Diamond was still talking. 'We both know you'll eventually get the nod to come for me. I know you'll probably beat this, but it'll take a while. By the time you do, I'll be even further away.' His voice dropped an octave. 'My advice: when you *do* get the nod, refuse it.'

Instead of telling Diamond he was about to leave the police for ever, a low growl started in the pit of Fluke's stomach. It travelled up his throat and erupted down the phone. He threw back his head and unleashed a deep, guttural laugh.

He heard the other end of the line go dead and he put his phone back in his pocket. He carried on laughing.

359

Bridie was right. Why did he have the arrogance to think he could deny who he was? Who he would always be.

Nathaniel Diamond had had a man killed using Fluke's own knife. A man who'd worked for the company that was trying to intimidate Fluke into selling his beloved cabin. The man he blamed for his partner leaving, for not being part of his child's life.

Fluke had the means. He had the opportunity, and he damn sure had the motive.

He was going to be arrested.

He was going to be charged with murder.

He had no obvious defence.

Everyone would assume he'd done it.

He smiled.

So this was how it began. The defining case of his career.

Well played, Nathaniel, well played. But remember, this is just round one.

Game on.

Enjoyed *Body Breaker*? Check out the first instalment in
M. W. Craven's Washington Poe series: the brilliantly twisted
and addictive *The Puppet Show*.

Read on for a sneak peek . . .

The stone circle is an ancient, tranquil place. Its stones are silent sentinels. Unmoving watchers. Their granite glistens with the morning dew. They have withstood a thousand and more winters, and although they are weathered and worn, they have never yielded to time, the seasons, or man.

Alone in the circle, surrounded by soft shadows, stands an old man. His face is heavily lined, and lank grey hair frames his bald and mottled scalp. He is cadaverously thin, and his gaunt frame is racked by tremors. His head is bowed and his shoulders are stooped.

He is naked and he is about to die.

Strong wire secures him to an iron girder. It bites into his skin. He doesn't care: his tormentor has already tortured him.

He is in shock and thinks he has no more capacity for pain.

He is wrong.

'Look at me.' His tormentor's voice is flat.

The old man has been smeared with a jelly-like substance that reeks of petrol. He raises his head and looks to the hooded figure in front of him.

His tormentor holds an American Zippo lighter.

And now the fear kicks in. The primal fear of fire. He knows what's going to happen and he knows he can't stop it. His breathing becomes shallow and erratic.

The Zippo is raised to his eyes. The old man sees the simple beauty of it. The perfect lines, the exact engineering. A design that hasn't changed in a century. With a flick, the top flips open. A turn of the thumb and the wheel strikes the flint. A shower of sparks and the flame appears.

His tormentor lowers the Zippo, drags the flame down. The

1

accelerant catches. The hungry flames flare, then crawl down his arm.

The pain is immediate, like his blood has turned to acid. His eyes widen in horror and every muscle goes rigid. His hands clench into a fist. He tries to scream but it dies when it reaches the obstacle in his throat. Becomes pitiful and muted as he gargles his own blood.

His flesh spits and sizzles like meat in a hot oven. Blood, fat and water roll down his arms and drip from his fingers.

Black fills his vision. The pain fades. His breathing is no longer rushed and urgent.

The old man dies. He doesn't know that his own fat will fuel the fire long after the accelerant has burnt away. He doesn't see how the flames burn and distort what has been carved into his chest.

But it happens anyway.

CHAPTER ONE

One week later.

Tilly Bradshaw had a problem. She didn't like problems. Her low tolerance for uncertainty meant they made her anxious.

She looked around to see if there was anyone to share her findings with, but the Serious Crime Analysis Section office was empty. She checked her watch and saw it was coming up to midnight. She'd worked for sixteen hours straight again. She thumbed her mother a text, apologising for not calling her.

She turned back to her screen. Although she knew it wasn't a glitch, with results like these there would be an expectation that she had triple checked. She ran her program again.

After making herself a fruit tea, she glanced at the progress bar to see how long she had to wait. Fifteen minutes. Bradshaw opened her personal laptop, plugged in her headphones and typed, 'Back at keyboard'. Within seconds she was fully immersed in *Dragonlore*, a multiplayer, online role-playing game.

In the background her program processed the data she'd entered. Bradshaw didn't check the SCAS computer once.

She didn't make mistakes.

Fifteen minutes later, the National Crime Agency logo dissolved, and the same results appeared. She typed, 'Away from Keyboard', and logged out of her game.

There were two possibilities. Either the results were

3

accurate, or a mathematically implausible coincidence had occurred. When she'd first seen the results, she'd calculated the odds of it happening by chance, and had come up with a number in the high millions. In case she was asked, she entered the maths problem into a program of her own design and ran it. The result popped up and showed it was within the margin of error she'd allowed. She didn't smile when she realised that she'd worked it out faster than her own computer, using a program *she'd* written.

Bradshaw wasn't sure what to do next. Her boss, Detective Inspector Stephanie Flynn, was usually nice to her, but it *had* only been the week before when they'd had their little chat about when it was appropriate to call her at home. She was only allowed to ring when it was important. But . . . as it was DI Flynn who decided if something was important, how was she supposed to know without asking her? It was all very confusing.

Bradshaw wished it were a maths problem. She *understood* maths. She didn't understand Detective Inspector Flynn. She bit her lip, then came to a decision.

She reviewed her findings and practised what to say.

Her discovery related to SCAS's latest target – a man the press were calling the 'Immolation Man'. Whoever he was – and they'd made an early assumption he was male – he didn't seem to like men in their sixties and seventies. In fact, he disliked them so much, he was setting them on fire.

It was the third and latest victim's data that Bradshaw had been studying. SCAS had been brought in after the second. As well as identifying the emergence of serial killers and serial rapists, their role was also to provide analytical support to any police force undertaking complex or apparently motiveless murder investigations. The Immolation Man certainly ticked all the SCAS boxes.

Because the fire had destroyed the bodies to the point they didn't even *look* like bodies, a post-mortem wasn't the only approach the SIO, the senior investigating officer, up in Cumbria had taken. He'd sought advice from SCAS. After the post-mortem, SCAS had arranged for the body to go through a multi-slice computed tomography machine. The MSCT was a sophisticated medical investigative technique. It used X-ray beams and a liquid dye to form a 3D image of the body. It was meant for the living but was just as effective on the dead.

SCAS didn't have the resources to have their own MSCT – no law enforcement agency did – but they had an agreement to purchase time on one when the situation merited it. As the Immolation Man left no trace evidence at the murder scenes or abduction sites, the SIO had been willing to try anything.

Bradshaw took a deep breath and dialled DI Flynn.

The phone answered on the fifth ring. A groggy voice answered. 'Hello?'

She checked her watch to confirm it was after midnight, before saying, 'Good morning, Detective Inspector Flynn. How are you?' As well as talking to her about when it was appropriate to ring her after hours, DI Flynn had also urged her to be politer to her colleagues.

'Tilly,' Flynn grumbled, 'what do you want?'

'I want to talk to you about the case, Detective Inspector Flynn.'

Flynn sighed. 'Can you just call me Stephanie, Tilly? Or Steph? Or boss? In fact, we're not that far away from London, I'll even accept guv.'

'Of course, Detective Inspector Stephanie Flynn.'

'No . . . I mean can you not just . . . Oh, it doesn't matter.'

Bradshaw waited for Flynn to finish before saying, 'May I please tell you what I've found?'

Flynn groaned. 'What time is it?'

5

'The time is thirteen minutes past midnight.'

'Go on then. What's so important it couldn't wait until the morning?'

Flynn listened to her before asking a few questions and hanging up. Bradshaw sat back in her chair and smiled. She'd been right to call her. DI Flynn had said so.

Flynn was there within half an hour. Her blonde hair was tangled. She wore no makeup. Bradshaw wore no makeup either, although that was by choice. She thought it was silly.

Bradshaw pressed some keys and brought up a series of cross sections. 'They're all of the torso,' she said.

She then went on to explain what the MSCT did. 'It can identify wounds and fractures that the post-mortem might miss. It is particularly useful when the victim has been badly burned.'

Flynn knew all this but let her finish anyway. Bradshaw gave up information in her own time and wouldn't be rushed.

'The cross sections don't really give us that much, DI Stephanie Flynn, but watch this.' Bradshaw brought up a composite image, this time from above.

'What on earth . . . ?' Flynn asked, staring at the screen.

'Wounds,' Bradshaw replied. 'Lots of them.'

'So the post-mortem missed a load of random slashes?'

Bradshaw shook her head. 'That is what I thought.' She pressed a button and they studied the 3D image of the wounds on the victim's chest. The program sorted through the seemingly random slashes. Eventually they all came together.

They stared at the final image. There was nothing random about it.

'What do we do now, Detective Inspector Flynn?'

Flynn paused before answering. 'Have you called your mum to explain why you aren't home yet?'

'I sent her a text.'

6

'Well, send her another one. Tell her you won't be back tonight.'

Bradshaw began tapping the screen of her mobile. 'What reason shall I give?'

'Tell her we're getting the director out of bed.'

CHAPTER TWO

Washington Poe had enjoyed his day repairing the dry stone wall. It was one of several new skills he'd learned since moving back to Cumbria. It was backbreaking work but the reward of a pie and pint at the end of the day was all the sweeter for it. He loaded his tools and a few spare rocks into his quad's trailer, whistled for Edgar, his springer spaniel, and then began the drive back to his croft. He'd been working on the outer boundary wall today so was over a mile from his home, a rough-stone building called Herdwick Croft. It would take him fifteen minutes or so to get back.

The spring sun was low and the evening dew made the grass and heather shine. Birds chirped territorial and mating songs and the air was fragrant with early flowers. Poe breathed in deeply as he drove.

He could get used to this.

He *had* been planning on a quick shower then a walk over to the hotel, but the closer to home he got, the thought of a long soak in the bath with a good book was far more appealing.

He crested the last peak and stopped. Someone was sitting at his outdoor table.

He opened the canvas bag he always carried with him and removed a pair of binoculars. He trained them on the lone figure. He couldn't be sure, but the person looked female. He increased the magnification and smiled grimly when he recognised the figure with the long blonde hair.

So . . . they'd finally caught up with him.

8

He put the binoculars back in his bag and drove down to see his old sergeant.

'Long time no see, Steph,' Poe said. 'What brings you this far north?' Edgar, the furry traitor, was fussing round her like a long-lost friend.

'Poe,' she acknowledged. 'Nice beard.'

He reached up and scratched his chin. He'd got out of the habit of daily shaves. 'You know I've never been good at small talk, Steph.'

Flynn nodded. 'This is a hard place to find.' She was wearing a trouser suit; navy blue with pinstripes, and judging by how lean and supple she looked, she'd obviously kept up to date with her martial arts training. She exuded the confidence of someone in control. A pair of reading glasses lay folded beside a file on the table. It looked like she'd been working before he'd arrived.

'Not hard enough apparently,' he replied. He didn't smile. 'What can I do for you, Sergeant Flynn?'

'It's Detective Inspector now, although it couldn't possibly make the slightest bit of difference.'

Poe raised his eyebrows. 'My old job?'

She nodded.

'I'm surprised Talbot allowed you to take it,' Poe said. Talbot had been the director when Poe had been SCAS's detective inspector. He was a petty man, and he'd have blamed Flynn for what happened just as much as he blamed Poe. More so perhaps – Poe hadn't hung around; she had.

'It's Edward van Zyl now. Talbot didn't survive the fallout.'

'Good man, I like him,' Poe grunted. When van Zyl was in North West Special Branch they'd worked closely together on a counter-terrorism case. The July 21st bombers had trained in the Lake District, and Cumbrian cops were vital in building up the

9

intelligence profile. It had been van Zyl who asked Poe to apply for the SCAS position. 'And Hanson?'

'Still the deputy director.'

'Pity,' said Poe. Hanson was a politically savvy man and Poe wasn't surprised to learn he'd somehow managed to wriggle out of it. Ordinarily, when a senior manager is forced out due to catastrophic errors in judgement, the next manager in line takes their job. That Hanson hadn't been promoted meant he'd not got away with it completely.

Poe could still remember the smirk on Hanson's face when he suspended him. He hadn't had contact with anyone from the NCA since. He'd left no forwarding address, had cancelled his mobile-phone contract, and as far as he knew, he wasn't on any database in Cumbria.

If Flynn had taken the trouble to track him down, it meant a decision on his employment had finally been made. As Hanson was still in post, Poe doubted it was good news. It didn't matter; he'd moved on months ago. If Flynn was there to tell him he no longer worked for the NCA then that was fine. And if she were there to tell him that Hanson had finally found a way to charge him with a criminal offence, he would just have to deal with it.

There was no point shooting the messenger. He doubted Flynn wanted to be there. 'You want a brew? I'm having one.' He didn't wait for a response and disappeared into the croft. He shut the door behind him.

Five minutes later he was back with a metal espresso maker and a separate pot of boiled water. He filled two mugs. 'Still taking it black?'

She nodded and took a sip. She smiled and raised the mug in appreciation.

'How'd you find me?' His face was serious. His privacy had become increasingly important to him.

'Van Zyl knew you'd come back to Cumbria and he knew

roughly where you lived. Some quarry workers told me there was someone living in an old shepherd's croft in the middle of nowhere. They'd been watching you do the place up.' She looked round as if evidence of this was negligible.

Herdwick Croft looked as though it had grown out of the ground. The walls were made of unrendered stone – too big for any one man to lift and manoeuvre into place – and it merged seamlessly with the ancient moorland it inhabited. It was squat and ugly and looked like it had been frozen in time for two hundred years. Poe loved it.

Flynn said, 'I've been here a couple of hours waiting—'

'What do you want?'

Flynn reached into her briefcase and pulled out a thick file. She didn't open it. 'I assume you've heard of the Immolation Man?'

Poe jerked his head up. He hadn't expected her to say *that*.

And of course he'd heard of the Immolation Man. Even in the middle of the Shap Fells, the Immolation Man was news. He'd been burning men to death in some of Cumbria's many stone circles. Three victims so far, unless there was another he hadn't heard about. Although the press had been speculating, the facts were there if you knew how to separate them from the sensationalism.

The county had its first-ever serial killer.

Even if SCAS had been called in to help Cumbria police, he was on suspension: subject to an internal investigation *and* an IPCC inquiry. Although Poe knew he was an asset to any investigation, he wasn't irreplaceable. SCAS had moved on without him.

So what was Flynn really doing there?

'Van Zyl's lifted your suspension. He wants you working the case. You'll be my DS.'

Although Poe's face was a mask, his mind worked faster than a computer. It didn't make sense. Flynn was a new DI, and the last thing she'd want would be the *old* DI working under her, undermining her authority just by being there. And she'd known him

11

a long time and knew how he responded to authority. Why would she want to be a part of that?

She'd been ordered to.

Poe noticed she'd made no mention of the IPCC inquiry so presumably *that* was still ongoing. He stood and cleared away the mugs. 'Not interested,' he said.

She seemed surprised by his answer. He didn't know why. The NCA had washed their hands of him.

'Don't you want to see what's in my file?' she asked.

'I don't care,' he replied. He no longer missed SCAS. While it had taken him a long time to get used to the slower pace of life on the Cumbrian fells, he didn't want to give it up. If Flynn wasn't there to sack or arrest him, then he wasn't interested in anything else she had to say. Catching serial killers was no longer a part of his life.

'OK,' she said. She stood up. She was tall and their eyes were on the same level. 'I need you to sign two bits of paper for me then.' She removed a thinner file from her briefcase and passed it over.

'What's this?'

'You heard me say van Zyl's lifted your suspension, right?'

Nodding, he read the document.

Ah.

'And you realise that as you're now officially a serving police officer again, if you refuse to come back to work it's a sackable offence? But rather than go through all that, I've been told I can accept your resignation now. I've taken the liberty of getting HR to draw up this document.'

Poe studied the one-page sheet. If he signed at the bottom, he was no longer a police officer. Although he'd been expecting it for a while, he found it wasn't as easy to say goodbye as he thought. If he *did* sign, it would draw a line under the last eighteen months. He could start living.

But he'd never carry a warrant card again.

He glanced at Edgar. The spaniel was soaking up the last of the sun. Most of the surrounding land was his. Was he ready to give all this up?

Poe took her pen and scrawled his name across the bottom. He handed it back so she could check he hadn't simply written 'piss off' on the bottom. Now that her bluff had been called she seemed less sure of what to do next. It wasn't going to plan. Poe took the mugs and coffee pot inside. A minute later he was back outside. Flynn hadn't moved.

'What's up, Steph?'

'What are you doing, Poe? You loved being a cop. What's changed?'

He ignored her. With the decision made, he just wanted her to go. 'Where's the other document?'

'Excuse me?'

'You said you had two things for me to sign. I've signed your resignation letter, so unless you've got two of them, there's still something else.'

She was all business again. Opening the file, she removed the second document. It was a bit thicker than the first and had the official seal of the NCA across the top.

She launched into a rehearsed speech. It was one Poe had used himself. 'Washington Poe, please read this document and then sign at the bottom to confirm you've been served.' She handed over the thick sheaf of paper.

Poe glanced at the top sheet.

It was an Osman Warning.

Oh shit . . .

Help us make the next generation of readers

We – both author and publisher – hope you enjoyed this book.
We believe that you can become a reader at any time in your life,
but we'd love your help to give the next generation a head start.

Did you know that 9% of children don't have a book of their
own in their home, rising to 12% in disadvantaged families*?
We'd like to try to change that by asking you to consider the role
you could play in helping to build readers of the future.

We'd love you to think of sharing, borrowing, reading, buying or talking
about a book with a child in your life and spreading the love of reading.
We want to make sure the next generation continue to have access
to books, wherever they come from.

And if you would like to consider donating to charities that help
fund literacy projects, find out more at www.literacytrust.org.uk
and www.booktrust.org.uk.

Thank you.

hachette
CHILDREN'S GROUP

little, brown
BOOK GROUP

*As reported by the National Literacy Trust